Liars

ALSO BY FRANCES VICK

Bad Little Girl

Liars

FRANCES VICK

Bookouture

Published by Bookouture in 2018

An imprint of StoryFire Ltd.

Carmelite House
50 Victoria Embankment
London EC4Y 0DZ
www.bookouture.com

ISBN: 978-1-78681-320-6
eBook ISBN: 978-1-78681-319-0

To M, J and T with all love

CHAPTER ONE

The Night the Snow Fell

The first snowflakes were hesitant and watery, but soon they were as big and solid as cats' paws. All night it pattered softly, insistently, on roofs, fences, on the cold ground. The squeaking sigh of snow crunched underfoot as people left the Rose and Crown and made their way, shivering and chuckling, back to their homes. The snow covered the pretty buildings, the un-pitted roads, the well-kept hedgerows, until only a few chimneys peeked from beneath the white. Only a few soft undulations showed where the pavement met the road. By morning, only one hardy dog walker managed to make it out into the stillness.

This woman, older, thin, moved cautiously towards the hills. Her dog, a pot-bellied and aged Jack Russell, sneezed as he sank up to his belly in the drift. The woman picked him up then. The dog quivered in her arms, half with cold, half with excitement, and yapped, once, twice.

'We'll be there soon, Huck,' the woman told him. 'Just let me go at my own pace. Don't want to slip. Don't want to slip, now, do we? Not on the hills.'

The hills – not hills, but slight folds and ripples in the earth, where once there had been a brickworks – lay at the very edge of the village. Only young children and elderly people thought of them as hills.

It was Saturday, 9 a.m. and not a sound. No one was getting into their cars. There were no breakfast radio shows, no sharp, parental annoyance on the school run, no mutinous mutterings from their children. The woman bent slowly, stiffly, placed Huck on the ground and unfastened the lead from his collar.

'There you go now. Have a run about.' But the dog seemed dubious, and his breath formed little husky puffs as he sniffed suspiciously at the snow. He looked round at the woman as if this weather was a personal insult she'd visited on him.

'Dafty! Go on!' The woman prodded his backside with one wellington boot. The dog sighed, put up one hesitant paw and plunged into the snow.

She smiled, watching his little tail bobbing up and down. Mornings made her happy. The quiet made her happy. She would pay for it later, she knew: the cold wouldn't do her rheumatism any good, but it was worth it. She closed her eyes and breathed deeply in the frigid air.

Huck barked then. It was his 'Look at this!' bark.

His tail stood straight as an exclamation point, and he whimpered and growled at something in the snow. As the woman moved forwards she saw a scrap of red material fluttering near a bone-white foot; the rough slump of a torso. The head, topped with greying brown hair, was twisted and one fixed, open eye, the eyelashes weighed with snow, gazed at the blank sky. As the woman stared at the face of her neighbour, a frightened sob escaped her and, hearing this, Huck whimpered, and gave one panicked bark. The world started again.

'Huck! Huck, away! Now!' Together they backed away from the body and moved, as quickly as they could, back to the warm house and the telephone.

On the way, the snow started falling again. By the time the police came, both dead eyes were filled with it.

*

'I-I knew it was Sal,' Mrs Mondesir told the nice police lady, later, wrapped in two cardigans, and sipping sweet tea by her own fire. 'So did Huck; I could tell. I could tell because he was so upset. He liked her. She'd always have a treat for him, you know. She was good with animals. I-I touched her foot. I've never felt anything so cold. I shouldn't have touched her, should I?' she whispered to the policewoman. 'They say on TV, don't they, you must never touch a body. Crime scene.'

'Don't worry,' the officer said. 'Can you tell me what happened next?'

'I just looked at her. Her neck. It was too long – it looked like a Christmas goose, you know? When you used to see them hanging upside down at the butcher's? Do you remember that? No, probably you don't. Too young.'

'Does she have any relatives? Anyone nearby we should contact?'

'Oh yes. Yes. She lives with her daughter. Jenny. Is she not in the house?'

'There's no one in the house that we can see. Do you have a contact phone number for Jenny?'

'Oh no. No. I don't,' Mrs Mondesir replied. 'That means she doesn't know! The poor girl doesn't know what's happened!'

CHAPTER TWO

A mile away, Jenny Holloway stood in her friend's parents' kitchen, studying a list pinned to the fridge:

Orchids rem change gravel!
Fan heaters 10-12, 2-4, 6-10.
Check bubble wrap for holes EVERY DAY.

She was keeping an eye on things while Freddie's parents were on a cruise, and they were very anxious about their greenhouse.

The kitchen – spacious, stylish, clean, was normally her favourite place to be in the house – but all night she'd suffered through various shifting nightmares, had woken late, and was still unsettled. She pulled a painful brush through her tangled curls and smeared on some tinted moisturiser that promised on the tube to make her look *Radiant, Rested and Rejuvenated*. It didn't work. A slightly browner face frowned from the mirror, blinked slowly, frowned. She dabbed concealer on the small bruise on her chin.

She put on Freddie's old parka and a big fur hat with lots of flaps and pockets that Graham – Freddie's father – had bought on a recent holiday to Crimea. Looking in the mirror again, she almost laughed. She looked like a caricature of a teenage runaway. Freddie despaired of her dress sense at the best of times, referring to it caustically as 'Asylum Seeker Chic'. She took a photo and sent it to him with the caption: 'Still got it!'

She took the shortcut through the church graveyard. Snow lay frozen in glittering, crusty crests over the gravestones; she paused to take a photo of a stone angel with an icicle dripping from its nose. She sent it to Freddie. He'd get a kick out of that.

After a while, the big detached houses close to the churchyard gave way to large semis and a neat heath used for cricket matches and picnics in the summer. Once upon a time, the heath had marked the very edge of the village, until the affordable housing section had been built next to it. Years later the houses were still roundly despised by 'real' villagers, who would gather in the shop or at parish council meetings to complain. Why did they have to be built here? Why not closer to the city, in one of those other, uglier, villages? They were such horrible little boxes, and the hills they backed onto was a popular spot for dog walkers, ramblers... having houses there ruined the peace, changed the ambience... couldn't Something Be Done?

Eight years ago, Jenny and Sal had been one of the first families to move into one of those horrible little boxes. On the day they arrived they saw a rabbit, an actual wild rabbit! Sometimes there were foxes – not the mangy, scavenging beasts she'd seen in the city, but fluffy-tailed, plumply alert creatures. Sal said they must have their den in the hills somewhere, and they'd put out scraps for them to eat until Mrs Mondesir told them not to because they might end up going for her Jack Russell.

It had been their New Start, in a New House and a New School and, for a while, it had seemed like it might all work out...

Jenny didn't see anyone that morning, and the only thing that passed her on the road was a police car.

'I didn't think anything of it,' she told Freddie later.

At her mother's front door, Jenny saw that the lid had come off the recycling bin. The empty bottles were very visible, only partially covered in snow. She quickly replaced the lid, hesitated, sighed and, riding a sudden wave of adrenaline, opened the door.

'Mum?'

A freezing breeze caught the door lazily, slamming it almost shut, before catching on the latch. The TV was on in the living room – a tinny Jeremy Kyle berated an alcoholic in front of a baying crowd. She crossed the room quickly, and turned it off.

'Mum?' Her voice was louder now. 'You in bed?'

Two drops of blood, as big as pennies, stained the carpet at the foot of the stairs and, on the bannister, like a sinister skid mark, was a smear of blood. More spots and drips of red on the wall ran vertically down to a broken picture frame resting on the stairs. Glass smashed into a starburst... a child perched on a donkey, huge grin, an ice cream in one chubby fist. Adrenaline hit again but, this time, she froze. Her stomach felt hollow, smoky. 'Mum?'

And then an unfamiliar voice came from the kitchen. 'Hello? Who's there? You'd better come here, whoever you are.'

And Jenny turned slowly, each inch an eternity, eyes wide and heart bump-bump-bumping. The police officer stood next to the kitchen table.

'I knew then that something very bad had happened,' she told Freddie later.

They sat at the kitchen table. The policeman eyed the semicircle of dirty glasses and plates at the base of the table and tried to keep his clean uniformed elbows off the tabletop.

'Your mother has been involved in an incident.' His voice was soft. 'Your neighbour next door was out walking her dog—'

'Is she OK?' Jenny asked.

He thought she meant Mrs Mondesir. 'She's had a shock but she's being looked after next door. Can I ask—?'

Jenny started to turn. He caught her arm, and she struggled. 'Let me go and see my mum!' she shouted.

'Miss Holloway? I'm going to need you to sit down. Please.' His kind eyes were tired. His smile was sad. 'I'm sorry to have to tell you that your mother has died.'

Jenny stared at him, nearly said something, but then seemed to deflate, empty out. She sat at the table like a puppet with its strings cut: eyes wide, mouth open. She asked: 'How?'

A few words pierced the fog. '... found... field at the back. Must have slipped on the snow...' Then he nodded at the glasses on the floor. 'Drinking, was she?'

'Yes,' Jenny whispered.

'Should she have been drinking?'

'No. Not really.'

'Can I call anyone for you?'

'What?' Her face was wiped clean of expression, kabuki-like. 'What did you say?'

'Can I call someone for you? Brother or sister?'

'I don't have any.' Her empty face stared, straight-ahead, at the back door, still open, squeaking. 'There isn't anyone.'

'A friend?'

There was a long pause. Jenny spoke as if the words were being dredged up from the deep. 'My friend Freddie. You can call him.' And she gave him the number.

'Did your mother have a partner? Boyfriend?'

Jenny flinched, then got up, slow as a sleepwalker. 'I think I'm going to be sick.'

She stumbled up the stairs, past the bloodstains and the glass, to the tiny bathroom and there she crouched by the toilet bowl until there was a knock and an 'Are you OK in there, Miss Holloway?'

'I'm—' She made a gagging sound. 'No. I'm… I don't know.'

'We've called your friend. Why not come out now, if you're feeling better?' He sounded anxious.

Jenny stood up shakily, crossed to the basin. In the mirror, her fearful face rose like a yellowish moon; she splashed it with water. *Your mother is dead, your mother is dead, slipped on the ice, in the cold. Your mother is dead. Dead in the snow like an animal.*

'Miss Holloway? I do need you to open the door now.' There was an urgency in his voice.

'Don't worry. Don't worry about me,' she murmured at the mirror.

'I want you to come out of the bathroom now. Can you do that for me?'

Your mother is dead your mother is dead your mother is dead.

'Miss Holloway!'

She unlocked the door. Later she realised that he was probably scared she'd hurt herself in there. Taken an overdose, or cut her wrists or something.

As they walked down the stairs together, towards the smashed picture, he asked: ' Do you know what had happened here?'

'No.' Jenny looked at the glass dazedly. 'No idea.'

When Freddie arrived an hour or so later, the policeman seemed a little relieved to hand her over to someone else. Freddie gently coaxed her out of the chair, out of the house and into his waiting car, where he buckled her in like a child, and, like a child, she gazed at him with sudden piteous fear.

'My mum died, Fred.'

'Oh darling!' He pulled her stiff body towards him in an awkward hug.

'I don't know what to do. What should I be doing?' she whispered into his shoulder.

He didn't answer. There *was* no answer. They drove back to his parents' house, where the remains of Jenny's breakfast were still on the kitchen table, there was still steam in the shower room, and everything was abnormally normal, strangely sane.

CHAPTER THREE

Later, that afternoon, Jenny found herself at the hospital.

The two officers, one old, one young, were quiet, professionally quiet. In the car over they'd been quite chatty; it had been easy to almost forget where they were going. Until she saw the sign.

Mortuary. Level Zero

A small, narrow corridor led to a wide grey door that wheezed on its pneumatic hinges. Inside, the room was partitioned by thick glass, smeared with the sweaty ghosts of many handprints, and through these prints, a body laid on a slab-like gurney.

'Take your time,' the older policeman told her.

'Do I...? Can I get closer?'

'No,' he murmured. 'Health and safety.'

Jenny looked at him, then at the floor, then at her own hands. Anywhere but at the body. 'I don't know what to do,' she whispered. 'I know what you need; I know you want me to identify her. I just... I can't...'

'Take your time, Miss Holloway,' the younger one repeated.

She took some deep breaths, in for five seconds, out for five seconds... *Do the visualisation technique Cheryl taught you. Your place of power... your still, cold, blue room, silent and safe. Bars on the window, bars on the door, and no one can get in, no one can harm you... safe for ever without end... Now, open your eyes. Do it now – get it over with...* She stood up straight, opened her eyes and approached the glass.

Sal was draped in a purple robe. It looked strangely regal. A bruise bloomed on her cheek, and her neck seemed too long. Too long and twisted. Jenny heard herself say: 'Why's her neck like that?'

'Her neck was broken in the fall,' the older policeman said impassively.

Her mother's hair, grey at the roots, and cut short, brutally short, made the neck seem even longer. Jenny pressed her forehead to the glass. Her mouth formed soundless words.

'What was that, Ms Holloway?' The elder policeman leaned towards her. 'Did you say something?'

'That's her. That's my mum.'

'Would you like to ask us any questions?'

Jen kept her eyes closed. 'What do I do next? The funeral?'

'We'll tell you when the body can be released,' the elder one told her.

Jenny opened her eyes a little. 'What? What does that mean?'

'Well, there'll be a post-mortem.'

'Why?'

'To ascertain the cause of death,' said the younger officer sadly.

'But, you said she fell. That's what happened, right?' Jenny's voice rose, and she turned from the glass. 'It was an accident. The policeman this morning told me so. You said that yourself.'

'Ms Holloway, any unexplained death has to be investigated.' The elder one looked at her kindly. 'It's routine. Please don't let it upset you.'

Jenny laughed then, a short, sharp mirthless bark. 'Oh my god, I couldn't do your job,' she muttered. 'I really couldn't.' Then she closed her eyes, leaned against the glass again, and when she opened them, she seemed calmer. 'I'm sorry. I didn't mean to be... horrible or anything; I don't want to make your day even worse, you know?'

'Can we give you a lift back home, Miss Holloway?'

'No.' She took some deep breaths. 'No, I have to… what did they say? I have to pick up her personal effects. Her teeth – her bridgework – came out, they told me.' She stopped suddenly, blinked. 'Actually, maybe I should go home. Yes. Shouldn't I?'

The younger officer took her by the elbow; the older one handed her a tissue.

As they walked back to the car park, she noticed that the cafe in the foyer was called The Spice of Life. Under other circumstances this would have made her laugh, but not today.

CHAPTER FOUR

You Can't Go Home Again

What does a person think about on the morning their mother dies? What will I remember? Some people get a call from a relative, or the hospital. Some people are there, at the deathbed, to hear, miss, hate or cherish those last moments. I didn't get any of that.

Death happens, and to some it's a shock, to others a release, but I haven't found the word yet. Is there a word for it? Maybe there are a lot of words for it. Maybe I need to use all those words.

Writing helps. My therapist has taught me that. She used the analogy of trepanning. 'Let the evil spirit out. It will be painful. It will be against your instincts.' I made some lame joke about her boring holes into my skull, but she didn't laugh. 'You're using humour to deflect attention,' she said. 'Release is against your instincts, feeling pain and acknowledging injury – it's against your instincts. It's not how you brought yourself up.' I must have paled, because that line *did* bore right into me. I did Bring Myself Up. I am self-made. But, sometimes – often – especially now, I feel like a child's first attempt at pottery – all misshapen and dented. The kind of thing only a mother would be proud of.

Let me tell you about my mum. Let me pull her out of this snarl, and set her upright in front of you. It's important that she's rescued from the mess her life became. She wasn't just a mess. She wasn't always a mess. She was wonderful. She was tall, like me, and lean. She looked like someone who ran, someone who worked out, even though she didn't. I've inherited that from her. I'm very lucky.

When I was small we would dance together. She had all these old records, singles from the 80s and 90s, 12 inches and albums. She'd put them on her little turntable and we'd dance to them – even the things you couldn't really dance to, like Nirvana and this other band called Chinaski. She was related to the singer somehow. I forget how. When she danced she'd shake her head and her hair – wavy pre-Raphaelite hair – would show all it's different russety shades. The light would come in through the kitchen window and shine through her hair like a stained-glass window. I thought she was beautiful. She *was* beautiful.

She sometimes used to pick me up from primary school and, when she did, she always wore dresses or skirts and blouses, never trousers, and her lean legs were pretty as a fawn's. Her skin was this beautiful matte golden colour, with little freckles, like a sprinkling of nutmeg, over her nose. I was so proud to be seen with her! Proud and loved and warm. Other kids' mothers were dumpy, or angry, or just not *there*, but my mum was so vivid. She was someone you remembered. Just looking at her did you good.

We used to go to Scarborough on holidays with Auntie K and her daughters (my mum's step-auntie, really, so my great aunt). K's boyfriend then was a big man called Granville who managed a hotel – The Windsor Castle it was called – and we'd stay for free – all crammed into two adjoining rooms. Mum kept all her 2p's aside so I could use them in the penny falls at the arcade. At night we'd stay up in the hotel bar, and Granville would make sure we had all the Pepsi we could drink. Mum and Auntie K might have a few drinks and sing. They both had lovely singing voices. The first time I heard Dusty Springfield, I thought, *That's my mum!*

It was just me and Mum, and it was perfect that way. We were poor, but so was everyone we knew, and at least my mum had a job – she worked as a receptionist at a dentist's surgery in town, and sometimes in a pub at night. She was very particular about her appearance – ironed hems, lacquered nails. Hair always washed and shiny. A little slick of lipstick.

Then she fell in love. She fell hard.

Right from the start I didn't like him. I knew he was a Bad Man. And with him around, things changed. She stopped singing. She started drinking more. One day I came back from school and she'd cut her hair off. I know it sounds silly, but it was as if all her strength was in that hair, and when she had it cut into a nondescript mum-helmet she started fading, fading fast. I date her decline from the haircut. The long, passive slide, hastened by The Bad Man, into what was the rest of her life.

I was thinking about her hair when the policeman was talking to me through the bathroom door, those glossy waves with the little glints of copper and gold. It seemed to hang in front of my eyes, beautifully, impossibly bright, and I wanted to tell him all about her: about her laugh and how she danced, about Scarborough, and how, on the beach, she'd let me bury her in the sand and then lurch out like a monster to play-scare me. She would be younger than I am now. Just a kid herself really, trying her best to raise me right, working hard to make me happy. I wanted them to understand, you know? This was not just a dead woman with a stretched-out broken neck. This was my *mum*, with her long legs and her wide smile and her ability to raise one eyebrow, and her dirty laugh and her glorious, glorious hair. You can't explain that to people though, can you? Not to the police anyway.

Someone can just... *die.* Someone can just cease to exist. Blink and they're gone. The last time I saw my mum, she'd been firing on all cylinders, spitting gin and slinging barbs, and now what? She went for a walk and died. She was there, and now she's not. Someone that vivid paled away to nothing? How can something natural feel so insane?

In the mortuary, I was alone with her one last time. But she didn't look like my mum. I couldn't even look at her for very long. It wasn't her. It was a body.

And that's when I began to cry, and just thought over and over *Mum, Mum I'm sorry*. I'm sorry.

XOXO Jay.

Jenny read the last line, mouthed the words silently to herself. Then she hit publish.

Freddie knocked on the study door, came in, and sat on the desk.

'Can you eat?' he asked.

She shook her head.

'Blog post?'

She nodded.

'Is that a good idea though? You don't have to share everything right away.'

'Oh, well, you know. It helps me to write,' she told him.

'I know. I know it does.' He squeezed her limp palm briefly. 'What can I do?'

'Just carry on being lovely.' She smiled at him.

'I just hope you won't get any crazies,' he said.

'Oh, I won't,' she told him firmly. 'They're good people.'

'OK, but let me monitor it, OK? Go and have a bath. Relax, try to have a nap? I don't want anyone to have a go at you.'

The first pings of response sounded within the hour. Regular readers rushing to Jenny's virtual side. Freddie kept an eye on the messages as he filled the dishwasher, happy to see that people were being nice. Apparently the post had helped Christie from Pontefract cry for the first time since her own mother's death two years before – 'RELEASE of tension!'; Liz from Braintree sent LOVE, and Maya Jayasinghe wrote (or cut and pasted) a touching haiku. Lisa Pike-was-Shay sent a link on an article about grief from the *Daily Mail*; ilovemykids1982 was concerned that Jay was putting too much pressure on herself to keep up the blog: 'You have enough on your plate with the counselling training, as well as work and the grieving process. TAKE TIME TO HEAL!!' but Trish Cole from Dover felt that the busier she was, the better, and signed off: 'From one neurotic to another, I appreciate your courage!' All the messages were positive. All expressed their absolute belief that Jenny was a Strong, Remarkable Woman who would Get Through This.

But then it all seemed to go wrong.

Theehedgewitch: *How did mum fall? Was she drunk? Drugs?*

Ilovemykids1982: *what? NOYB*

Theehedgewitch: *just asking unexplained death suicide?*

Ilovemykids1982: *Oh my god crawl back under your rock!*

Theehedgewitch: *All I can say is that at the end of the day you have one mother and that's it, why weren't she looking after her??? Why was she alone???*

EmmajCrawford: *awful news but @Theehedgewitch has a point. When my mother was sick I was there for her fair question imho*

Theehedgewitch: *THanku! Just sayin*

Ilovemykids1982: *ffs!! If you think she wasn't! The whole blog is about that! Read dont troll :-(*

Lilagracee: *A quick archive search would have told you that Jay did everything she could to help her mum, she gave up her job and* *everything to look after her! Does that sound like someone who doesn't care @Theehedgewitch??*

Ilovemykids1982: *Thanks @Lilagracee. For you newbies there Jay has been through a lot and weve all been on the journey with her so walk a mile in her shoes!*

Lilagracee: *Exactly. For example: I'm experimenting with pureed food. I'm like the mother of the world's largest baby – even Mum has to laugh! Today it was pumpkin, broccoli and sweetcorn (I know, right? Delicious.) What delicacy can I prepare for tomorrow? Carrots peas and kale? *shudders* In other news I borrowed some power tools and put up the handles she needs beside the bath and at the top of the stairs. I'm becoming quite the renaissance woman! Joking aside, Mum is making improvements day by day. I'm so proud of her! The MRI shows that she has scarring from previous mini strokes, which is why we have to be very careful, but the physio is definitely getting easier for her to manage. I can't thank you enough for all your messages of support! But, keep them coming! I need you guys!*

ilovemykids1982: *its just humbling*

Theehedgewitch: *you call me a troll but i'm entitled to my opinion there is such a thing as online bullying you know*

ilovemykids1982: *OMFG*

Lilagracee: *@Theehedgewitch Police always investigate an unexplained death UK law doesn't mean anything suspicious*

Laundryloony2: *Disgusting that Jay is being cross examined in this way!*

HollybFootitt: *She's just asking a question tho, no reason to jump on her imo*

Laundryloony2: *Oh really how would you feel if your mother just died and you were asked this???*

HollybFootitt: *My mother passed when I was a child, actually so don't talk to me about it*

Laundryloony2: *Just goes to show!!!!*

HollybFootitt: *????*

Lilagracee: *I really don't think this is necessary, come on ladies*

Ilovemykids1982: *Theehedgewitch I hope your mum dies bitch*

HollybFootitt: *WTF??*

A few years earlier, after she dropped out of university, Jenny often visited Freddie in London, where he was sharing a flat with five bisexual anthropology students and a bashful, bemused Greek. She wasn't doing much at the time, just kicking her heels at Sal's house and applying for temping jobs, but somewhere along the line she must have mentioned something vague about 'maybe writing some stories or something' and that's where the 'Jenny is a writer' idea came from. Every time she visited, without fail (usually at last orders at the student union bar), Freddie would bring out his tub and start thumping; she was *talented! Seriously, in school? She was so good. Inventive. Seriously! Tell her, will you?* Then they'd have another drink, head to a club and all careers advice was put on hold until the next hungover morning. When he graduated and moved back home – well, not home, but the nearest city, where Jenny was working as a receptionist in a doctors' surgery, his ambition for her coalesced into a firm objective. It wasn't right that she was wasting herself on stupid menial jobs. *You're better than that.*

'This whole benign bully thing? You can stop that any time you want you know,' she told him.

They were moving Freddie into his new flat. Very grown up. But then Freddie had done what you're supposed to do and had finished university, and his parents, Ruth and Graham, had done what parents are supposed to do and helped him with a deposit to buy a flat.

'You've got to be cruel to be kind.' Freddie had aped the local accent.

'You catch more flies with honey than with vinegar.' Jenny's pale face had shone with sweat as she struggled with a box marked 'Kitchen shit'.

'Fortune favours the bold.' Freddie took the box off her.

'Good. Better. Best. Bested,' she replied smugly.

'Now, you see, I don't even know what that means,' Freddie told her. 'So that *proves* you're cleverer than me, and you shouldn't be on minimum wage. So, in a very real sense, I'm brilliant.'

'I like it there,' she lied. 'The people are nice.'

'It's between the magistrates' court and the dole office. Literally nobody there is nice.'

'You're a snob,' she told him, smiling, and passed him a beer.

'I'm not though. I'm…' She watched his expression descend from happy banter to serious pondering, and felt herself tense. 'It's not snobbery. It's worry.' He swigged his beer and turned to her. 'Have you thought about talking to someone?' This was the new tack he'd decided to take with her: her lack of ambition was a psychological issue that could be fixed. 'Not finishing university. Jen, you broke down for a reason—'

'I didn't *break down*. I quit. That's all. I couldn't afford the debt.' She frowned at a handful of knives. 'We don't all have to go to university.'

'Put that down, will you?' Freddie took the box from her, put it on the work surface. 'We've never really talked about what happened.'

'That's because nothing *happened*.' Jenny frowned. 'I just got sick of it. I wanted to get a proper job—'

'Living the dream, dishing out methadone scripts and scrubbing up tramp vomit?'

'Someone's got to do these jobs, Fred.'

'You're *right*. But that someone doesn't have to be *you*. You're better than that. It's like you're *punishing* yourself or something—'

'You need to lay off the self-help books.'

'Well, maybe you could do with reading a few,' he told her. 'Or maybe talking to a proper counsellor would help? Something's holding you back. The refuge? That had to be tough; I mean you were only fourteen? Fifteen…?'

Her face hardened. 'You see, that's exactly what I don't like about the whole counselling idea. Poking about in the past, looking for something to blame everything on. It's-it's childish.'

'So, Marc, your mum drinking, the refuge… none of that hurt you in any way, is that what you're saying?' Freddie asked her softly. 'Nothing to see here, move on. Is that it?'

'It's just paying someone to whine at them,' she muttered.

'OK, would you say that if it was me that was going for counsel-ling? Would you call it whining then?'

'No. But—'

'There you are then.' Freddie's face shone pink and smug. He drained his beer. 'Look, I'm back now, I'm on your doorstep, and I'm not going to quit. I'm giving you fair warning. This is my thing now. It's Project Jen from now on.'

'It's expensive though. I'd only get five sessions free,' Jenny frowned, but she was wavering. Freddie pressed his advantage.

'I'll lend you the money.'

'Well. There's Cheryl, the woman who does counselling sessions at the surgery. She's nice…' began Jenny doubtfully. 'I could see if she takes private clients—'

'Do it,' Freddie told her, took her empty bottle and replaced it with a full one. 'Just give it a go?'

'No. It's stupid.'

Freddie shook his head gravely. 'It's not. Stupid is wasting your life. Stupid is giving up on yourself. And that's what you've been doing for the last few years. Admit it.'

Later, when Jenny started training to become a counsellor herself, it was Freddie who brought up the idea of blogging. '"Counselling journey?"' She winced.

'OK, all right, it sounds cheesy but think about it. When you started this whole thing, navigating all the different training paths was so hard you nearly quit before you began, remember? If there'd been a blog or a site or whatever, where you could see someone else was having the same kind of experiences, it would've helped wouldn't it? And blogging might, I don't know, give you a creative outlet.'

'Project Jen is still up and running then?'

'It's my thing now. I told you.'

'I have precious little time as it is, between college and work.'

'OK, how about this: it'd be more of an online journal. I mean you're meant to keep some kind of reflective diary for the course or something, aren't you?'

'Yeah. That's a nightmare actually. It feels really artificial doing this diary at the end of each session. I feel like Anne Frank.'

'OK, so if you made it into a blog, you'd be doing what they want you to do with the diary and all, *and* you'd be helping other people and getting feedback and it'd be like a—'

'You're about to say *community,* aren't you?' Jenny grimaced.

'I was. I'm sorry but, look, it's *hard* what you're doing. I just think that writing about it might help you. Everyone needs support, and this way you'll be getting support from people who really understand what it is you're going through… keeping up with the coursework, as well as going through therapy *yourself* and—'

'I don't know,' she muttered. 'It's not really *me*. Blogging.'

'Well, a bit ago, training to be a counsellor wasn't "you" either, was it? And what if you're not "you" anyway? Use a pseudonym. No one has to know it's you. One of the Kardashians checks into hotels as "Princess Jasmine".'

'"One of the Kardashians"?'

'Okay. Kim. It's Kim.'

'What about "Sigourney Beaver"? Is that one taken?'

'You might get the wrong kind of readers with that one.'

'"J-Ho"?'

'Again—'

'"J. K. Growler"?'

'Enough. Stop. Not even this level of facetiousness can derail Project Jenny. See if you can do it first, then decide on a name. A non-porny name.'

And so she'd talked it over with her tutor, who'd agreed that, in principle, a blog could be viewed as a reflective diary portion of the course, so long as it was anonymised. And so, online, Jenny became Jay.

During the few weeks she spent on cautious research, she discovered that the Internet was a murky river swelled by horribly written streams of consciousness. She read blogs about childcare, about depressing Tinder dates, about gardening, weight loss, teeth alignment, and artisanal breakfasts. Freddie was right, there wasn't much out there about training to be a counsellor – how gruelling it could be, how emotionally demanding, unexpectedly hilarious, and fascinating it was. There was a gap she could fill.

It didn't take long for her to get a following, especially once Freddie drafted in his ex-boyfriend to do something complicated sounding with Google to get more hits. Soon more people – mostly women– were reading her posts and seeing something of themselves in her and her situation. Freddie was right: she was a naturally inventive writer, funny, insightful, charming. She soon came to rely on the appreciation and support she received from her readers.

When Sal had the stroke, and Jenny moved back to the village to take care of her, she changed the blog name from the almost criminally dull *Jay's Counselling Training* to *You Can't Go Home Again* – a strange, evocative phrase that had come to her out of the ether. It fitted perfectly; she was home again, but it wasn't a home; she was the grown-up daughter, of a now infantile mother… the axis had changed. The messages and comments she received showed her that the world was full of women a lot like her: women with demons, women with pasts, women who loved her, who needed her. And, now that she had her 'community' (a hateful phrase but an accurate one), she realised how lonely she'd been without them.

'I told you! Didn't I tell you?' Freddie had asked delightedly. 'I mean, this could be your *thing*, I mean, you're *helping* people, Jen!'

*

Now though, that precious community was divided as the sniping continued, mushroomed. *Ping ping ping.* Jenny watched it unfold on her phone screen, but didn't step in to calm things down. Instead she stared into the mirror until the steam obscured the pale oval of her face, the snaky mass of hair, the quiet, hooded eyes. Each question shouted in caps lock was horribly valid:

WHY WEREN'T YOU WITH HER THAT NIGHT?

SHOULDN'T YOU HAVE BEEN BETTER AT THE JOB OF LOOKING AFTER HER?

WHAT KIND OF A DAUGHTER ARE YOU ANYWAY?

There was a knock on the door. 'Jenny? You're not on your phone, are you?' Freddie's anxious voice told her that he too had been reading the comments. She left a long pause.

'I probably shouldn't have posted anything,' she admitted finally.

'Just, don't respond, OK?' Freddie told her. 'Please? Or let me help?'

'Fred?'

'Yes, darling?'

'They're right. What they're saying – it's true.' She was still staring at her reflection.

'It's not true though,' Freddie said flatly. 'Don't read anything else. It's all bullshit.'

Jenny noticed, with a detached interest, the nerve jumping beside her mouth. This hadn't happened in years, this old twitch. This Tell.

While Jenny was in the bath, Freddie had panic-ordered Chinese, and far too much of it. Jenny gamely ate a few spring rolls and poked about in some noodles, but an hour later, the dining table was still strewn with barely dented containers of congealing food.

'You can't let them get to you,' Freddie said.

'Is it still going on?'

'A bit,' he admitted. 'But they'll get sick of it soon.'

Jenny coughed. 'So I have to call the council on Monday.'

'Why?'

'About the house? They'll want it back. It was in Mum's name, so...'

Freddie shifted uncomfortably. 'How long have you got then?'

'Couple of weeks. I'll have to call Kathleen.' Kathleen was one of her shadowy 'aunties', who now operated a bar in Tenerife.

'Well, shouldn't she come back to help? If she's a relative.' Freddie huffed indignantly.

'She hasn't got the money to get on a plane just to babysit me.' Jenny looked at him and smiled. 'That's what she'd say anyway.'

'It's not babysitting, it's support.'

'No.' Jenny made a vague gesture. 'I've got to clean Mum's place, and I'm not sure Kathleen would be much of a help anyway.'

Freddie thought of Sal's grimy house, the stained carpets, the dirty windows. There might not be a lot of furniture to dispose of, but there would be a hell of a lot of cleaning to do. 'OK. Listen. I'll take leave and give you a hand with the cleaning,' he answered firmly.

'Oh, you don't have to do that,' Jenny murmured.

'Babe, you don't have to do everything yourself, you know. I think you're expecting a bit too much of yourself,' Freddie told her. 'Look, all this happened *today*. You're not just going to bounce back. You're going to have to be a bit more realistic.'

She smiled bleakly at him. 'None of this feels real though. I feel like I'm in a play or something. And I'm under-rehearsed. Everyone else seems to know what they're doing but me. It was stupid, I know, but I thought that if I wrote about it, I could... comprehend it.' She looked over at her laptop. 'But that didn't work. Everyone'll blame me. I know it. Everyone will start having a go.'

'You don't have an obligation to let the world know everything that happens to you. Your only obligation is to get through the next few days and weeks as best you can, and rely on your friends – your real, *actual* friends – to help you. Not these trolls.'

'They're just saying what everyone else thinks – Kathleen, the people in the village, the police and everyone'll think the same thing. I wasn't there. I should have been there, and I wasn't,' she said flatly.

'Don't get paranoid... Try not to get... maudlin. I mean—'

'No, you're right. What am I doing?' She looked at him bleakly. 'I mean, all I have to do is tell everyone that the woman I was caring for is dead, arrange the funeral. Find the *money* for the funeral somehow. Give the house back. Find somewhere to live. Oh, and when I have time, do a bit of grieving. I don't know what I'm getting so stressed out about. Sorry, *maudlin* about.' She opened her laptop, winced at the comments, closed it again.

'I'll help you,' Freddie told her. 'You're not doing anything by yourself, OK? You're not. And that *maudlin* thing – that was a stupid thing to say, I'm sorry.'

'It really was,' Jenny replied. 'Dick move.' They sat in woeful silence for a minute. 'You're right though. I can't just… collapse,' she said eventually. 'Things have got to be done, and I have to do them. There isn't anyone else.'

'Leave the blog for now though?' he asked. 'You don't need these people making you feel worse.'

She looked seriously at him. 'I do need them though.'

He was about to ask about the bruise on her chin, now undisguised by make-up, a green/blue smear, but he didn't. He'd already upset her enough. Instead he sat with her, watching the storm on the blog begin to blow itself out. @Theehedgewitch was cornered into accepting that she'd started the argument. @HollybFootitt confessed that she'd never allowed herself to grieve over her own mother, and maybe that's why she'd been such a bitch about things, and @Laundryloony2 posted a soothing Gandhi quote that Freddie was pretty sure wasn't Gandhi at all, but Beyoncé. Once things calmed down, Jenny felt able to sleep. It was as if they'd granted her clemency.

CHAPTER FIVE

Jenny woke late the next day with an unfamiliar brown taste in her mouth and a slight headache. Freddie had already left for work but had left her a note saying he'd try to get back early. He didn't want her to be on her own too much.

With her hair tied back, with no make-up, she looked so much like Sal. She stared at her haunted face in the hallway mirror: a face with brownish pouches around the eyes, crushed-looking cheeks, and, between the brows, a deep comma of worry.

Half an hour later she was making the calls.

Kathleen, who never cried, who prided herself on never crying, sobbed down the line from Tenerife.

'She was better! When I spoke to her last week, she said she was feeling better! Said she was going to try to go back to work!'

Jenny swallowed, hard, and met her mother's eyes in the mirror. 'She-she hadn't been looking after herself,' she managed.

'What? What d'you mean not "looking after herself"?'

'Well… she'd started drinking again.'

Kathleen's voice cracked with tearful indignation. 'Well why didn't you *stop* her?'

Jenny's voice cracked too. 'I *tried*! I really tried, Kathleen, I did!'

'And what? She had another stroke? What happened?'

'No. She fell. They said she fell and hit her head. She'd had a few drinks.'

'Where? In the house?'

'No, outside. It was snowing; it was the middle of the night; I don't know why she was out, I— Kathleen, don't cry, please? If you cry, I'll start, and—' Jenny moved the phone away from her ear and watched her reflection wince, watched the hand holding the phone shaking, watched until it stilled. She heard the snap and fizz of a cigarette being lit. Kathleen thanked someone in a wobbly voice that sounded old, fearful. 'I'm sorry, Kathleen, I am. I tried my hardest, but… I'm sorry to ruin your day. Don't feel you have to come back or anything, you've got the bar to look after and—'

'Oh bugger the bar!' Kathleen drew a shuddery breath. 'And, I know you did your best with her. She was her own worst enemy was Sal.' Blowing the smoke out, Jenny could hear the little wheeze in her throat. That familiar little wheeze. 'When's the funeral?' she said eventually.

'After the post-mortem,' Jenny answered softly.

'What? Why're they having a post-mortem?'

'I don't know. They said they had to. Unexplained death.' Jenny pushed one hand through her hair and closed her eyes, pivoted her body away from the mirror. 'It's all just—'

'I can't take it in, Jenny. I can't.' Kathleen sounded scared, again. Kathleen was never scared. 'It's just… a shock. Thought I'd go first, you know?'

'You're tough as old boots,' said Jenny.

'I *was*,' Kathleen answered seriously. 'I was, but I'm not feeling it now.'

'Kathleen, I'm-I'm sorry I had to tell you like this. On the phone. I had to though, I couldn't not have told you. I mean, you were like sisters.'

'Oh, don't!' And her voice was clotted with sobs again. 'Don't. Listen, I'll come back – when? Tomorrow? I'll come back tomorrow.'

'What? Why?' She caught a quick flash of her reflection again. 'No, it'll cost you money to come back—'

'Bugger that. Roisin'll sub me. She's got her divorce money through.' Roisin was one of Kathleen's taciturn and faintly intimidating daughters. 'I'll get back as soon as I can, OK?'

The next few calls were easier. Mrs Hurst who ran the cleaning business Sal had worked for had already heard via the village grapevine. Kathleen's other daughter, Maraid, took it well, but then nothing seemed to impinge on her stoicism. Jenny then left a voicemail for her therapist, Cheryl, and called her personal tutor to explain that she wouldn't be able to make the next few workshops and might be late with the next essay. He specialised in grief and trauma, so he was very sympathetic. The last person she called was Andreena, a relatively new friend, but already like family. She came over.

CHAPTER SIX

Andreena's expressions were vivid, extreme. Like an expanding thundercloud, they spread rapidly over her face, only to disperse just as quickly. Some people found that unsettling. Jenny had met her when she'd been temping at the Council Tax department three years ago, just before her stint at the doctor's surgery. She was warned about the fearsome HR manager who had refused to give up her office when the rest of the department went open-plan; who wore huge gold crosses and signed off her emails with a blood curdling bible verse.

But Jenny had soon discovered that Andreena was nowhere near as terrifying as her reputation, and it was probably the fact that she was a Union representative that genuinely scared the management. Charmingly, she had a childlike love of cat memes and a genuine, fierce loyalty to those close to her. And the bible verses? They weren't that bad once you got used to them. She tended to stick to the Psalms anyway, and avoided Leviticus after one of her nephews came out as gay.

When Jenny heard Andreena's little Fiesta putter down the drive, she ran to open the back door. Her friend was carefully unfurling her six-foot frame from the small car. The turban she wore added a further four inches to her height. She advanced with her arms open, like a statue of the Virgin Mary, and Jenny was enveloped in a strong, almost painful, hug.

Over coffee in the kitchen, Dree held Jenny's hand, glared at her affectionately and asked: 'How are you?'

Jenny frowned. 'I'm not sure. Shocked, still, I think. I find myself doing normal things and then thinking I'm weird for being able to function normally. It's... I—'

Andreena held one hand up and managed to smile and frown at the same time. 'You shouldn't feel guilty.'

'No?' Jenny looked at her clasped hands, serious eyes under knotted brows. 'I wasn't with her. If I'd been with her I wouldn't have let her go out for a walk. The one night I spend away...'

Andreena's brows pinched. Her mouth pulled down at the edges. 'Are you eating?' Andreena thought food cured just about everything. 'I brought some things over—'

'Oh, Freddie bought loads of food—'

'Fruit. And some curry, and, what's this? Cake? Banana bread...'

'Oh, Dree, you didn't have to do that—'

'And brandy and soursop tea to help you sleep.' She seemed to have come to the end of the bag of provisions. 'Eat and sleep. It's important. If you try to be too strong, you'll break,' she said firmly. 'I've seen it. I know.'

'I don't feel very strong,' Jenny muttered. 'I can't seem to pull myself together. I need to go to college. I've got to call the council.'

'Now, you see, you're robbing Peter to pay Paul.' Andreena's face shone with delight that she'd found such an appropriate idiom. 'Listen; when my brother called me, told me "Mummy's passed", I was strong, too. I went to work. I cooked. I cleaned. I was' – she emphasised the last word with a little hand squeeze – 'fine. I booked my ticket and didn't cry on the plane, or when I saw Hopeton waiting at the airport; when I saw Mummy in her coffin, I didn't break. "Who needs to cry?" I said. All these fools are crying, and it wouldn't do a bit of good, and Mummy didn't like crying. Now, you know what happened when I came home?'

'What?' Jen whispered.

'I went to bed and I didn't get *out* of bed for a month. It all hit me – *pow* – like a plank, and I was no good to man nor beast.' She grimaced with an odd sort of satisfaction.

'Mmmm.'

'It's not healthy to be British. Carry on, carry on until you die. No. Cry. Don't be afraid. Don't think about other people. Stop that now,' she said in a low, serious voice. 'You look after your*self*, you take help from your *friends*. You *grieve*.'

And she stared meaningfully at Jenny, until she did begin to feel herself crying; first, quietly, and then loud, ugly tears. And Dree patted and cooed, gave her kitchen roll, made her sip tea until she calmed.

Then she said: 'Tell me. Tell me what you're thinking.'

Jenny's voice was wobbly; she looked at her knees. 'I did a rotten job of looking after her. I'm a rotten daughter. I know it. Everyone knows it.'

Andreena made one of those noises peculiar to her, a kind of quizzical, amused squeal. 'How were you a bad daughter? And who is this *everyone*? Tell me?' She waved one bangled arm around the room.

Jenny took a deep breath, dabbed at her eyes with more kitchen roll. 'There are things I should have done. I should have stayed the night with her, Dree, I should've. If I'd done that, she'd still be here.' She watched fearfully as Andreena sat back, her face a curious mixture of conflicting expressions. 'You see? You *do* think I'm—'

Andreena's voice was as sharp as her face was kind. 'Don't tell me what I *think*. Tell me what *happened*.'

'No. No, you'll think badly of me,' Jenny answered. Through her tears she could see Andreena's face soften. She took a deep, shuddering breath.

'Tell me,' Andreena said softly. 'Tell me and maybe you'll feel better. Nothing can be that bad, can it?'

'I don't know about that. It *feels* that bad,' Jenny sobbed.

'Jenny,' Andreena's face was world-weary now, 'if you think I can't guess what happened, you're silly. Believe me. Nothing gets past me.'

'What d'you think happened?' Jenny whispered. She stared at her own shaking fingers, knotted together on her quivering knees. The nerve by her mouth twitched like a fishing line snagged in weeds.

Andreena sat back on the chair, then opened the small bottle of brandy and poured a generous dollop into their mugs. It merged, turbid and nasty looking, with the dregs of the tea. She pushed it towards Jenny.

'I think that your mum was a difficult woman. I think that she drank too much. I think that maybe she said something nasty, and that's why you came here. For a break. I can understand why, it's a nice house.' She looked around the clean kitchen. 'Is that what happened?'

'Yes,' Jenny whispered.

'Is that all that happened?'

'What d'you mean?'

Her voice was so soft now. Andreena put one firm hand on her knee. 'Did she hurt you? That's what I mean.'

'No! God, no! Mum wouldn't do anything like that—'

Andreena reached one swift hand to Jenny's jaw. 'You're bruised here.'

Jenny hastily pulled her hair out of its ponytail. She let the tears come.

'Listen to me.' Andreena's voice was low, husky, hypnotic. 'You're a loyal person. You're a good daughter.' She put up one hand to ward off any disagreements. 'It isn't easy to admit that bad things are happening, is it? And so you push it down and push it down, and you break. Eventually you break. And you do something that normally you'd never do.'

'What do you mean? "Something you'd never do"?' Jenny looked at her friend like a python's hypnotised prey. 'Did you do something… bad. To your mother I mean?'

Andreena blinked slowly, and when she opened her eyes, they were dim with memory. 'I ran from her. I ran away from Jamaica because of her. I loved her, but she'd do things… ach.' She pushed a rough hand through the air. Bangles clinked and clashed. 'But you? You *moved back* to be with yours! And one night, one night only, you run away.'

'And look what happened.'

'You run away. To be safe,' Andreena told her seriously, and touched the bruise on her chin. 'That's good. That's a good thing to do.'

'But if I'd been with her, she wouldn't have *died*.' Jenny looked at her. 'That's what people are going to think! I posted something on my blog about it. Maybe I shouldn't have done. I wasn't thinking straight. I'm just so used to writing what I'm feeling, you know? But then some people started being awful, and there was a big row, and it just… That's what everyone is going to think. That I… did something bad.'

Andreena smiled solemnly. 'Well maybe they will. Crazy people make a lot of noise. And on the Internet?' She puffed out some air, her hands made the shape of an explosion.

'They're *right* though, aren't they?' Jenny muttered.

'They are? And how many of them have your worries? Hmm? Listen to me now. People will always chat nonsense. They've been doing that since the beginning of time but, unless they're paying your rent? Pay. No. Mind.' This was Andreena's favourite maxim. 'Listen. If you can look after other people, you can look after yourself. Am I right? Now it's time for you to do that. No guilt. No excuses. Live for yourself now.'

'That doesn't seem right,' Jenny whispered.

'It is though,' Andreena said.

'How did you get out of work today?' Jenny asked her after a pause.

'I told them there was a problem with my daughter,' Andreena answered. 'And I was right, wasn't I?' Jenny was beginning to cry again, and Dree pulled her close. Her coat smelled of cinnamon. Her hug was, as always, fierce with love. 'Start to live for yourself. Never blame yourself for things that happened in the past. Anything. Promise me?'

'I promise.'

That night Jenny suffered through a heavy medicated sleep with nightmares that were not really nightmares but heightened memories. The sudden shocking thud of a head against the wall. The broken picture and the blood on the carpet. Sal's stretched neck and the snow. *I'm sorry to tell you that your mother has died.*

Her shouts woke Freddie in the room next door, and he stumbled in, all bed hair and panic. 'Oh God, what happened?'

'Nothing, just a bad dream, I'm sorry. I kept trying to wake up and I couldn't. Those sleeping pills I took…' She was sweating, face clenched, the demon panic sitting on her chest.

'You were screaming something.'

'Oh God, I'm sorry! What did I say?' She sat up in bed, still shaking.

'You kept saying "Get up! Get up!"'

She settled back into the rumpled pillows. 'You and I were being chased. We were being followed. You fell, and I was trying to help you up. The snow… the snow kept burying you and I couldn't dig you out fast enough.' She laughed shakily. 'That's all I remember. Shit. That was horrible!' She passed a sweaty hand through her hair. 'No more of those pills for me. I'd rather not sleep.'

'I'll stay with you, OK? Until you get back to sleep.'

And he did, though he dropped off first, his pink round face losing years as he slept. Cherubic and innocent. Jenny closed her eyes, went into her place of power – the blue room, that safe space, but it seemed to have lost its magic. Sal's long neck snaked through the sturdy bars; her weak cries could be heard through the walls, and Jenny, unsafe, exposed, felt fear. It was dawn before she finally fell into an exhausted slumber. And she didn't dream, thank God.

CHAPTER SEVEN

The next day, Freddie and Jenny headed to Sal's house to start on the cleaning.

'So, what, we get the furniture sorted first? We won't have time to do the carpets.' Freddie puffed beneath his bin bags. 'We'll need a proper cleaning service to do them I think.'

'No, Kathleen said that Maraid will lend us her Vax.'

Freddie thought of the state of the carpets. He wasn't sure a Vax would do it either.

Jenny had been skittish all morning. The sleepless shadows beneath her eyes gave her a haunted look. She drank a few sips of coffee, put the mug down, forgot it, and made another, forgot that too. They stopped in the village shop on the way to the house, and Jenny spent an inordinate amount of time talking about the relative effectiveness of various cleaning products, insisting that they get new scrubbers, bleach, stain remover, while Freddie hovered behind her, his face creased with concern. When it came to pay, she realised that she'd come out without her purse, so Freddie had to buy it all, packing the bags while Jenny kept up her rambling monologue on what to clean and how to do it, and the woman on the till looked on with an uneasy sympathy, eventually offering shy condolences.

'I was very sorry to hear about Sal,' she said, stopping Jenny in mid flow. 'She was a lovely woman. We used to see a lot of her. Before the stroke, you know.'

There was an awkward pause. 'Thank you,' Jenny mumbled.

'If there's anything I can do?'

Jenny smiled crookedly. 'Well, if she ran up a gin bill, you could write it off. That'd help.'

The woman's face froze in confusion. Freddie winced. Jenny seemed to come to a little. She shook her head in a dazed way, as if she was shaking off a cloud of flies.

'I'm sorry. I don't know why I said that. If there *is* a bill, then of course I'll—'

'There's no bill,' the woman told her. Confused disapproval flowed from her every pore.

Freddie took Jenny by the elbow, and together they walked slowly, and in silence now, towards the estate. At the bend in the road, she stopped like a stalled horse.

'We'll do as much as you can stand, OK? It'll be all right. Just let me know when you've had enough, and we'll go home, OK?' Freddie told her.

Despite standing empty for only two days, the house smelled neglected and damp. The glasses were still on the floor; the sticky kitchen table was now covered with a thin patina of dust. Freddie walked ahead of Jenny, an advance guard, while she hung back by the door. She only came into the room fully when Freddie crunched one boot on the glass that still littered the stairs.

'Here, pick up the bigger bits and we'll wrap them in newspaper,' she told him. 'Watch it, though, because it's all over the stairs.'

'What happened?' Freddie picked up the photo, shook it free of glass, and pulled one shard out of infant Jenny's face.

'Accident, that's all.' Jenny was picking up splinters, her fingers drifting over the blood on the carpet. 'She knocked it off going up the stairs.'

'What about the blood?'

'That's mine. I tried to clean it up, but I got sidetracked getting her to bed and—' She showed him a half-healed cut on one thumb.

'OK then, I'll clean this up,' Freddie said eventually.

'No. No, I'll do it.'

And, still without looking at him, she plunged her hand into the shopping bag.

'No, Jen, not that!' Freddie grabbed at it. 'It's spray bleach. You need the stain remover.' She didn't let go, though, and her face, behind her loose hair, seemed set in a snarl. He almost recoiled. 'Jen – let me do this, come on.'

'No. I'm fine. I can do it.'

'For sure, but not with bleach.' He leaned down to look into her eyes. 'You're not OK.'

'I'm fine.'

'You're *not* though.' He led her stiffly to the kitchen. 'Look, you make a start in here and I'll – deal with the stairs. OK?'

She nodded, took a shuddery breath. From her coat pocket, her phone rang. 'Missed it.' She looked at the screen, pale and tired. 'Kathleen. I'll go outside to call her. She can be funny about people overhearing her on the phone.'

She wasn't outside for long, and from what Freddie could see, Kathleen did most of the talking, while Jenny answered only: 'Yes, yes, of course, yes.'

She came back into the kitchen and shrugged her coat off.

'Everything OK?'

'Yup.' She kept her head down, and grabbed a handful of scrubbers with one shaking hand.

'You're sure?' Freddie asked. 'You don't look like everything's OK. Did she upset you?'

'She said that Maraid will only lend me the Vax if I give her the telly and the nest of tables.'

'Are you kidding me?' Freddie was all indignance. 'She's family, for God's sake! I mean—' The sight of Jenny's strained, pale face stopped him. 'That's bullshit, though. Really.'

Jenny made a shaky, vague gesture. 'Families. That's just what she's like. I'm not going to argue with her about it, I don't have the energy. Plus she scares the shit out of me, Maraid.'

'But, it's your mum's stuff, I mean, by rights it's yours, surely—'

'I don't *want* any of her stuff!' Jenny cried, almost savagely. 'It's all… shit. It's all cheap shit!'

'Babe – sit down.'

'No. I just want to get on with the cleaning now.' That rage had left her voice, left her weakened, grim. 'Let's just do that, shall we? Make a start anyway.'

'Do you want me to call Kathleen back? I mean—'

'God no!' Jenny said. 'She'd kill me if you did that. No, I'll just let her have the TV. It'd only remind me of Mum anyway. I don't want to argue about it. Right. You do the stairs, and I'll start in here.' She moved briskly to the sink.

'Take it easy though, will you?' Freddie hovered behind her. 'Any time you need to stop, just stop, OK?'

And so Freddie spent the half hour carefully spraying and dabbing at the blood on the wall, which he soon had down to a pastel smear. The carpet cleaner, driven into the cheap shallow weave, fizzed pinkly with dissolving blood. From the kitchen he heard the scrape of crockery being dragged out of cupboards, the splash and gurgle of water in the sink.

All morning they scrubbed and dusted and aired the place out, until their eyes and fingers stung with bleach, and the scent of lemons drove out the cigarettes.

By early afternoon they stood on the cusp of Sal's bedroom, spooked as children.

'I can do this for you,' Freddie told her.

Jenny let out air through pursed lips. 'No. I'm not going to be a pussy about this.' She took one determined step into the room. Then another. Then stopped. 'I can still feel my mum. Isn't that weird?' She looked over her shoulder at Freddie. 'I keep imagining she's in the next room. Andreena told me the other day that when her mum died she saw her afterwards. Just walking around her house. Behind her in the mirror.'

'God, that's creepy!' Freddie shuddered.

'She said it was a nice thing, like her mum was telling her that everything was all right, that she needn't feel bad. She said she saw her on and off for a whole year, until she stopped grieving and accepted what'd happened.' She turned around fully to face him. 'You don't believe in ghosts, do you?'

'Not really.'

'Me neither,' Jenny replied. There was a pause. On the bed, a gaudy flowered wrap lay spreadeagled, it's sleeves puffed as if they still held phantom limbs. 'Look at that. She loved that thing. She claimed it was silk. It's not though. It's only polyester.'

'Jen, really, why don't you let me do this?'

'No. We'll do it together.'

'Or we can come back tomorrow maybe?'

'No.' She pulled a bin bag off the roll, a loud rip in the stillness. 'If you do the wardrobe, I'll do the chest of drawers, OK?'

'OK.' Freddie opened a window a crack to let in some fresh air. In its reflection he watched Jenny hesitantly approaching the bed, placing one spread palm on the gown, letting it hover, and then grasping it suddenly, bagging it up and throwing it into the bag with a grimace.

By 4 p.m. they had stopped for the day.

'We can go for a drink on the way back if you want?' Freddie opened the door, peered at the darkening sky. 'They might still be serving food.'

She followed, hesitated, stopped. 'No, you know what? I think I'm going to stay here. Just this one night.'

'What? I don't think that's a good idea—'

'No. I want to. I don't know why, but I think it'll help. Honestly.' She smiled at him. 'Don't worry.'

'OK, I'll stay with you—'

'No.' Jenny was firm, serious. 'I think I should be on my own for a while.'

CHAPTER EIGHT

Jenny didn't stay in the house for long. Half an hour later she texted Freddie to make sure he was at his parents, and then took a taxi to the train station, keeping her head down; she didn't want to risk anyone in the village seeing her, wondering where she was going, mentioning it to Freddie. That was the problem with villages... they were boring places filled with boring people who had nothing better to do than Notice Things. At the station she bought a ticket to the city and, in the train, sank into a still meditation, here and not here, present and past, and when the train stopped she merged with the rush hour crowds in the dark streets, under the dark sky, just another grey bobbing face.

Then she turned east, and the streets were emptier here. Striding through the semi-derelict covered market, past dirty drifts of swept-up snow, past a pub with broken panes covered with plywood, named, incongruously, Pretty Windows, and up the hill, the winding, bleak hill to what, years ago, was Home. Her mind meandered around the narrow alley of the word. *Was this still Home? Home is where the heart dies. Home is where the hatred lies. You can't go home again.* The years hadn't dimmed her memory. If anything, going over the same memories again and again had scored them deeper into her brain like scars. Here was red brick on red brick under a lowering sky; halal butchers and Polski Skleps; dull-eyed teens and overtired toddlers. Here was The Fox, the pub where Mum had worked, where she'd met Marc. Here was the taxi rank they'd run to that night. Here was the drain down which her family photos had swirled. Here was the wall against which she'd been pinned, legs dangling, his fingers crushing her windpipe. Everything was the same, and everything smelled of rain, coppery and dense as blood.

She got to their old house, the front door still scabrous black. No handle, just the flimsy Yale lock that a child could open using any old bit of plastic. The only things different were the curtains. These were nets with grimy bunched bottoms, whereas theirs had been blue with little grey flowers. Maraid had run them up on her sewing machine when they'd first moved in with Marc. Quiet. It was so quiet on this street. You could hear everything on this street. You learned not to say anything on this street. You had to keep secrets on this street.

Like a sleepwalker, Jenny walked down the alleyway to the back of the row, stopping just at the edge of her old back garden behind the still-broken wall. The garden had been paved since they lived there, and all the sad little flowers that Sal had planted must have died years ago.

She stared at the house and felt the scummy tide of pain, of grief, of rage rush towards her. Home was where it had all started. Home was where everything wrong…

From far away, she heard a car backfiring. Jangly music in some guttural language pumped out of a nearby window. A thin cat, one-eyed and friendly, undulated over the broken bricks. She put out one hand and stroked its ears. The animal purred, tense, purred and tensed and, in Jenny's mind the two Sals merged and detached, merged again a blurring confusion, a foggy duo. Dancing Sal, who sang like Dusty Springfield. Dresses and shiny hair, red nails and laughter. Older Sal, cut down short like her hair, trembling before Marc, and never singing a note. And behind them both? That was the thing she didn't want to see. Blood in her hair. She imagined small dykes carved in the snow, first deep then shallow, then mere grazes: the evidence of a useless struggle to right herself. Sal wasn't a natural struggler. It would have been better if she hadn't bothered. It would have been quicker.

The wind picked up, blowing fresh sleet, limey light filtered through the black clouds hovering over The Fox and spreading towards the city.

The cat crouched, shivered. Up close, Jenny could see that it didn't have one eye; its left was just so infected that it had closed behind a gummy scab of pus. No collar. Fur sparsely covering its bumpy, knotted spine. It gazed at her, closed its good eye into a cat smile. Even now, it wanted to please, even now, when it looked close to death. Jenny gently picked it up, feeling it curl gratefully against her chest with a rusty purr. 'I'll keep you safe,' she whispered. 'I promise.'

She stopped at the shop on the corner to see *if they had any boxes and maybe a bag to keep it dry?*

The woman on the till shook her head sorrowfully at the animal. 'I've seen that around for the last few weeks. Poor thing.'

'She doesn't belong to anyone then?'

'No. She mustn't. Nobody would let a cat get into that state.'

'I want to take her to a vet,' Jenny said.

The woman shook her head again, with just a touch of smugness. 'Not sure that'll do any good. Look at her. She's on her last legs.'

'She's purring though,' Jenny said, a little wildly. 'Listen!'

'Oh, they purr when they're dying,' the woman told her. 'It's to make it easier for them. It means they go happy.' They both gazed at the cat.

'I want to try though,' Jenny said.

'Tell you what.' The woman disappeared into the room, and came back with a dusty cat box. 'Put her in this. And if she gets better, let me know.' Together they shoved the cat into the carrier. 'Keep the carrier.'

'You'll need it for your cat though, won't you?'

'No. He died. That's how I know about the purring.' The woman smiled. Her eyes were wet. She gave her some cat treats for the journey.

And so, Jenny made her way back down the hill, the bulky cat box pressed against her chest. Behind her, her old house, her old school, the pub, everything was grimly bathed in darkening grey, and so she began to trot to stay ahead of the snow, back through the market, past trundling pensioners, and made it to the city centre just before the storm broke, huge and thrilling. She huddled with others under a shop awning, everyone infected with that giddy friendliness that bad weather brings.

'Coming down fast!' A man said half to her and half to himself. 'Look! It's as bad as the other night, isn't it?'

In the box, the cat shifted and mewed. Its one good eye shone huge through the grill.

'Don't worry,' she whispered to the animal, 'I'm going to get you better, and keep you safe. I promise. You and me, girl.'

As the snow thickened this small, hard kernel of resolve grew. *She would be safe. From now on, she would be safe. She deserved to be safe.*

CHAPTER NINE

'Thanks so much, Cheryl. I was passing when the snow started, and my phone's out of juice. Can I call a taxi? I didn't interrupt anything though I hope?'

'Not a thing,' Cheryl told her. 'Get warm.'

They were sitting in her living room, rather than in her office – a small extension adjacent to the kitchen. Jenny had never been here before. A log on the fire popped and crackled; the one-eyed cat, its wound gently sponged, luxuriated on the rug, briefly started, stared indignantly at the flames, and then settled down again.

'She's in a state, isn't she?' Jenny murmured.

'You found her outside your old home?' Cheryl passed her some biscuits.

'Yes. A lady – the one who gave me the carrier – said that she's been wandering around like this for weeks.'

'And she didn't take her in herself?' Cheryl frowned.

'I never thought about that.' Jenny frowned. 'She *liked* cats, that was obvious.'

'But she saw this little thing every day and never tried to help her?'

'Huh. No. Weird, isn't it?' Jenny gently stroked the cat's back with one toe. Its purr was immediate, and grateful.

'But quite common too. People don't want to get involved,' Cheryl intoned. 'It's interesting that you found this animal, uncared for and lonely, in the same place where you were uncared for and lonely.

'And people saw her, but never helped. Just like they saw *me* and never helped.'

'Exactly. Why did you go there today?'

'I don't know. I thought it might make things clearer in my mind, I suppose. Scene of the crime. That's a stupid way of putting it, sorry.' Jenny hunched forward. 'I... I needed to get away.'

'But you went somewhere that's unpleasant? That holds bad memories?'

'Well, maybe it's a kind of self-punishment. Something... happened today and I lied to Freddie about it.' She looked at Cheryl through her eyelashes. 'You know how much I hate lying. To him, especially.'

'What happened today?'

'The police called.' She stared at her hands, clasped, unclasped, clasped again. 'They want to talk to me tomorrow.'

'Why?' Cheryl's calm was slightly cracked.

'Mum. Unexplained death. I suppose it's what they have to do?' Jenny looked at the fire, clasped her hands tighter. 'I lied and told Freddie it was my auntie Kathleen on the phone. I didn't want him to worry; he's already worried enough about me, and he's taken time off work and—'

'All decisions he made himself.'

'Well, yes. But I don't want to be a burden. I don't want people to feel they have to sort everything out for me, you know? I should be able to do all of this myself. No one needs the... hassle of looking after me.'

Cheryl squinted. 'Why can't people love and support you? Why would that be a hassle for them?' She too hunched forward. 'The police. When are you going?'

'Tomorrow morning. They're sending a car.' One tear plopped onto her knee. Then another. 'I'm scared, Cheryl. What if they think I did anything?'

'Why would they?'

'I don't know. I really don't know. But I'm scared of them. I was taught to be scared of the police. They were always coming round the house for Marc. I think that's why I came back today, to the old house, to try to put all that fear in the past? But that didn't work, did it? I'm still scared, and now I have a dying cat to deal with on top of it all.' She tried to laugh.

'What is frightening you the most about tomorrow?'

'Talking about Mum. Telling them about the drinking, and… everything. It feels wrong. It feels disloyal to her.'

Cheryl nodded. 'Your role is to be the protector; the gatekeeper of secrets.'

'Yes. I suppose.'

'Roles are given by a director though, aren't they?'

'What?'

'Who gave you this role? Who trained you?'

'Mum.'

Cheryl nodded. 'And the production of your life hasn't been well-structured so far, has it? The director was out of her depth, confused and, dare I say it, lazy.' She held up one hand to ward off an assumed disagreement. 'What I'm saying is that you don't have to play the same role anymore. It's a whole new production now. You don't owe your mother that kind of allegiance any more.'

'I should tell the truth?' Jenny whispered.

'You must,' Cheryl replied. 'The truth is the only thing that will set you free.'

It was late by the time Jenny got back to the house. The furtive stench of old cigarette smoke was rising beneath the bleach. She coaxed the cat out of the carrier. It put one cautious paw on the lemony linoleum, sniffed, took a turn about the room, its tail a question mark. Jenny opened a tin of tuna and watched it eat every last strand, and then took it upstairs with her. They lay together in her childhood bed, and all night it purred, a rusty rumble, while Jenny tried and failed to sleep.

The truth will set you free. It sounded simple. But she knew that truths are strangely subjective. A few months ago, she'd watched and half-understood a TED talk on quantum physics, the gist of which was that The Observer Creates Reality Simply by Observing. It had filled her with a strange comfort at the time – this idea that objectivity doesn't truly exist. Now, though, it had the opposite effect: her truth – Sal, drunk, slipped, fell and died – was, after all, The Truth, but what if the police, merely by poring over the story, altered it to make it theirs? It was so simple to trust the police if they'd never let you down, but Jenny remembered how strangely immune to common sense they could be. How many times had they stood in Marc's kitchen, glanced dispassionately at Sal's bruised face, at Jenny's obvious fear, and ignored it? The police only saw what they wanted to see.

CHAPTER TEN

The next morning, two policemen arrived to pick her up, one young, one older. Jenny sat in the back seat and they gave her their helmets to hold in her lap. Inside she noticed that each had a little ring of foam inside them to cushion their heads, and in one of the helmets there was a biro drawing of a smiley face and 'KIERON!!' in shaky capitals.

'Who's Kieron?' she asked.

The older officer looked at her in the rear-view mirror and said: 'My grandson. Did that last week. Little bugger.'

'How old is he?'

'Five. Five going on seventeen. I tell you.'

She let a pause go by. 'Do you see a lot of him then?'

'Weekends. We have him at the weekends. His mum's young still; she likes to go out. You know how it is with kids. You never get a minute to yourself. Got any kids yourself?'

'No,' she said. 'I love kids though.'

He crinkled his eyes at her in the mirror again. 'More trouble than they're worth.'

He was a nice man, she could tell. They both were. Nice, normal, ordinary people who just wanted a 'chat', and her fear lessened a little.

Unfortunately, they said goodbye to her at the desk and handed her over to another officer – an older Dawn French-type woman with very small eyes, like blue marbles sunk in dough. Her smile was brisk, perfunctory, and when she showed Jenny into the interview room, she told her that the 'chat' was going to be taped.

Jenny sat down. 'I feel a bit nervous,' she admitted.

'Nothing to be nervous about.' The woman smiled, and it almost reached her eyes. She wasn't like the man talking about KIERON!! He'd been natural, while this woman sounded like she was reading from a script titled: 'Put Accused At Ease With Niceties'. The weather. The job market, how hard it must be to come back home after all these years, and this last observation clunked like a hasty gear change, and Jenny knew that the preamble was over.

'You came back to look after your mother... six months ago. Why was that?'

'She had a stroke.'

'She was very young to have a stroke? Forty-two was she?'

'Forty-three.'

'It's difficult looking after a parent.'

Jenny nodded.

'It's what you have to do though, isn't it?'

Jenny nodded again.

'You mentioned to PCs Burns and Newell that your mother had been drinking the night she died?'

'Who?'

'The officers who took you to the hospital?'

'Oh, yes. Sorry. I'm a bit... it's all merged into one. Sorry.'

'It's a distressing time.' She nodded. Her smile winked on. 'But just take your time. Your mother was drinking the night she died?' The smile winked off.

Jenny began to shake then and the shakes crawled up her body and settled in her chest and in her shoulders. She felt like she did when she was small and had to read in front of the class. 'I'm sorry,' she managed to shake out. 'This is hard.'

'Take your time.'

'It feels disloyal that's all. I talked to my friends about it but—'

'Was your mother a problem drinker, would you say?'

Jenny closed her eyes. 'Yes. She hid it pretty well, but when she came out of the hospital and couldn't work, it kind of took her over again.'

'And she was also taking medication?'

'Yes.'

'How many pills did you give her?' she asked softly.

'I didn't give her any. She said she'd already taken her beta blockers. I wasn't sure that was true, but I didn't want to give her any more in case it made her sick. She... she was pretty tipsy.' Jenny swallowed this last word, and looked at her hands.

The woman coughed and shuffled some papers.

'Her blood alcohol was .32.'

Jenny looked up. 'Is that a lot?'

The woman raised one eyebrow. 'Yes.'

Jenny let out all her breath, nodded to herself, and then sat up straighter. 'I think she was stockpiling alcohol and hiding it. I just... I didn't confront her. I should've, but I didn't.'

The woman's blue pebbly eyes rested on Jenny's. 'You were in the house all day you said?'

'Yes, but I did some shopping at six. Or six thirty. But it could have been seven. I just don't know for sure, I'm sorry.'

'And was she already drunk?'

'Not too bad. But when I came back from the shops she was. I tried to get her to eat something – I opened a tin of soup, but she wouldn't eat it. I tried to get her to bed then; I want to say it was around nine?'

'Do you know how the picture on the stairs got damaged?'

Jenny squeezed her eyes shut. 'Oh I don't want to say.'

'Can you tell me?'

She opened her eyes again. They were dull with pain. 'She didn't want to go to bed. She... look, she didn't know what she was doing, all right?'

'Can you tell me what happened?'

'She... pushed me. Not on purpose, just sort of pushed past me, but hard. And I fell, hit my head against the frame. It was an accident.'

'And the bruise here? On your chin?'

'Oh this? That was my own stupid fault. I slipped on the ice on the way back from the shop, that's all.'

A silence grew into each corner of the room.

'And after the picture broke?'

'Well, it seemed to sober her up a bit, to tell the truth. She said she was sorry, and we had a hug, and that was it.'

'And the frame and the broken glass stayed where it was?'

'I wanted to clean it up, and I started to. Cut myself too, look.' She showed the officer her thumb. 'And got blood on the carpet. Mum said she'd clean it all up. She said it was her job; she'd broken it, so she'd fix it. She was cleaning it up when I left.' Jenny shook her head. 'That was stupid of me. I should've stayed.'

'You told the officer at the scene that you didn't know how the blood got there, or how the picture was damaged.'

'I... I know I did,' Jenny admitted. She looked at her hands, twisting together in her lap 'I wasn't thinking, or rather I *was* thinking, but not properly. Shock I just... it felt awful to tell the truth about it. Like I said, it felt... disloyal somehow. She wasn't herself. She was drunk.'

'And what time did you leave?'

'I don't know. Something was on the TV – *Teens Who Kill*, I think it was called, but I don't know what time that's on, or even the channel. I remember before I left I turned the TV down. Her neighbour – Mrs Mondesir – she complains about the noise sometimes. Mum tends to leave the TV on all night. Tended to.'

'And did anyone see you leave?'

'No? No, I don't think so. Why?'

'Was it snowing when you left?'

'Yes. Why?'

'We're trying to work out exactly how long she was outside before she fell. We're appealing for witnesses.'

There was a silence. 'You mean people that might have seen her? But surely if anyone had seen her, they would have helped her—' Jenny began.

'We'd like to talk to anyone who saw your mother, yes, but also anyone who saw you walking to the Lees-Hills' house, and at what time,' the officer said evenly.

Jenny stared at her. 'What does that mean though? Do you mean I need an alibi?' She tried to laugh, but it sputtered into hitching, fearful breath.

'This is all routine, and I don't want you to worry about this, or *concern* yourself or—'

'But how can I not though?' Jenny's voice was high as a little girl's. 'Am I *suspected* of anything?'

The woman's face was empty of all expression. 'It's just timings we need to be certain about. When your mother left the house, how long she was out there, things like that.'

'God, I've been thinking that too. Over and over.' Jenny seemed to be speaking to herself. 'I think about her in the snow.' She looked up. 'It's so horrible, thinking of her like that, alone. And maybe shouting for help and no one hearing…' And then Jenny began to cry the big hitching sobs that she hadn't allowed herself before. She cried until her eyes shrank into little red pinwheels.

The woman stopped the tape, and she handed her a tissue. After a while, Jen quietened.

'It's just that she's all alone, still,' she managed eventually. 'All alone in the snow and now all alone in the hospital, and I can't help her, you know? I can't *end* this for her, give her a decent funeral. I know you've got to do your job, though, and I understand, but it's just... hard, you know? I just want everything to be over, not for me, but for her. I want to do right by her.'

CHAPTER ELEVEN

You Can't Go Home Again

[Unpublished post]

I hadn't really realised before that, while the answers you give to the police are approximate, they don't really register approximations, so what you say is taken as absolutely what you'll always say. So I've decided to write everything down, just so I keep track of things, remember them in the right way. My family was bad. I come from bad stock. But that doesn't mean I'm bad. I have to keep hold of that.

When I was a kid, the police were always hovering around. Kathleen's partner went down for possession of stolen goods. One of her daughters was convicted of benefit fraud. Marc was always being asked down to the station for a 'chat'. When Mum met him he'd just got out of prison for aggravated burglary.

This is the thing, I'm very familiar with the police in a way that most people probably aren't. I've been brought up to fear them and hate them, and the fact that I don't fear and hate them any more tells you how far I've come. But in the police station, I felt it all come back. When you come from a family like mine, there's something about the police that makes you feel pugnacious and scrappy and, well, guilty. Even if you've done nothing wrong.

It bugs me that I didn't tell Freddie that they wanted to see me. A lie of omission is still a lie.

I'm also worried that, despite what I told the police, I don't have a clue what time I left Mum's house. And what if they make something of that? What then?

Remember when Mum first started to see Marc? Remember how things changed, imperceptibly, day by day? I noticed it and she didn't. How the endearments became more and more barbed, until they were cruel jokes; the pats became grabs; the one drink after work became more before and after. No more lipstick, no more nail polish. Her tread became heavier and, finally, her glorious hair, severed and swept up by a truculent teenager in the salon at the bottom of the hill. I thought, then, very distinctly, Don't let this happen to you, Jay. Keep control of yourself Jay.

I don't feel like I'm in control anymore. I don't feel safe. I used to, but now I don't, and I can feel panic plucking at me. Fear does terrible things to a person.

Jenny went to hit 'publish' but changed her mind, saved it as a Word document and closed her laptop instead.

CHAPTER TWELVE

The cat seemed even smaller and thinner on the stainless-steel table. She quivered under the vet's dry hands.

'A stray?'

'Not really a stray, more homeless, I think.' Jenny touched its ears, immediately raising that grateful, rusty purr. 'Is she going to be OK?'

The vet frowned and cocked her head to the side. 'She's underweight, and has ringworm. And her eye is pretty badly infected. I'll need to give it a good clean under anaesthetic and then give you a two-week course of antibiotics.' She stroked one ear. 'You've been through the wars, haven't you little one? Pick her up tomorrow at ten.'

'OK. Um, I don't have insurance or anything. I mean, she's not my cat. It sounds awful but how much will all this cost?'

'It depends what we find but more than two hundred pounds, I'd say.' The vet left a significant pause.

Jenny nodded to herself. 'OK. Yes. I'll find it somehow.'

'We might be able to set up a payment plan.'

'That'd help, thanks.' She gave the cat one last stroke. 'Got to take care of her, haven't we?'

'And does she have a name?'

'God, I haven't thought of that… Claudine? That's a good name. See you tomorrow, Claudine!'

Claudine closed her good eye in response.

*

The police called her just as she was leaving the surgery. Just another chat. There was no need for her to come to the station, they'd pop along to see her this time if that was all right?

This time, the fear was different, less diffuse. She saw herself reflected in the surgery window, strangely distorted, deathly pale, and so much like Sal.

Like Sal dead in the snow.

She hurried home and spent half an hour putting on make-up, each careful dab and stroke blurred the resemblance to Sal, and her sleep-deprived, indistinct features became gradually more definite. More her own.

Safe. You're safe. Safe. You're safe. Everything you can do to stay safe, you've done.

Then the doorbell rang.

It was the Dawn French woman with a younger officer she vaguely recognised. They sat down after commenting on the weather *(Rain. You'd never know we were nearly snowed in a week back, would you?)*. They refused tea. Was that a bad sign? Sal had never offered the police tea whenever they'd come round, so Jenny couldn't tell. *Close your eyes, take some deep breaths. Damp the panic down, stamp it down. Don't let them see it.*

'Are you all right there?' the younger officer said.

'I'm… scared,' Jenny admitted. 'I've never really had any dealings with the police before. It's all a bit… overwhelming.'

The Dawn French woman, sitting heavily on one of the spindly kitchen chairs, shuffled forward with a creak. 'Well, like I told you yesterday, it's all routine. There's nothing to be concerned about. Just dotting the i's and crossing the t's.' She smiled.

What did the smile mean? What kind of a smile was that?

Jen smiled at her tiredly. 'I think I just watch too much TV, that's all.'

'It's nothing like the TV shows,' the woman said. 'It's a lot more mundane than that. No, we just want to double-check: when did you leave your mother's house the night she died?'

Jenny closed her eyes. 'I want to say ten? Around ten. But I can't swear to it, I'm sorry.'

'No, that's fine. And did you see anyone on your way back to the Lees-Hill house?'

'No. No one. The weather was too bad.' She frowned then. 'I do remember seeing a car on the high street though, and thinking how horrible it would be to drive in all that snow.'

'Car?'

'Yes, it was red, I think, but I couldn't tell you the make… and a man was driving – I saw his face by the traffic lights.'

'You didn't mention that before.' The woman shifted. Her shirt rolled up slightly, and Jenny could see the pink and white crenulations The elasticated waistband of her slacks had dug into her flesh.

'God, sorry. I didn't think about it before. You asked if I'd seen anyone in the street, and I hadn't. I'd forgotten about the car until now.'

'And you saw the man's face?'

'Yes, but only from the side and just for a second or two. White guy, short dark hair.' She made a helpless gesture with her hands. 'That's all I saw. Why?' Her face froze. 'Wait, do you think that man had something to do with Mum—?'

The woman looked alarmed. 'No. No. Nothing like that. A person came forward today.' She took out her notebook. 'He was driving back from the airport. He says he saw you walking past the Rose and Crown at 10.30 p.m. He remembers because it was snowing hard and you weren't wearing a coat.' The woman put the notebook down, and her blue eyes rested on her kindly. As kindly as they could, anyway. 'So, what this means is, we have no reason to ask you any more questions.' The room sang with silence.

'I don't really understand?' Jenny managed after a moment.

'The post-mortem reports "Death by Misadventure". Basically, it's as we thought; sadly, your mum slipped and fell on the ice. The alcohol in her system and the medication probably made her more unsteady, and we know from talking to you and others that she'd had similar accidents in the past. All this, coupled with someone seeing you walking back, means that there's no case.'

'You mean against me? Is that what you mean?' Jenny's voice broke. 'God, I didn't even think of that!'

The woman was apologetically solemn. 'We have to investigate an unexplained death, you understand.'

'Oh, yes, of course!' Jenny said quickly. 'It's just… It's only just dawned on me how bad this could have been. *Worse* I mean.' Despite the flooding adrenaline her eyes remained stubbornly droopy, fatigued. She put one shaking hand up to her hair, and through her tired mind the phrase drummed: *It's over it's done with over it's done with.* 'So, I can organise her funeral?' Her voice broke further.

'Yes, that's something you can do now.'

Tears, large and hot, welled and spilled, and the tension rolled off her in palpable waves, making her stutter, making her shake. *It's over it's over it's over…*

When they left, a peace, heavy as a shroud, fell on her shoulders. She slept for the next three hours and didn't dream. When she woke, she saw that her make-up had transferred itself onto the pillow, like a vivid Turin shroud but, rather than changing the pillowcase, she lay back down, drowsily, with her smudged eyes open, smiling. One clenched hand furled open, closed, opened again.

CHAPTER THIRTEEN

You Can't Go Home Again

Hi guys.

I want to thank everyone for their messages, public and private. It's been a hard couple of weeks. A few times there, I really thought I was going under... reading all the positive things people said helped me look after myself though.

There were a lot of negative things thrown at me too. Sometimes I wonder if you realise that This Is Real Life. This is *my* life, with no filter, no defences. I've chosen to put myself out there, and it's hard, it's painful. Just because this is a blog, and not a TV show or something, doesn't mean that I'm not real, that what's happened isn't real, and what people say about me doesn't really hurt. But here's the thing: People have every right to their opinion. I'm all about truthful disclosure, and some people find that threatening. And when people feel threatened, they act on their basest instincts – they attack, they obfuscate, they lie. The last few days have taught me that I have to allow for this sort of thing, and accept that I have no control over the opinions of some Haters, just as they have no control over what I choose to share.

So, what I mean to say is, I won't be silenced, and neither should you be. This isn't a cult of personality, you're free to dislike me/mistrust me/argue about me. I'd prefer it if people were more accepting, nicer, less aggressive, but I started *You Can't Go Home Again* with the idea that it should be a dialogue rather than an echo chamber. I feel very strongly that We Are In This Together, that we can be a family to one another. And families argue and then make-up; they fracture and re-bond, become stronger. I'm stronger than I was a few weeks ago. I believe in myself more. In a funny way, everything that's happened has given me a sense of my own worth, a small but growing sense of entitlement. And there's nothing wrong with entitlement, is there? We're all entitled to respect, to comfort, to safety, to success. Just one small, good deed can change a person's whole life, and we should be alive to that possibility, and welcome it.

Something quite wonderful happened to me today.

I don't want to go into the whole story, it's all too raw, but, as you know the police (briefly) investigated Mum's death. What I didn't tell you was that, since nobody saw me leave the house the night she died, they appealed for witnesses, and for a few horrible days I felt as if I was some kind of suspect. This, coupled with shock and – yes, some of the abuse that I received via the blog – almost drove me to a breakdown. For the first time ever, I really felt that I could be losing my mind. Grief, horror, misplaced guilt – it all knocked me down, but then, something happened that made me regain my faith in people.

A witness came forward to say that he'd seen me that night, and suddenly, I could do right by my mum, give her a decent burial. I asked the police if they could thank him for me. They said that, yes, he'd agreed to that. I passed on my number, and... he texted me this morning. Before I knew what I was doing, I'd invited him over for a coffee. Bear in mind that the house is still a mess – half of the furniture has gone, and I only have one chipped mug and a wine glass. I almost texted back to say, Actually can we do another time? But that seemed rude, so I didn't. I'm really glad I didn't.

When I was a kid, I spent a lot of time at friends' houses, but they very rarely came to mine. I could never be sure what kind of a state Mum would be in, and I told myself that she'd be mortified if anyone saw her drunk, but really, I think I was protecting both of us.

So, in a funny way, this man was my first visitor. Apart from the police.

He's my age, and, weirdly, we went to school together! He remembers me, but sadly I don't remember him at all. He told me that he'd noticed me at school, because he thought I seemed sad sometimes, insecure. And then he said something that really struck me: 'I should have reached out to you then.'

And I felt my thoughts start to untangle and resolve into one, simple emotion: Gratitude.

When you look after a relative, when you're a carer, you're so removed from other people. You exist in a realm of sickness, age, worry. It's debilitating. I said something like that to him, and he knew exactly what I meant. Why? Because he, too, is looking after a close relative.

We sat in the darkening kitchen and talked for hours. We talked about work, about holidays, about ambitions, about all the things that get put away when you're a carer, all the things that you hope, one day, will regain their rightful place in your life again. And the guilt, of course. The guilt that, no matter how much you love your parent, you miss your own life, and want it back. When he left, we both felt better, and we agreed to meet again, soon.

So, let me leave you with this: think of the small, good things we can do for others that are large and life-changing. Never underestimate the value of these small things. Don't give in to fear, but rather share your feelings, reach out to others. We can form our own families, forge our own bonds. All you have to do is be honest. All you have to do is come from a place of love.

XOXO Jay

Lilagracee: Such a relief for you and amazing Revelation! You keep shining lady!

Laundryloony2: Going on a date ;-)

Lilagracee: Not everything's about that take some time

Brittanywalsh: He sounds nice

DaisyChain: To those who have given up on love... trust life a little bit

HollybFootitt: If you can't love yourself, how can you love someone else? Self-love is NOT narcissism! Pleased to see Jay *finally* believing in herself.

Brittanywalsh: sad2 here about bad messages tho just discovered YCGHA and have2 say i love it.

Lilagracee: @Brittanywalsh welcome to the family!!!

Laundryloony2: Going on a date??!

CHAPTER FOURTEEN

A funeral, with the invitations, the venue, the flowers, the refreshments, is the stunted shadow of a wedding. The morning of Sal's funeral was incongruously sunny. Brownish remnants of snow clung to curbs melting muddily into the drain. Kathleen, a trim, attractive woman in her late fifties, had come up a few days before to help give the house a last once-over, and pick out the outfit Sal would be dressed in: the same periwinkle blue suit she'd worn to Maraid's wedding and Roisin's divorce party. Jenny could hear her talking to herself quietly – 'Grace and Dignity – come on Kath, Grace and Dignity!' and every now and then stifling a sob.

The two women sat in the shining house waiting for the cars to arrive. The smoke from Kathleen's cigarette curled into the lemon-scented kitchen. Claudine padded about, her fur glossier, her eye almost healed.

'What you going to do with the cat then?' Kathleen asked.

Jenny stroked Claudine's ears. 'Keep her. She's nearly better now.'

'Did you put the wine and beer in the fridge?'

Jenny wandered to the door and leaned against it. 'I did, but I'm not sure people'll be drinking.'

'People expect a drink after a funeral,' Kathleen said firmly. 'I've done more funerals than you, so I know. They need a bit of help relaxing. Helps the grieving process. And anyway,' she looked up, 'we're Irish, aren't we? The Irish love a drink at a funeral.'

'We're not Irish,' Jenny muttered.

Kathleen thought about that. 'Well, my nan was. And your auntie Miriam's mum was.' Kathleen squinted through her cigarette smoke. 'I think?'

'Miriam's not my real auntie though.'

'Oh, is she not? Well…' Kathleen took her cigarette to the open door, stubbed it out on the doorstep and immediately lit another. 'Everyone's a bit Irish, aren't they?'

People arrived just as the hearse did. The coffin was all but obscured by a huge arrangement of yellow chrysanthemums spelling out 'SAL'. Kathleen nodded with approval at her own good taste. Then she went forward, clutching at the hands of her daughters, before moving on graciously to welcome those she didn't know – Mrs Mondesir, frail and uncertain; Freddie who arrived with his parents, Ruth and Graham; Andreena; Mrs Hurst who Sal had worked for. Kathleen was right, she did know more about funerals and, under her expert eye, everyone was introduced, made to feel welcome and ushered back into their own cars within a few minutes, with none of the scattered, self-conscious small talk that Jenny had so dreaded.

It was only when she climbed into the car that she realised just how much this was costing Kathleen; she slumped into tearful anxiety, muttering: 'Grace and dignity, grace and dignity' under her breath. It was somehow horrifying to see her reduced to this state. She took Jenny's hand, squeezed it too tightly. 'You're a good girl, Jen.'

'I'm not good enough,' Jenny murmured, looking out of the window. 'I wish I hadn't left her that night. I'll never forgive myself for that.'

Kathleen gave an almighty sniff and fumbled in her bag for a tissue. 'What's done is done.' She blew her nose. 'She was so proud of you. So *proud.*' She gave a tiny nod. 'And I'm proud of you too.'

It was the nicest thing Kathleen had ever said to her. It was probably the nicest thing she'd ever said to anyone.

By the time they reached the church, Kathleen had recovered somewhat; it was Jenny who needed the support as she walked down the aisle following the coffin, strangely small, carried by the undertaker's men, who smelled ever so slightly unwashed.

Kathleen ushered her into the first pew. Freddie, sitting just behind her, dropped a comforting hand on her shoulder, and she clung to his fingers, trying to control her breathing, trying to calm down. She had to. She was giving the eulogy. She'd been up most of the night, trying to write it, but she still only had partial notes and no real idea of its structure. There was one reading – a poem about dancing and joy and eternity – read in a self-conscious monotone by Maraid. Then, after the obligatory hymn, pitched too impossibly high for anyone to sing it well, Jenny stood and walked slowly to the altar.

For a second or two, she gazed at the coffin. Blond wood, nickel-plated handles and, inside, she knew, a blue frilled satin lining. Sal would be nestled in there, blue on blue. *Had they put some make-up on her? Had they brushed her hair? Did they do that in this country if it was a closed coffin?* Jenny didn't know. She'd been asked if she wanted to 'view the body' at the undertakers, but she'd refused. Kathleen had, but it had upset her too much to talk about. Now, in front of all these people, that was all Jenny could think about. What did she look like in there? Was her neck still twisted? Her nose still bloody?

Jenny cleared her throat in the quiet and willed her brain *to stop, just stop*. The notes quivered in her hand. She began, and her voice sounded rusty, rarely used.

'My mum, Sally Holloway, was more than a mum to me. She was my friend.' Jenny stopped then, looked down and closed her eyes. Freddie half rose anxiously. The mourners watched uncomfortably as Jenny swallowed hard, looked at the coffin and muttered something to herself. Then she smiled tightly, and said: 'I'm sorry, I'm nervous.' There was a small pulse of polite sympathy from the crowd.

'Let me start again. I have these notes, but I don't need them. I know what I want to say; I just hope I can say it well,' she said more clearly, more forcefully. 'My mum was only nineteen when she had me. She had plans to go to college, and maybe even university. She wanted to become a nurse, but then I came along, and she had to give them up. She loved me enough to give them up. It could be said that if it wasn't for me, she'd have had a very different life. Probably a happier one.' Andreena made a sad growling sound, and several people shook their heads. 'Only a week ago, we were talking about it. I asked her if – well, not if she was sorry she'd had me, but, if circumstances had been different…? She shut me down right away.' Jenny swallowed, recollecting Sal's words. 'She said "Never EVER think that you weren't meant to be." She said: "We're a unit. A team."'

Kathleen at the front sobbed, and said quietly: 'I can *hear* her say that.'

'And she told me she loved me.' Jenny looked at the coffin. 'Not that there was ever a doubt in my mind about that. As a family, we were never short on love. She always put me first, even if it meant moving away from the city she loved, her closest friends and family. She-she missed you all, so much'. She looked directly at Kathleen. 'She loved you all so much.' Now Jen, too, began to cry. She wobbled on her heels and put one hand on the coffin to steady herself. Chrysanthemums shook, and Freddie half rose again, ready to catch her if she fell, but then she opened her eyes again, smiled at a late arrival, a man, tall, dark, in a sober grey suit, standing at the back of the church, and became steadier.

'And so, when I think about Mum, I think about her strength, not her weakness. I want you all to think of her like that, too. I think about her laugh, her silly sense of humour. I think about watching old movies with her. I think about us dancing to the radio; playing on the beach at Scarborough; the time I made a mud pie in nursery and she actually ate a couple of mouthfuls to make me happy. And I think about how brave she was, how resilient, despite everything.' Jenny paused then. She looked at the ground. 'On the night she died, we went through some old photos. I told her that she didn't look any different to that beautiful girl with the baby. I told her she was my best friend.' Now her voice caught. She managed the last sentence through hitching breaths. 'I'm so glad that I told her that. I'm so glad she got to hear that. Because,' she touched the coffin with one shaking hand, 'it's true, Mum. And it always will be.'

Kathleen, buttressed by Roisin and Maraid, was sobbing loudly now. Jenny wavered on the altar, as if not quite knowing what to do next. Freddie sped up the aisle and gently took her elbow, and led her back to her seat.

As the coffin made its jerky progress back to the hearse, 'The Wonder of You' boomed too suddenly from the church speakers. Kathleen burst into fresh sobs. 'Oh, she loved that song!' and Jenny, her face drained of colour and expression, moved to the door. People stopped her to murmur sympathy as she passed by, her half-closed eyes swollen with tears and exhaustion.

Outside in the car park, the undertaker, unctuous and stooped, presented himself to her. A huge port wine birthmark stained his face.

'A very loved woman,' he intoned.

'She was. Thank you,' Jenny murmured.

He smiled, took her hand. She felt the business card in her palm.

Hurton and Sons: We pride ourselves on our compassionate and caring manner. Ample parking at rear.

'Think of us next time.' The birthmark rippled when he spoke, like paint bubbling in heat.

'What?' Jenny said sharply.

People stared.

'If you've been happy with our service, think about us next time.' The servile smirk was still there, but looked a little more fragile.

'Why? D'you think anyone else in my family's going to die soon? You got inside information or something?' Jenny hissed, with sudden, sharp, rage.

Then Andreena muscled her way over, and he melted away like a ghoul.

Jenny opened her palm and showed her the card. 'Touting for more business,' she smiled grimly.

'Let me go and find him, I'll tear a strip off him—'

'No, Dree, it's OK.' Jenny's sudden fury seemed to have exhausted her even more. 'I'll make a complaint later or something.'

'But—'

'No, really, Dree, I can't cope with any drama. It's just—' She put one vague hand out, and let it drop.

'You're shaking, are you cold?' The man who had been hovering at the back of the church suddenly appeared. 'Here, take this.' He took off his jacket, warm and smelling of a sharp tangy aftershave, and draped it around her shoulders.

Andreena's face underwent one of her lightning quick changes. Anger morphed into soft appreciation.

'Oh, Dree, this is David.' Jenny's face coloured a little. 'It was David who saw me walking back, on, you know, that night. He's the one that told the police.'

David put out his hand. Firm handshake. 'Nicetomeetyou.'

Andreena looked hard at him. Approval flowed from her. 'So kind of you to think of our Jenny! So good of you to come to pay your respects!'

Freddie, who had been talking to Kathleen, hurried over. 'What was that about?'

Jenny showed him the card curled up in her palm. 'They "pride themselves on their caring and compassionate service."'

'You're kidding?' Freddie pinkened.

'David – this is my best friend, Freddie. I mentioned him, didn't I? Fred, this is David. He's my alibi.' She laughed a little wildly. Her knees buckled. David and Freddie exchanged an anxious glance.

'Sit down.' Freddie took her by the elbow and led her to a memorialised bench carved in the shape of a butterfly. The others gathered around, too. 'Listen, do you really want people coming back to the house? Won't that be a bit much?'

'Oh, no,' Jenny told him. 'It's a wake. And we're Irish, didn't you know?'

Back at the house, guests nosed politely around the funeral – 'Good service'; 'Lovely send-off'; 'Very dignified' – but no one stayed long.

Mrs Mondesir was the first to leave – she had to get back to feed the dog; Mrs Hurst had to go back to work; Freddie's parents consoled Kathleen before Roisin and Maraid, in their brusque way, ordered a taxi to take them all back to the station. Kathleen clung to Jenny in the front garden, and pressed papery lips to her cheek. 'Grace and dignity. It's how she would've liked us to behave. You take care, my love.' Andreena, too, had to get back to look after her own children and left after embracing everyone – including David – telling them that they would all be in her prayers. Soon, only Freddie, David and Jenny remained, sitting at the scrubbed clean kitchen table.

'It was OK, wasn't it?' she asked them.

'You did brilliantly,' Freddie told her. 'The eulogy, everything.'

'It's the first funeral I've ever been to,' she told them. ' You don't know about these things, do you, until you have to do them. You don't know if you're doing the right thing?'

'It was very moving,' David said.

'I have an idea.' Freddie picked up an unopened bottle of whisky from the work surface. 'A toast. To Sal!' They all stood.

'To Sal,' echoed David.

'To Mum,' whispered Jenny; downed her drink, gagged. 'God, it tastes like it's been made in a toilet! Who brought this?'

'I think Kathleen did.' Freddie winced and looked at the label. 'Lidl's finest.'

'You know what? Roisin works at Lidl. I bet she lifted it.' She shook her head. 'God, that says it all, really. Drinking stolen gut-rot at a funeral. Weirdly, that's made me feel better.' She smiled tiredly, ruefully, at them both. Claudine trotted into the kitchen and gave a cracked miaow.

'She's braver now everyone's left,' Jenny said. 'Come on, darling, let's get you fed.' She opened a pouch of food, while Freddie picked up the whisky bottle, poured it down the sink, and made a pot of tea instead.

'Thanks for coming; you didn't have to, you know,' Jenny was telling David.

'I wanted to. I wanted to help as much as I could—'

Jenny smiled and flushed pink. Freddie waded into the awkward pause.

'So you guys went to school together?'

'Well, briefly. Jenny was in my form room, but we didn't really know each other. And then I left the school soon after.'

'Oh that makes sense. I didn't go there until Sixth Form, so I suppose that's why we didn't meet.' Freddie told him.

'Me and Fred did English A level together.' Jenny smiled fondly at Freddie. 'We bonded over a shared love of *A Streetcar Named Desire*.'

'Well, a shared love of Marlon Brando, to be honest. And we both obsessed about James Dean, and we both read Sylvia Plath. There hadn't been much of that at St Columbus – that's where I was before. All boys. A lot of rugby.' Freddie winced. 'So, how come you didn't go to Sixth Form?'

David was sitting stiffly upright, tense, jaw clenched. He looked as if he was having a mute, urgent conversation with himself. 'Um, well, I… had a stroke when I was sixteen. Just before GCSEs,' he answered eventually, through tight lips.

'Oh my god, David, I'm sorry! I—' Freddie said.

David's lips relaxed into a smile and he waved a gentle hand. 'No, don't worry. It's a long time ago, and I'm fine now. I don't generally talk about it, that's all. I had a hole in my heart, undiagnosed, from birth. So I had to have surgery, then rehabilitation, so I lost a lot of time. Eventually I went to boarding school did my GCSEs and A levels in two years so I wouldn't be going to university too late.'

'Wow,' Freddie said, 'GCSE's *and* A levels in two years? That must've been harsh?'

'I'm a quick study.' David smiled.

'So what boarding school did you go to? St Columbus took boarders; wouldn't it be weird if we'd, like, effectively swapped schools? Was it St Columbus?'

'No. Hazlewood. It was called Hazlewood School, but I think it's closed down or merged with somewhere else now,' David answered. 'Then I went to Durham University—'

'Where's Claudine got to?' Jenny asked. 'Fred? She didn't go out, did she? I'm meant to keep her in.'

'No, she's in the living room, tearing at the carpet again. So, Durham? I *knew* someone who went there. Ryan Needham? He did Anthropology, I think,' Freddie said.

'She's limping. Look, Fred – Claudine's limping, don't you think?' Jenny got up, crossed the room anxiously.

'No, she looks fine to me. So, Ryan – did you ever meet him?'

'Yes, I know Ryan.' David smiled again. All straight, white teeth.

'That's so weird!' Freddie said. 'Is he, like, a really good friend of yours? If so, it's best to let you know that Jenny hates him.'

'I don't *hate* him. I don't *know* him.' Jenny came back into the room with Claudine in her arms. 'I just don't think he was very good for you, that's all.' She looked at David, her face serious. 'He-he wasn't honest.'

There was an awkward pause. 'She's more protective of me that *I* am of myself,' Freddie told David. 'Anyway, it was nothing. Facebook, that's all. We were messaging for a few months a while ago but we never managed to meet up. At least now I know he wasn't a catfish or something.'

'Oh no. Ryan's very real.' David's forehead puckered. 'Do you want me to put you back in touch? I mean—'

'No,' Jenny interrupted. 'Don't do that. I don't want to see you go through that again, Fred.'

'See what I mean? She's like a Tiger Mom. Protective. Sheathe your claws, Jen, that's all over with. I think some things just aren't meant to be,' Freddie said with finality.

'Well, for what it's worth, I think it was his loss. Ryan is… he's not very constant if you know what I mean,' David continued seriously. 'Like Jenny said, he's not a very trustworthy person.'

There was something definitely special about David, Freddie thought. He was also very attractive in a terribly British, David Niven, sort of way. 'So, what's Ryan doing now?'

'Fred—' Jenny warned.

'He's in America. I was coming back from dropping him off at the airport when I saw Jenny, you know, that night.'

Freddie shook his head. 'So weird. Spooky.'

Jenny refilled everyone's cup. 'David looks after his mother, too.'

'Yes, when Mum took a turn for the worse I moved back. My father died last year and there was no one to look after her, so... I'm lucky, in that there's enough money for me to be able to just stop working for a while. I suppose I could have got nurses, or even put her in residential care, but I just...' He opened one palm, and shrugged.

'Couldn't do it,' Freddie said softly.

'No.' His face pinched a little, a sadness settled. 'But that's not really an appropriate thing to be talking about today, is it? I'm sorry.' He smiled at Jenny, at Freddie. His voice was soft. 'I really have to get back, actually. I'm very aware that you're tired, and probably just want the place to yourself now.' He put one hand up to stop Jenny's objection. 'But if you need help with anything, or just want a coffee and a chat, well, you have my number?' He hesitated. 'Maybe it would be OK if I called you in a few days?' A nervous sheen of sweat shone on his top lip.

'No, I mean, yes, that'd be fine!' Jenny, too, seemed shy.

'Good. That's good.' He seemed mightily relieved. Then he shook both their hands – a charmingly old-fashioned gesture, Freddie thought – and left.

Freddie managed to wait until he was out of earshot before saying: 'God, there's not many men about like him, are there?'

'No. He's very nice.' David leaving seemed to have taken all the life out of her. Even her clothes seemed to droop with exhaustion.

'The Ryan thing? That's so strange...'

'Fred, please don't read too much into that, I'll worry about you.'

'Well don't. I'm not putting myself through that again, I promise.' He took her hand. 'You're knackered. Look, let's go back to my parents' tonight. I think you might need a break from this house.'

'No. No, I'm OK. It's probably best if I'm by myself.' Her eyes closed slowly again, and she stifled a yawn.

'I'm not going to just leave you here—'

'Fred, really. To be honest, I'd quite like to be on my own. If I'm with people, I know I'll feel weird, like I have to talk about things, and… I don't want to feel like I'm being rude—'

'No, no, absolutely, I get it. I'll call tomorrow, OK?' He pulled her in for a hug. 'You've done amazingly well today. Amazingly.'

'Thanks, darling.'

'Keep your good eye on her,' he commanded Claudine. Then he hugged Jenny again.

'I love you, Jen,' he told her.

'Love you too.' She sighed.

CHAPTER FIFTEEN

'I hope you told her she'd be more than welcome to stay here?'
Ruth asked, handing Freddie a glass of cloudy liquid.

'Of course. She wanted to be alone though.'

Ruth nodded. 'A little peace. I can see that.'

Freddie took a sip, grimaced. 'What is this?'

'*Akvavit*,' Ruth told him. 'We got a taste for it on the cruise.
We've got wine if you prefer though?'

'No. I'll soldier on.' He took another sip. 'In the end it was just
me, Jen and David something. Crane?'

'You mean Catherine's son?' Ruth asked. 'The house by the
green?'

Freddie shrugged. 'I don't know. Tall, dark, handsome. About
our age. He looks after his mother?'

'Yes, that'll be him. Was he at the funeral? I didn't see him. How
was he?' Ruth seemed oddly excited.

'Nice boy, from what I recall. Nice boy.' Graham came in with
a bag of Kettle chips and sat down with a sigh.

'He always was a lovely boy.' Ruth nodded. 'Especially considering... Well, you know.'

'Ruthy...' sighed Graham.

'I know what?' Freddie leaned forward.

Ruth frowned at her husband. 'Graham, it's not gossip if it's old
news! It was years ago, now.'

'Still...'

'Catherine had that friend staying with them. Lived in some sort of granny flat in the garden. He looked like – oh, who's that man? Dick Van Dyke! Like him, white hair, distinguished sort of. And he had a phony accent too – not Maori Parpins awful, but Michael Caine in *Zulu* awful.'

Freddie nodded sagely. 'That was a terrible accent.'

'What was his *name*, Graham?'

Graham coughed, answered unwillingly. 'Tony.'

'*Tony*! Yes! Well, he had some kind of house at the end of their garden, and he and Catherine used to spend *all* their time together, drank the pub *dry* on quiz nights – they both thought they were very knowledgeable, you know the type. Shouting out the answers, stage whispers. All that.'

'Got the answers wrong most of the time too,' murmured Graham.

'So, what, were they having an affair?' Freddie asked.

'Oh come on—' Graham growled.

'No. Well, I always thought he was gay, but who knows? Maybe he made an exception for Catherine.' Ruth poured herself another drink. 'Anyway, one day the flat – or shed, or whatever it was he lived in – burned down.'

'Oh my god, what?' Freddie poured himself another drink too. 'So what happened to him?'

'He survived, but still. Catherine put about the story that it was an accident with a gas stove or something, but I remember there was talk about petrol,' Ruth said significantly.

Graham rolled his eyes and put the bottle on the other end of the table, out of Ruth's reach. 'Don't talk rubbish, Ruth,' he murmured.

'We worried about David at the time. There was so much gossip, and he always seemed to be a very sensitive boy. Can't have been easy for him, with the whole village talking about his mother that way. Did he seem well?'

'He seemed fine. What's wrong with his mother?' Freddie asked. 'He mentioned she was sick, but I didn't want to ask.'

'Dementia? Rebecca at the Rose and Crown said it was dementia. Or Parkinson's. One of the two. David stopped working to look after her full-time, not that he needed to work anyway, family money, you know. And Catherine too – she came from money. Though why they'd live *here* with all their money is beyond me.'

'He's been ill too, you know.' Freddie sipped his drink with a grimace. 'He had a stroke.'

'Oh, I never heard that. Did you hear that Graham?' Graham pursed his lips and shook his head ever so slightly. 'Recently?'

'No, when he was fifteen or sixteen. He had a hole in his heart. Ended up having to miss GCSEs and everything.'

'Lord. That would be around the time of the fire.' Ruth shook her head. 'He's really been through the mill that boy, hasn't he?'

'I think he likes Jenny.' Freddie smiled.

'Well, she could do a lot worse by the sound of it,' replied Ruth.

'He's... he's really calm. Gentlemanish,' Freddie said.

'You approve of him?'

'I do.' He poured himself another *akvavit*. 'He seems lovely.'

That night, with a few more *akvavits* under his belt, Freddie found David on Facebook. His profile picture showed him looking relaxed, smiling. From the angle it was taken, it looked like a selfie. On the wall behind him, only half in shot, was a framed picture... One tanned arm in a splash of sunlight, a small hand resting on a fold of material, blue, patterned with stars. It felt familiar. *Where had he seen that before?* It was probably a print of something famous, *a Klimt thing?* There was something pleasingly whimsical about someone as solid as David having a soft spot for visionary art. It made him seem even sweeter. Smiling, Freddie wrote:

Hi David. Lovely to meet you today, even though it was under horrible circumstances! I can't thank you enough for all the support you've offered Jenny. Anyway, hopefully we can all meet up soonish? Freddie

Then he pressed return. A minute later David replied.

Very nice to meet you too, and thanks for the kind words about Jenny. I didn't really do much, but I'm glad what I did do was helpful. She's a very special girl. I'm not on FB much, but occasionally I check messages, and thankfully today was one of those days! Friend request sent, and yes, we should all meet up again soon. Cheers! D

Everything about this reply – so modest, polite and charming – pleased Freddie enormously. It seemed odd that someone as solid and grown-up as David should be friends with the skittish, extreme-sport-loving Ryan Needham. But then Freddie was still 'friends' with lots of fools he'd met over the years, too. People he no longer had anything in common with, people who posted and liked faintly embarrassing things, people who verged into racism whenever there was a terrorist attack…

Against his better judgement, he started scrolling through David's friends (205 – a decent amount, but not too many, indicating that he actually knew all these people in real life), until he found Ryan Needham. Here was the profile picture of him in snowboarding gear. The same motivational memes on his semi-private wall. *He was a bit of a wanker, Ryan, he really was, and wasn't he getting a little bit too old for all this intrepid stuff?* Free diving. Rock climbing. Triathlons. Fitness was all very well, but… Freddie looked at Ryan, gazed down at his own burgeoning stomach, looked at Ryan again, realised he was considering messaging him, remembered how much *akvavit* he'd had, and shut the computer. Jenny was right; he really didn't need to fall into that hole again.

In the morning, he noticed that David had taken down his cute profile picture and not replaced it. Now he was just a blank silhouette.

CHAPTER SIXTEEN

You Can't Go Home Again

Hi guys!

Long time, no post. I am fine though – thanks for all your messages. It's been three weeks since the funeral; three weeks since I had to move out of my home and give it back to the council, and I have to admit, I shed a few tears over that. The house was a sanctuary for me and Mum; in a very real sense, it saved our lives. It's fitting for it to go to another needy family. I hope it works the same magic for them as it did for us.

So now I'm engaging with the world again. I found the perfect flat – not too far from college, not too far from the city centre, and not too far from my therapist (all bases are covered!). The rent is a bit steep, but that's what you get for trading up – I have one flatmate rather than five like I did in the last house. It's clean, it's warm, it suits me down to the ground. My college has been AMAZINGLY supportive too. With everything that happened I let my coursework drop, and I didn't get round to organising a work placement, which I have to do to pass the course. I called my tutor yesterday, all apologies, fully expecting him to say they'd thrown me off the course altogether, but he said that they not only wanted me to stay, they had recommended me for a placement with an amazing organisation. It's like the best placement I could have hoped for! Obviously I can't mention the name, but it's a charity dedicated to helping people cope with trauma, and this couldn't have come at a better time for me. When I put the phone down I cried with happiness!

I'm still in a dark place, but, with the help of you guys, college staff, friends and family, I'm fashioning a ladder out of the pit. I can't let my own traumatic experiences hold me back any more.

I want to talk a little about the importance of openness. So many of us have been brought up – trained really – to hide our emotions, to put others first come what may, and stifle our own. As a result of this conditioning, being genuinely open feels very, very strange. I feel a mixture of intense vulnerability and guilt when I realise I'm reliant on someone.

Of course I'm entirely open and honest in this blog, that goes without saying, but, it's easier because it's a step removed from real life. I can't see your faces as I spill my fears; I can't project boredom and disdain onto you; I can stop and run away for a while if I have a sudden attack of anxiety. In person, though? I censor myself. I try to earn love by being 'useful', 'kind', 'reliable' and 'a good listener'. Selflessness is the currency I use to buy acceptance and avoid rejection.

Since Mum's funeral though, I've been experimenting with *drum roll* self-confidence! I'm trying to talk, honestly, to people, knowing it will be frightening, knowing I'll feel guilty, knowing I might run the risk of alienating them, but doing it anyway. For example, before Mum's funeral, a family member demanded that I give her ALL of Mum's furniture, including the TV. Now, I'd already promised to give the furniture to a homeless charity, and the TV? You know what? I wanted to keep it because I don't actually own one myself. But, what did I say? 'Oh yes, of course, I'll help you get it all in a van. Even better, why don't I help PAY for the van?'

Today I had a mini epiphany. I called her and said, 'Actually I want to keep the TV and a few other things.' And I waited. And I didn't apologise. And she huffed and puffed, but I just repeated, calmly, respectfully, that I wanted to keep some things. No backtracking, no compromising, just honesty. And you know what? The sky didn't fall in. I didn't have a panic attack. Even if this family member hates me now, that's her problem, not mine.

I AM NOT A BAD PERSON FOR PUTTING ME FIRST.

That's what I want to leave you with today. Write it down, on your hand, spell it out in fridge magnets, send yourself an email – do whatever you want to tell yourself that today, OK? You are important. You deserve a space in the world. You can come first.

Jay XOXO

CHAPTER SEVENTEEN

Freddie looked around the spartan kitchen, the pictureless walls. 'What's your flatmate called again?'

'Matt.'

'So, isn't Matt here much?'

'No. I barely see him. It's a bit weird. And I don't have Claudine, now either.'

'Oh no, what happened?' Freddie asked: 'She's not sick?'

'Oh, she's fine, it's just I signed the tenancy here without really thinking about how it's not good to keep a cat in a flat, and it turns out that Matt's allergic to cats anyway, so David's looking after her. I really miss her though. God, I'm never happy, am I? The last house was too crowded and grotty, this one's too quiet and clean. I can't afford to keep a cat; I miss my cat.' She grimaced and made a little 'boo hoo' gesture with her fists close to her eyes.

'I still don't know why you don't you just move in with me,' Freddie said. 'Tyler's contract will be up soon.' Tyler was Freddie's Christian lodger. Their relationship was so polite it was painful, and Freddie was counting the days until he left to go back to Canada.

Jenny sighed. 'I signed a year's tenancy though.'

'Well, I can lend you the money to get out of that, just—'

'No, Fred. You can't lend me any more money. I won't take it, and then you'll just get angry, and you're terrifying when you're angry. You're like the Hulk. But ginger.' She passed him a beer. 'Take this. It's my way of controlling you.'

'It just seems stupid.' Freddie was serious. 'You're living some-where you don't like, and I'm living with *someone* I don't like. It doesn't make any sense.'

'You're getting pinker,' she said soberly. 'Your clothes are starting to rip.'

'Stop it, I'm serious.'

'Well, so am I. Fred, it's about time I grew *up*. I can't live like a student or sponge off my best friend. It's not right. It-it isn't the way I want to live my life. That's all.' She took a sip of beer in a decided way. 'Anyway, if I lived with you, you'd see what a slut I am. Men – twenty-four hours a day. It'd sicken you if you had to live with that. I almost sicken myself.'

'Speaking of men,' Freddie said, 'have you seen anything of David lately? Apart from cat-related meetings, I mean.'

She hesitated.

Freddie watched the play of expression on her face, sincerity battling brittle sarcasm.

'We've been to the cinema a few times,' she said shortly.

'What, like a date?' Freddie's tone was teasing.

'*No.*' Jenny blushed. 'We just like the same movies, that's all.'

'What did you go and see with him?' Freddie asked.

'The new Ryan Gosling one?'

'OK, let me tell you something– there's no way he'd voluntarily watch a Ryan Gosling movie if he wasn't properly into you!' Freddie said.

'*You* like Ryan Gosling though! We went to see *La La Land* together,' Jenny said.

'No. I *fancy* Ryan Gosling. I *suffered* through *La La Land*. There's a difference,' Freddie told her. 'OK, so cinema? Anything else?'

Jenny went to the kitchen to get another beer. 'A couple of meals out!' she called back.

'Ha! You see? Oh, get me another one too. No, wait, actually no. Calories.'

She came back into the living room looking pensive. 'But it's not, you know, anything...'

'Why not? Why isn't it anything?'

'He's *nice*...' Jenny drifted to the table, fiddled with a stack of Matt's cycling magazines.

'Look, just sit down. I'm not going to give up, so you might as well be comfortable.' Freddie patted the sofa seat next to him. 'Talk to me.'

'He's *solid*. He's a grown-up. He's been through a lot – you know, the stroke, his dad dying, his mum getting so ill. But even though he has so many of his own problems to deal with he always makes room for me. Drops me a text most mornings to check in, wants to hear about the course. All that. It's...' She shook her head, and her smile was puzzled. 'I don't know what to make of it.'

'What's that mean?' Freddie frowned. 'I mean, is he weird about it or...?'

'No. No, I don't think so, but then I wouldn't know because I've never met anyone who's wanted to look after me. Apart from you. That sounds really self-pitying, I know, but it's true. It's.... a novelty.'

'Novelty?'

'No, not a novelty – that was the wrong word, because it's not like I'm going to get sick of it, it's more...' She made a vague gesture. 'Anyway, he'll probably get bored of me soon. *I'd* get bored of me soon.'

'Well that's just stupid,' Freddie said firmly. 'What's wrong with being taken care of, being kept safe? And what happened to this "Putting Yourself First" thing?'

'Oh, you read that?'

'Of course I did, and it was great to read. I didn't know Maraid asked for *everything*. That's fucked up.'

'Well, I didn't want to...'

'I mean, everything though? She seemed all right at the funeral. A bit—'

'Terrifying?'

'No. Which was surprising after everything you've told me about her. More... quiet. Self-contained.'

'That's what they say about serial killers: "Nice man, kept himself to himself".' She sat down with a sigh. 'She knows how to do things on the sly. She's clever that way.'

'Are you not worried she'll read your blog? Come gunning for you?'

'Oh God, no. No.' Her face was just slightly disfigured by a sneer. 'Maraid doesn't read.'

'Anyway, it was good to read the whole "Put Yourself First" thing, it really was, but now you're talking like that's just something you wrote, not something you really believe.'

Jenny said hesitantly: 'I... *do* believe it. I mean, I did when I wrote that piece. I felt very strongly about it. But then, you know, all your insecurities come back, and you think: "Oh, he just feels sorry for me".'

'So you're doing exactly what you said you *weren't* doing: you're telling your blog audience to believe in themselves and value themselves and all that, but you're not following your own advice. Why not invite him round for a beer now?'

Jenny looked alarmed. 'Now? He lives miles away! That will just make me seem weird.'

'OK then, how about this: invite him over for a meal? No cinema, or restaurant. Nothing to distract you from the agonising terror of Being Alone With Someone You Like.' He smiled.

'Well, when you put it like that.' Jenny glanced around the room. 'Here though? It's a bit... grim. Bare.'

'Well, put some pictures up! Make the place your own! I'll help you with that. Do what you want to feel like it's your place and then invite him round.'

'Right, and I'll wear a cocktail dress, and cook a roast and when I take off my glasses and take my hair down he'll say "But Miss Holloway... you're... you're *beautiful*!"'

'You're not going to get out of this by being snarky.' Freddie took both her hands and looked very seriously into her eyes. 'Do you like him?' She nodded, avoiding his gaze. 'Then *show* that you like him! He's really nice!'

She nodded again, smiled. 'I know.'

'And he really likes you. Call him! Set it up.'

She frowned. 'No. I'll-I'll tell you what I'll do. I'll meet him for a coffee some time. I need to give him some information on a carers' group that might be—'

'"You are important... you don't have to buy love by being useful or kind",' Freddie quoted, closing his eyes. 'Look, I'll be your chaperone if you want. He really wouldn't thank me for it, but if it'll make you invite him, so be it.'

'Oh God, Fred this is all so silly. I shouldn't need you to hold my hand. I sort of do though. Do you mind?'

'Holding your hand? Well, I'm not going to lie, you could do with a manicure—'

She punched him lightly. 'No! I mean being here with David.'

'Of course I don't mind. But put up some pictures, please? It looks like a rehab clinic or something. And by the way, where *is* the TV?'

'Um...'

'Jesus Jen, you didn't—'

She nodded shamefaced 'I caved. Kathleen called and banged on and on about how Maraid needed the TV and why was I so selfish and...' She shrugged.

'So the blog post was a lie then?'

'No, when I posted it I was really sure of myself, but then...'

'They got to you?'

'Mm.'

Freddie shook his head. 'You can't let people walk all over you, Jen.'

'I know,' she muttered. 'I just… I have a bit of an Achilles heel when it comes to family.' She looked up. 'Is that the right phrase? Achilles heel?'

'You *know* it's the right phrase. Don't make out you're this ignoramus,' Freddie said testily. 'Don't… undervalue yourself like that.' He took her hand. 'For Christ's sake Jen, if you could just believe in yourself more, just be a bit more like you are in the blog… if you managed that you'd be unstoppable.'

'You think?'

'I know. In the meantime, we'll start with making this place look like you actually live here. Then, when you invite David over, he won't think he's in a halfway house for ex cycling junkies.' He sneered at a copy of *Cycling World*. 'Look at this – "You need 600mm ERD, built 32x2 onto a hub with flanges of 60mm from the hub centreline". It's like Sanskrit.'

And so they spent the next hour going through Jenny's belongings, consisting of holiday photographs, a few mass-produced prints – the obligatory Klimt, Hokusai's *Wave*.

'Wouldn't it be nice to have a photo of your mum?' Freddie asked gently.

'There aren't any. Marc trashed them all. He threw them all out when we left. The only one I have is this one.' Young Sal sitting on a striped towel, squinting into the sun. Jenny – about six years old – squatted next to her, her small face punctured, almost obliterated.

'What happened? How come it's got a hole in it?' Freddie asked.

'The night, she, you know. She pushed me into it, and my head must have caught it. It smashed, and then she trod on it.'

'Jesus, Jen,' Freddie said softly. 'She hit you?'

'No. Not hit. More of a sideswipe. She didn't know what she was doing.' Jenny's voice was low, her face averted. 'That's where the glass went through it.' When she touched the edge of the photo, her fingers made it tremble. She smiled. 'I remember that day. I fell off a donkey and cried so much that Mum bought me a stick of candyfloss to cheer me up, and so did Kathleen and her boyfriend and a few other people, and I ended up being sick on the bus home.' One finger gently caressed her own younger face.

'I feel awful now,' Freddie said. 'I didn't know she... hit you. I saw the bruise, too, and I didn't even...' He shook his head at himself. 'If I'd known that she'd hit you, there's no way I'd have told you to get it framed.'

'No – you know what? I'm glad you did.' She raised her head. 'It's important to remember the good times, isn't it? She wasn't always like that. She...' She looked down at her hands, swallowed hard. I should get it framed again. It's all I have left of her, isn't it?'

'I bet I can get it repaired.' Freddie pocketed the picture. 'Let me see if I can. And I'll get it framed too. 'You're right. It's... it's important to remember things, good things. It's your history.'

'It is.' She nodded.

'Does David know about – any of that stuff? The refuge? Marc?' Freddie asked gently.

'No. God, no!' She shook her head vehemently. 'I don't want him to either. I don't want anyone to feel sorry for me.'

Freddie closed his eyes and quoted: '"You deserve a space in the world. You can come first".' He took her hand. 'Does he even know about the blog?' Again, she shook her head. 'Why not?'

'It's... I don't know why not. It's complicated. I... Don't tell him, Fred?'

'No, of course I won't, but, Jen, why not? It's something to be proud of. Your whole history is something to be proud of! You survived when lots of other people wouldn't have. *I* sure as hell wouldn't have. David seems lovely, so maybe try to… let him in more. Trust him. What you wrote a few months ago? About making your own family? You were right about that.'

'You think?'

'I *know*. *You* know it too. You're so… *loved*, Jen. You are!'

CHAPTER EIGHTEEN

A week later and Jenny stood by the work surface, her eyes pink with onion tears, hair escaping her ponytail. David and Freddie would be at the flat in half an hour.

As she cooked, she hummed tunelessly to herself, then, with ten minutes to spare, she ran to the bathroom, patted some make-up on and struggled into a slightly wrinkled dress. Then she watched her reflection widen its eyes, biting its lips, until the doorbell rang. The wide-angled view through the spyhole showed David and Freddie standing together, a little awkwardly, on the doorstep. David held flowers. Freddie held a bottle of wine. She counted to three and opened the door.

When David saw her, he radiated pleasure.

'You look lovely!'

'Thanks. This is my posh dress.' She accepted a kiss from Freddie, and shifted sideways to allow them to come into the dim, narrow corridor and then into the too-bright kitchen.

'This is very nice.' David looked around amiably.

'Oh, it's a bit bare,' Jenny apologised. 'Matt doesn't really go for a lot of decoration. I've managed to make my room look a bit more lived-in though.'

'Matt?' While David's smile remained, his forehead creased.

'My flatmate?'

'You didn't mention that you had a flatmate.' His smile flattened.

'Oh, didn't I? Sorry. He works shifts, so we barely see each other.' There was a pause. 'Anyway, come this way for the grand tour!' It took less than three minutes to wander through the small flat. 'And this is my room.'

'That's a lovely picture.' David pointed at the wall above her bed where she'd put up a photograph of herself. 'Where was it taken?' He looked at her and smiled.

'Turkey.' Jenny smiled back. Something seemed to pass between them. 'That was in Marmaris, wasn't it? Fred?'

'What?' Freddie seemed distracted. 'Oh, yes. Yes. You'd just bought that sarong from that pushy man on the beach, remember?' As he peered at the photo, a thought darted into his mind, snagged, twitched.

'We went all over the place, didn't we Fred? We almost ended up crossing the border into Syria by mistake. That could have been disastrous. And we nearly got arrested for illegally camping in that butterfly valley – wasn't it a protected area or something, Fred?'

'What? Oh, yes, yes.' Freddie dragged his confused gaze away from the picture. 'We only got away with it because that fat police guy fancied you. Lucky.' He turned to David. 'You've seen *Papillon*, right? If she hadn't flirted with the him, we'd be in solitary somewhere, eating bugs.'

There was a silence. David, still smiling, said: 'I'm afraid I don't understand the reference.'

'Oh what? *Papillon*! Steve McQueen, Dustin Hoffman? Great film. Easily one of the best Steve-McQueen-fails-to-escape movies.' Freddie beamed.

'I'll be sure to look out for it,' David said politely.

There was a pause.

'Well, that's the end of the tour.' Jenny led them all back to the living room. 'I just need to poke about in the kitchen; drinks are on the table though, if you want one? I'll just be a minute.'

Left alone, Freddie waggled a bottle at David. 'Start on the best and work down to the cheap?'

'Mmm.' David stood irresolutely, one hand fiddling with the back of a dining chair. 'So, Matt, is it? And what is it he does again?'

'I think he's a nurse.' Freddie struggled with the bottle opener. 'I'm terrible at this.'

'Let me.' David took the bottle off him. 'So Matt isn't often here then?'

'No, not much I don't think. I've only met him once or twice.'

'So he's not a close friend of Jenny's then?' David persisted. He pulled out the cork with a grunt of effort.

'No. She answered an advert in *Loot*. Thanks.' Freddie accepted a glass. 'Cheers. I wanted her to move in with me, but the timing was all wrong, and she says it's too far away from Cheryl. Her therapist? I hope she'll change her mind though. I mean,' Freddie glanced at the closed kitchen door and lowered his voice, 'it's OK here and everything, but it's not, you know, homely. And it's not cheap either. She would have got mates rates from me.'

David frowned again. 'It must be a bit… difficult to live with a stranger. A male stranger. A single girl. It's a bit—'

'Oh, Jenny's lived with loads of people, don't worry about her!' He registered David's expression, and rushed to explain. 'I mean, she's always lived in shared houses, with men and women, and she's very good at looking after herself – boundaries, all that. And Matt is very nice and tidy. He has a girlfriend that he spends a lot of time with too.' He stopped then, aware that he had furiously back-pedalled himself into a blatant lie; he had no idea if Matt had a girlfriend or not. *Shit.* 'Anyway, living alone is sort of horrible. Have you ever done it?' he asked, as Jenny came back.

'Yes, but I never really enjoyed it. I can't relax in a house by myself.'

Jenny nodded. 'I've only done it a few times, like when I was staying at Freddie's parents' when they were on the cruise. I had to leave the downstairs lights on every night.' She laughed and shook her head. 'Don't tell Ruth!' she told Freddie. 'I'm not cut out for living alone. So, even though me and Matt don't see a lot of each other, it's nice to know that there's someone in the room next door, you know?'

After a pause, David said: 'When I moved back to the village, I couldn't get over how quiet everything was. Where I'd lived before – it was always quite noisy, even at night, but suddenly I was in a house where I could hear everything. It's probably worse in a big house, magnified…Things rattle, doors slam. To be honest I've more or less shut the top floor of the house off. I sleep in what used to be the study next to the sitting room.' He smiled. 'You Can't Go Home Again.'

'Ah! So you've finally pierced her facade! You know she's really a blogging superstar!' Freddie grinned.

'I took a look at it today,' David said. 'When I had a moment.' It was a strange, ambiguous phrase. Elderly. His face expressed absolutely nothing.

'I 'fessed up the other day,' Jenny told Freddie, then turned back to David. 'But, you know, I started it on a bit of a whim, and I just jot down ideas every now and again. And it's more for the course than, you know, for *me*.'

'Bollocks!' Freddie told her. From the corner of his eye, he thought he saw David flinch. 'It's not just for the course, not any more. It's brilliant. It's practically a public service. Don't put it down like that!'

David winced again, ever so slightly. After a small pause, he said: 'It is a great achievement. But I wonder, does it make you feel a bit… exposed? People knowing everything about you like that, being able to… reach into your life and do what they want. I've read about… what are they called? Trolls?'

'Well, that's why she keeps it anonymised,' Freddie said quickly. 'And people are very nice. She gets a lot of lovely messages and stuff. Support. Don't you, Jen?'

'Well, not always,' Jenny admitted. 'I had some pretty nasty comments a while ago. That was difficult.'

'What kind of comments?' David asked.

'Well, when you write about death, or any kind of trauma, it's powerful stuff. It can really affect people. I think some people reacted without thinking, and there was a bit of a row in the comments section, that's all. It kind of blew up and then blew away, thankfully.'

David nodded sagely. 'These were the comments after your mother's... passing?'

David's speech was flecked with those sort of antiquated phrases – 'When I had a moment'; 'Mother's passing'. It was as if he'd been cryogenically frozen for the past fifty years or so, and was only just now thawing out. Strange. Irritatingly strange, because Freddie really wanted David to be perfect for Jenny.

'It was pretty awful while it lasted, wasn't it, Jen?' Freddie said. 'A real grimy window into humanity. But Jenny handled it brilliantly, I thought. Didn't dignify anything with a response.'

'"Grimy window into humanity". That's a good phrase, Fred, I'm stealing that one,' Jenny said. 'But yeah. It was... unnerving.'

David coughed. 'I suppose I don't have that... talent. To be that open with people I don't know well. It's definitely something I need to work on. I think, if I'd been in your position, Freddie, seeing the kind of things that were being written, I wouldn't have been able to resist posting a few replies myself. But that's me. I have an—' He closed his eyes. '"Enlarged sense of justice".' He opened them, smiled. 'Someone told me that once, and I still can't really understand why it's a bad thing?'

Freddie gazed at him. *Was that a dig? Did he think he should have weighed in to the argument? Defended Jenny? Should he have?*

'Anyway, it's all over with now.' Jenny was smiling, but her voice was firm. 'You have to be a grown-up about these things. Live and learn and all that.'

There was a brief, not too comfortable, silence.

'And on that note – the past and all that,' Freddie reached for his coat. 'I've got something for you.' From out of his pocket, he produced a brown paper oblong. 'Here.'

'Oh Fred.' She smiled. 'I know what this is.' The paper ripped, and Jenny's repaired toddler face stared up from her lap.

'They did the best they could with the hole.' Freddie said. 'There's still a bit of a tear, but there you are, in all your chubby glory.'

'Oh Fred, thanks. That's really… special. It's lovely. Come here!' And she hugged him hard. 'This is the only photo I have of me and Mum together.' She wiped her eyes, handed it to David. 'And Freddie got it fixed for me!'

David held the frame between finger and thumb – as if it were a strange insect, or a fragment of an obscene letter – and his ever-ready smile faded, faded into something unreadable. 'But I don't understand. Why don't you have any other photographs?'

'Oh.' Jenny made a dismissive gesture. 'Long story. Dull.' She reached for the picture.

'No, really, why?' David was insistent. His soft eyes seemed aggrieved, offended, and he didn't give the picture back.

'Well, my mum was in an abusive relationship, and when we left him, he destroyed them all. Nearly all of them anyway. There might have been more that Mum threw out.' Jenny shrugged. Freddie looked at her anxiously, trying to catch her eye, but couldn't.

'I don't understand that either. Why would she have done that?' David asked, frowning.

Jenny shrugged. 'I don't know if she *did,* she just might have. She-she'd do things like that sometimes. I don't know.'

David's voice hardened just a little. 'But why? They were your photos too. They belonged to *you*. They were precious. Didn't she think of that?'

Jenny gazed at him. 'Well, like I said there might not have *been* any more photos. I don't know. All this happened a long time ago, it doesn't matter—'

'It *does* matter though,' David muttered. 'You only have this photo? That's all you have?'

'Well, yes,' Jenny answered after a pause. Finally, she looked over David's head and met Freddie's eyes. Her expression said: *Help!*

'At least it's a nice photo!' Freddie said, with forced jollity. 'My parents have shitloads of photos of me, and I hate every single one of them.'

David frowned sorrowfully. 'I just… I would've thought…' He shook his head. 'I'm sorry. Things like that really… get to me. Other people deciding things for you, taking things from you.'

'I think sometimes parents don't really understand how precious things like photos are for their kids,' Jenny said carefully. 'But maybe it's more careless than callous?'

David sighed, and the anger that had crept into his face crept back out. 'You're right. Yes. It needn't be a… cruel thing. It's a pity though. Sorry.' He handed the picture back. 'When you're a child, you need to feel safe and… respected. If that doesn't happen, you have double the work when you're an adult.'

'Absolutely! And that's the kind of thing I'm blogging about,' Jenny said eagerly. 'I really think we have to learn to value ourselves, nurture ourselves, you know? Without thinking it's selfish, or wrong.'

'I agree. But shouldn't nurture come from someone else? We're pack animals, aren't we?' There was something wolfish about David's smile now. 'We make more sense working as a unit than alone. That's why I think living alone isn't natural, or, you know, living with a stranger just to split the rent. It's not how we're meant to be.'

'You see, I agree with you,' Jenny said, 'but all my life I've tried to go the opposite way, even though I don't like it.' She shook her head. 'I want to be Oh So Independent.'

'And if you admit that you don't like it, it feels a bit pathetic,' David said. 'Society tells you to go against your nature, so you spend years chasing an ideal that you don't even want, while passing up what you really need.'

'Well, yes.' She nodded. She looked a little dazed. 'That's it. That's the thing.'

Later, when Freddie thought about this evening, he pinpointed this as the moment Jenny and David fell in love. It was what he'd hoped for her – it was a fairy tale. It should have been lovely. It should have been something he'd allude to in his wedding speech: 'I was there at the beginning…' But… no. It wasn't like that at all. It was more complicated than that.

Later still, in the months during which his mind worried at this memory like a terrier with a rat, his emotions changed, morphed into something more concrete. At the time though, he was just puzzled – *what was wrong?* Something was damming the natural flow of the evening, like a corpse caught in the weeds.

CHAPTER NINETEEN

David offered to give Freddie a lift back to his flat. He insisted.

'It's out of your way,' Freddie said doubtfully. 'I don't want to make you late; I know you have your mother to get back to.'

'No, no, it's raining. Please, let me save you the walk.'

When they were in the car, after the perfunctory conversation about where they were headed was exhausted, Freddie felt unsettled. David seemed stiffer. The relative easy candour he'd displayed in Jenny's flat had gone. After a few minutes of awkward silence, Freddie grasped at one of the few things he knew they had in common.

'So, have you heard from Ryan lately?'

'No.' David drove slowly, deliberately. His hands never wavered from the ten to two position, and his eyes never left the road. 'I'll probably see him at the school reunion.'

'Oh, you went to school with him as well then?'

'What?' David slowed even further.

'You went to school as well as university with Ryan?'

'Oh. Yes.' The car had now slowed to a crawl. 'Both.' There was a long pause.

'There's still a bit further to go,' Freddie said eventually, nodding at the speedometer.

'Sorry,' David answered absently. 'I drive like an old woman.' He sped up fractionally, and the conversation died again.

Then Freddie's phone rang. His latest ring tone – Barbra Streisand singing 'Who's Afraid of the Big Bad Wolf?' – had seemed hilarious when he downloaded it but, now he was alone with David, its volume and sheer inanity was just embarrassing. Unfortunately, because he was sitting on his coat, and the phone was in the inside pocket, they were treated to a whole verse and half the chorus, cutting off just after 'Big bad—'

After a few seconds it started again, just entering the verse when the car suddenly swerved and David shouted: 'Can you turn that *off?*'

'I'm trying,' Freddie told him. 'Sorry!' He unbuckled his seatbelt and managed to wrench the coat out from under his thighs, just as Barbra hit the high G. It was Jenny, but he rejected the call. He didn't want to annoy David any more.

They drove in silence until they arrived at Freddie's flat.

'Sorry about the phone,' Freddie said quietly.

'No, it's fine,' David said seriously.

'It's a stupid ringtone,' Freddie said. Then he waited for a few seconds to see if David would apologise about overreacting.

Instead he waved it off with a magnanimous gesture. 'It's really no problem.'

He smiled. It winked on like a bright light. Then, after a hesitation, David gave Freddie a rough, stiff hug. Freddie's head only came up to his shoulder, and he found his cold cheeks being pushed into tweed. *His father's jacket?* It had to be. It smelled old. 'Good man,' David said. 'Nicetomeetyou.'

Then he let go, trotted back to his car, raised one rigid hand in farewell, and drove off.

Freddie could see his face, illuminated by a dim street light, the smile sliding, a sheen of sweat on his white face. Freddie walked into his building, locked the door behind him, and sat for some minutes on the sofa in the dark, feeling confused. Feeling… scared.

His phone buzzed – a text from Jenny:

Nice night, don't you think?

He was about to call back, but didn't. David didn't like Barbra Streisand, that's all. It didn't signify anything. Millions of people didn't like Barbra Streisand, annoying ringtones or polite chit-chat. Lots of people wore tweed. Lots of men got physical affection wrong. Jen was happy. David was nice. Freddie had Done A Good Thing by getting them together. Just... *don't overthink it.*

He wrote back:

Lovely! Bit knackered call you tomorrow xxxx

Just clean your teeth, Fred, he thought. *Clean your teeth, wash your face, set an alarm to wake you in time to get to the gym, ignore said alarm. Don't go to the gym. Just a normal Sunday.* He flossed, rinsed, gargled and retired to the dark quiet of his room and... thought about David. Good son. Kind to his mother. *Just like Norman Bates. Shut up, Fred. Stop it now.* But that photograph of Jenny? The one on her wall? Something about that stayed stuck in the folds in his mind like a splinter.

After a while he knew he wasn't going to sleep without figuring out what it meant.

So, sighing, he got up again and got out his laptop, opened his photo folders, and found Turkey 2013. Jenny on the beach in Marmaris. Brown and blue and yellow stars. He placed one hand over her torso, leaving only the arm, the sarong, the splash of sunlight. That was it. That was it! It was the same picture that had been in the background of David's profile picture. He was practically sure, almost positive.

What was David doing with a picture of Jenny that was taken before they even met?

Now, wide awake and fizzing with adrenaline, he found David's Facebook page again. The blank silhouette profile was still up, *but maybe his old one was in his picture folders somewhere?* But no. There were no pictures at all, which was strange. Or not? Maybe David didn't advertise his whole life online, like some people did. Like Freddie did. *Stop looking for things to worry about. Go to bed. Just stop it now.*

But when he finally managed to get to sleep, it was a thin, fitful rest, and he woke early to the sound of birds, with his mind still clogged with misgivings.

CHAPTER TWENTY

You Can't Go Home Again

I've been thinking a lot about determination. On the one hand, we're told that we have to follow our dreams, never give up *insert cliché here*, and on the other hand we're told to put others first, Do-as-you-would-be-done-to and don't make waves.

There's a cognitive dissonance here that I've struggled with, and I know that a lot of you have too. I think the struggle is harder for people like us – people who haven't grown up with self-respect, and have had to learn it on the way. If our early life experiences have told us that we don't 'deserve' comfort and happiness, it's hard to accept love and appreciation from others. We don't 'deserve' it, or we're suspicious of it.

All this is my overwritten way of telling you that I'm seeing someone, and it's great and sweet and exciting and SCARY. You know that old Groucho Marx line – 'I would never be a member of a club that would have me as a member'? Well that's the thing that knocks me flat. If someone likes me, I find myself being facetious and glib – using all the usual tools to stay separate, stay safe.

I'm really trying not to do that this time though. I even managed (glibly, facetiously) to tell him how I feel. And here's what he said: 'I believe in you. I have confidence in you. If you can't find those things within yourself, just borrow a little from me.' And it was so beautiful, so kind, that I felt some of that tension inside me loosen.

If someone loves you and admires you, perhaps you can take it as read that you are loveable and admirable and act accordingly. Graft that onto yourself and assimilate it, learn to use it, like you would a donated organ.

Perhaps, just by having endured the pain of the past, you have earned what you want, what you need? Perhaps the rest of your life can be lived in fullness rather than lack?

Take care. Jay XOXO

CHAPTER TWENTY-ONE

'You're sure it's OK?' Jenny looked over her shoulder at her reflection. 'It's not too, you know, severe?'

David shook his head. 'Not at all. It's smart.'

'I quite like how 1950s it looks.' She smoothed her hair back from her face. 'It looks better if I get my hair out of my eyes. Fred?'

'Weren't you talking about getting it cut?' Freddie replied.

'Oh, I was probably talking about it, but I'll never get round to it.' She shrugged at him. Then, as David's eyes drifted to the frizzy tendrils dangling over her shoulders. 'Unless you really think I should get it cut? Should I, David?'

'Well, you could probably do with it,' he admitted. 'Why not go to that hairdresser next door now and see if they can fit you in?'

Jenny frowned doubtfully at him. 'That's, like, a designer place; even if they have any space I couldn't afford it after buying this. No. I'll wear my split ends with pride! You're sure the other suit won't do?' she spoke to them both, but David answered.

'No. This is the suit you should get. Definitely.'

When she went back into the changing rooms, David turned to Freddie. 'Will you tell her to get her hair cut? Let it be my treat?'

'She won't let you,' Freddie told him. 'And I couldn't make her either. I can't make her do anything. Don't even try. That way madness lies.'

Jenny called from the changing room. 'I'm just trying on these shirts too! Listen, you guys go to the pub and I'll see you there in ten minutes.'

Both men nodded and smiled awkwardly. Both David and Freddie had assumed they were would be spending the evening alone with Jenny, and they were feeling the strain of the other's company. They'd arrived separately to meet her from her placement at only to find her tiredly confused and apologetic. 'God, I must have double-booked, sorry! I thought I was meeting Fred tomorrow and you today… But listen, let's go out together for a drink? I have to do some shopping before though. I need a suit for this interview? With the council? I told you about it, didn't I? God… my memory is terrible. Too much going on.'

They walked stiffly to The Bristolian – a pub over the street – David held the door open so that Freddie had to duck and scuttle under his arm. It gave him a disagreeable feeling, as though he was being treated like a child.

They found a booth by the door. David frowned at the walls plastered with posters, at the wide, horseshoe-shaped bar. One finger tapped on the table, picked at the varnish that had bubbled with age. It was Freddie who broke the silence.

'I haven't been in the place in years.' He looked around. 'Believe it or not, they've tidied it up a lot. It used to be a kind of punk place. Gigs on and all that.' David nodded politely, and tore a stretch of varnish off the table. It curled like flayed skin. 'So, how's your mother?'

'Fine. Well, not fine, but, you know.'

'Is she mobile? I mean do you need help in the house and—'

'What I can't work out is how she's going to keep working at the – what is it called – illness centre—'

'Oh, you mean Jenny? It's the Wellness Centre.'

'"Wellness Centre".' David's voice was ever so slightly tinged with vitriol. 'As well as working full-time and keeping up with college. How will she manage it?'

'She's very resilient you know,' Freddie told him. 'She'll just make it happen, that's all, even if it means hardly sleeping, and working all the hours God sends. It's a real vocation.'

'I just can't see how she can do it.' David shook his head. 'She'll collapse.'

Freddie smiled reassuringly. 'She won't though. She knows what she wants now, and she knows how to get it, but you know, there's sacrifices to be made on the way, and that's what she'll do. She's very determined, very tough when it comes down to it. So, don't worry about her too much, OK?'

David made a noise, somewhere in the middle of dour cynicism and impatience, and Freddie's attempt at establishing a rapport, already terminal, died there.

When Jenny swung through the door, both men were mightily relieved.

'OK, so, that's the suit I'm going to get!'

'Where is it then?' Freddie asked.

'Aha, I have A Plan,' she told him. 'So, I tried it on in the shop to see what it looked like, but I'll actually buy it on eBay for loads less money. You see?' She tapped her head. 'Always thinking.'

'You're a *rara avis* my love,' Freddie said.

'I'm a skint *rara avis*. But I can still buy you each a drink, what'll you have?'

'No, I'll get them – David?'

'Anything. No. No, just a juice.' He got up distractedly. 'I just need to go out for a few minutes.' And he shouldered his way out of the door.

'I think it's his mum,' Jenny said after a pause. 'He's worried about her. He's left her today with an agency nurse, and had a few nightmares with them in the past, and Catherine doesn't respond well to change, and so strangers in the house... they throw her.'

'Have you met her?'

Jenny hesitated, nodded. 'I have. Last week. She's lovely. It's really sad.'

'You didn't tell me you'd met her.'

Jenny winced apologetically. One finger tapped the torn bubble of varnish. 'David is... private. I think it's been so hard taking care of her, harder than he thought it would be, and he feels a bit guilty that he finds it hard. I asked to meet her because I thought it might help him if he shared his feelings a bit. It's lonely, looking after a sick parent, and David... well, I don't think he confides in many people. He doesn't have a Freddie.'

'Not sure he wants a Freddie.'

'*Everyone* wants a Freddie.' She twinkled at him.

'I think he's a bit pissed off that I'm here,' Freddie admitted. 'I think he wanted you all to himself tonight.'

'Well, maybe I was a bit economical with the truth,' she admitted. 'I kind of deliberately double-booked you. I just wanted you to get to know each other in a more casual way, not at dinner or anything like that, just, *oh, hey, let's have a quick drink* – that kind of thing. Don't tell him that, though, will you?'

Freddie shook his head. 'It's backfired then. He doesn't seem very comfortable with me.' Jenny nodded soberly.

'I thought that might happen, but it's shyness, honestly. He really likes you; he told me. And he knows that wherever I go, you're there too.'

'Like an evil twin?'

'Exactly like an evil twin.' She smiled. 'Don't get paranoid. He's... he's a bit stiff, but he really is lovely, you're lovely, and that's it. Right!' She slapped the table. 'I'm going to get drinks.' And she disappeared into the lounge bar, where the bar staff lurked, and reappeared ten minutes later with a tray of drinks and two packets of crisps clasped in her teeth that she dropped on the tabletop.

'David not back?'

'Nope.' Freddie tore the crisp bags open and arranged them fussily on the table.

'I'll give him a call... oh, wait, he's texted me.' She frowned at her phone. 'Oh, what?'

'What?' Freddie said through a mouthful of crisps. 'Is he all right? He's not gone home has he? I told you he didn't want me here.'

'No, he's not gone home, but I tell you what he has done.' She looked up from her phone. 'He's bought me that suit! And booked me an appointment to get my hair cut!'

'Bloody hell!'

'I know!' She stared at the phone again. 'How lovely is that?' Then she sat down. 'I can't accept it though. I can't. Can I?'

'Why not?'

'It was £200, that's why not.'

And at that moment, David came through the door, so boyish and charming that Freddie found himself smiling back. He swung three carrier bags onto the tabletop, and wagged one finger at Jenny.

'Now don't tell me off. I couldn't let you buy a second-hand suit, it's just not right. So,' he opened the first bag, 'here's the two that you liked – you can't just have one suit, can you?'

Freddie opened his mouth, tried to catch Jenny's eye, but she was stroking the suit, eyes soft, cheeks pink with happiness.

'And obviously you needed shirts, so I bought these three – I think the shade is perfect for you, and they're nicely fitted. I asked the saleswoman and she agreed that, with your colouring, you can wear blue. Any kind of blue looks lovely on you!' His voice rose with excitement. He handed Jenny a bag filled with boxes. 'And here are some shoes. Again, I thought it would be best to just buy all three pairs. I looked at them, and they were all perfect and they all work well with each suit. And these,' he handed her a wrapped box, 'I just thought they were special. They're just for fun. Hope you like them.' He sat back, still with that smile on his face, looking like an expectant puppy.

Jenny opened the box, her mouth fell open, her cheeks pinkened.

'What is it? Show me!' Freddie leaned over. 'Jesus.' He stared at the shoes, stared at David. 'I've seen enough drag shows to know they're Louboutin.'

David flinched ever so slightly, but kept his eyes on Jenny. She didn't say anything, so he asked anxiously: 'I did get the right sizes in everything, didn't I? I can go back and change things if—'

Jenny drew out one of the Louboutins, turned it over, and watched her reflection swim back at her from the red lacquer. 'Wow.'

'Do you like them?' David asked eagerly.

'They're gorgeous. It's all—'

He interrupted her. 'So your hair appointment is in half an hour. And after that why don't we have some dinner? Not here, obviously.' He looked around at the pub with visible distaste. 'But anywhere you'd like really. Somewhere nice.'

'I just can't believe you *did* this.' She dragged her eyes from the shoes and looked up at David. Then she glanced at Freddie. 'But I can't—'

'You can.' David was firm.

'Well will you let me—?'

'Pay me back? No.' He sat back, took a sip of his juice. 'All of this is really down to Freddie anyway.'

'What?' Freddie asked.

David smiled, with just a touch of condescension. 'Something you said made a real impression on me. "Knowing what you want and going for it"?'

'Well, I meant… I was talking about Jen, and the career and all that…' Freddie trailed off confusedly. 'I didn't mean buy the shop.'

'No, it was very useful. I took it to heart, really.' He looked at his phone. 'So, shall we eat? What's a nice place, Freddie? What would you recommend?'

'There's a nice Thai place round the corner?' Freddie answered weakly. 'We went there on a work do once, the all you can eat buffet is nice and—'

David wrinkled his nose. 'No. I think we can do better than that. I'll just nip outside to make a call. It's too… loud in here, don't you think? Why does the music have to be so loud?' And he bounded out of the door again, leaving Jenny and Freddie facing the boxes and bags strewn on the table.

'Bloody hell,' Freddie managed after a while.

'I know.' Jenny opened the shoebox again, took a dreamy peek. 'The shoes alone are £300.'

'What're you going to do? I mean—'

'Jenny?' A man with a greying mullet and a Celtic Frost T-shirt shambled towards them. 'Sal's kid? Jenny? Dougie? Remember me?'

Jenny froze, half turned. 'Hey, Dougie.'

'Boyfriend?' He nodded at Freddie.

'Just a friend,' she answered tightly.

'And how's Sal getting on now then?'

'She's dead,' Jenny said shortly. Then she stood, picked up the bags.

'Christ! What? Sal?' Dougie wobbled in his boots. 'How? How'd that happen then?'

'Got to go, Dougie.' Jenny got up quickly. 'Freddie, come on.' She pointed at the door. Freddie nodded dumbly to Dougie, and followed Jenny out like a dog.

'Who was that then?' Jenny didn't hear him. She was casting about in the darkening street, looking for David. 'Jen? Who was that? Why'd we have to leave?'

'Just some... old friend of Mum's. One of the old gang. Marc and all those types.' Her mouth tightened with distaste. 'One of those bastards.' She shivered. 'Where's David got to then?'

'Call him?'

'No, better not, he doesn't like to be called,' she answered absently. 'We'll just wait. That's all.'

'Well can't we wait inside? It's freezing out here. What d'you mean he doesn't like to be called?'

'He just— He just doesn't like to be called, that's all,' Jenny said shortly. 'And I don't need Dougie and his old crew asking about Mum.'

'How come he didn't know? About Sal I mean.'

'*I* don't know, Fred. Maybe he missed the leaflet drop. Or *maybe* I didn't fancy inviting every dodgy drunk she used to knock about with to the funeral?'

'All right.' Freddie's voice was hurt. 'I didn't mean anything—'

'No. You didn't mean anything.' Her voice was hard. Then she looked at him, and it softened. 'I know you didn't. I'm sorry. It just... it freaks me out when I see people from all those years ago, that's all. It makes me think I haven't come that far after all.' She smiled tightly, but it was still a smile. She checked her phone. 'I have to get to the hair salon. Here, can you take one of the bags?'

'What are you going to do about all this stuff?' Freddie asked, puffing under the weight of the bag as they trotted across the road.

'I can't keep it. Can I?'

It was difficult to gauge her meaning. *Was she asking for his permission, or stating a fact?* He looked at her pale face, sad now. The wind streaked around the corner, blowing her hair back from her forehead, exposing her creased forehead, her pinched eyebrows.

'I can't, can I? Keep this stuff?' she asked again.

And Freddie thought about Dodgy Dougie and His Old Crew. Such a sinister phrase. It sounded like a pub band from the 70s, reformed after serving their sentences for various sex crimes… The Old Gang. What must it be like to be Jenny? To have a past like that, all those demons, all that pain. So close to happiness, but never quite reaching it… and so he did what he knew would make her feel good. 'Yes, you can,' he told her. 'You deserve everything good Jen. He wants to buy you nice things and, well, you *deserve* nice things.' She looked so grateful that he went further. 'He's really… nice. David, he really is.'

'He is, isn't he? I know he's a bit… old-fashioned, but he really *gives* a shit, you know? And there haven't been many of them in my life. It's just been you, really. And now him, and—'

'Speak of the devil!' Freddie was relieved to see David bearing down on them. He didn't especially want to carry on singing David's praises, or listen to Jenny doing it either.

He accompanied them as far as the salon door, and then made his excuses. Early meeting. Presentation. Prep to do beforehand.

'Oh, Fred, don't go,' Jenny said anxiously.

'Yes, can't you stay out a little longer? Have dinner?' David was less convincing. 'I managed to get a table at the new place on the wharf. It's meant to be very good.'

Freddie paused for a second. *That place is Michelin starred…*

Then his phone rang, and Barbra Streisand had her predictable effect on David. He stiffened, and when Freddie silenced the phone, shuddered.

'No, I'd love to, but I just can't,' Freddie said firmly. 'But have fun, and, Jen, send me a picture of your hair after? And tell them to go easy on the product. Serum is not your friend.'

As he left he heard David giving Jenny precise haircut instructions: 'Only an inch or two off the length but layers for body. And a conditioning treatment…'

CHAPTER TWENTY-TWO

You Can't Go Home Again

[Unpublished post]

A while ago I was watching some American talk show, and the peppy host was interviewing a mother and her child. They'd been in a terrible car crash, and, despite being injured herself, this mother had somehow managed to rescue her child by lifting the entire car off him and dragging him out. She tore all her muscles doing it, but she didn't let herself feel the pain until her baby was safe. Then, and only then, she collapsed. She said something that really struck me: He's more important than me. Any mother would do the same.

Huh. I thought. Any mother? Really?

The other day I saw one of Mum's old friends. Ran into him in a pub. A pub I haven't been to in years. A pub I've never liked. He was exactly the same, just greyer. The same dried patches of spit at the corners of his mouth. Hands still shaking and nicotine stained. Fewer teeth. He knew Marc too. They all knew Marc.

I was with people I loved, people who cared about me, but as soon as I saw this man, the old fear swept in and I had to run away, chased by my own childhood, poking and prodding at me.

For the first time I have someone who needs me (yes, I'm hearing Stevie Wonder too). I thought that if I made my place in the world, if I was loved and valued, everything would be all right, and yet The Bad Thing isn't going away. It's coming back with more force. Maybe that's what happens? Maybe your mind waits until you're safe to process all the unsafe memories?

So, *trigger warning*: This post is about abuse. I need to write this, but not at the expense of your comfort. Please, please don't read further if it might in any way harm your own recovery.

OK, here goes.

My mum had a boyfriend. We moved in with him when I was eight, and for a few years nothing bad happened. To me, anyway. Then it started.

He'd come into the bathroom when I was in the shower, sit on the toilet, just 'having a chat', but he'd stay until the water ran cold, and he knew I couldn't stand it any more, and I'd have to get out. Then he'd hand me a towel. That was all. Later I had to 'pay' for the towel by kissing his cheek. Sometimes I had to let him dry me. I'd be about eleven then. Mum once told him not to be so affectionate with me. That's what she said, 'affectionate'.

I hate writing this. I hate it.

Mum didn't know. No. No, I'm being honest, I have to be honest. Perhaps she did know? I think, on some level, she had to, because her attitude towards me changed. I stopped being her child and became her competition. She seemed jealous of me. She borrowed my clothes, somehow managing to squeeze herself into my twelve-year-old's jeans and tops, as if this was some twisted love triangle, and we were fighting over this man – this balding man, with his cigarettes and pot belly and coke habit.

Then she stopped buying me clothes altogether. Maybe it was her way of punishing me for what was happening? I don't know, but soon only my school uniform still fitted me. One day Marc came back with a bag full of clothes – I don't know where he got them from – but they were teenagers' clothes, kind of slutty – crop tops with slogans on them. Tight jeans. I remember Mum trying to make a joke out of it – 'You never get me anything nice!'. She tried to normalise it. 'Let's have a fashion show – Jen, model your new clothes for us.' And she made me put on every outfit, in every permutation. I didn't want to wear this stuff, but I had no choice, I didn't have anything else to wear. People stared at me in the street, and girls said nasty things. Once, on non-uniform day, I was kerb-crawled by a man, all the way home from school. That was scary, but I didn't want to tell Mum in case, somehow, she blamed me.

I want to say I'm remembering all this now, but it's not true. I'm re-remembering it. I'm letting myself think about it.

There's other things, but I don't want to write them down. Maybe some time, but not now.

When you've experienced abuse, it's very difficult to understand safety, permanence, comfort. When you've experienced abuse, it colours everything, alters your perceptions. To this day I can't, hand on heart, say I feel safe.

But I will say this – I'm going to try, as hard as I can, to recover. And that means putting down my burdens, letting myself be looked after, pampered. Babied? Maybe. But there's nothing wrong with that. That's what I deserve.

Anyway. Apologies for the self-indulgence. And, as ever, take care of yourselves!

Jay XOXO

CHAPTER TWENTY-THREE

'I'm telling you, Fred, it's just, God, *awful*, the things some of them have gone through,' Jenny said through a mouthful of food. 'I mean, I can't talk about the details obviously, but. God.'

'Is this the group sessions or the one-to-one?'

'Both. But the group sessions are probably more intense.' Jenny had been on placement now for two months and, since their truncated evening at The Bristolian, Freddie hadn't seen a great deal of her. Between work, college and her placement she barely had any free time. This hurried lunch was in lieu of several missed dates.

'So, what are the group sessions like?' he asked.

'Strange. Fascinating, but strange. They say all the right supportive things to each other, listen respectfully and all that, but then immediately counter with their own experience. So there's almost this one-upmanship going on, you know? "Yes, I totally understand how lost you must feel after your ninety-year-old nan died, because I felt the same when my entire family died in a car crash". "Yes, your miscarriages are awful; when my eleven-year-old died of cancer…".' She laid down her fork, and took a sip of water. 'There's these two competing dynamics. One is, like, intense empathy and the other is a kind of competitive narcissism, you know?'

'That sounds shit,' Freddie told her.

'It is. But it's fascinating too. Just seeing how people work to impress each other in strange ways, you know? It's all about feeding the ego with sympathy.' She pushed her plate away. 'But, yeah, it's… intense.'

'Are you eating enough?' Freddie pointed at her half-eaten plate of food.

'Oh.' She waved one hand in an irritated way. 'You sound like David.'

'What?'

'No, not in a bad way.' The irritation disappeared. 'I mean, he said the same thing the other day. I'm probably not though, in fairness. I forget to eat lunch most days. Too busy.'

'You need to look after yourself a bit more,' Freddie told her anxiously. 'You don't want to burn out. And what about the blog? That's been pretty quiet lately.'

'I know. I know.' She sighed. 'I just haven't had the time—'

'I'm not criticising. It's just, you always found it useful, a safety valve.'

'David's a bit iffy about the blog at the minute.' She pushed her hand through her hair.

'Why?'

'Oh, he's very private. And he worries about me – especially after all the comments after Mum died, you know. He doesn't want me to go through that again.'

'It's nice that he's supportive,' Freddie said carefully. 'But you have to do what feels right for you, haven't you?' It felt strange to pick his phrases so carefully. But he hadn't seen her in such a long time, and she was so tired and stressed that he didn't want to tire her further with any criticism of David – however minor.

'Can I tell you something?' She looked out from under her hair. 'About David?'

His heart sped up a little. 'Of course.'

'He has a real problem with Matt. He wants me to move out of the flat and in with him and Catherine.' She flopped one tired arm onto the tabletop. 'What d'you think?'

'Why does he have a problem with Matt?'

'It's my fault really. I shouldn't have… I knew he'd freak out a bit.'
She frowned. One finger picked at an already bitten nail. 'Sometimes
I think Matt's been in my room. It's silly, it's just a feeling.'

'Oh what?' Freddie spluttered. 'You didn't tell me that! What?—'

'But I'm probably imagining it. I'm so tired when I get back I
can't see straight. I'm probably just being paranoid.'

'But why d'you think he's—?'

'Oh, like I said, it's silly. Just sometimes the door's open when
I know I left it closed. Things in my drawers look different, like
they've been touched. But it's all just… nothing. Anyway, stupidly
I told David and, well, you know how protective he is of me. He
really wants me to move in.'

Freddie paused. The idea of her moving in with David was…
alarming. 'You could come and stay with me?' he said eventually.

'No, I can't leave. I've got ages left on the lease. And anyway, if
I stay with you, that'll hurt David's feelings.' She shook her head.
'No, I'm just being silly. I'm just tired and… anyway, listen, what're
you doing this weekend? David's invited us to his house for a meal.'

'You're sure I'm invited?'

'Well, yes. Of course.' She smiled. 'Why wouldn't you be?'

'He's not invited me before,' Freddie replied. 'I don't think he
likes me much.'

'He does!' Jenny was over-bright. 'He thinks you're brilliant.'

'Oh come on, Jen…'

'He just takes a while to open up, that's all. He likes you. He does!'
Freddie ducked his head, absurdly aware that he was suddenly close
to tears. Silly. Childish. But he was used to people liking him. And
he wasn't used to seeing less and less of Jenny. The fact that she was
trying so hard to deny the obvious was painful. Sweet, but painful.

'I'm a third wheel nowadays.' He tried to mitigate the self pity
with a laugh, but that only made things worse. His throat closed.
His head felt hot.

Jenny took his hand. 'Look, I know that David is a bit reserved, but that doesn't mean he doesn't like you. If it means anything at all, it means he doesn't know you. It's taken me a while to get my head around it too, but all it is is that he's very English, you know? He's not impulsive, he's careful. He kind of lets his actions speak for him. Like when he bought me all those clothes, and the shoes. That was his way of telling me he loved me. Some people are just like that, aren't they? They don't say what's on their mind; they show you, and I know that making a meal is a big deal for him.' She smiled. 'He's actually planning menus! We had a long conversation last night about how much you might like mussels.'

'Not at all. You told him that, right?'

'Yep. And then he started worrying about desserts.'

'That's sweet.'

'It *is* sweet. *He's* sweet. That's one of the things I like about him – he's… different. He thinks about things, he's very deliberate. Because he really wants you to like him, he's nervous around you, and maybe that shyness comes across as… being standoffish? Anyway, a meal, well that's his way of asking if you'll be his friend. Genuinely. Please come? You're my two favourite people, and I need you to get along so I can be happy. Not going to lie, I'm being incredibly selfish, here, OK? Please?'

'Yeah, that's the thing about you. Completely self-centred.' He grinned and blinked a tear away. 'Absolute bitch. I should warn David about you.'

'Warn him this weekend then. That's your chance to save him.' She squeezed Freddie's hand, and became serious. 'I've missed you, Fred. Just because I'm seeing someone, it doesn't mean that you and me—'

'Stop.' He dabbed at his eyes. 'Christ, all right. I'll come. Don't say anything else about it or I'll dissolve completely. What's wrong with me?'

She patted his hand again. 'Menopause?'

He'd been planning on mentioning the ringtone thing, and telling her about the profile picture but, now, after such a long time apart, and after this heartfelt exchange, how could he? He hadn't so far, so why would he now, after David was making such an effort to be his friend? And they didn't signify anything anyway – Jenny was in love with a nice man, a man who worried about and cared for her, a decent man who was just a bit on the shy side, and Freddie feeling a bit left out and lonely, jealous even, had blown things out of proportion. That was all.

CHAPTER TWENTY-FOUR

The following Saturday afternoon, Jenny and Freddie drove back to the village together, and she navigated their way to David's large half-timbered house, secluded, hidden from the road by a tall line of conifers. The curving drive, bordered by well-tended flower beds, led to the front door: a massive slab of wood with a whimsical brass knocker in the shape of a mermaid. When David opened the door he was smiling, wearing an apron with a William Morris-type print on it, and his hair was a little dishevelled.

'Hello! It's so lovely to see you!' He smiled, hugged Jenny and pumped Freddie's hand heartily. 'I'm making a curry, but I haven't made it before, so apologies if it's… come in, come in!' He shut the front door behind them. 'Here, let me put a light on, it's so gloomy, isn't it?'

He was nervous, bless him. Freddie felt himself relax. He gazed around at the parquet floor and slightly shabby wood panelling on the walls. The place smelled of musty lavender.

'This way, Freddie. Oh, mind the boxes – I'm sorting some things out.' David led them past two rooms that looked largely empty, and then the hallway widened into a kind of vestibule at the centre of the house from which led three small corridors. The walls were covered with framed photographs.

Freddie pointed at one. 'Who's this cutie?' A small boy was grimly clutching a kite in one hand and a resigned-looking grey kitten in the other. 'Is that you, David?'

'Yup.' He reached up and took it down, smiling. 'That's my old pet cat Tinker. I think that was taken on my fifth birthday?'

Freddie looked from the picture to his face and back again. 'You haven't changed that much!'

'Oh God, I hope I have,' said David. 'Here's another, look.' An indistinct, frowning figure stood next to a bike. A silver balloon attached to the handlebars read 'HAPPY BIRTHDAY!' 'This was taken just a few weeks before I first met Jenny.'

'How do you remember that?' Jenny asked.

'Oh, I have a long memory,' he replied. 'For the important things.'

'Is this your dad?' Freddie pointed to slightly larger photo, framed in wood.

David glanced at it briefly, and shook his head. 'No. That's a family friend who sadly isn't with us any longer.'

'Oh. Sorry.' Freddie, flushed with optimism since calling the infant David a cutie and getting away with it, was now sure he'd managed to put his foot in it by mentioning a dead friend.

'Oh don't be. This place is full of pictures and memories, and… Well, like I said, I'm doing a clear-out at the moment. Right, just down here is my mother's room,' he said. 'I told her I'd introduce you. Do you mind if we just say hello?'

He tapped at the open door and pushed it without waiting for a reply. Everything in this room was soft, tufted, in varying shades of pink and apricot; it looked like the inside of a seashell. In the corner, a shrunken woman was nestled in a peachy velvet armchair. Her cerise coloured quilted dressing gown seemed to have bled all the colour from her skin.

David moved soundlessly over the deep pile of the pink carpet, and crouched over her. 'Mum? She raised her head. 'I'd like to introduce you to Freddie.' He pointed at the doorway. Freddie gave an embarrassed little wave, which the woman didn't register.

'This is Jenny's friend – Jenny's and *my* friend, I should say. I was telling you about him the other day? Do you remember?' He left a pause. The woman smiled vaguely. 'They're staying for dinner.'

'Nothing for me.' The woman had a surprisingly strong voice. 'I ate at the club.'

David half turned to Jenny and Freddie with a slight frown. 'So, Mum? If you see Freddie in the house, you're not to worry, OK? He's my friend.'

'Oh I won't worry,' she told him. 'You're doing very well.'

David left the room and closed the door quietly. 'She has good days and bad days, and today is a bit of a bad one.'

'Oh God, I hope us being here hasn't, you know, disturbed her or anything,' said Freddie.

Jenny answered. 'No, no. It has nothing to do with you being here. It's just the illness; it fluctuates. That's why nurses are hard to get and keep, aren't they, David? Sometimes they have nothing to do, and sometimes it's too big a job for one person. It can change within the hour.'

'But, she liked you, Freddie, I could tell,' David told him.

Even though David had obviously been primed to be as friendly and welcoming as possible, Freddie was still touched. This was the David he'd first met at the funeral. A decent, serious man. Sober, interested and sweet.

They followed him to the kitchen at the back of the house, a large, modern extension.

'This is lovely!' Freddie looked around admiringly.

'Yes, I managed to put a bit of pressure on them to modernise the place a bit. Just before Dad… passed. OK, so I have red wine, white wine, beer?'

'Red wine, please,' Freddie said.

'Hang on, Fred, I brought that bottle of Prosecco! It's in the car; I'll go and get it.' Jenny pulled the keys out of his pocket.

Even though David was being so nice, and Freddie was more relaxed than he'd been around him in months, both men quailed when she left and self-consciousness filled the vacuum. Freddie nosed about the room like a puppy waiting for praise, while David busied himself with a manly looking corkscrew, his lips pursed, as if he was whistling. Seeing this, Freddie only just managed to stifle an insane urge to whistle 'Who's Afraid of the Big Bad Wolf'. Desperate, he grasped for the blandest topic at hand.

'It's a lovely house.'

'Well,' David said absently, yanking the cork out with an effort, 'it will be once I get the building work finalised.'

'And how are *you*, Claudine?' Freddie picked her up and placed her on his lap. 'Having fun scratching all this furniture?'

'I had her declawed,' David said absently.

'Oh really? But don't cats need their claws? I mean—'

'What does she need her claws for? She won't be getting into any fights here.'

'No, I meant… I don't know what I meant. Is it even legal to have a cat de-clawed? I mean…'

David looked at him, and smiled bleakly. 'What d'you mean? I can do anything to her. She's my cat, isn't she?'

As if offering her opinion, Claudine playfully sunk her claws into Freddie's thigh. He jumped up, and the rattled animal sped out of the room, and David laughed, not an entirely good-humoured laugh. 'Did you really think I'd had her de-clawed?'

Freddie grimaced confusedly. Between the scratches and the weird turn of the conversation he was struggling. 'Well, you said you had—'

'I was *joking*.' David laughed. 'As if I'd hurt her like that. It was just a joke.' David nodded at the open door, put one finger up, and crossed the room to shut it. 'I need to ask you something. Matt.' His voice was low.

'Matt? Matt: Jenny's flatmate Matt? What about him?' Freddie sat back down, wincing.

'You know he's been breaking into her room? She told you that?' David shook his head grimly and thrust a glass of wine at Freddie.

Freddie hesitated. 'Oh well, I don't think he broke *in*. She didn't tell me anything like that—'

'Have you met him?' David interrupted.

Freddie blinked. 'A few times, very briefly.'

'What's he like?'

'Well, he seems very nice, I mean—'

'What kind of a man does something like that?' David interrupted again. 'I mean it's strange enough that a single man would rent a room to a single girl, you know? That's strange, isn't it?'

Freddie tried to laugh. 'Well, no. I mean it's not the 1950s, is it? And anyway, he's not single. He has a girlfriend and spends a lot of time with her.' Happily, Freddie knew now that this was the case.

'Still. To rummage about in other people's things. Private things.' David seemed to be working himself up into a quiet rage.

'Look, I really don't think... I mean, I don't *know*, but then neither does Jenny. She told me that she's so tired after work that she forgets things, and that's probably the explanation. It's more likely to be that, isn't it? Rather than him *breaking* into her *room*—'

'D'you think I should have a word with him?' David asked urgently.

'What?' Freddie shook his head, as if dizzy. 'I don't—'

'Just to let him *know*... that *I* know what he's up to.'

'Let him know? But he hasn't been up to anything! Jenny isn't sure of—'

'Or I could go round there and put a lock on her bedroom door. That'd send a message, wouldn't it?' He topped up Freddie's wine. 'Of course, what she should do is just move in here with me. She's told you about that? That I want her to move in?' David said this very quickly.

Freddie opened his mouth, shut it, opened it again. 'Um…' he managed.

'Because she's not safe where she is. Is she?'

'I think—'

'See? Now we just have to convince her.' He smiled grimly. When Jenny skipped back into the room, his face softened. 'And here she is!'

'Sorry I was a while – the bottle had rolled under the seat and I took the handbrake off by accident and then the car started to roll towards the flower beds… it was a bad sight gag. Anyway, what've you two been talking about? You look shifty.'

'Oh, I was just reassuring Freddie that I'm a responsible pet owner,' David said lightly.

'He absolutely loves Claudine,' Jenny told Freddie. 'I'm not getting her back.'

'And he was asking about Matt,' David said smoothly. He didn't seem to be the same person who'd just been speaking so alarmingly of locks and sending messages. 'Freddie's concerned too, aren't you?'

'Oh, Fred, I told you, I'm just being a bit paranoid, that's all.'

'But – and Freddie was just saying this, and he makes a good point – you are Matt's tenant, and he has a duty to make you feel as secure as possible. Why don't you let me put a lock on your bedroom door? It might make you feel better, and worry us less,' David told her seriously. 'What d'you think, Freddie?' Freddie nodded dumbly. 'Well then, I'll come over in the week with my trusty toolbox.' David smiled then. His teeth were as white and even as piano keys. 'Now we can both stop worrying about her, can't we Freddie? I have a cold bottle of champagne in the fridge – what say we drink that, and keep your prosecco, is it, for another time? D'you mind getting it, Jenny?'

When she was gone, Freddie started to splutter, and David was all apologies. 'Sorry. I'm genuinely sorry about that... I'm just so worried about her and I knew that if I told her you were just as concerned, she'd take it a bit more seriously. She hates the idea of worrying you.' He smiled winningly. 'So I lied. A white lie, but, still, I'm sorry. But we're on the same side, aren't we? I *want* us to be on the same side.'

Then Jenny came back with the champagne and David opened it with a great flourish.

'My mother always said that when you toast you should look everyone in the eyes so they know how important they are to you.' He handed out the glasses 'To Friendship!' They all clinked glasses, gazing at each other as requested.

A year or so ago, Freddie had briefly dated an actor and spent many a dull hour sitting in on rehearsals for a very insignificant production of *The Seagull*. One day, all Chekov'd out, he wandered into the wings, and came across the discarded costumes, the dusty ropes. As the draft from an open door wobbled the inept trompe l'oeil of the false proscenium, Freddie had gazed around, seeing the silhouettes of the actors through the safety curtain, listening to their voices, flat and artificial in the empty theatre, and it was all just so silly. It was a conceit that relied on complicity rather than honesty. He reflected that one heavy step would bring the wobbly walls of the set down and stop the performance dead. That's all he had to do, just stamp a bit, force it to fall, and they could all stop pretending and go home. He hadn't done it though. He'd waited and left when he'd planned and he hadn't split up with the actor until a few weeks later when a stormy argument about The Beatles forced him to (The Beatles – more specifically, the general overrated shitness of The Beatles – was one of Freddie's few red lines). He had the same feeling now, in David's house – the same feeling, but worse, and he couldn't escape – not without abandoning Jenny.

And so, Freddie did what any normal person would do under the circumstances. He decided to get drunk enough to cope with the weirdness and get through the day as best he could.

'So, basically, I'm going to have to get a better job if I want to keep on seeing Cheryl and keep my placement at the same time.' Jenny sighed. 'That way I'll have enough money to still finish the course by next year and get registered, but if I *don't*—'

'What then?' asked Freddie.

'I'll have to, I don't know, up my temping hours or take a second job or something. Or I could defer for a year, but I really don't want to do that. There's too many balls to juggle at the moment, you know? And I haven't even updated the blog or anything for ages.'

David said: 'Don't you think you're trying to do too much?'

'I say that to her all the time, but she doesn't listen,' Freddie added.

'Oh I'm all right. This year will be the hardest. After that things will get easier.' She nodded, as if she was convincing herself. 'Some people use work to help them through grief. I think maybe that's not a bad thing. I mean, if you *know* that's what you're doing, you're not fooling yourself or anything, maybe it's useful? Cheryl and I were talking about this the other day—'

'Oh, *Cheryl*. Of course. Your therapist.' David's voice seemed to put quotation marks around the word. 'Why are you still seeing her anyway?'

'I have to see a counsellor myself as part of the course,' Jenny said after a short pause. Her voice was small, confused.

'So when you stop the course you can stop seeing Cheryl?' David frowned.

Jenny shook her head. 'God no! I don't *think* so. I don't know really. I think there's still a lot of work to do, to be honest. And it's standard practice for a therapist to see their *own* therapist. It's to help you stay on track, discuss good practice, all that.'

David smirked. '"Discuss good practice".'

'I know, I know, all the jargon is a bit...' Jenny smiled apologetically.

'You know what it sounds like to me?' David sat back. 'It sounds like a pyramid scheme. People see a *counsellor*, who sees their own psycho*therapist*, who probably sees a *psychologist*, who probably needs a *psychiatrist*, and they're all complicit in trying to fleece as much money as they can from someone who's arguably saner than all of them put together.' He laughed. 'You have to admit, it's a great way to make money.'

'I don't think many people go into it for money,' Jenny admonished him softly. 'I'm not going to make my fortune out of this, you know. But, I'll be doing something important.'

'And something you're great at,' Freddie said warmly. He hadn't spoken in a while. His voice was a fraction too loud.

David held up his hands in mock surrender. 'No offence. I'm no expert. It really is great that you're doing what you want to do.' He topped up her wine again. 'So long as it really is what you want to do, and not what you've been *persuaded* to do.'

'The careers adviser at school told me that I should be an admin assistant,' Jenny said.

'He told me I should be an air stewardess. He thought he was being funny,' Freddie added. 'What about you, David? What were you meant to be?'

David frowned. 'There wasn't a careers person at our school,' he said.

'Didn't you see the same one we did in Sixth Form? He did all the schools in the area. That guy with the ginger beard? The one with the limp?' Freddie asked.

'I wouldn't have seen a careers adviser,' David said again, smiling. 'I was homeschooled, remember.'

'But I thought you boarded at… where was it?' Freddie screwed up his face, trying to remember. 'Hazleton? Or Hazlewood? Or somewhere?'

'Yes. Yes, I did, but before that I was homeschooled. After the stroke.' David stood up, started collecting the plates. His averted face was tense. When he left the room, Jenny leaned into Freddie,

'He's a bit sensitive about the stroke,' she told him sternly. 'Can you back off a bit?'

'Well how could I know he'd take it there? He went from bad careers advice to a stroke in, like, one sentence?' Freddie hissed.

'Maybe we just shouldn't talk about school at all,' Jenny said. 'Are you going to be all right to drive? How many have you had anyway?'

'And what's his problem with therapy?'

'I don't think he has a problem with it,' Jenny told him. She glanced at the door, lowered her voice. 'Maybe he had a bad experience or something.'

'No need to be aggressive about it though, was there?' Freddie whispered loudly. 'I mean, especially seeing as you're in training? That was just rude… Oh, and talk about *aggressive*, you know the Matt thing? The lock? It wasn't *me*—'

But then David came back pushing an old-fashioned dessert trolley. 'I didn't make anything, I'm afraid. I don't have the knack, but I did buy in a selection of things. Let's see, we have cream cakes, and… what're these? Scones? Scones. And a trifle.' He passed around delicate china bowls. 'It's all a bit random, I'm afraid.'

'It's lovely,' said Jenny firmly.

'I love trifle. It's proper school dinner stuff, isn't it?'

'So, at boarding school, David, was it all a bit Harry Potter? All dormitories and gowns and… and… wizard orgies and, OK, I haven't read any Harry Potter, so I don't know what I'm talking about…' Freddie trailed off.

Wizard orgies? Jenny mouthed at him.

'It was OK,' David said shortly.

'Did you miss your parents?' Freddie leaned forward. 'I always felt a bit sorry for the kids at St Columbus that boarded, but they were probably perfectly happy. I mean their parents could have been absolute bastards. Their *kids* were bad enough.'

David flinched slightly. 'I missed them at first, but then I got used to it,' he replied quietly.

'Well, you were that bit older, weren't you? When you're older you can cope better with things like that… separation. I suppose—' Freddie reached for the wine bottle and pulled it towards himself with his fingertips. 'It's all about what you're *used* to – *shit!*' The bottle tipped, rolled and fell. Freddie leaped up, gesturing widely with his too-full glass splashing yet more wine in a wide arc. It splattered over the table, over himself, onto the sofa, and onto the floor. 'Shit! Shit, sorry!' He drunkenly backed away from the mess, and yet more wine ran down each trouser leg, puddling further into the very antique-looking rug. 'Oh god, do you have a cloth?'

David was up, inspecting the rug. He made an assessing hissing sound, and shook his head.

'I'm sorry! Can I… if I get a cloth?' Freddie said weakly, but David was already on his way to the kitchen.

Jenny knelt down, patting the stain with a napkin. It spread like blood through the fine fibres of the rug. 'I think it's silk or something,' she said, and looked at Freddie. 'Careful, you're still dripping.'

'Is it bad?' Freddie stepped back onto the parquet and winced. 'It's probably an heirloom or something, isn't it? Shit!'

'Yes it's bad! Why're you being so weird?' She was still on her hands and knees. She sounded angry. 'Seriously, stop drinking.'

When David rushed in with a bowl of soapy water and various stain removers, she and David dabbed, tutted and murmured at the mess. 'Can he take them off?' David indicated Freddie's dripping trousers. 'At the top of the stairs' – dab dab dab – 'chest of drawers? There's some of Dad's old trousers in there.'

'Freddie!' Jenny hissed, as if David's words needed translating. 'Top of the stairs. Trousers!'

'What, in a *room* at the top of the stairs, or…?' Freddie asked, but David didn't reply. Jenny gave him a severe look, and went back to pressing anxiously at the stain. They looked for all the world as if they were resuscitating a patient.

Freddie, pinching the thighs of his jeans away from the skin, backed out of the room and made his way up the stairs, head swimming, and feeling like an idiot. To Friendship. *David likes you, he does he does, so please come to tea?* And what happens? Things get weird, things get worse and the clumsy sidekick runs to the wings, reappears in a dead man's trousers. Slow handclap. Exit left.

He couldn't see any chest of drawers at the top of the stairs. It had to be in one of the rooms. He pushed open the nearest door and walked into a large, musty-smelling room that was mostly empty, except for two packing crates by the window, a bulky 1930s wardrobe and a CD player, its dusty plug still in the ancient-looking socket above the skirting board. Freddie walked slowly to the wardrobe, opened it. The spotted mirror on the inside door reflected his pink and white face and wine-soaked jeans. There were a few old suits hanging up, and Freddie took the nearest one down. It smelled a bit mildewy, but the trousers looked as if they'd fit. Maybe.

As he jumped and wiggled, trying to fasten them, he managed to knock into the wardrobe. A couple of hand weights rolled out onto the wooden floor with a clunk. He grabbed them, and put them back, wedging the two between an old gym bag stuffed with paper and a small cardboard case marked 'Precious Memories!' in one of those old Letrasets.

Precious Memories? That was intriguing. And, after all, he wasn't in any hurry to go back downstairs and talk to David…

He tried to take a moment to think. *Fred, you're pissed. Maybe scrabbling about in people's personal possessions isn't the best idea?* He crouched down, the wool of dead man's trousers straining over his thighs. *Just go back downstairs, apologise, switch to water* – his fingers unlatched the catch – *buy a new rug, if needs be. Yes, that's it, go back downstairs and offer to buy another… Jesus, are we really doing this? Fred? Really?*

'Of course we are,' he muttered to himself.

'Precious Memories!' was divided into three sections with stiff corrugated cardboard, cut specially to fit, and each section was packed with seemingly meaningless objects. A compass. A pink Post-it note. A very old newspaper clipping about fly-tipping. A lady's chiffon scarf marred by a wine stain. Nothing precious, all trash. It was all pretty boring. *Why keep it then?*

He closed the lid, shut the wardrobe door and wandered over to the nearest packing case to see if there was a bag or something he could put his wet jeans in, but it just seemed to be full of paper, old binders and loose photographs. He dug deeper, pulled out an empty holdall and shoved his trousers in it.

Now he had nothing to do but go back downstairs and face David.

Knowing he was deliberately dawdling, he looked out of the window. The room faced the back garden. The faint indentations of what had once been the foundations of a building scarred the grass, and, just beyond, what looked like a wooden cross was planted at the end of the shrubbery. It had something written on it, but Freddie couldn't read it from this distance.

The cross, the empty room, 'Precious Memories!', the curtainless windows… it was all depressing. It was also sinister. Uncanny. The whole house was strange. David was strange. *Admit it. Admit it to yourself. Yes you're drunk, yes you've behaved badly, but… but David. There's something about David. Jenny can't see it, but he's not right.*

He walked slowly out of the room and onto the landing, feeling heavy with this new, fully admitted knowledge. There was something about David, something wrong and rotten at the core of him…

He was so absorbed in his thoughts that, when he felt the hand on his arm, he cried out in shock.

Catherine Crane was standing, thin and paper pale, by the bottom step, half hidden in the shadowy corridor. Her hand was firm, almost steely. The quilted dressing gown drooped on her frame like a shroud, and when she smiled she looked like a bird with teeth.

'Mrs Crane?'

She held out her other hand to him, placed it on his chest, and her grip softened. Her eyes, he noticed, were the same light grey-blue as David's, but not as cold, and filled with love.

'We *missed* you. We didn't want you to be away for so long.' She clung to Freddie's arms, swayed.

'Are you all right? Mrs Crane?'

Now she was leading him falteringly down the corridor. She smelled of Chanel No. 5 and denture cream and something else… something not fresh. 'It's all about presentation, isn't it? Clothes maketh the man.'

'You mean the trousers? I'm sorry, I had a bit of an accident. David said it was OK if I borrowed these.'

'No matter what anyone says, I know it was an accident.' She told him firmly.

'And I'm so sorry about the rug. I'll fix everything, get everything clean I promise,'

'You feel *better*, you *do*, now, don't you?' She stopped, gazed at him, dim eyes piteous with love. 'What's passed is passed? Mmmm? Hazlewood works wonders.'

Finally Freddie realised that she really didn't know who she was talking to. 'Shall I go and get David for you?' Freddie took a little step backwards, but one thin hand tugged at his elbow with surprising strength.

'I ate at the club,' she told him firmly. And then she began to shake.

'Fred?' Jenny came around the corner. 'Where've you been?'

'Finding trousers. And then David's mum—'

'Catherine?' Jenny came forward. 'Are you OK?'

She nodded at Freddie again, saying: 'I ate at the club.' A stream of mustard coloured urine ran down one leg and puddled in her slipper.

'Oh lord, can you get David? Fred? *Go* and get *David.*' Jenny was already cradling Catherine by one elbow and steering her back towards her room. 'Catherine? Let's get you cleaned up.'

'I missed him,' Catherine told her. 'But Hazlewood worked wonders.'

'Yes. Yes, I know. Let's get you comfy… *Fred*? Go and get David, will you?'

Freddie ran to the sitting room, but David wasn't there. He found him in the kitchen, frowning over his phone. Cloths, stained pink with wine, were scattered on the draining board, like so many shot birds. 'David, your mum—'

'What?' David paled and came forward. 'What's happened?'

'She's… she needed to go to the toilet and well, there's another rug to clean, I'm afraid.'

'Oh God.' David put the phone down on the work surface and shouldered past him. 'I'm sorry!' he said.

'Oh no, it's not, I mean, I hope she's all right,' Freddie called weakly at his back, and followed a few paces behind, his dead-man's flares flapping around his wine-stained ankles.

Jenny was sitting with Catherine on the tufted pink chaise longue, murmuring empty conversation. The older woman seemed to be almost asleep, her greying hair nestled and mingled with Jenny's tawny curls, and the fabric of her nightdress fluttered with each tiny breath. Jenny looked up at David and smiled. 'She's OK. Just got a bit confused, that's all.'

'I'm sorry.' David sounded close to tears. 'I'm so sorry that—'

Jenny shook her head. 'What's to be sorry about? It's OK. Everything's OK.'

David let out a painful noise; an angry sob.

'Catherine? David's going to sit with you now, is that OK? Here he is now.' Jenny ever so gently eased Catherine's head off her shoulder and swapped places with David. David, his face averted, stretched one arm across his mother's shoulders, mechanically. Both Jenny and Freddie tiptoed out of the room, not looking at each other until they were safely back in the sitting room.

'Wow,' Freddie whispered then.

'I feel so sorry for him,' Jenny whispered back.

'She was talking to me like she thought I was him.'

Jenny nodded. 'Same to me. Poor woman. Poor *David*. Look, let's clean up a bit, fill the dishwasher and stuff, and then we should probably leave.' She gazed at his trousers. 'Wow. That's all you could find?'

'Dead Dad trousers.'

'Where are your jeans?'

'In a bag. I left it at the bottom of the stairs.'

They quietly cleared the sitting room of dishes, rolled everything back to the kitchen on the dessert tray, and began stacking the dishwasher. By the time they'd finished, David was at the door. His face was pale, and there were small red dots around his eye sockets, as if he'd been crying. He said: 'I can't apologise enough.'

Jenny came forward. 'You don't *have* to. Come on, David, if anyone understands it's me, right?'

'I just wanted everything to be perfect.' He swallowed his words. 'It's so important that you—'

'David,' she took his hand, 'you don't have to worry. About anything. Please don't? OK?'

He nodded, but he kept his head bowed.

The phone he'd left on the work surface rang, but he didn't make any move to pick it up. So Freddie did instead. Andreena. Why was Andreena calling David?

Jenny took the phone off him. 'Hi, Dree. Listen, I can't really talk now, can I...'

And Freddie realised, with a start, that the phone he'd seen David looking through only a few minutes before wasn't his at all – it was Jenny's – and something in the atmosphere cracked, like hot water poured into a cut-glass bowl, and only Freddie and David could hear it.

David disappeared, then came back with the holdall. 'You can keep the bag,'

'OK,' Freddie answered dazedly

'Everything in that room is rubbish.' David said then. 'Next time you come it'll all be cleared away. Burnt.' He thrust the bag at him. 'You're not driving.' It was a statement rather than a question.

'Don't worry, he won't be,' Jenny told him. 'That was Dree, she wants to meet you. Properly.'

'I'll be very glad to,' David said stiffly. Then his face relaxed, and he smiled. 'I'll make a meal, she can come over here.' He reached for Freddie's free hand. 'Nice to see you again.'

'Mmmmm.'

'And don't worry about the mess you made, it's all fixable.'

Freddie couldn't do anything but nod dumbly back.

David stood at the front door, watching them get into the car, watching Jenny gingerly pull the seat in, and frown at the dashboard. Just as they were about to turn, David walked leisurely to the passenger window, rapped on the window. He smiled.

'Be careful.'

'Oh, we will, don't worry.' Jenny was worriedly checking her mirrors. 'I'm too much of a nervous driver to be anything else.'

Then he backed away, and held one hand up, stiff and still in the air.

They stayed silent until they were out of the village and on the main road. Jenny was nervy and preoccupied, prone to making sudden, crunching gear changes and fearful glances in the rear-view mirror. Freddie sat in the passenger seat feeling guilty, feeling fearful, and still quite drunk.

'OK, so that was... kind of awful.' he said eventually.

Jenny flicked on the indicator, but managed to put windscreen wipers on instead. 'No. No, it's fine. David wasn't angry or anything. Can you push something? I don't know how to turn this off.'

'When I went to the kitchen, you know, after the thing with his mum?'

'God, I hope she's all right,' she murmured.

'In the kitchen? I saw David—'

'That rug too. I hope the *rug's* all right. Do I take a left here? Fred?'

'Yes. Left. Well, I saw him looking through your phone.' He said this last bit in a rush.

Jenny made the left, sighed. 'God, I hate motorways… it's the joining them that scares me. And the lorries – look at this guy! Freddie, should I let him pass or what?'

'Did you hear me? I saw David looking through your phone. In the kitchen.'

Jenny frowned in the mirror, harried, a bit exasperated. 'No, you didn't, don't be silly.'

'He was though! And when I saw him he just kind of *looked* at me.'

'God, how pissed are you anyway?' Her eyebrows crumpled together. 'David and I have the same type of phone, you know. It was his phone you saw, not mine.'

'No, honestly, Jen, it *wasn't*. He was looking through it, and he put it down when I came in, and that was the same phone Andreena called. I know it was yours. I'm *positive*.'

'You're pissed is what you are,' she muttered.

'And what about this – that picture of you? The one I took in Turkey with you in the sarong?' His voice rose. 'I saw it on David's Facebook page when I friended him, a few months ago and, get this, as *soon* as I friended him he took it down.' He stopped, looked at her eagerly. 'So how did he have *that* picture on *his* wall before he'd even met you?'

Jenny frowned. 'What wall? His Facebook wall?'

'No. Well kind of, on his *wall* wall. It was in a frame, hanging up just behind his head on his profile picture. I'm positive.'

'Well if you were that positive, why didn't you tell me at the time?' she asked reasonably.

'I don't know.' He hated how hesitant and lame he sounded. 'I maybe wasn't *that* sure, but then I saw him looking through your phone, and it made me sure.' He paused, got nothing from her set profile, and went on excitedly, knowing on some level that he was doing exactly the wrong thing. 'And, he's so jealous of Matt, too! Banging on about getting a lock on your door and everything.'

'*You* were worried about that too though!'

'Ah! No. David *told* you I was worried, but when you were out of the room it was him that was telling me how worried *he* was.'

Jenny shook her head. 'Basic syntax, Fred.'

'He told me he'd had Claudine de-clawed!' Freddie said wildly.

'Fred—'

'And your family pictures: when you said about not having any photos, he got really angry—'

'He didn't get angry; he was surprised, that's all.' She sounded stern now. 'He thought it was sad. It *is* sad. *You* said it was sad.' She slowed, took the motorway exit. After a long silence she said, 'Why're you doing this? No, wait, I know why you're doing this.'

'I'm worried about you, that's all. Jen? David… there's something not *right* about him. The things he says, and he twists things. Like saying I was worried about Matt, I told him to buy you those clothes. He's *weird* Jen. I don't want him to be, but he *is* and I'm scared for you.'

She didn't reply but shook her head with such quiet rage that Freddie shut up like a clam. They didn't exchange another word until they'd arrived at his flat.

'I've sobered up now,' he said. 'I can drop you back at yours if you want? Or why don't you stay here?'

'College work to do,' she said tightly, not looking at him, turning to leave.

'OK. I'll call you tomorrow? Or you call me?' he called.

She didn't respond, carried on walking quickly away, angry fists in her pockets.

'Jen! I'm *sorry*.'

She didn't look back.

It was getting dark, and the cold air bit. It would take her ages to walk home. He almost got in the car with an idea of driving around until he found her, persuading her to come back, but, in the end, he decided against it. Despite what he'd told her, he was still a bit drunk, and couldn't be sure of his instincts. He thought about Jenny going back to her grim flat. He imagined David calling her, all sobriety and care; he imagined her apologising for him – 'Freddie is protective, that's all' – imagined David's measured response, something along the lines of: 'It's wonderful that he respects you so much', or some such phrase packed with hurt and covert dislike... he'd sound so dignified and restrained, making Freddie seem even more childish and hysterical by comparison. There was something wrong with David – something uncanny, unconvincing. There was something condescending in his devotion to Jenny. How could he love her, and lie to her? How could he love her and loathe her friend? It was a strange devotion if it was tinged with contempt. But Jenny couldn't see it. She was too close. Freddie knew he could have made her see things his way if he'd just... handled it better. But he wouldn't give up. He couldn't. Jenny – sweet, brave, Jenny. Outwardly cynical, inwardly too-trusting, Jenny needed him.

And so, after taking off the dead man's flares, and swallowing paracetamol with a third cup of tea, he started digging for David. The real David.

Where to start though? There were so many entry points. The fire. The stroke. The private school. Homeschooling. Catherine had said he was away for so long. They'd missed him. Hazlewood. *They work wonders.* Start there.

There were quite a few Hazlewood Schools, but only one that accepted boarders, and even then only up to the age of thirteen. David was older than that when he'd had the stroke – the final year before Sixth Form, so he must have been fifteen or sixteen, and he'd gone to Hazlewood straight from hospital… Perhaps Freddie had conflated the hospital and the school in his mind? He searched for 'Hazlewood Hospital' on the off-chance.

The first hit made him fizz with excitement.

Turrets and spires. Smiling people lounging on the lawn. A friendly faced woman with a discreet name badge sat at a desk, smiling at someone with their back to the camera.

> Here at Hazlewood, we devise a personalised care package to suit your needs with a wide range of therapies and fee structures… depending on how long you want or need treatment, we use a range of therapies which we can offer to you individually or in group therapy session.
> Our Child and Adolescent facility supports young people with a range of diagnoses including:
> Depression or anxiety
> Emerging personality disorder
> Eating disorder
> Emotional/social and behavioural difficulties
> Psychosis
> Self-harm/suicidal ideation

This was a mental hospital. Who goes to a mental hospital after a stroke? Was this the rehabilitation he was talking about? *Hazlewood works wonders. We missed you.* How long had he been there anyway?

He opened a new document, and noted down everything that now seemed doubly sketchy about David:

> *Looking through J's phone*
> *Therapy as a pyramid scheme*
> *Matt paranoia*

Profile picture!
(Lying about) Mental hospital!!!

He hesitated. Should he include other, less concrete, fears? Buying Jenny the shoes, the clothes, styling her according to his wishes, as if she were a little doll. And what about the dead man's clothes? The box marked 'Precious Memories!', the grave at the end of the garden, and the mad woman in the pink bedroom? But, while it was all very gothic and added to the atmosphere of general weirdness, he had to admit that none of these things amounted to evidence of anything; it was all background colour though, wasn't it? It lent context and support to the idea that All Was Not Right With David. And what about the sudden rage at Barbra Streisand? Well… Freddie had to be fair; it was an incredibly annoying ringtone. He'd picked it *because* it was annoying… even his own father, normally calm as a Hindu cow, had threatened to smash his phone if he didn't change it. Even Barbra herself probably hated it. *Enough, enough with Barbra, focus… what had happened to make David ill enough to get put in a mental hospital? The fire?* It was worth researching. Half an hour later though, he still hadn't turned up anything about this Tony guy, or a fire in the village. Maybe the family had kept it quiet? Remember the day of the funeral? When Mum said that there'd been talk in the village about petrol… a suicide attempt… *or maybe not a suicide attempt at all?*

He pushed the computer away, and took a shower to clear his head. The problem was that he was doing this by himself when he was used to working out difficult problems in tandem with Jenny. They worked better together, and always had. Look what happened when they went to different universities? Jenny had only lasted a term or two, but when they were together again, she believed in herself enough to start a whole new career. They were good for each other. Maybe that was it; Freddie had taken a back seat – given them space – all the other awful clichés you wanted to use, and, left alone, she'd got herself sunk into this mire with David. Perhaps all he had to do was tell her everything in a well-ordered, not-drunk-covered-in-wine way. Two Heads Are Better Than One. A Rolling Stone... *stop that now. It's no fun on your own.*

So he called Jenny, left her a voicemail, kept it brief so she could tell he was sober and serious. 'Could they meet tomorrow? Here or in town? It's important.'

She texted back:

8.30 a.m. Tiffin Coffee Bar.

Her brevity spoke volumes. He nearly called her again, but stopped himself. He drafted three emails, but didn't send them. Instead he sat in the darkening room, looking at his list, and rehearsing his opening line. 'David has problems.' 'David has lied to you.' 'David might be dangerous.' 'Let me help you.' After all, it was his duty to help her. It was all his fault. He'd done everything he could to get them together; he'd been David's biggest fan; poor Jenny thought she'd found her Prince Charming, and tomorrow Freddie was going to break her heart. It was for the best, but it was still so sad.

CHAPTER TWENTY-FIVE

In the end he was so nervous that he didn't use any opening line at all. He just opened the laptop to the Hazlewood homepage and pushed it towards her, then watched her expression as she read, that little comma of worry appearing between her brows. A muscle jumped beside her mouth. She was tired. This always happened when she was tired or stressed. After a minute she pushed it back to his side of the table, saying nothing.

'I'm sorry,' he said quietly.

'What for?' There was something hard and unreadable about her expression. 'I don't know what this is or why you're showing it to me, or—'

'David? Hazlewood? This is the school he said he went to, but it's not a school, it's a mental hospital.'

'No, it's a clinic.' She looked up. 'The term "mental hospital" went out with "gollywogs" and "gaylords".' She stared hard at him. 'What're you doing this for, Fred?'

'OK, I know it's a shock, but come on, Jen, I had to tell you... he's been lying to you.'

'And you've been spying on him.' She sat back. '*I* seem to be the only honest person I know.'

'I'm scared for you. He's lied about being in hospital—'

'No. You have no proof he was ever *in* hospital. All you have is a clinic that you *think* might be *similar* to the name of his boarding school. That's all you've got, and you immediately start calling *him* a liar.' Her face, furious and cold, was almost frightening.

Freddie tried to keep his voice calm. He had to stay calm, stay with her, let her be as angry as she needed to be. She'd burn herself out eventually, and they could talk, finally, properly, and figure out what to do.

'I know it's hard. I know it must be – but Jen, I don't *want* David to… I don't *want* him to be a liar, but I spent hours on this last night, OK? There isn't a boarding school by that name *anywhere* in the country. Not kids of fifteen or sixteen. Anywhere, Jen.' His voice, despite his best efforts, had risen after all, and his carefully rehearsed, sequential arguments, fractured, fell apart. 'After I saw him going through your phone – and it was your phone, I'm positive – I thought back to how jealous he was about Matt without even meeting him, and how angry he seems about psychiatry, and then, when I found out that he's been lying about being in hospital? His mum *said* "Hazlewood". I had to tell you, didn't I? I mean, you'd have told me, wouldn't you?'

Jenny's face tightened further into a frown. 'Maybe he had some problems when he was younger. Maybe there was some post-traumatic stress after having the stroke. You don't just get over something like that, Fred.'

'Well we only have David's word for it that he even *had* a stroke.' Freddie's voice rang with fervour now. The tired-eyed waiter glanced over before going back to his phone. 'Mum didn't know *anything* about him having a stroke.' She flapped an irritated hand at him – *keep your voice down.* 'But she told me about that man in the picture we saw?' Freddie said this in an exaggerated whisper. 'The friend of the family? He nearly died in a fire at the house, at the same time David supposedly had this stroke. And David's mum and Tony – that guy in the picture? – they were having an affair, and—'

'What?' Now Jenny's voice rose. 'Where'd you get that from?'

'Mum. She heard it at the time. Village gossip—'

Jenny's eyes were hard now. One white-knuckled hand kneaded the other on the sticky tabletop. 'That's it, Fred. You said it. It's gossip, and it's *cruel*.' Her voice, low as a cat's warning growl, was very, very serious.

After a pause Freddie said: 'I know it's hard to hear. I wish I didn't have to say it, but—'

She sat back, stared at him with hard eyes. 'Why're you doing this? Are you *that* bored? Jealous?'

'Don't be—'

'Maybe there *was* a fire. Maybe David saw things he shouldn't have. Maybe something traumatised him and his parents felt that he needed therapy? Well, if so, then *great*! More parents *should* help their kids.'

'Jen, listen—'

'No, *you* listen! You're making out having mental-health issues is a crime! For Christ's sake, Fred, how are things in the 1920s? You, of all people—'

'This isn't about me—'

'And also, since I'm in therapy, does that make me "mental hospital" material too?'

'OK, OK, I shouldn't have said "mental hospital".'

'Fuck's sake, Freddie. I'm *training* to be a therapist. There's nothing *wrong* with therapy.' She seemed completely focused on this point.

'I know that. I do. But, if David had had some kind of breakdown, why would he keep it a secret?' Freddie asked lamely.

'Precisely because of things like this! People are ignorant! They jump to conclusions; they gossip and they judge. They think that once a person's ill, they never get better.' She shook her head again, and shut the laptop with a brisk movement. 'I never thought you'd be like that, Fred, I mean, you're the person who told *me* I should get help.'

'But you didn't lie about needing help,' Freddie said. 'You didn't tell people you'd had a stroke.'

'No, I didn't. But if I'd dropped out of school before Sixth Form I might have, or my mum might have, just to save me the embarrassment of having to explain my own private business to people who still use the term "mental hospital" and think it's OK." And anyway, I *did* lie. Just by not telling people, I lied for *ages* about how awful I felt; I just lied by omission, and that's the only difference between my situation and David's – *if* he even *was* in treatment.' She stopped, took some deep breaths to calm down. After a minute she faced Freddie, face still pale, but hectic pink spots showing on her cheeks. Her eyes were sad, disappointed. 'You were the only one that helped me, Fred. You saw through me, you persuaded me to get help.' She shook her head. 'I had *you*. David hasn't had *anyone*. That's not his fault, is it?' She stopped, began to speak, stopped again, before managing the words. 'You don't like him. It's as simple as that isn't it? Be honest, Fred.'

'I do. I *did*… I just… look, I don't *want* to think badly of David. I kind of helped get you together in the first place, but what do you want me to do, Jen? Just ignore everything? There are so many things that don't add up. Like the Facebook picture I told you about? How did he have a photograph of you, that *I* took, before he'd even met you?' He took her hand. 'I've tried to square that in my mind, but it just doesn't make sense. That's a bit *stalkery*, isn't it? I mean did he hack your account, or *my* account, or—?'

'You want to know how he got that picture?' Jenny said flatly. 'OK, I'll tell you.' She sighed, and her tired, cold eyes met his. 'I gave it to him. That's how he got it.'

It was one of the few times in his life that Freddie was genuinely lost for words. His whole body stilled and the air hummed with some strange electricity. 'What? *When*? I saw it on his Facebook page the day of your mum's funeral; you didn't even *know* him then— it's impossible.'

'But I *did* know him then.' Her voice was still flat. 'I'd known him for a long time before the funeral. I just didn't tell you, that's all.' The hum in the air became a buzz of confusion. He'd had the same sensation before passing out. Jenny signalled for a glass of water, made him drink some, and let emotion creep back into her face and voice. 'Are you OK? Fred?'

'I'm-I'm not sure. What did you say?'

'I've known David for a few years. Not *known* him, known him, but *Facebook* known him. So he didn't hack my account, or your account, or anything like that, and he hasn't been stalking me, OK? You don't have to worry about that.' She looked up from her clasped hands.

'But why didn't you tell me?' Freddie sounded like a hurt child. 'Why did you lie like that?'

'It wasn't a *lie*. It was more of a secret. I didn't want you to get hurt, Fred. It was all for you.' Her tone hovered into reproof, like a disappointed adult speaking to an immature teenager.

'How is this about me?' Freddie managed.

She sighed again. 'Ryan Needham?'

'What about him?'

'When you and Ryan were – talking – Ryan friended me too, remember? Just before you and him split up.' She said this last bit with a slight emphasis, as if using very faint quotation marks. 'Well, Ryan and David are friends from uni; you know that, David told you a while back. So that's how David found me – I popped up on some "People You Might Know" thing and he messaged me: "Hi, remember me from school?" "Yes, how are you doing?" that's all.'

'I don't—?'

'Then a week later, you and Ryan split; you were broken up about it and I was… worried. And pissed off on your behalf, so I messaged David to see if he knew what had happened, if Ryan was normally such an absolute bastard.'

'And you didn't tell me any of this?' Freddie mumbled.

'Well, how could I? Fred, you were in bits, and I felt so… useless. I wanted to send Ryan a message through his friend, you know, that what he'd done was shit, and people who loved you were pissed off, and… I wanted to know… something. I don't know. I wanted to rant on your behalf.'

'And?'

'And I *did* rant, and David felt awful about the way Ryan just dropped you – he'd done the same thing loads of times apparently, but David was particularly pissed off about it happening to you because you seemed like such a nice, genuine person. In fact, he distanced himself from Ryan because of *you*. *That's* how much he liked you before even meeting you.' Her voice throbbed with sad reproach. 'Anyway, David and I… we kept chatting on Facebook, that's all, but the longer it went on, the harder it got for me to tell you; it just felt wrong, insensitive.' She touched his hand. 'I hated keeping it from you though.'

'So, how come I didn't see David on your friends list then?'

'Well you might have done, but you didn't know his name, did you? And he never put anything on my wall. I told him not to; I didn't want you to see anything that might somehow link back to Ryan. I was only thinking of you. We just messaged each other, sometimes called each other, never met up. It was all very low-key. Then, when Mum died, David was in the village as well, and that's when we finally met face-to-face.'

'So at the funeral? You'd known each other for ages but you put on this act that you'd only just met?'

Jenny winced. 'It wasn't really an act. I mean, if you think back, I never said it was the first time we met. I didn't, like, explicitly lie to you.' She shifted. 'It all got convoluted and silly, and I hated keeping things from you, but I'm telling the truth now. All of it. And it's a good thing, Fred, can't you see? Now you know that you don't have to worry about David – the picture and—'

'What about the dinner at your house? I was playing cupid, but he'd been there loads of times before I suppose?'

'No.' She shook her head. 'That was all true. It really *was* the first time he'd come round, and we really *had* only been out on a few cinema and restaurant dates.'

Freddie shook his head. He sat in the too-small booth like a dazed, slumped bear. 'When did you give him the picture then?'

She gazed over his shoulder, thinking. 'That would be just before Mum died. He saw it on my Facebook wall and asked if he could make a copy of it. I said yes.'

'OK, so let me get this straight: he lives in the same village as you for months, and you never meet——'

'We *did* meet, we just didn't very often, and only after Mum died.' There was an edge to her voice. 'I've explained that.'

'And you knew him for years and never thought to tell me?' Freddie was all incredulity.

'I've explained that too. I was trying to save your feelings,' Jenny said tightly. 'And, if you remember, I had quite a lot on my plate at the time. College. Work. Therapy. You pining for Ryan. Looking after Mum, Mum *dying*, then having to convince the police I didn't *kill* her and then arranging her *funeral*. And after that, finding myself homeless. So, you know, dealing with your jealousy wasn't on top of my to-do list. Jesus.' She shook her head. 'David said you'd be like this. He warned me.'

'Oh, did he?' Freddie told her. 'It's nice to know that both of you have a firm handle on my feelings.'

There was a pause. Jenny sighed. 'I should have told you earlier. I'm sorry. I shouldn't have sprung it on you.'

'I'm not pissed off because you sprung it on me!' Freddie told her. 'I'm pissed off because you lied to me.'

'It wasn't really a lie, though,' said Jenny. 'I just didn't tell you the whole truth, that's all.'

'What's the difference?'

Jenny left a long pause. When she spoke again her voice was quiet, flat. 'All I can say is sorry, Fred.'

'No, why've you been hooking up with some guy you know nothing about and—'

She raised her voice. 'I don't have to tell you everything! And we weren't hooking up, we were messaging each other, which is exactly what you and Ryan did, and I didn't get all snotty about it.'

'I didn't lie to you about it, though,' Freddie said. 'I didn't worry you.'

'And I've said I'm *sorry*, but I was trying to do the right thing! What was I supposed to do? Just say: "Oh, I'm sorry your relationship with Ryan has gone south, but mine with his friend might be just beginning, please be happy for me?".'

'Yes! And I would've been happy for you, too!'

'I doubt that,' Jenny muttered.

'What d'you mean?'

'Nothing. Look, I'm tired, you're tired.' There was a resigned anger in her voice.

'No, what did you mean?' Freddie tried to keep his voice even.

'I mean that misery needs company, Fred.' She sounded so cold all of a sudden. 'If I'd told you about David, you'd have tried to make me feel guilty. I don't know if it's conscious or not, but that's what you do. That's your default mode. You make everything about you; you're doing it right now.' Her voice didn't rise, but that low growl was back. 'I've sat here, listening to you slag off my boyfriend; I've explained to you, reassured you, told you everything, and it's still not enough. You want me to apologise for being happy. That's what it comes down to.'

Freddie stared at her, at the concentration comma between her brows, as if it and it alone could tell him exactly how the conversation had got to this point. 'Why're you being like this?' he managed eventually.

'Like what?'

'Like *this*? You're not being you.'

'I've got to go to work. I'll call you when you've calmed down.'

'Wait, I *am* calm!' Freddie said, not calmly. 'Hazlewood. What about that place? He hasn't told you about that, has he? Ask him! Go on, ask him about Hazlewood!'

Jenny gazed at him. 'No.'

'No?'

'No. It's his business, it's not mine or yours.' She frowned again, opened her mouth, hesitated and shut it.

'Well if you don't ask him, I will!' Freddie said recklessly.

Jenny flinched. 'David is very... valuable to me,' she said softly. 'I'm not going to harm that for anything in the world, and neither are you.'

'If you don't ask him, it's because you're afraid of what he'll tell you,' Freddie replied.

She got up. 'Grow up, Freddie,' she said, and swung out of the door.

CHAPTER TWENTY-SIX

David was waiting for her in the lobby of a venerable old restaurant in town.

'You look beautiful,' he told her.

'Oh, no, really?' She touched her hair. 'I think I look frazzled. It was so hot in that office. Stuffy.'

'I thought we'd have a drink before the meal.' David led her to a table tucked beside a covered baby grand piano. They were the only people in the room, bar one horse-faced waiter.

He helped her off with her coat. 'So how was work?'

She made a face. 'Too dull to talk about.'

'Here.' He passed her a glass of white wine.

'Anyway, I only have another week and then I'll have to find something else. The temp agency is useless, but Andreena told me that there's a job going in her department, so, there's that, I suppose. If I got that, it'd be permanent. I'd even get holiday pay.' She waved an imaginary flag.

'I can tell you're not happy,' David said after a pause.

'I'm just a bit tired. Tired and overworked that's all. And Freddie—' She stopped, smiled and shook her head ruefully. 'No. I'm going to stop moaning.'

David's face tightened He poured himself another glass of wine. 'What's Freddie done to upset you now?'

'Nothing. We had a bit of a row, that's all.'

'Was it something to do with me?' His smile was pained.

'David—'

'It was, wasn't it?'

'It's his problem, not yours or mine. It'll blow over.' She frowned at her wine.

'If he's upset you, I'd really like to know.' He spoke softly, insistently. 'I don't care what he's said about me, but if it's hurting you, or-or *us*, then, please, tell me.'

Jenny took her time undoing her topknot, shaking it out and pushing a hand through the sudden cloud of her hair. 'Freddie's just… protective of me, that's all. Like you are.'

'I wouldn't call it protectiveness. I'd call it…' His expression hovered between fear and distaste. One finger tapped on the tablecloth. 'I bet I know what he told you.'

'David—'

'No. Let me speak. I need to… tell you something,' The pale oval of his face was damp. 'I'm sorry it's taken me so long.'

'You don't have to tell me anything. There's nothing to—'

He interrupted her again. 'There is. I do. I haven't been entirely truthful with you.' The handsome planes of his face seemed to shift and blur with the effort of telling this truth. 'I feel terrible.' I have all along. The thing is, I've not been entirely honest with you. Not just you, but… everyone. I've lied.' These words drifted into the quiet and hovered. 'And I can't lie any more, especially not to you. Even if it means I lose you, I have to tell the truth now.'

'David—'

'School. I lied about school. I didn't go to boarding school, I went to… well, a hospital, I suppose you'd call it. When I was sixteen, I had a breakdown.' He let out a long shuddery breath. 'That's why I didn't go to Sixth Form. There. That's it. I should have told you, but the longer I didn't, the harder it got.' He paused, put one hand over his face, and rubbed hard, leaving a red glow on his pale forehead. 'I'm guessing that that's what Freddie told you?'

'Yes,' Jenny said softly. 'He wasn't being horrible though, he was just—'

'Concerned.' David twisted the word, making it sound false, bitter. 'I knew that if he found out, he'd be "concerned".' David rubbed his face again, and then dropped both hands onto the bar. He looked exhausted. 'So that's the deep, dark secret. And if, you know, you want to stop seeing me…'

Jenny shook her head. 'I don't want that. I don't want that at all.' She watched as his hands crept together, his right thumb pressing into the knuckles of his left, hard. 'Do you want me to tell you exactly what he said?'

'Please,' David said shortly, and she couldn't see his face, couldn't see if he was close to tears.

'He said that you'd had some therapy. In a place called Hazlewood.'

'I did. And also in The Wolsey Clinic. After Dad died a year ago, I had a relapse. I-I loved my father.' And here his voice did break. 'When he – passed – so suddenly, knowing that it was just me and Mother left, it-it hit me hard. I checked myself into The Wolsey, almost expecting to get… ill. Just as ill as before. But I didn't. It turns out that I was a lot stronger than I gave myself credit for. I only stayed at The Wolsey for a few weeks, and then left, came back and looked after Mother. Listen, I want you to understand that this latest stay at The Wolsey, it was more of a prevention-as-cure stay. I was struggling with depression and grief. I wasn't *mad* or anything.' He laughed nervously.

'Shhh.' She put one firm hand on his. The thumb stopped moving but his hand still shook. 'Of all the people in the world, I'm going to understand this, aren't I? Look at me.' She raised his chin with firm, cold fingers. 'I love you, David. You believe that, don't you?' She smiled at his grateful, tearful nod. 'So, maybe it would help if you told me exactly what happened? About Hazlewood?'

And he began to tell her.

Catherine and Tony. *Had Freddie mentioned Tony?*

'Yes, he was the man in the photograph; the family friend. Mother's friend anyway, and an artist. Of sorts. He plugged away. He taught in schools and colleges, but then his contract wouldn't get renewed, and he'd travel for a while – Mum gave him money to do that; I don't think Father was very happy about it. Then he'd come back and get another job, and the whole thing would start all over again. He never had anywhere to live, so he always stayed with us until he got on his feet, but—'

'He never got on his feet?'

'He didn't, no.'

He told her how Tony first lived in the house, and then moved into a specially built 'summer house' at the end of the garden. He was only supposed to stay for a year, he said, but, inevitably, he stayed for longer than that. David had watched as the 'summer house' became more and more broken down and cluttered with half-finished paintings, shabby furniture that 'just needed a bit of TLC', and stacks of newspapers, records, books.

'I felt sorry for my father,' he said. 'He was such a gentle soul, and he respected Mum so much; he worshipped her. I asked him, just once, how he was able to put up with the situation but he just said: "Tony is your mother's guest." And that was the end of it.'

'So were they, I mean…' Jenny paused delicately.

'Having an affair? No. He was… that way. Gay. You know.' A faint blush fanned across his taut cheeks. 'I think Tony was her soulmate in a lot of ways, but they weren't – involved – like that. It didn't stop people thinking so, though.'

Jenny thought about Freddie saying *village gossip*. 'It can't have been easy for you?'

'No,' he said shortly. 'I coped with it by just shutting down. I pushed everything down. I tried to be as adult as possible. I thought that if it didn't seem to bother me, eventually it *wouldn't* bother me.'

'But that doesn't work.'

'No,' he said. 'Tony took over. Mother spent more and more time with him, Dad sort of retreated, and Tony...'

'What was Tony like?' Jenny pressed his hand with hers.

'He didn't *like* me,' David muttered. His voice high, tremulous with little-boy hurt. 'He was always being sarcastic about me. He'd do things to annoy me, frighten me.'

'Frighten you?'

David nodded. 'He'd tell me he'd been in my room, he'd read my diary, things like that.'

'And had he?'

'I don't know. But it made me very nervous, because I *did* keep a diary and I didn't know if he was joking or not. There was nothing awful in the diary, nothing to be ashamed of, but somehow, thinking that Tony had read it made me *feel* ashamed. And scared. Angry. So I began to hide it in a different place every day. I started to keep everything – store things away in hiding places – away from him. It became a bit of an obsession, collecting things, categorising things, storing them away.'

'What kind of things?'

David blushed, 'All sorts of things – scraps of paper, notes from Mother, things I found in the street that seemed interesting. Looking back, I think this is when I started to become ill. I know this probably makes me sound—'

'It makes you sound like someone who developed OCD,' Jenny told him. 'I've suffered from that before too. I think it's a control thing – I can't control X aspect of my life, but I *can* control how many times I've checked that the door is locked, you know? It crops up when you feel helpless.'

'Yes! That's it, and I did feel helpless. I *was* helpless. Tony: he thought he was joking, but it had a terrible effect on me.' He took a deep breath. 'And then there was the fire.'

Tony was a smoker. Catherine worried about him, worried that he refused to fit smoke alarms in the summer house, worried that the piles of papers, brittle bits of wooden furniture and paint thinner he kept in close proximity to each other was a disaster waiting to happen. 'Then my parents went on holiday, I was sixteen, so they thought I'd be fine on my own. Mum asked me to keep an eye on Tony, and I'm sure she asked Tony to keep an eye on me.' He smiled ruefully. 'But we didn't really have much to do with each other. When Mother wasn't there, he seemed to lose interest in… tormenting me. I spent a lot of time in my bedroom, and he was always in the summer house. Then, one day, I smelled smoke.

'I remember running down the stairs. The kitchen wasn't where it is now in those days, so I had to go out of the front door and kind of double back to the garden. If I hadn't taken such a long time to get there, maybe it wouldn't have been as bad. I ran as quickly as I could, but the flames were so high, and the heat…' His eyes were far away. 'I heard Tony shouting, and I just ran towards the noise.'

'That was brave,' Jenny told him.

'It was stupid,' David said flatly. 'I should've called the fire brigade. I didn't think, though. I panicked. When I got to Tony, I tried to grab him.'

'What was he doing?'

'He was beating at the flames with something, and he was screaming.' David closed his eyes. Squeezed them shut. 'I shouted his name, and he looked right at me. We stared at each other. His hair was on fire. He held out his hands, and I managed to grab one, and tried to pull him towards me, but the skin kind of melted, came off.'

'Jesus!'

David opened his eyes. 'Then there was an explosion, and I don't remember anything else. The fire brigade found me curled up at the base of the big oak at the end of the garden. Even though I was unconscious I was still crying.'

'Did Tony… I mean, was he…?'

'He survived,' David told her. 'But he was very badly burned. He had to have skin grafts, and he was in hospital for a long time. He never really recovered. He stopped eating, stopped taking care of himself, lost weight, kept getting infections, things like that. Mother tried the best she could, but he just gave up. He died a few years later. Mother was heartbroken. And then she started showing signs of dementia. I've always wondered – worried – that Tony dying was the thing that ushered in her illness. If only I'd saved him earlier, she wouldn't have become so ill and—'

'No. You can't think like that. You can't,' Jenny told him. 'Listen to me, you've spent all this time telling me about how you got things wrong, but where was your mother? Didn't she notice the things Tony was doing, how he made you feel?'

'No.'

'Did you try to tell her?'

'No. I wanted her to be happy.' His smile was sweet, sad. 'That's what I always wanted.'

'And after the fire? What about you?' Jenny leaned into him. 'How were *you*?'

'I was lucky. Minor burns to my face and arms. This hand was the worst.' He held up one big hand. The palm was criss-crossed with tiny white hatchings, the skin stiff-looking and waxy. 'They said that if I'd been a little bit closer to Tony, I might have died. The thing that exploded was a big can of turps, and it was a few feet away from where I was standing when I took his hand. It literally blew up in his face.'

'And afterwards?'

'I went to hospital. I couldn't talk – I wanted to talk but for some reason I couldn't. They were worried about me, Mother and Dad.'

'Well, of course they were.'

'And so, they sent me away. To Hazlewood. They said that going back home would be bad for me, bad for my recovery. I was there for almost a year.' He finally met her eyes. His were a little red-rimmed. 'So that's the truth. That's why I didn't come back to school. Mother told me to tell people I'd had a stroke. She told me that if I said that, I wouldn't have to be embarrassed.'

'"Embarrassed"? That's what she said? Wow.'

David looked down at his knees. 'She thought she was doing the right thing. I don't blame her. Anyway, if you want to end… this. If you feel as if I've…'

'David—'

'*Lied* to you—'

'David, listen, please—'

'I mean, I *have* lied. But from the moment I met you, I felt… happy. And I didn't want anything to take it away – take you away?' His voice cracked, shuddered.

'That's not going to happen, David.' She glanced at the ugly oil painting just behind his bowed head – a grimacing Judith thrust her knife into Holofernes's hairy neck. Her own face reflected in the glass made her smile. Love superimposed on murder. 'You don't have to worry, you really don't.'

'I'm making a bit of a fool of myself here.' He laughed, swallowed hard. Jenny finished her drink while he recovered himself a bit.

'I had to tell Freddie that we've known each other for longer than we said. That was the thing that really upset him.'

David paused. 'Ryan?'

She nodded. 'But I explained that I didn't want to tell him about you when he was still so cut up about the whole Ryan thing.'

David frowned at her. 'That's a lot of effort just to keep Freddie happy.'

'Well, it's to keep all of us happy really, isn't it? Anyway, I wasn't very successful. He's really angry with me.' She shrugged sadly. 'All I wanted was for everyone to get along, us all to be friends, but—'

'He's possessive.'

'He is, but he doesn't know the whole story. If I explained it to him – the breakdown, Hazlewood – he'd understand though, I'm sure he would, and then we could—'

'Start afresh?'

'Well, yes. He's not a bad person, David, he really isn't. He just gets carried away, and he can be a bit over the top, but his heart's in the right place.'

David shook his head. 'No, I think you're giving him too much credit. He comes to my house, pumps my mother for information, upsets her… upsets *you*, tells you *lies* about me. No. He's not someone I trust—' His voice was rising, loud enough to attract the attention of the waiter, who started their way, his face fixed in equine dismay.

'David, calm down. Please.' She glanced at the waiter, shook her head, watched him back away. 'I really don't think he pumped Catherine for information, I think she just mentioned Hazlewood, that's all, and he remembered the name and—'

But David didn't calm down. 'And tried his best to split us up by telling you I'm mad. That's what he did, didn't he? He doesn't want you to be happy if *he* isn't, so he's sabotaging us; it's as simple as that. Why would I want to know someone like that? Why would *you*?'

'He did handle this very badly,' Jenny admitted. 'I told him that, and he seemed to take it to heart. I'll explain—'

David put one hand up. 'No. I don't feel like… exposing my past to him or anyone. Apart from you. I'm not talking about him any more.' He looked at Jenny with something like challenge.

'All right, but we'll have to talk about him sometime—'

'No. No we don't.' David's voice was childish again, peevish. 'Anyway, our table must be ready.' He waved at the waiter, stood up, and soon they were sitting at a too-large round table, beneath another gory Caravaggio. 'I used to come here with my parents, years ago. It's special. That's why I wanted to bring you here.'

Jenny looked around at the painting hanging above, the heavy wood panelling, the deep pile carpet over which the waiter's footsteps whispered. 'Not a very family-friendly place. Very formal.'

'My father liked it. He liked the steak. He always ordered the steak,' David said evasively. His eyes were far away.

Jenny looked at him, considered bringing the conversation back to Freddie, but the thought of doing that was too enervating. When David was like this, it was best to just back away. 'What did you eat? When you came here with your parents?' she asked.

David thought for a while. 'D'you know, I don't remember eating anything. Funny.' There was a pause. 'All I remember is the ice cream. They used to make this wonderful chocolate sundae. I was very rarely allowed one though.'

Jenny picked up her glass. 'OK, this is what's happening then: we'll have steak in honour of your dad, and chocolate sundaes for dessert. And we won't talk about Freddie, or Ryan, or anything… anxiety-inducing. OK?'

'OK.' He smiled at her.

'So now we have to clink glasses. That's the charm.' She held out her glass.

'Will you promise me that you won't call him? I don't want to feel like this again anytime soon, and all he seems to do is upset you.' He held his glass up too. 'Can we have a break from Freddie altogether, at least for a few weeks? That's all I'm asking.' He looked at her; a supplicant before an angel. 'In a while I'll get over it, but at the moment my feelings are so hurt…'

Jenny nodded. David smiled thankfully.

They looked into each other's' eyes. Clink clink.

CHAPTER TWENTY-SEVEN

Freddie and Jenny didn't see or speak to each other for three long weeks. Freddie had already noticed that she'd stopped posting on the blog, but her social media – relatively dormant for the last year or so – had suddenly come to life with artfully filtered photographs. One, of a smiling Jenny and David underneath a cherry tree, was captioned: 'Spring has sprung!'

A saccharine cliché like 'Spring has sprung'? Really? Freddie shuddered. And the posts only got blander: 'Homemade gnocchi! Yum #spoiledgirl'. A photo of Claudine stretched out on a rug that Freddie recognised as the one he'd almost ruined with wine was captioned '#Happy Kitty + Happy me = awesome'.

Jesus.

Normally, when he saw something truly nauseating like this, he'd immediately share it with Jenny, in full knowledge that she'd also hate it, and probably hate it more. Now, all the caustically funny responses had built up in him as usual, but he had no one to share his hatred with: Jenny was the origin of this kitschy horror.

He understood, finally, that annoyingly precious euphemism 'My Other Half'. He felt as if he'd lost a huge part of himself. He was like an amputee, still feeling the itches and aches of their missing limb, trying and failing to work with something that was no longer there.

When they eventually met, accidentally, just outside Freddie's office, he almost didn't recognise her. Jenny was wearing an unfamiliar silk striped shirt paired with slim black trousers, and her hair fell in silky, precisely managed waves. They stopped in the middle of the street, buffeted by passers-by, and both were hesitant, shy. She said she'd just left work. Tax Office, Andreena's department.

'And how's Dree?'

'Good.'

There was a pause. 'You look lovely,' he told her.

'Do I?' She pinkened. 'I just got this top. David bought it.'

Another pause. 'It's lovely. So. How's David then?'

'He's good. Yeah.'

The town hall clock struck five. Freddie thought, *if this was a sitcom, we'd both start speaking at the same time, and then apologise, and then start speaking at the same time again.*

She raised her eyebrows. 'This is like a rom-com, isn't it? We should talk over each other, saying the same thing.'

And Freddie laughed. 'Yeah, and then we'd go for drinks and there'd be a montage. What would the music be?'

She thought for a minute. 'Van Morrison. "Brown Eyed Girl",' she said decisively.

'Now, you see, I was thinking something more Motown-y, Diana Ross-ish.'

'What's that Michael Jackson song about a rat?'

'"Ben". And I could take that as an insult.' Freddie smiled.

Jenny smiled back. 'I've missed you, Fred.'

'Me too.' He felt tears in his throat. 'It's been awful.'

She nodded at him seriously. 'I thought you sort of hated me.'

'Hated you? God, no! No. I've called and emailed so many times, though I thought you hated *me*. Then your number changed, and I couldn't get hold of you. I even went to your old flat—'

'Oh God, what did Matt have to say about me?' She shook her head. 'I left halfway through the lease, you know. David went to collect my things and he said Matt was nuts. Spitting mad.'

Freddie remembered Matt's decidedly un-nuts manner when he'd turned up on his doorstep last week. Rushed, slightly pissed off about being left in the lurch, but not weird in any way. *Could this be another one of David's little lies?*

'Anyway, Fred, let's go and get a drink? What's that old-man pub that used to do karaoke? The one by the canal? Let's go there, and I'll tell you all about it.'

Freddie's smile was wide, foolish. 'OK!'

The Narrowboat, previously catering to stoic all-day drinkers and the mentally ill, had, in recent months and with touching hope, rebranded itself as a gay bar – all infused gins and ironically chosen adverts from the 1970s. A few hardened alcoholics remained, resolutely standing in the place where their favourite tables used to be, a shaky, odorous stand against progress. There was no karaoke any more, but there was a jukebox that pumped out 80s and 90s hits with a leaning towards power ballads. Freddie and Jenny sat in a corner booth, ate chips, drank weak cocktails and gradually became used to each other again. By the third drink, and the second playing of Heart's 'Alone', though, Jenny still hadn't explained about Matt, and he was ready to ask questions.

'OK, Matt told me you'd moved out, left him with unpaid bills. What happened there?'

Jenny swirled her straw in the gin-y ice. 'Well, you remember that he was going into my room?'

'I remember you *thinking* he was going in your room, yes. Did you catch him at it?'

'I didn't, David did. He saw him coming out of my room holding my underwear – can you believe it? So David had it out with him, and Matt couldn't really deny it, could he? So David packed my things up and took them to his house. I'm staying there until I sort myself out.' She shook her head. 'It sounds funny now, but at the time it was awful. Just the thought of him going through my stuff and everything being all leery and—' She shuddered. 'David made me change my number so he couldn't contact me again. It was sort of horrible.'

David made her change her number? 'Oh,' Freddie answered carefully. 'So your number changed?'

She nodded. 'So yes, if you've been trying to call and couldn't get through, that's why. Sorry.' She shifted uncomfortably. 'I only got the new number a bit ago, and, you know, all my contacts aren't in my new phone, and – look, I'll call you now, so you have my new number.'

She could have emailed. She could have come round to his flat. She could have— *Stop it. Stop it Fred. She's here, safe and happy, and you're having a drink and a gossip like old times. Don't ruin it. Don't scare her off.*

'It's OK. You're super-busy.' He took a sip of gin. 'And *You Can't Go Home Again*? No new posts for a while?'

'I'm still *writing* posts, but I'm not posting them. You're right, I'm too busy. Work, college, same old same old. Travelling in from the village takes a while – David drives me most days, but if he can't I take the train and that adds ages onto the journey. And Catherine needs a lot of attention, of course.'

David brings her in. Of course he does. 'So Catherine? How is she?'

'Not great. In fact, today David had to take her to the hospital; she had a fall. He normally picks me up from work, so today I was supposed to get a taxi straight to the station, but I went rogue and did some shopping instead. I better call him actually, let him know where I am. I'll just pop outside.'

Why outside? Why not here? Freddie hesitated, almost said something, but didn't.

When she came back, she was shivering and her hair was dusted with fine rain. 'Freezing out there.'

'Everything all right?'

'Well I had to leave a message. He's probably still at the hospital, or driving, or–' she frowned. 'I'll text him too. If I'm not there when he gets home he'll worry—'

'Jenny.' Freddie's voice faltered. 'If you're going to… get into trouble… for staying out with me… I don't want to cause any—'

Jenny put up one hand. 'No. You know what, it's time we all put this behind us. All the stuff that happened between you and me, we should just get over it.'

Freddie nodded dumbly. 'But I know that David probably doesn't like me, especially after—'

She put up a hand again. Her nails, he noticed, were long, glossy, manicured. As long as he'd known her, she'd never been able to stop biting her fingernails. Now they were so perfect that they had to be fake. 'Here's the thing. I'm David's first *serious* relationship.' She frowned. 'I'm his… first, full stop. You understand?'

'What? He was a virgin—'

She nodded. 'Don't, for God's sake, tell him I told you that, OK?'

A foolish smile eked its way over Freddie's face. 'Wow. Really? That explains quite a lot actually.'

She nodded. 'He was in hospital at the time most of us start the boyfriend/girlfriend thing and his home life, Fred, it was… bad. Really bad.'

'So he *was* in a mental – sorry, psychiatric place! How? I mean why? What happened?'

Jenny frowned at her manicure. 'I can't really go into that. It's not fair to David, but' – she raised her eyebrows and gave a grim smile – 'let's just say we have a lot in common, me and David. And in many ways he had it worse than me.'

'But why didn't he tell you? Why make up that lie about the stroke?'

'He panicked,' Jenny told him. 'He was embarrassed and scared and he didn't want to lose me. You can understand that, right? So he told a lie, and, because he's not very good at lying, you saw through him and assumed the worst.'

'And you didn't?' Freddie was eager with gin. 'You never researched the Hazlewood thing, you never had any idea?'

She shook her head. 'I'm not great at lying either, so I can't tell when people are lying to me. Not lying, but you know, hiding the truth a bit.'

Freddie let the air out of his lungs through pursed lips. 'So, is he OK now?'

'Yes, he's fine! He's just... slow to trust. He's insecure. So, I... represent a lot to him. I'm on a bit of a pedestal, and when he met you, he felt jealous.'

'He knows I'm gay though?'

She rolled her eyes at him. 'He's inexperienced. He's not brain damaged. Anyway, all this time I've gone with it. He wants to make a fuss of me, he wants me all to himself and I can understand that.' She stared into the gloom of the bar. 'But, yesterday, I had a long conversation with him. I sat him down and I told him that if he loves me as much as he says he does, he has to give you another chance.'

'You said that?' Freddie almost felt tears. She nodded. 'And what did he say?'

'He agreed with me. That's the thing about David, he really does want to... get better at stuff.'

'"Get better at stuff"? Sex stuff or friendship stuff, or—'

'Stuff,' she said tightly. 'Let's just leave it at that.'

'So...' Freddie, touched, a bit overwhelmed, reached, as he always did in times of confusion, for facetiousness. 'Could this be the start of a beautiful friendship?'

Jenny's face relaxed a little. '"A man is known by the company he keeps".' She nodded sagely.

'"Out of sight, out of mind"?'

'Ah, but "absence makes the heart grow fonder",' Jenny replied.

Freddie paused, then countered with: '"It's an ill wind that blows no one any good".'

She winced at that. 'That many double negatives hurt my brain. Can't follow it. Gin might help?'

'"A nod's as good as a wink to a blind horse",' Freddie said, and went to the bar.

The cute barman smiled. 'Having a nice evening?'

Freddie smiled back. 'I am. Old friend. Sister from another mister.'

'Double up the gins for an extra £1?'

'Why not.'

'"A fish rots from the head down"!' Jenny called over.

'It's a game we play,' Freddie explained to the bemused barman. 'Idiotic Idioms.'

The barman opened the little tonic bottles with a flourish. 'You Can Lead A Whore To Culture—'

'But You Can't Make Her Think!' Freddie finished.

The barman winked.

Freddie made his way back to the table, 'OK. I've potentially pulled, and we're on the doubles.' He took a sip of his drink. 'Jesus, that's strong. That's more like triples. We're going to need food.' She was texting furiously. 'Everything OK?'

'What? Oh yes. Yes. Just…'

Freddie's ginny bonhomie lessened, just slightly. 'David OK?'

'Fine,' she said it decisively, if not completely convincingly. 'Oh, here, I need to show you something.' She dug into one of her bags. 'This shirt? Isn't it lovely?'

Freddie wasn't good at fashion. It was one of the things he and Jenny had always had in common – an absolute indifference to designer clothes. When she handed him a plain black shirt, he handled it gingerly, with the awkward bemusement of a grandfather with a newborn. He didn't know what to say, 'It's, yeah, it's lovely.'

'Stella McCartney: £500.'

He still didn't know what reaction she wanted, so he went for shock. 'Holy shit!'

'I know, right?' She nodded brightly. 'Gorgeous though, isn't it?'

Freddie looked at it. It was just a shirt. 'It's lovely. Yeah. I mean, I'd have to see it on…' He handed it back, and she folded it up with fond glee and placed it reverently back in the bag. £500? Washed back into nervousness, he lurched towards a safer topic. 'So how's the job?'

'Today was my last day. That's why I treated myself.'

'What? Oh, did the contract end, or…'

'Nope. I quit.' She nodded, gin-proud and pert.

'What? Why?' *How could she afford £500 shirts with no job? How could she afford £500 shirts at all, come to think of it?*

'I walked into the office this morning and I looked around and just thought "Nope". I mean, it was really nice of Andreena to basically get me the job and all, but £9 an hour, data entry. It's not a dream come true, you know?' She frowned and stabbed at her ice again. 'And so I called David just to sort of talk it over, and he said that he *knew* it'd be like that, but he let me take the job anyway—'

'He "let you"?' Freddie couldn't stop himself this time.

'He didn't say it like that. I can't remember how he said it, but it was useful.' She turned one hand over and met his eyes. 'He said that he always knew I'd see my own worth, not sell myself short any more. It's the counselling that's really my passion. I should stop letting things get in the way of that.' She slurped up the last of her ice.

'OK, but what'll you do for money in the meantime? Are you going to be a kept woman?' He tried to make his voice light, non-judgemental.

'No! No. I'm just going to help him look after Catherine.'

'What? He's going to pay you to look after his mother?' A bit of ice went down the wrong way and he found himself sputtering untidily.

She handed him a napkin. 'Well he's not *paying* me. That'd be weird. No, he suggested that, because I have caring experience, and Catherine trusts me, I could help him out. It makes total sense. I'll have loads more time to finish my dissertation, I'll qualify quicker and be able to set up on my own in a year or so. I'll use one of the rooms in the house as an office.' Jenny was sitting upright and pert, ginny eyes bright, and proud little smile forming on her face, just waiting to be congratulated.

Freddie didn't know what to say. He faked another ice cough, excused himself to go to the bar for a glass of water. The barman looked concerned.

'No, it's OK. Something went down the wrong way that's all. You know, while I'm here can I have two gin and tonics? And double them.'

'Two gins. Stat!' He was really, really, very cute. 'What's the problem?'

Freddie glanced over his shoulder at Jenny, texting again, turned back. 'You've seen *The Stepford Wives*?'

'The original or the remake?'

'Oh, God, the original, of course.'

'Got it on Blu-Ray.' He nodded at Jenny, now absently drumming each perfect nail on the tabletop. '"I'll just die if I don't get that recipe… I'll just die if I don't get that recipe…"'

'She's not quite at the Nanette Newman stage. But, yeah. Listen, £500 for a shirt. That's nuts, right?'

The barman nodded sagely, pointed at his own shirt. 'EBay. £2.'

Freddie resisted the urge to propose to him, right then and there, and reached for his money, and was told that the drinks were on the house.

I'll have to come back here, he thought.

Back at their table, Jenny was looking at her phone again.

'Is that David?'

'Yes, he just wants to know when I'll be back, that's all. I didn't say I'd be this late. I thought I *had*, but he says I—'

Buzz buzz.

'It's not late though, it's—' Freddie peered at his own phone, 'not eight yet. I got you another drink.'

She flushed. 'I better not.'

'Oh come on, just this last drink, and then we can go and get food. David can meet us there? It'll be nice.' Gin always made Freddie expansive and sociable.

She hesitated, relented. 'OK. I'll just see what he says.'

She pulled her phone out of her bag, and Freddie saw that it was bristling with missed calls. 'I'll go outside. Can't hear in here.' Still flushed she was scampering away from their table now, the phone in her hand, vibrating like an angry wasp.

Within a minute, she returned, suddenly tired. 'I have to go, sorry. Catherine needs me. I seem to be the one person who can calm her down at the minute. David said she won't let him give her her pills; she'll only let me do it. He's frantic. I've got to go.'

'I thought she was in hospital?' Freddie asked.

'Only for tests,' she answered, gathering her coat,

'Oh.' Freddie tried not to look too woebegone. 'OK, well, say hi to David from me, and tell him I hope his mum feels better soon.'

'Yes. Oh, and David was sorry he couldn't meet up with us. He said some other time.' Her face was averted. When he stood to give her a quick hug goodbye, she felt stiff, tense.

He watched her leave, and tried to unpick his thoughts. He felt terribly guilty. If David was a survivor of abuse, then surely he had every right to his privacy, every right to make and maintain an environment that made him feel safe and kept him well. On the other hand, Jen was riddled with tension that increased with every text, every call she received from David; she was intimidated into cutting her evening short. The new haircut, the posh clothes, the acrylic nails, didn't quite disguise how tired her face was in repose, how thin she was getting, the little quiver of her hands when she reached for her phone.

Freddie thought about this while he finished both drinks and then gave into the temptation to begin researching 'Controlling Relationships' on his phone.

Ten Tell-Tale Signs You're in a Controlling Relationship
1. Isolating you from friends and family
Yes.
2. Criticising your dress sense
Well, all of a sudden she cared about designer clothes, which was weird.
3. Making you feel and/or placing you in debt
'So you're going to be a kept woman?' That slight start, the vehement denial.
4. Using guilt as a tool
'Catherine needs me.'
5. Spying, snooping on you
Looking through her phone. Constant texting – where are you, where are you?
6. Overactive jealousy
Well, he was very suspicious of Matt. But then Matt had turned out to be creepy, so…
7. Thwarting your professional or educational goals by making you doubt yourself
Slagging off the counselling profession as a pyramid scheme. 'Letting' her give up her job so she could care for Catherine and work on her dissertation. These two things cancelled each other out, but David was controlling, not necessarily consistent…

8. Makes you feel that you're unable to make your own decisions
'He said he knew it'd be like that.'
9. Calls you several times a night
YES!
10. Using threats or violence
No.

He sat back, feeling that this last 'No' was a bit of an anticlimax. *Did he want Jenny to be hurt?* Jesus, Fred. No, no, of course not. But David checked all the boxes but that one. Freddie read through the list again; his right hand was tinted white and red from clutching his phone so hard, and in his gin-soaked mind he thought – *if David isn't violent now, he will be soon.* That was the way things went with men like him… secretive strange men who lived with their mothers and stayed virgins until their twenties. He was a jealous man, an angry man… Jenny had admitted that already.

The beginning of a migraine throbbed behind his eyes.

The place was filling up now, and the music was louder. A group of men stood close to the table, their glances making it obvious that he should leave to make way for them, and so Freddie wobbled upright, waved to the barman, and started walking back home, hoping the cool air would sober him up a bit. Halfway home he caved in and called a cab.

Back home he made himself a sloppy sandwich and ate it over the sink while texting Jenny:

> *Lovely to see you, let's not leave it too long next time? and yes let's sort out a playdate soon for you me and D? NO GIN! I already feel like shit xxxx*

Then he went to take a shower.

She hadn't replied by the time he got out, and so he called her – once, twice, three times, each time leaving an exaggerated groan as voicemail. When his phone pinged, it was a text from an unknown number.

> *Don't call again.*
> *Jenny?* Freddie wrote back. *What's wrong you OK?*
> *It's David. Don't call her again.*

Freddie froze, then began shaking with adrenaline. He dialled David's number and the call was answered without a word. 'What the fuck?' Freddie spluttered. 'You can't—'

But David had already hung up, and when Freddie called back, the phone had been turned off.

CHAPTER TWENTY-EIGHT

Freddie spent the next few hours reading up on domestic violence and coercive relationships. He read harrowing accounts of imprisonment, manipulation, rape, and the more he learned, the more he realised that Jenny could be a poster child for the cycle of abuse; she'd had no father and an alcoholic, neglectful mother, an abusive stepfather, and now she was all alone in the world, ripe for the picking for any abusive nut job who told her they loved her. It was textbook. How in hell could Freddie have let this happen? What kind of a person just sat back, wallowing in their own hurt feelings while their friend was suffering through… god knows what?

Feverish guilt drove away the last mists of gin, and by the morning, he knew what he had to do.

The next morning Freddie called in sick to work, and drove back to the village, full of paracetamol and vigorous, righteous anger. Now he parked near enough to David's house so that he could spot him leaving, not close enough so he'd be spotted himself, but he had no idea if David *would* leave the house at all. He slouched in the passenger seat for two uncomfortable, boring hours, watching the curve of David's drive for any activity. Cops in cop shows always hated stakeouts, and now Freddie knew why… cops on cop shows also had the foresight to bring coffee and donuts with them. Freddie had nothing but half a bottle of flat Coke and a phone full of articles about abuse.

Finally, at 2 p.m. David's BMW nosed out from behind the conifers. Freddie ducked down to hide the ginger beacon of his hair, and managed to maintain a partial view of the BMW disappearing down towards the slip road leading to the motorway. If he was going that way, chances were he was going to the city, which would hopefully give Freddie enough time to see Jenny, talk to her, and make her see sense.

He made his way up the drive and towards the door, trepidation increasing with each step. His chest was clenched, and despite the spring warmth, the hairs on his arms stood stiff. Claudine ambled out of a flower bed and pushed her head against his legs. He picked her up, happy for the warmth, appreciating the purr. 'What's the news, kitten?' he asked her, clattered the mermaid's tail door knocker against the wood. 'Cover me. I'm going in.'

Jenny opened the door, dressed in dungarees and an old T-shirt. Very much Old Jenny and not Sleek Stepford Jenny, which had to be a good thing.

'Freddie! How come you're here?'

'Are you OK?' he asked.

'Yes. Yes, of course I'm OK, why wouldn't I be? Why aren't you at work?'

'Took a sickie. Can I come in, then?'

'Of course.' She sounded ever so slightly unsure, but stepped back to let him into the gloomy hallway, where he almost collided with a tremulous pillar of cardboard boxes. The top one wobbled, fell and spilled out papers, scarves, a small knitted hat.

'We're doing a clear-out,' Jenny explained, kicking the scarves out of the way. 'There's some building work starting in a week, too.'

'Oh, yes?' Freddie was determined to keep his manner as normal as possible. All the articles about abusive relationships said this was essential. *Let the victim take the lead in disclosure. Don't push, but be as accepting and open as possible.*

'Yes. The plan is to knock through the larger living room, the small sitting room and the kitchen, as well as a couple of the smaller rooms upstairs. But they've been used for storage since the beginning of time, so, there's a lot of work to do…' She sounded a little bit more animated, describing all the changes, and led him past some more boxes, past the conservatory – half-demolished and covered with tarpaulin – and into the kitchen proper. 'So, the conservatory's going altogether, and that room will be knocked through, and made wider. And we're going to do something about the garage. We haven't decided what yet though.'

We we we we we. 'God. Lots of work,' Freddie managed.

'Yeah. Well, it needs doing.' She looked about vaguely. 'But you know, once you get started, there's no end to it. And the planning department are being, well, you know…'

'Mmm,' Freddie answered. He'd never, ever in his life thought he'd be having this conversation with Jenny of all people. *What was next? Cushion covers? Ocado deliveries?*

'So everything's OK?' Freddie said carefully.

'Well, yes. Why wouldn't it be?' She seemed to be slightly nervous.

With immense effort, Freddie tried to remember his research. *Resist asking too many questions… allow space for her to talk about her own feelings.*

'So, what's in the boxes?' he managed.

'Oh Lord, you've seen *Hoarders*, right?' I don't know. There's books, there's clothes, there's all sorts of stuff. Catherine kept *everything*. So did Piers. I think David doesn't really want to part with it all either – that's why he's putting it all into storage.'

'Is he here?' Freddie asked casually, sipping boiling tea.

'No, he's at the storage place now to take a look at it. He wants to make sure they're above ground, just in case they have, you know, rats or something. He doesn't want anything to get gnawed at.' She grinned, but it didn't illuminate her face, just made her look more tired. 'Fred what's wrong? You didn't skip work to talk to me about *Hoarders*.'

'David called me last night.' He watched her face stiffen, then arrange itself into bland ease.

'Oh, OK? And…'

'He told me not to call you. He—'

'What was that?' Jenny half rose.

'I know, right?' Freddie exclaimed, all his careful self-training gone. 'He said I couldn't *call* you *ever again*—'

'No, listen,' Her thin face, her corded neck – it all communicated incredible, sudden strain. 'The car. Shit, he's back. Fred, just… go upstairs. Please?'

'Why?' Freddie said stoutly. 'Why aren't you allowed to have a friend over? What's he going to do if he sees me, hit you?'

'It's not that I'm not "allowed". It's complicated. He'll just get upset, and I really don't need that.' She was pleading with him. 'You can come back down later once he's gone again. We'll talk properly, and I'll explain things, I promise, but please, Fred, for me?' She pointed towards the stairs. 'Take your coat with you!' she hissed.

And Freddie did as he was told, making it to the landing and ducking into the nearest bedroom just as David put the key in the door.

It was the same room that he'd been in a few months ago, now housing more boxes, as well as the same two packing cases and the same ugly wardrobe dominating the corner by the window. Freddie edged towards that, his heart clattering in his chest, the sour taste of adrenaline at the back of his throat. All he could hear from downstairs was the muted bass of David's voice, and the half-imagined nervous treble of Jenny's. He braced himself for an explosion of anger, footsteps on the stairs, David marching in. A dramatic confrontation, furious argument, and a filmic denouement with Freddie rescuing Jenny, both of them running like children down the drive to safety... that would be great. But none of that happened. Instead Freddie spent the next half hour wedged between the wall and the wardrobe, miserably aware that he needed the toilet.

To make things worse, the wardrobe door wouldn't stay shut. Every few minutes Freddie pushed it to with one finger, wincing against the creak, and every few minutes it would swing open again, the sound monstrously loud in the silent room. David was bound to hear it if he came up the stairs and, if he came into the room, he'd see Freddie immediately... If he moved that bag of papers and the hand weights a bit – pushed them further back – that might make the door stay shut. Was it worth it? As if furnishing a reply, the door groaned open again. Freddie shuffled forwards. The bag was spilling with shopping lists, phone messages... 'Vet called re Tinker' said one. 'Gruyère if possible?' said another. A birthday card opened to a pop-up wine glass with 'It's Wine O'clock!' printed in cartoon bubbles. 'T ALL LOVE C'; a decade-old copy of the *Telegraph*. Jenny hadn't lied: this family really did keep everything. An old copy of the *Radio Times* from 1992 slipped out and a photograph fell out from its folds... a blurry woman in brown, faintly familiar looking. Freddie tried pushing the bag in further. The door still wouldn't shut because there was something caught in the hinge; Freddie wiggled it free. A photograph of a stone-faced baby, furiously asleep in a cot, a pink bow on its bald head. On the back in blue biro was written 'Jenny's first Xmas '93'. He felt time stop with a jolt.

Some people are born with the happy knack of discerning the grown adult in a baby's face, but Freddie wasn't. A baby was a baby as far as he was concerned, just like a cat was a cat and a dog was a dog... and anyway, Jenny didn't have any baby pictures. Marc had destroyed them all. The only picture she had was the one that he, Freddie, had had framed for her. But the date was right… He peered at the picture, trying to make sense of it. It *was* her. It had to be.

If this was here, what else was here?

He put the baby photo down on the floor, and then, carefully, as silently as possible, he reached into the bag again, finding nothing of any meaning until, among the receipts and general detritus, he found a newspaper clipping. A recent one.

> *17th January 2017*
> *Police are investigating after a woman's body was discovered this morning.*
> *Emergency services were called to the village of Marston at 7.30 a.m.*
> *Local sources have identified the dead woman as Sally Holloway, aged 43, of Dene's Walk, Marston.*
> *A police spokeswoman said: 'The woman died some time in the evening of 16th January. The death is not being treated as suspicious and formal identification has not yet been made. A report will be prepared for Her Majesty's coroner and the woman's family are being supported at this difficult time.*

The back of the clipping was covered with blocky capitals. A list:

16 Edi 628 9:08 HHN 502 9:23 LGG 746 9:38.

No dates.

He put this next to the baby photo.

'Precious Memories!' was still nestled in the corner of the wardrobe. There'd been another newspaper clipping in there too, hadn't there? Something about fly-tipping, but he'd only looked at one side of it.

From downstairs he heard the French windows open, heard David in the garden, talking loudly about a patio, about garden furniture. The soft burr of Jenny's voice told him that she was there, too. If they were both outside, they weren't likely to hear any rustling of papers from the upstairs bedroom. Freddie thought quickly. Here was his chance – maybe his only chance – to properly look through David's strange set of mementos and get real, genuine evidence that he could present to Jenny and save her. Already, with the baby picture and the newspaper clipping, David was looking distinctly stalkerish.

With one shaking finger, Freddie pressed the 'Precious Memories!' rusted release catch, opened the lid and began scanning the random, unconnected pieces of trash that now seemed a lot less random. There was some sinister underpinning to these carefully curated items. Something that made them *precious*. The dirty chiffon scarf. A series of train tickets that had been carefully laminated. One, a return ticket, was surrounded with doodled hearts. There was a pink Post-it note with Jenny's handwriting on it – he could tell it was hers because she'd never wrote the @ symbol properly; she just wrote a normal 'a' and circled it. It seemed to be a list of train times. A photograph of a patch of ground and, in the far corner, was a little cross with the words TINKER written on it. Some pinkish gravel in a sandwich bag was sellotaped to a piece of cardboard. And, yes, here was the newspaper clipping he'd seen before – Freddie noticed how yellowed it was – the print had smeared and the folds were cracking. David handled this a lot. David thought this was important enough to keep hidden and keep going back to. Freddie turned it over and read.

1st March 2009 – Body of Man Identified.
Police have identified a man who was found dead in the
canal two weeks ago as missing person Marc Doyle.

*Officers were called to Carrington Street in the city centre
two weeks ago after a body was found in the water. Following specialist forensic tests required to identify the deceased,
officers have been able to confirm the man as 38-year-old
Marc Doyle of St Ann's.*

*The death is being treated as suspicious and a file will be
prepared for the coroner ahead of an inquest which will take
place in due course.*

Marc? What in hell was David doing with a cutting about Jenny's
sort-of ex-stepfather?

With shaking hands Freddie got out his phone, and took some
careful pictures of the clipping, the strange numbers and letters,
the train tickets. On the other side of the Post-it note was written:

*You mustn't think bad of me because I'm writing quickly I
am not writing quickly because I am not a nervous man. I
like writing and I am not afraid of you because inside me
lives god and my nerves are calming down a lot and I feel
myself improving and how are you? It's important you're well
and happy? I feel myself getting more well, and happier, and
that means.*

He didn't recognise the handwriting. *David's?*

He looked at the 'TINKER' photo again; there was something
familiar about this nondescript patch of earth... he'd seen it
before... Yes! That same cross was at the end of the garden, near
to the scars the fire had left on the lawn. *What did it mean? Why
have a photograph of your cat's grave?*

'Here?' David's voice sounded from the garden, just below the
window. It made Freddie jump. 'A full bed or a rockery?'

'Maybe a bit further that way?' Jenny said.

'At the end, you mean?' David asked doubtfully. 'Isn't that a bit too far from where the patio will be?' His voice was moving away, while Jenny's was still close, and a fraction too loud.

'Well, if we extend further, we could move all the plants away from the *front* door?' It was a strangely emphasised phrase.

'D'you mean the patio door?' David seemed to be coming back towards her.

'Yes, sorry I meant that. Not the *front* door.' Again, that emphasis. She was signalling to Freddie that he should leave now, safely, from the front, as David was being kept busy at the back. *Clever girl!*

And so Freddie crawled to the bedroom door and put one cautious foot on the top step, paused, and trotted halfway down before he was stopped dead by a voice.

'What is it?' Catherine called from her room. 'David?'

Freddie remained rigid on the stairs, one toe on the next step, hand clutching the bannister.

'David? Come and talk to me David!' Freddie held his breath. 'Holes. Holes! What about Tinker? Tell me. Tell me and I won't tell.'

Still Freddie didn't move, barely breathed. The silence grew monstrous, pregnant. From the kitchen, he heard Jenny call to David in the garden: 'Look, I have some pictures on my phone – stay there and I'll get it!' And a moment later she was at the bottom of the stairs, gesturing wildly towards the open front door. Freddie pointed towards Catherine's room, and she pulled the door to, all the while waving him down the stairs.

'Who's there?' Catherine asked nervously as he passed her door.

'Just me,' Jenny told her, and mouthed: 'Go!' at Freddie.

'Who?' Catherine was just behind her door now. Her voice was strong; it rang with authority. 'I have a right to know!'

Jenny made a telephone gesture with one hand and waved at the front door with the other. Her eyes pleaded with him *to go, just go*.

'How could you do that to Tinker?' Catherine shouted.

Freddie ran then, down the drive.

Back in the car, he allowed himself a few minutes of stillness, of calm, enough time to let the sweat that had run down his sides dry stickily, and his breathing to return to normal. As he turned the engine on he got a text from Jenny.

> *I will explain EVERYTHING, promise but don't call or text.*
> *Have to take Catherine to hospital for tests in the morning,*
> *so might get a chance to call you then? OK?*

Safely back home Freddie studied the photo of the scribbled numbers and letters. But when he googled 'LGG' all the results were for some kind of probiotic drink. And also… airports? LGG *could be* Liège Airport in Belgium. HHN turned out to be Frankfurt Hahn. EDI was Edinburgh. Why did David have all these written down? Could the numbers correspond to flight times? They had to. He looked up flight statistics, and let out a little yell of triumph. He was right!

An hour later, he'd narrowed the flight times down to scheduled arrivals to their regional international airport. The only number that didn't fit was '16'.

A date?

He typed '16' and the name of the city. Nothing. '16 David Crane'. Nothing; 16 and the name of the county, nothing. As a last resort he tried the name of the village, and up popped a familiar local news article. Sal's death. 16th January. The same news report that David had clipped and kept safe in 'Precious Memories!'

Freddie flopped back onto the sofa cushions. The cursor blinked insistently next to Sal's name, and Freddie looked at that, looked at the date, looked at the flight times, struggling to get his fingers under what this might mean. David had flight times from the evening of Sal's death. Well, David had been coming back from dropping Ryan off at the airport on that night. That was how he'd been able to see Jen walking through the village; that was how he'd been able to provide the police with her alibi. On the surface, it made sense, *but why have the details of three separate flights written down?* David hadn't given a ride to three people taking three separate flights from the same airport at the same time, had he?

Freddie fingered his phone nervously. No message from Jenny. He couldn't call her because it might put her in danger; she'd more or less told him that. David might be monitoring her Facebook page, her emails, everything… scratch that, he *must* be. Controlling communication was the number-one weapon of choice for abusive partners. There was nothing Freddie could do, but worry, and wait until she was able to call him, confide in him. If she ever did. *God, this was awful.* This was everything the Controlling Relationship websites had warned him would happen. And people like David always had a history of this sort of thing. They don't start being psychotic at the grand old age of – well, how old was David anyway? Twenty-five? Twenty-four? Even though he'd appeared out of nowhere: the perfect son, the doting boyfriend, he must have a past, and a dark one too? A person doesn't end up in a psychiatric unit for years because they were a bit insecure. David must have done this sort of thing before.

What about Ryan Needham?

Freddie opened Facebook, went to David's profile – the picture was now a sepia-tinted one of him and Jenny – and found Ryan, resplendent in snowboarding gear, in his friends list.

OK. Deep breath. This isn't about you. Do it for Jenny.

Hi Ryan. It's Freddie Lees-Hill. Turns out we have a friend in common, David Crane? Small world!

He didn't get a reply. He hadn't really expected one. *Small world? Who said small world anyway?*

To kill some time before, and if, Ryan messaged him back, Freddie did some research on Marc Doyle, and found the same newspaper item that David had already clipped out of the paper. Another search resulted in a grainy photo of a rough-looking man standing in front of a pub, wearing a baseball cap. It was part of a death notification in the *Post*, and it didn't say anything about how he'd died, just that 'he was taken from us too soon'.

Freddie closed his eyes. Marc Doyle *taken from us too soon*; Sally Holloway found dead. *I am not afraid of you because inside me lives god. Tinker. Holes! How could you do that to Tinker?*

When he tried to sleep, his tired brain pawed at Tinker. It meant something to David. Tinker meant enough to David that he still kept up her grave… Lots of people were sentimental about dead pets, but who takes a photo of the grave and keeps it hidden in a wardrobe? Tinker was important. It meant something to Catherine too: *How could you do that to Tinker?*

What *had* David done to Tinker?

CHAPTER TWENTY-NINE

Freddie called in sick again the next morning, and then spent the next few hours slouched in his car, keeping an eye on David's drive. At eleven he saw the BMW turn onto the slip road, Jenny sitting with Catherine in the back, while David drove. He gave them a few minutes, and then made his way through the field to the boundary of David's back garden, his newly bought spade and trowel clinking together. Just through the rustling conifers he could see Tinker's grave. *Holes,* Catherine had said yesterday, and it had to mean something. David kept everything, he was obsessive, secretive, and whatever he'd buried by Tinker's grave must be significant enough to keep, but too disturbing to keep in the house.

It was cold, kneeling in the dirt, and a fine rain fell. Freddie's hands slipped and jarred with the unfamiliar tools. Rain dripped down his back and pooled in his underwear. After half an hour of digging in the wet, resistant earth, he was almost ready to give up when his spade hit something solid with a dull twang, and he knelt, scraping the trowel around the edges of something metal, square, until he was able to thrust his fingers far enough into the soil to touch it, grip it, wiggle it looser.

A tin box, about twelve inches long. The faded picture of playful kittens on the top was damaged, cracked; one of the kitten's faces had warped in the time it had been in the ground, so that the metal bulged at its mouth, distorting its face into a sneer. It was creepy. As he levered and coaxed the box out of the hole, he felt... not vindication, but dread. His mind yammered *no way back now. No way out of it now.* And when the box was out, and sitting next to the mound of earth, it began to rain harder and Freddie, crouched still, the cold seeping into his bones, forced one unwilling hand to drag it a little closer to him, to open it.

The first thing he saw inside was a large grey rock, squarish and broken. It looked like a bit of a paving slab, or a patio block. It rested on top of a plain white carrier bag. Freddie picked up the rock, lay it reverently on the ground, and then opened the bag. The crackling rustle merged with the sound of rain like a sinister whisper. Freddie reached inside and brought out a baseball cap – sweat stains around the headband, and mud stains on the side and the peak. Inside the cap was a knife, about four inches long, still sharp, the blade slightly bent at the very top, and it too was stained with mud. *With mud?*

'Not mud. Blood,' Freddie whispered to himself.

Freddie sat dazed for a minute and then, quickly, took some photographs of the hat and the knife, and then put everything back in the bag in an approximation of how he found it, and pushed it away from himself, telling himself to *bury it again, just bury it, get rid of it.* This seemed imperative. But burying the box was harder than he thought – it seemed that it didn't want to edge back gracefully into the grave it had inhabited for the last few years. Some of the soil had fallen back into the hole, and Freddie had to dig some more, scraping against tree roots with the trowel. He worked for a few minutes, sweating, until the trowel grazed against something – seemed to cut through something. Freddie took out his phone, and used the light to see what it was, and what he saw made him squeal and drop the phone.

It took him a few minutes to recover, and he was still stiff with fear as he put one, unwilling hand into the hole… his index finger brushed against the loathsome thing and he resisted the urge to snatch his hand away, telling himself that it was just bones. Just an animal, long dead. And it had to be moved to make room for the box, it had to be. He put his phone on the ground, took a deep breath and gingerly pushed at the small, fragile skull that had something in it. An oblong of silver foil, carefully folded, pinched in at the ends. Not knowing why, Freddie carefully opened it. Inside, like tiny splinters, were the animal's teeth, sellotaped into two neat rows.

'So that's what he did with Tinker,' he half moaned.

Gritting his teeth, avoiding looking, Freddie spent long, anxious minutes digging to the left of Tinker's remains, making the hole big enough again so that the box might be easily buried again and then jammed it back into the muddy hole. Then he replaced the silver foil in the animal's mouth, and started filling everything up with earth, trying to remember exactly what the ground had looked like before he started digging – there hadn't been that little slope, had there? *Had there?* Put some leaves on it, pat it down. He was faintly aware that he was crying a little now, and the sweat crawled cold on his skin.

Freddie considered staying at his parents' house that night. He felt cold, frightened, and he wanted to be looked after and reassured, but they were bound to notice his muddy clothes, his distraction, and he couldn't trust himself not to tell them everything. He couldn't do that, not before talking to Jenny. So he drove back to the city. The rippling waves of fever rose, and by the time he parked, negotiated the stairs and unlocked his door, he knew he was sick, but he had one more thing to do before he showered, had a well-needed drink and tried to sleep.

He messaged Ryan.

I'm not being stalkery I promise but I need to ask you some questions about David. Please!

Instantly Ryan responded:

Who?
David Crane? He's going out with one of my friends?

There was a pause.

Yes I know David.
How do you know him?
Download this.

Ryan attached a link to an encryption app.

Why?

Ryan was silent for a long time.

I'm only comfortable talking about D if you use this. Only way I can do it.

Freddie did a quick check, but it seemed legitimate enough, so he downloaded it.

I'm back. How do you know David?
I went to school with him. Why?
He says it was university.
Both.
Did he give you a lift to the airport last month?
Yes. Vegas. Why?

Freddie frowned at the screen. None of the flight codes were for Las Vegas. He doubted that their regional airport had any flights to America. As far as Freddie knew, you could only get to Europe and Scandinavia from there...

Do you see a lot of him?
Why?
I'm sorry, it must be really strange me contacting out of the blue again and asking all these questions.

Silence.

Freddie's fear billowed... this had been a mistake. *What was he doing? What if Ryan told David about this? It'd make things worse for Jenny...*

Not spoken to D for a long time. Didn't know he had a girlfriend.

Then:

What's he done now?

'What's he done now'? That indicated that he'd done bad things before... *Tread carefully here, Fred, tread carefully.*

I'm worried about my friend. I found some things?

Long silence.

What kind of things?
Pictures of my friend as a child. And some other things he shouldn't really have of hers.

I can't help you if you don't tell me what kind of things. This has happened before you see.

'Knew it!' Freddie whispered to himself, texted back.

You mean he's done this with another girl before?

Ryan said after a long pause:

Can we meet up somewhere to talk about it? It'd be better than this I think.

OK. Phone me, message me, but please don't tell David about this conversation.

I don't have contact with D any more for various reasons. You know he was in hospital? And he didn't have a stroke?

Yes I worked that out. That's sort of why I'm worried – what if he's had a relapse?

Long pause.

No I don't think it's that. I don't believe he was ever ill, he's the sanest person I've ever met.

Longer pause, and then Ryan said:

I think I can help. I'll call you tomorrow or the day after. Would you be able to meet face-to-face?

For sure.

And Ryan left the conversation.

A second later it disappeared completely.

Freddie only semi-slept that night, sweating through the sheets and existing in a kind of half-world in which he knew he was sleeping, even while he shivered at the end of David's garden, feeling the cold, wet earth on his hands. His flatmate found him wandering about the kitchen in his boxer shorts muttering about buried treasure. He persuaded Freddie back to bed, managed to make him drink some water and take aspirin, and then, at a loss as to what to do next, he called the only person in Freddie's phone he knew the name of. Jenny said she'd be over within the hour.

For what seemed like a long time, Freddie burned and froze, reeled and wilted, and Jenny was there through it all. She sat on a kitchen chair next to his bed, reading. He could see her quiet, delicate profile, her mass of hair, her long slim fingers. She was beautiful. He said so, too, or tried to, but she hushed him, laid one cool palm on his cheek.

'You feel a bit better. Up. Up. Take this.' And he gratefully swallowed cool water. The room was dim, quiet.

'I love you, Jen,' he whispered.

Her face, unsmiling, hazy, hovered above his. 'I know.'

Later he heard her on the phone. She was saying: 'David, listen—' She was pacing the small living room. 'No, just *listen*, will you?' Freddie half raised his head. He wanted to tell her that she didn't need David's permission to do anything, that he wasn't the boss of her. 'No. No! It's more complicated than that...' she was saying.

Freddie fell asleep before he found out what was *more complicated*.

CHAPTER THIRTY

Freddie's fever finally broke, and he woke, crushed and stiff on his sweaty bed. He reached for his phone. Midnight, but what day was it? How long had he been ill? Painfully, he inched up the bed and propped his head up against the mashed-down, still damp pillows. Looking at his phone made him feel more connected, more conscious. Two texts: one from the Canadian – *did he need anything from the pharmacy?* He'd be staying at his girlfriend's. Another from a blocked number. Freddie blinked slowly and opened it.

When can you meet? Ryan

Freddie closed his eyes. The memory of 'Precious Memories!' swilled back in a scummy tide. The knife. The hat. The animal's teeth. He swung his legs over the side of the bed. The world swam up to greet him. After a long minute he was able to totter into the darkened living room, towards the kitchen.

Jenny shifted and woke on the sofa as he wandered back with a glass of orange juice.

'Fred? What time is it?'

'Midnight.' His voice was hoarse. 'How long have I been in bed?'

'Since the night before last.' She sat up, yawned, put the heel of one hand to her eye and rubbed hard. 'I was going to give it till this morning and then take you to the hospital.'

Freddie sat heavily next to her. He could smell the hours of sweat and sickness on his skin. She put a hand on his forehead.

'You feel better. Thank God!'

'How come you're here?' Freddie managed.

'Tyler called me.'

'I'm surprised David let you come.'

'Oh Fred, don't do this—'

'You said you were going to call me to explain things, and you didn't. I didn't know if you were OK... or... or...'

'I wasn't able to call. It... I just couldn't. But I'm here now, Fred. Fred, don't be like this.'

'I'm not being like anything,' he muttered truculently.

'Take a shower, OK? Then we'll talk.'

When he emerged wrapped in towels, she was still sitting primly, neatly, on the sofa, looking into the half distance. Her silenced phone lay on the floor, lit up, vibrating.

'You're not going to answer that?'

'No.' She looked at the screen. They watched as 'David' flashed on and off, on and off and, when the screen dimmed, she turned it over. The face-down phone vibrated again.

'He's not giving up, is he?' Freddie commented. He sat down heavily. Even though the fever had receded, his head still pounded with pain.

'He's worried.' The fake nails had gone. She was worrying at the gnawed edge of her thumb. Bite, look, bite, look. 'He's... he gets very worried about me.'

'Where did you tell him you were?'

'I said Andreena was sick and her kids needed looking after. He doesn't have her number or address, so he can't check. I'm meant to text every hour, but I must've missed it. That's why he's calling all the time,' Jenny said softly, her hands twisting together in her lap.

'You're "meant to text every hour"?'

'He—'

'He's a psycho, Jen,' Freddie said flatly. He was exhausted, in pain, and didn't have the energy to be subtle. 'He's nuts. He's dangerous, and you can't go back to him.'

She looked at him. One tear plopped on to her folded hands 'Don't be horrible, Fred, please. It was hard to come here, but I *did* come. You don't understand how hard it was to leave. He's just been getting more and more... agitated. And he – OK, he's jealous, I can see that now. And maybe he has a *problem* with jealousy. But, I can't abandon him because he has a problem, can I? I mean—'

Freddie let all the air out of his lungs in one exhausted breath. 'Jesus Christ.'

'If I can help him through this, then I *have* to, don't I? I mean...'

And Freddie, so incredibly tired, reached for his own phone. Knowing that what he had to do next would exhaust him even further. 'I've found some things out. I've got some things to show you. Once you see them, I guarantee you that you'll never be going back.'

'But—'

'Shhhh. Take a look at this.'

Half an hour later, they were still sitting on the sofa, the phone between them. Freddie had shown her everything.

Jen was scrolling back and forth, studying the pictures again. She put one trembling finger on her bald baby face 'That's me. It's one of the ones we never got back from Marc after we left him. I don't—'

'What about these train tickets? Does the date mean anything to you?'

'I don't know. I don't know what any of this means,' she answered tonelessly.

'And there's other things that I can't really figure out *what* they mean either, like, these plane times? They're from the date Sal died?' He showed her the hat and the knife. 'He had these buried in the garden. He really really didn't want anyone to find them.'

Jenny was very still. 'Why does he have these?'

'Babe, why does he have any of this stuff? That's Marc's hat, right? And the knife?'

'It's his hat, yes. The knife… no… I haven't seen that before.' But she seemed uncertain.

'Jenny? The knife? Have you seen that before?'

'No.' She sounded more definite now. 'Marc carried knives though. It must have been his.'

'The only thing I found that doesn't seem to fit is this.' He found the photo of the chiffon scarf. 'It must be important to David, but I really can't figure out how. It's not yours, is it?'

When she saw the scarf, her body jerked forward, her hand reached for the phone, plucking it from his fingers. She enlarged the photo with shaking fingers until the muddy stain at the centre separated into pixels, *maybe not mud, though, maybe blood.*

'Jen? Have you seen it before?'

She put the phone down, shook her head. 'No. No. I thought I had, but I haven't.'

'Maybe it's Catherine's?'

'Maybe.'

'But why would he keep it? I really think everything I've found is about *you*. Your photos, your handwriting. I think David's obsessed with you, Jen. I think he's been following you for god knows how long. I mean he has things from years ago – like your baby photo – right up to just before you met him, and he shouldn't have *any* of it. The scarf though… it doesn't fit. You're sure it's not yours?' On the floor, Jenny's phone once again brightened, vibrated. They watched it until it stopped.

'I've never seen it before,' Jenny said then.

'If he's been following you, what if he's been monitoring your phone calls, emails, everything?'

The phone rang again. They looked at each other with serious eyes. Hesitantly she reached for it.

'What're you doing?' Hissed Freddie

'I have to answer. If I don't answer he'll get more suspicious. And what if he comes round here? I *have* to Fred.' She pressed answer 'Hi! Sorry, what time is it?' Her voice was just the right side of sleep-befuddled. She was a good actor when she needed to be. Within David's indistinct mutter – words quickly muddying together – Freddie heard his own name, and Jenny was calm, mollifying, credibly tired. 'No, Not yet. Mmmmm. No, maybe eight? I'll call. I know. I know all that, really.' Her voice was emollient. 'I don't want you to worry. You don't have to worry, OK?'

When she ended the call her composure began to fracture. She said in a shaky voice: 'OK, he's all right. He still thinks I'm at Dree's, but I have to go back tomorrow—'

'What? You're not going back!' Freddie shrieked. His head hurt. 'You're not going back!'

'I've got to. Think about it, Fred. I'm the only person who can talk to him, make him see some sense.'

'No. Not true.' Freddie shook his aching head 'I've been reading a lot about abusive relationships, and everyone says that you should never go back! It's not your job to help him, you can't—'

'There's… more to this though. It's more complicated than that. There's some things I haven't told you—'

'What things? That he's *damaged*? That only you can help him? That's what men like this *do*! They make you feel needed, and… and *beholden* to them. I *knew* it was weird that he just showed up at exactly the right time to give you that alibi,' Freddie interrupted.

'What do you mean by that?' Jenny stared at him.

'I mean it was as if he waited until you were at your most vulnerable, and then swooped in to save the day.'

'I don't know what you mean.' Her lips shook, having trouble meeting to cover her teeth. 'You mean... Mum? He... knows something about that night?'

'I don't know.' Adrenaline and the remnants of fever had swamped his fatigue, but now he felt dizzy again. Weak. 'Maybe it's her scarf? Maybe...' Sick exhaustion stopped him then. Sweat blistered his forehead, and when he closed his eyes a sickening vagueness rushed into his head. 'I don't feel well,' he said to himself.

'Go back to bed,' Jenny told him, sitting as still as a doll while he panted for breath. 'Go back to bed, now.' She walked to the kitchen.

'You have to... we have to do something though, Jen!' he called. 'Please?'

She returned and held out two pills with a glass of water.

'What are these?' He blinked at her, dizzy.

'Paracetamol,' she replied. 'Take them,' she commanded, watched him swallow them with difficulty, and went back to the kitchen to get him another glass of water. 'I need you healthy if you're going to help me,' she told him from the doorway.

'What are you going to do?'

'I'm not sure.' She sat down on the floor.

Freddie pressed the cool glass against one pink cheek. 'Ryan said David was the sanest person he'd ever met. I think it's fair to say that Ryan isn't the best judge of character.'

'Ryan? Ryan *Needham*?' She leaned forward. 'You've *spoken* to him?'

'No. On Facebook.'

'You told Ryan about all this? Jesus, Freddie, why?' She seemed close to panic.

'Because I was *worried* about you!' Freddie said. 'You didn't answer my calls; I found all this shit out about David, and Ryan was the only person I know who knows David. I wanted to get someone else's opinion on this stuff.'

She picked up his phone quickly. 'Can I see what he said?'

'No, he made me use this encryption thing. Then he erased the conversation. Or it automatically erased itself, I don't know. God,' he rubbed his head. 'What were those pills again?'

'Co-codamol. It'll help you sleep.'

'Jen? I think we should call someone. The police? I really think we should.' His eyes were closing.

She looked down at her phone, humming and glowing with David. Then she looked up. 'Not yet. Not yet.'

'Jen—'

'Let's see what Ryan tells us first, OK? Please?'

They curled up together in Freddie's bed, huddled together like children in a storm.

CHAPTER THIRTY-ONE

He slept like the dead, and woke, dry-mouthed and bristly the following morning just before midday.

'Jenny?' His weak voice echoed in his head. He felt hungover. 'Jen?'

She wasn't in the living room. A note was propped up on the coffee table:

> *I called work for you, and told them you have the flu. Don't call me, don't text.*
> *I'll call you later today. Will explain everything I promise.*
> *XOXO*

There was also a message from Ryan.

Can we meet tonight? Narrowboat at 8? There are things about David that I think you should know. I've told Jenny too.
How do you know Jenny? replied Freddie.
Will explain tonight. I want to help. Please don't talk to anyone/ tell anyone about this.

Again, Ryan ended the conversation, and again it was deleted a few seconds later.

CHAPTER THIRTY-TWO

You Can't Go Home Again

[Unpublished post]

I've been walking around all morning. Visiting old haunts that haunt me. I went back to my old house and I knocked on the door. A young girl opened it – she was about ten or eleven. I told her I used to live there, and she shrugged. Why aren't you in school? I asked and she told me she was sick. She had an accent – Eastern European sounding, but she looked at me as if she knew me. She said: 'I like your top' and I thanked her. I said my boyfriend had bought it for me. Do you have a boyfriend? She said no.

Good. I'm glad she said no. I don't know what I would have said if she'd said yes.

A little boy wandered up behind her then, and clung onto her leg. His face was filthy and his nappy sagged with urine. She gazed down at him and rested her hand on the top of his head. That's when I stopped feeling like I was looking in a mirror. I haven't got any brothers or sisters. No cousins, aunts or uncles. Not real ones. No toddler will ever come to me for comfort, pressing his little body into the curve of my waist, to make a neat, tessellating whole. There is No We of Me. Sometimes I doubt if there's even a Me of Me. It feels like there's two parts of me that have never quite met in the middle, like a cleft palate. From a distance I look whole, but I worry that up close, and when I speak, people can see my hidden deformity. Maybe when I was a child it garnered sympathy, but now only disgust. Adults, after all, should be Whole.

David and Freddie don't see it. Cheryl does, a little, but thinks it's curable. Does this make them stupid, or does it mean I'm wrong?

The little girl looked at me with penny-dull eyes. Her brother yawned. I said goodbye abruptly and walked to The Fox, where I ordered a drink I didn't want. I'm sitting there now.

Sometimes people look over at me, in an appraising kind of way. I must look out of place here, with my £500 top and my £80 hair and my careful, practiced make-up. My reflected face swims out of the screen of my phone. Black, then lit with a call. Then black. Then lit.

I don't feel safe. I'm not safe. I thought I was, but I'm not.

Why Ryan? Why Ryan after all these years?

CHAPTER THIRTY-THREE

Throughout the train journey back Jenny stared at her doubled reflection in the grimy window. *Safe Safe Safe* the wheels told her: *you must be safe you must be safe you will you will you will.* Talk to him. Just talk to him, and he'll listen. He'll listen like always. Look, here he is now – David lit and David dark. David Lit. David Dark. David Lit.

She made her voice light. 'Hi! Sorry, have you been worried? The reception at Dree's house is terrible… No. No, listen David, it's not what you think. No. I'm coming home now. I'm nearly home. We'll talk when I get home, OK? Don't be… upset. Please? I can explain.'

*

He was waiting for her at the station when she got off the train. The clock struck two.

She made herself smile at him. A smile says you're in control. A smile hides the ruin within. A smile buys time.

CHAPTER THIRTY-FOUR

Freddie dutifully took the pills that Jenny had left for him, and while his temperature had definitely gone down, he still felt insubstantial, unsteady.

He did as he was told and didn't call her, but God it was difficult. So many times his thumb strayed to her name and hovered, hesitated, retreated. *No, just trust her. She said to trust her. She's not stupid, and now she knows the facts she'll do the right thing. She will.*

However, as time ticked, being alone in the house grew harder to bear. He shouldn't have slept. He shouldn't have let her go. He should tell the police about David, not made her that stupid promise…

*

He killed time by having another long shower, and when he got out, he saw that he had a missed call from her. No message though. Surely that meant he could call? He pressed her name with one shaking finger, held the phone next to his hot skin, and listened to it ring ring ring itself out. When he tried again it had been turned off.

He closed his eyes then, feeling dizzy, feeling sick. Something bad had happened… it must have done… he imagined her hiding, maybe somewhere in that huge house; suddenly her phone rings, and David, incensed, follows the sound, finds her…

A few seconds later he got a text from an unknown number.

It's Jen, I'm using this phone. DON'T call the other one! Will
explain later. Have you heard from Ryan?
Yes, where are you? Is everything OK?
I'm with him now. Lot's happened but need to tell you face-
to-face… don't worry though we're both safe.
Meet now then? Come here?
We're driving. Narrowboat nearer and yours might not be
safe. Will explain I promise XOXO
What's happening????

She didn't reply.

His imagination, sluggish with fatigue, slid further into fear.
Jenny and Ryan, speeding towards the city, white with terror,
bristling with evidence, David in hot pursuit. And all Freddie could
do was wait. Shrugging on his coat, he left the flat, and started to
walk to the pub on the other side of town.

The mist that had receded during the day was rolling back in from
the hills to the city, and even though he dawdled as much as he
could, he still arrived at the virtually empty pub half an hour early.
The same cute little barman was serving, and he did the same cute
little thing with drinks – a double gin for the price of a single,
which Freddie took before thinking that he probably shouldn't be
drinking when he was ill and taking those pills Jenny had given him.

He texted the number Jenny had called from.

I'm here now.

There was no reply.

Are you OK Jen? What happened?

No answer.

Knowing he shouldn't, he called her, but the phone was turned off. *Don't panic, Fred, don't panic. Doesn't mean anything. Could have run out of battery… she could be in a tunnel or something. Who knows.* He drank another gin – too quickly – feeling the effects almost immediately.

Then Ryan messaged him:

Is Jenny with you?
No! She was with you, wasn't she? What's happened?
We got separated she said she was coming to see you, look around for her.
She's not here I would've seen her what's happened?
Find her!
What's happening?

Then the whole conversation deleted itself.

CALL ME!

He texted Jenny, and almost immediately his phone buzzed with her message back:

Come and get me something bad's happened I'm under the canal bridge behind the pub please come now!

And Freddie put his phone away and dashed to the back door. The cold hit him with an almost physical force and the gin and pills made him more unsteady. The steps to the towpath were slippery. The canal was black and still as tar.

Freddie's heart sped up. His face glittered with heat. Sickness and fear combined.

'Jen?' he called and his voice sounded young, so young to his own ears. 'Jenny?'

QUIET!

Ryan messaged:

I've found her. Please hurry!

The side of the bridge showed abruptly through the fog.
Ryan told him:

I can see you, stay there.

And Freddie did. The gentle lap of the water was close, in the distance, music, and then, behind him, was Ryan.

Freddie didn't feel the knife in his back and, spinning around clumsily, he didn't feel it in his chest either – four stab wounds in total the police counted later. He was too busy looking at the face of his attacker. His eyes widened, his mouth opened as if to speak, and then folded in on itself, primly, like an old maid, and, quickly, he slipped into cold blankness. Cold water. And then he felt nothing at all.

AFTER

CHAPTER THIRTY-FIVE

You Can't Go Home Again

Hi.

This is the hardest thing I've ever had to write.

Today I found out that my good friend – my closest friend – is dead.

I'm writing it down so I can understand it. If I fix it to a screen and pin it down with punctuation, then this horrible fact will stay still long enough for me to comprehend it.

Is it strange to want to write? Should I... what should I be doing? What can I do?

His father called me this morning. I've known him since I was sixteen, and yet I didn't recognise his voice, he sounded so old, lost. Dazedly polite. So sorry to wake me... I heard the pause, and the whistle of approaching tears – the same sound my own lips made when I made my own calls after Mum died. I knew then. I knew. And my mind filled with a mosquito-like whine, and the world dipped dizzily, like there'd been an altitude shift, a drop in normal pressure.

I went to their house, and sat stiffly on the sofa between them. Catatonic Mother and emptied-out Father and I didn't have a thing to offer them. No way of making them feel better, only ways of making it worse. But I sat and I held their hands and hoped to God I could – I don't know – stop everything that had happened. Go back a few months... Hell, go back a few years. Start over.

I went to the mortuary with them. My friend was in the same room as my mum had been. The same greasy glass. But not a purple robe, just an off-white sheet. I think his mother had a tiny hope that, with me there, three would be the charm, that the combined force of our grief would reverse this terrible wrong and it wouldn't be our loved one there, on the slab, marbled white and pink. No. It would be someone else's darling, someone else's tragedy – nothing that we would have to own. I would have to own.

On the way out I ran to the toilet to be sick, rested my head on the toilet seat and, for a tiny moment I felt like I was back at Mum's, on that morning, the policeman hovering outside asking if I was OK.

When I opened the door, my friend's parents were standing waiting for me, looking like lost children. Do they think I know the ropes, that I can do this Death thing for them? For a second my body tensed. Then I took their hands, and we wandered to the automatic doors, the blind leading the blind.

Theehedgewitch: sorry for your loss

HollybFootitt: *hugs*

SExyStace: Don't blame yourself hun? Why you think your too blame? Can't turn back time.

Laundryloony2: stop everything that's happened?

CHAPTER THIRTY-SIX

Notes for Cheryl

The blind leading the blind.
That was disingenuous.
I'm not blind. I haven't been for a long time. I just didn't want to see, that's all. But now, after what's happened to Freddie, I don't have a choice. I've been forced to see just how little control I have.
I wasn't honest. I wasn't truthful. I kept a lot from Freddie: my phone going missing, then breaking – messages deleted, suddenly out of battery. My possessions disappearing, and showing up later, just slightly out of place. Everything I'd allowed to be blamed on Matt could have been (was?) David all along: all a ruse to make me feel unsafe where I was safe, to prod me into moving voluntarily into the least safe place possible. If I'd told Freddie about how bad things are in the house, how bad they've been for weeks, he'd have MADE me leave, I know he would have. I would have moved in with him, and he'd still be alive. I didn't tell him that David locks the doors from the outside. How sometimes, when I drink the special 'energy' smoothies he makes for me, I pass out and wake hours later. Sometimes still fully clothed and stiff because I haven't moved, sometimes I'm naked and bruised. How Catherine – scared, lonely Catherine – pleads with him to be kinder. To let her see more of That Nice Girl. That's

what she calls me now: That Nice Girl who helps with pills.
'Can't I watch TV with That Nice Girl?' but David keeps
her locked in her room more and more. I hear her crying
sometimes, but I don't dare go to her.

The poor woman's mind is perilously adrift, and her only
mooring point is David. David the loving son. David the
perfect boyfriend. David who, I'm only just beginning to
understand, has done some terrible things.

I used all sorts of excuses: David's just protective of me;
David is socially anxious; David is in recovery; David is
tired/stressed/traumatised…

David's made a coward out of me.

Time to stop that. Time to face facts.

David isn't well. David is ill. David is…

Dangerous.

Freddie deserves to be honoured with the truth. What I'm
writing now is the real truth. My hope is that I'll somehow
be able to leave, get out of the house with all these notes
intact, go to the police and tell them everything. But, in the
meantime, I have to keep David happy and calm. That way,
I have a chance. If I don't, then what happened yesterday
will happen again.

Freddie wasn't the first person David has killed.

When Freddie showed me the hat, I knew it was Marc
Doyle's. I recognised it straight away. Freddie thought
that David has been stalking me for years. Could that
be true? How else would he have any of these things?
But even then, I believed and didn't believe. I thought I
could… fix things.

So I came back. I left Freddie sleeping, hopped on a train
and thought that, somehow… when I saw David, I'd be
able to fix everything. Stupid.

He was waiting for me at the station. He didn't ask about Andreena's children, but I volunteered a lot of information anyway. Perhaps I overdid it? Perhaps that's what made him suspicious? He was quiet in the car, distracted, and when we got back to the house, he took me by the elbow, steered me into the kitchen. That's when he told me that he knew I hadn't been at Andreena's.

I paused. 'Yes I have,' I managed, unconvincingly.

He shook his head. He started to cry. He told me how much he loved me; how much he had trusted me. He'd opened his house, his heart, to me, and look how I repaid him? What did I have to say for myself?

'Freddie was sick,' I managed. 'I had to look after him, and I knew that if I told you, you wouldn't let me go ...'

'Wouldn't let you?' He opened his eyes in wide, exaggerated pain. 'How can I stop you from doing anything?' He sat back in his chair. His tears had all dried up. 'You know what hurts? You know what he thinks of me, and you go there anyway. What lies did he tell you about me this time?'

'It's not lies, David. I've seen—' I stopped.

'Seen what?'

I should have stopped there. Stupid. But I was angry, tired of being bullied, wrong-footed. I wanted to knock him off balance with the truth. 'Freddie found some things,' I blurted. 'I had to stay to talk to him about it.'

'What things?'

I wised up then. I didn't mention the hat or the knife. I told him that Freddie was still worried about David's stay in Hazlewood, that it had taken me all night to finally make Freddie understand that David only suffered from an anxiety disorder, that he didn't have to worry about me.

'So, does that mean he'll stop snooping on me?' David asked.

'Yes,' I replied. 'That's why I stayed over with him, to make absolutely sure that he understood about Hazlewood, and he wouldn't ever bring it up or upset you.'

David seemed satisfied with that. 'And he didn't say anything else? Only about Hazlewood?'

I managed to look puzzled. 'No. Why? What else would there be to find?'

That made him back off a little. My plan was to call Freddie once I was safely alone, like I'd promised, so I told David that I was going to take a shower and have a nap. When David left the room though, I couldn't find my phone. He walked in on me downstairs, hunting for it.

'Your phone? Is it not here? Maybe it dropped out in the car. No, you have your shower and I'll find it for you.'

What could I do? If I insisted on looking for the phone myself he'd get suspicious. So I said, thanks. Yes. I'll have a shower. Thanks.

I stood under the spray until the water went cold and, when I came out, David was there. He handed me my phone – it was on the drive – it must have fallen out of my pocket. The battery was completely dead. He'd put it on to charge while I had my nap. He told me I looked pale, that he was worried about me. 'I made you one of my smoothies,' he said. 'Superfoods. Spinach, banana, pomegranate…' He sat me down and watched me drink every last drop of it. Whatever it was he put in the smoothie hit me hard. I felt dizzy, sick. He told me to lie down, rest, and tucked me into bed like a child. As I lapsed into unconsciousness, I understood how much I'd underestimated him. I thought he'd believe me. I thought I still had some kind of power over him, but no. David had, efficiently, ruthlessly, proved me wrong.

*

When I woke up it was dark, and my limbs and head were heavy, drugged. I managed to get to the door; it was locked, but David hadn't taken the key. I beat on the door with my feeble fists until I heard Catherine stirring.

'Catherine, can you unlock the door?' I shouted. 'Just follow the sound of my voice.'

She looked scared when she opened the door. She said that David was upset. Why was he upset?

'Is he in the house?' I asked.

She shook her head, then nodded, then smiled.

'Catherine? Please? Is he in or out?'

But she just stood there until I led her back downstairs and into her room. Every step I took exhausted me more. I was wavering at the bottom of the stairs when David came in through the back door. His skin was cold, and he smelled of earth. I panicked. I didn't want to get Catherine into trouble. I stammered out that I'd made her unlock the door, that it wasn't her fault, that—

'Shhh,' he said. 'The door wasn't locked. Why would I lock the door?' I looked in his eyes, and there was nothing there but sincerity. Did he believe what he was saying? 'I think you're ill. You're not thinking straight. I think you caught Freddie's cold. Go back to bed.' He took me by my elbow, led me back to the stairs.

'Freddie – I said I'd call him,' I said.

He shook his head then. 'It's far too late for that.'

'What do you mean?'

'It's 1 a.m. What do you think I meant?' He frowned gently at me. 'You're ill. You're feverish. Go back to bed and I'll bring you some aspirin.'

He gave me some more pills. I tried not to take them; I said that I felt a lot better, but he smiled, shook his head, and had me swallow them, and sat with me until they began to take effect. As I was falling back to sleep, I heard the key in the door turn again. Then it was morning. My phone was on the bedside table, fully charged. That's what woke me up. Graham, calling with the news.

*

David let me post on the blog, but he watched me do it, and then took the computer away, along with my phone. He didn't want me to be upset or disturbed, he told me. For a while we sat on the sofa, watching/not watching the news, and I could feel him glancing at me, squeezing my cold hand. He wanted to know, what could he do to help?
'You're right. I'm ill,' I told him. 'I'll go to bed.'
He liked me telling him he was right. He liked it so much he didn't give me any more of those pills, and that's how I managed to stay conscious, write all of this down on scraps of paper. If I write it all down, I have some kind of… testimony. If anything happens to me, these notes will signal the truth. I have to find a good hiding place. And if I manage to get out of here, I'll give it all to Cheryl. He doesn't know where she lives. Plus, I made sure to tell him we weren't friends any more. I even used his insult about her: I called her a snake-oil merchant, and he liked that.

*

I hid each paper in a different place all around the room – stuffed into the toes of shoes, rolled up inside the curtain pole, between the mattress and the bed. If he finds one page, that would be bad, but he can't find them all. This is my insurance policy.
I told him that I felt much better, that it would be best if I kept busy. No point moping. He approved of that. If I

seem matter of fact, stoic, there's a chance he'll let me out of the house. He needs me awake and active anyway because Catherine isn't well, and she won't let him tend to her. She's skittish and fearful – probably because she's heard me crying over Freddie. She knows something is wrong. I'm the only person she trusts at the moment. – David always told me that's one of the reasons he loves me so much; I'm so patient with his mother. He's jealous of that, I can tell. He's jealous of our bond, hurt that she fears him, angry that when she does speak, she only speaks to me. The angrier he gets, the more frightened she becomes until I gently ask him to leave her with me: I'll calm her down. And when we're alone, in her own way, she tells me a lot. On the night Freddie was killed, the night David drugged me and locked me in the room, she heard him leave in the car, returning 'a while later'. 'How much later?' I asked, but in her poor, fogged mind, it wasn't later at all. It was eight. They watched University Challenge together. Tony was there. He'd borrowed Tony's old Beetle, and, since I was a guest, did I need a lift to the seaside? I got her into bed, and held her hand. Just before she fell asleep, she looked straight at me. Her eyes were more lucid than I'd ever seen them. A stuttering, frustrated determination seemed to energise her.

'You must take care of yourself, Jenny,' she said.

She's never used my name before, and it seemed to take the last of her strength, and she fell asleep while I was still holding her hand.

I'm still in her room now, writing at her desk, using her old lavender-coloured notepaper.

I have to take care of myself, but I also have to keep Catherine safe. She's my responsibility. She's my family now.

*

It was blustery, cold the next morning. All night long the wind had bothered Catherine; the rhythmic scrape of branches against the panes, the sudden clatter of rain on the windowpanes woke her and kept her awake. By 9 a.m. she was quiveringly nervous, refusing tea, toast, countering each offer with the querulous demand. 'How could you do that to Tinker?'

I managed to give her her pills and, by midday, she was a little calmer. She even agreed to wash her face and clean her teeth, and I walked with her to the bathroom, keeping up a comforting murmur.

Then, somehow, she must have tripped.

I can't write about this now, I don't have the time. They're waiting for me downstairs. David's shouting for me.

CHAPTER THIRTY-SEVEN

Jenny's scream was loud enough to reach David at the other end of the house. Catherine was spread on the bathroom tiles, one leg twisted and exposed all the way up to her buttock, bulging varicose veins showing. There was blood in her hair, in her ear, blood on the lid of one terrified eye – fixed, staring. As soon as she saw David she panicked, howled, tried to get up.

'No, Catherine, no!' Jenny told her. 'You might have broken something. You might have a concussion. Just stay there. David? David!' she shouted sharply. 'Call an ambulance now. Now!'

She stayed with the older woman, kept up that murmur, gently stroked her hair and crooned, until the paramedics arrived.

David was hysterical. He got in their way even as he shouted at them to *hurry, hurry! She's in there – there I said!* His fear made Catherine cry. His aggression made the paramedics question whether they should even let him come to the hospital at all. Jenny – the calm centre of the storm – was the one who guided the stretcher out of the house, saw them all out safely, soothed Catherine as the oxygen mask was slipped over her face – *don't try to talk, don't try to talk* – before dashing back to collect her coat and lock the front door. Back in the darkness of the ambulance, she took up her accustomed place next to Catherine.

'You're going to be fine,' she told her slowly. 'Just took a tumble. That's all. Going to be fine.' As she ducked down further, her long hair, loose, fell over her face, and she smiled gently, reassuringly. 'Just a tumble. Just a fall. Don't worry. Don't try to talk.'

*

At the hospital, when David's attention was completely occupied with doctors, Jenny excused herself to go to the toilet, and walked away; first, at normal speed, but then, once she was back in the lobby, quicker. The fear showed on her face as she weaved through the throng of tired nurses, jaded doctors and the worried well. By the time she was at the exit, she was running.

BEFORE

CHAPTER THIRTY-EIGHT

David. Eight Years Earlier

David could never remember the date. Strange, it was the most important thing that had ever happened to him, *would* ever happen to him. It must have been after Christmas because it was still cold, but the decorations in the school hall had been taken down, and that ghastly fake snow had been wiped off the windows. He was sitting next to Francis Brennan. He remembered that, because Francis always sat fractionally too close, and the smell of him made David sweat. The date on the board said…? February? Valentine's Day? Why not? That was fitting. It was Valentine's Day.

The girl was standing outside the class doors. Her new blazer was too big. Her skirt, not new, was shiny on the seat. Her remarkable hair hid her face from the form tutor, Mr Bream, and the head, Mr Jackson. Both men were smiling down at her.

Francis nudged him. 'New girl,' he said. And winked.

As if Francis liked girls.

David had shuffled his chair away from Francis again then; he did every minute or so, in tiny increments, until his chair stuck out into the aisle. He turned to the door once more.

Girls around him were doing the same, while the boys shrugged and turned to each other, laughing, the noise increasing each minute, until the dull roar caused Mr Bream to open the door and cough sharply.

Jenny Holloway. New. Welcome. Fit in well. Seat next to Jeanine Finney.

Jenny walked to her seat, just across the aisle from David.

Jeanine Finney patted the chair next to her with a kind of queenly largesse, and David heard her asking if she'd just moved here, and Jenny was saying yes, last week.

'She's half-caste, I think? Isn't she?' Francis said then, and his voice, like everything else about Francis, was insultingly difficult to ignore. David froze. Jeanine stiffened and smiled embarrassedly, seemed to shrink into her blazer. Even Francis seemed to register the atmosphere, but, as usual, he made a bad thing worse.

'Not being racist. David? Wasn't being *racist*.' His whisper was louder than any whisper ought to be. For a fraction of a second David allowed himself to look directly at Jenny – it was an assault on his senses. She smelled of apples and cinnamon, her skin glowed with an inner light, and her hair was a golden cloud of spun sugar. He also saw how her cheeks burned with shame, he registered that her toes, in her flimsy new school shoes, curled, and one small hand clamped to the side of the table, the knuckles white, and right from that first moment, David knew exactly what she was thinking. She was about to run. To cry. And she'd hate herself for crying, he could tell.

Francis tittered, nudged David – 'Dark meat is so sweet.'

David saw her flinch, saw one foot arch, as if she was about to get up and bolt, and he knew what he had to do.

He picked up Francis's compass from the table and jammed it into his thigh, pushing forward, and jerking it up because that was the way to cause maximum damage. He'd seen it once on a TV drama about the SAS. It was a very effective technique: Francis paled, then purpled. His shriek was high-pitched enough to cause the class to laugh, but, when it went on, and it became obvious how hurt Francis really was, the laugh petered out into excited murmurs. David gave the compass one more vicious push for good luck, pulled it out of Francis' flesh and put it in his pocket. Then he leaped up, backed away from his table, and made himself look shocked watching the spread of blood pan across Francis's meaty thigh, drip down his knee and drop-drop-splat onto the floor. Good job he'd stood up quickly, because the blood could easily have got onto his own trousers, and he knew from experience that blood was a bugger to get out...

Mr Bream muscled his way over. Francis was examined, the students babbled and, in the ensuing panic, Jenny was able to relax without anyone else peering at her and making comments.

It was the first favour he ever did for her. It still made him proud.

David was very calm as he was led away by the head teacher. He dropped the bloody compass beside the bins in the cafeteria and, during his grilling, he was able to say, truthfully, calmly, that he had no weapon on him.

'You can search me.'

'So Francis stabbed himself? Is that what you're saying?' The head teacher, relatively new to the job, reminded David slightly of Lenin. He had that same waxy sheen about him, the same pomposity. He wore cufflinks too, which David thought was absurd.

'Mr Jackson, I can't, hand on heart, tell you *what* happened.' David made his face furrow. *Hand on heart?* was that a phrase a normal boy would use? He leaned forward slightly. Just having a man-to-man, conversation. They were both reasonable people, weren't they? 'Francis... well, I hate to tell you, but Francis has... God, this is awkward.'

Mr Jackson was interested, he could tell, but he wasn't letting the stern head teacher mask slip yet. 'Spit it out!'

'Francis… he *touches* himself.' David let himself blush. 'Down there, you know.' He nodded with solemn significance.

A shiver of distaste passed over Mr Jackson's face. 'Go on.'

David paused. He hunched into his school blazer, making himself look smaller, more vulnerable, ashamed. 'I don't really want to, sir. I don't want to get him in even more trouble.' David was good at that. Turning things around with such deftness that the victim became the perpetrator and vice versa. It was dizzying. It was one of his major talents.

'David,' Mr Jackson's face was still stern but slightly less angry, 'we're not going to get anywhere if you don't tell me the truth.' He paused. David waited. 'What was Francis doing?'

There! He'd got him. They were talking about Francis doing something now, not David. Now he could relax and have a bit of fun 'When the new girl came in?' He peeped out from under his eyebrows. 'Francis… Francis got very… excited. If you know what I mean.' He noted Mr Jackson's wince. 'I sit next to him. I think Mr Bream thinks that if Francis sits next to a boy he won't get… you know… excited.'

Wince. Hands in steeple shape. Voice quiet. 'Go on.'

'Lately he's been doing this thing – I think he thinks it's funny? When he gets… excited? He sort of mimes punching himself – down there.' David shook his head bleakly. 'I've tried to tell Mr Bream about it, but—'

'And have any of your classmates seen this… behaviour?'

David shook his head with all honesty. 'I don't think so. Francis sits by the wall, you know. He's hidden from the rest of the class. It's only me who has to… see what's going on.'

Mr Jackson sighed. 'Go on. The new girl?'

David blushed again. It wasn't hard to blush; he wasn't faking it. All he had to do was think of Jenny. 'The new girl, she had to pass our desk, and when she passed, Francis said something… racist.'

David swallowed. Pebbles of indignation rumbled and bubbled beneath the smooth stream of his voice. He looked up. 'He said something about her being a "half-caste"? I'm not sure what it means, but I *think*...' Mr Jackson winced again, and David nodded sadly. 'And then he said something even worse. Awful.'

'What was that?' For the first time Mr Jackson considered David with sympathy, with respect. 'Don't be afraid, just tell me.'

'He was... excited. Really excited, you know? And when she passed he said: "Dark meat is sweeter" and he kind of did that punch himself thing? That he does as a joke? But he had a compass in his hand. He mustn't have noticed.'

The silence lay heavy when he stopped talking, and David let it. This could go either way, he judged. Mr Jackson could either side with Francis Brennan – a fat little prick on the autistic spectrum who gave everybody in the school the creeps, or with David – a volunteer hall monitor, a decent student, an all-round good-egg with no history of violence.

'You're sure that's what happened?' Mr Jackson rested his pompous, serious gaze on David's face. 'This is a serious accusation, David.'

David nodded solemnly. 'I know. And, look, for what it's worth I really don't think Francis can help it. Touching himself. It's like an addiction or something but, more than that, he doesn't understand...' He let his voice trail off.

'Social cues?'

David nodded. 'He just has problems with things like that. But the racism? I mean, nobody can condone the racism, can they?'

Mr Jackson shook his head, his jowls swinging, 'Absolutely not.'

'But, sir, about Francis... please don't come down too hard on him. And, if it's easier for the school to blame *me* for what happened, then I'm willing to carry the can.' He squared his shoulders in a way that he knew made him look both brave and touchingly young.

Mr Jackson smiled then, and David knew it was all over. 'David, don't be silly. There's no way you're taking the blame for something you didn't do.'

'But I really don't want Francis to get into trouble,' David said anxiously.

'This isn't your problem, David. And I'll speak to Mr Bream, see if we can't get you moved next to someone else.'

He was allowed to leave then. He made sure to drift by the cafeteria and pick up the compass. When he got back to the classroom, Francis's blood was only a ruddy smear on the floor. Francis, himself, was absent.

Later, in the lunch hall, he saw Jenny sitting with Jeanine Finney and her friends. She was absolutely dazzling! Looking at them together, David couldn't understand how and why he'd had a crush on Jeanine for such a long time. Next to Jenny she looked strangely lumpy and skittish, like an overbred horse. Even her laugh sounded like a neigh...

He sat down at the next table, with Jake Shearsmith and a few other people from his form.

'What happened with Francis?' Jake asked.

David made a brief wanking motion, shrugged, whispered: 'Self-harm or something.'

'That's some sick shit,' Jake grimaced happily. 'Did he, like, have it out and everything?'

On the next table, Jeanine was asking Jenny more about where she lived. Her answer was too soft for him to catch, but Jeanine's braying reply – 'Oh, the new builds?' – told him everything he needed to know. He hoped hard that Jenny didn't pick up on the curl of pity and disdain in Jeanine's voice.

She was such a bitch.

'Dave?' Jake again. *Dave.* David hated being called Dave.

David nodded, cracked a smile, 'Forgot he was holding a compass.'

Jake, delighted, hooted with laughter, and by the end of the day the whole school buzzed with the knowledge that Francis Brennan – you know, the weird fat one? The one who lives with his nan and says he has an IQ of 150? – stab-wanked himself in maths class.

CHAPTER THIRTY-NINE

'I can't imagine what was going through his mind.' That afternoon, Mother's voice was whimsical and amused; it was her three-glass-mood. 'He could have nicked one of his testicles.'

'Mum…' – David pointed at his eggs on toast – 'I'm trying to eat.'

'Well, he *could* have. Or an artery. Tony, isn't there an artery down there?'

Tony considered this. 'Maybe? They're everywhere, aren't they? Arteries?'

'Can you pour me another? Chablis? Fridge? No, really. I can't understand it. And you've been sitting next to this boy for how long?'

'All year,' David replied through a mouthful of egg.

'And you never thought to mention it?'

'Maybe he liked it,' Tony put in. 'Nothing wrong with it—'

'In school, Tony? Be serious.'

'I didn't like sitting next to him,' David said tightly. 'I never liked it.' Having almost convinced himself that the wanking story was genuine, he felt genuinely aggrieved that Tony was making light of his traumatic experience.

'Well what's happening to the boy now then?' she asked. 'Is he excluded or…?'

'Cold showers and shock treatment. That's what they used to do in my day!' put in Tony. 'The poor boy's probably being psychoanalysed to death somewhere right now… *tell me about your mother*?'

David picked up his plate, put it in the dishwasher. He liked to keep things clean. 'I'm going out.'

'It's freezing out there, though, David?'

'I need fresh air.'

As he left he heard her tell Tony: 'Do you know, I think this episode has really got to him.'

'Well, cheer up. There's every chance that this Francis boy will end up like Jeffrey Dahmer. David will be able to say, I was there at the beginning! Sell his story. Get a book deal—'

'Stop being glib. Is that bottle finished?'

'*Au naturellement.*'

'Is there another in the fridge?'

'*Bien sûr.*'

'Chop chop then!'

Mother was right, it was freezing outside, and David had left wearing only his school clothes. He didn't want to go back to the house and see Tony again, so he went to the garage and put on one of his father's tweed jackets – the one he used to garden in. Gratifyingly, it almost fit, perhaps it was a bit long on the sleeves, but that wasn't too noticeable. David enjoyed wearing Piers's clothes; he felt closer to him when he did. Sometimes he'd notice, and say something wry like 'The clothes maketh the man', or 'I'm sure I've seen that jacket somewhere before?' Whenever this happened, David felt a great contented warmth. He and his father had a very strong, unspoken bond. The only thing that would damage this bond – in David's mind – would be embarrassment. David hated the idea of embarrassing his father; after all, Mum did enough of that… but that was Tony's fault, not hers. Never hers.

David made his way down the drive and into the main village, quite a large village, and larger still since the new houses had been built on the northern edge. They weren't council houses but they *looked* like council houses, and David knew that, for some reason, that was A Bad Thing. Father had been one of those on the parish council who had vociferously lobbied to have the plans rejected, and when he failed, he had resigned. He missed it though, David could tell. It had kept him away from the house, away from Tony. Now he had spare time, but he spent more and more time at work, or in his study. Tony had usurped him. David felt very sorry for his father because of that.

On the way to Jenny's estate, he thought over the events of the day. What he'd done interested him because it had illuminated a talent for violence he didn't know he had.

David wasn't violent by nature; he wasn't impetuous or tormented enough to be violent. What he did have was a deep-rooted dislike of bad manners. What Francis had said for example – yes, it was racist, unwelcoming, and just plain weird; but for David, the bigger offence was that it was simply *bad form* to say those sorts of things, to pick on the different, to mark them out. Usually David suffered silently through other people's social foibles, but today was different. Today, David had Acted. He'd set right a wrong, and he'd got away with it. Something fundamental had shifted: in stabbing Francis, and saving Jenny from further embarrassment, he felt as if he had passed some crucial test, and the gates to his new calling were creaking open, slowly slowly, exposing a path he never even knew existed. A very Significant Day that would definitely make it into 'Precious Memories!' Perhaps overshadow every 'Precious Memory' he had.

David turned right through the graveyard that ran parallel to the main street. Crossing the street, he passed the Rose and Crown – where Mum and Tony would be later, hunkered down hilariously in the snug. Then he followed the stream, past the bakery, down to a small bridge which led to Dene's Walk, the new builds, and behind them, the hills.

Then he paused for a few minutes, thinking about Jenny, making her solid in his mind.

She was a thin girl, with long legs and no tits to speak of. But it wasn't right to think things like that. That wasn't nice. Start again.

She was slim, not thin. Her hair had been pulled back into a ponytail, curly, and filled with strange colours, tawny, yellowish, gold. Her skin was – olive – he supposed you'd call it. A uniform, beautiful, matte olive, and next to her, everyone – even the acknowledged beauties of the school like Jeanine Finney – were pale, pockmarked. Criminally ordinary.

Where had she come from? It was a strange time of year to start a new school. She must have come from the city. Or abroad? He already knew that he was going to watch her, because he liked her so much already. David rarely interacted with the people he really liked; he just watched them, either on TV or in real life, thought about them, knew that he liked them, and left it at that. They didn't have to be friends or anything. The irascible man who owned the Chinese take-away, for example – David liked him; he liked the way he pretended not to speak or understand English; he liked the way he feigned deafness when his squeaky daughter shouted the orders at him, but he'd never spoken to the man, and, save for ordering chow mein – he was training himself to eat Chinese food; he didn't like it, but it was all part of his training – he'd never spoken to the daughter either. When he heard the man on the phone in the kitchen, heard that his English was fine – he even had a slight estuary accent – David was enormously pleased, and the man went to the top of his 'Like' list.

He paused at the end of the close. Looking around at the new houses, he understood his father's offended dismay. Tiny, boxy, weak-looking things with windows set high and narrow like peevish eyes in a stupid face. The bricks were the nasty colour of oatmeal, and each identical door was topped by an improbable, flimsy-looking awning in plastic-coated wood. Each had a frosted glass window at the top where the bathroom was. Each had a patch of grass, about a few metres square, in front of the door, like a sad little welcome mat. The streets meandered around in concentric semicircles, but there was a spur of land to the east that jutted out of the pattern. All David had to do was work out what house she lived in – look for signs of moving: boxes, packing crates, bright lights shining through curtainless windows. Rooms emptily messy with unpacked belongings.

He closed his eyes, and Jenny, already buried down into the soft tissue of his brain, like a tick, led him down the middle of the deserted road towards exactly the scene he'd pictured – squashed boxes stacked carelessly in the desiccated front garden of the last house on the left.

On the rare occasions that David did something impetuous, the same phrase would canter through his mind – *Don't think, do. Don't think, do.* That's what he was hearing when he plunged the compass into Francis, and that's what he was hearing now too. He closed his eyes again then, opened them, and turned back, dodged between the houses, crossed the end of the neighbour's garden, and headed to the hills. There he found a kind of grassy nook between two rocks that not only sheltered him from the cold, it also allowed him to see a little bit of what he was sure was Jenny's door and kitchen window, while still being hidden himself.

Like always, his instincts had not let him down. He could only see one person in the house – Jenny's mother, he assumed. The TV was loud. Loud enough to upset him, even at this distance. He needed to work harder on that. It was a weakness that could easily trip him up if he wasn't careful.

He waited in the cold for an hour before hearing the sigh and squeak of worn tyres. Illuminated by the security light, he could see that

Jenny's hair had escaped her ponytail and was drifting, beautifully, around her pink cheeks. He could see her breath steaming, the light quiver of her slim fingers. He heard her tired grunt as she got off the saddle and leaned it against the wall. She wasn't wearing her school uniform any more. *Where had she been?*

'Mum?'

His flesh thrilled with the sound of her voice! Slightly gruff, throaty, with a local accent, but not harsh, not grating. Unconsciously David half stood up, to be closer to her, to hear her more clearly. *Don't think, do.* And he scuttled closer to the house, into the garden, and crouched behind the bins below the kitchen window. If he made any noise, the sound of the TV would mask it.

'Where've you been?' the mother was saying. Through the open window, smoke billowed from her cigarette. 'I've been worried.' She didn't sound very worried. The TV laughed and laughed and laughed, and David's chest felt hot and his head started to throb. The woman shut the window then, and they must have moved into another room. Though he waited for another quarter of an hour, he couldn't hear anything else intelligible from the house because the TV was on too loudly, and the noise was almost a physical assault. *Why so loud?*

When he got up, his head hurt and his legs were stiff with the cold. He'd need thicker trousers for next time, gloves too. Noise training too. If it was going to be this loud every time, he'd have to toughen up.

David made his way back between the houses, and onto the street. He breathed great gulps of silence, imagining it running down his throat, into his organs, his bones and filling him with calm. *Calm calm calm.* In the middle of the road, he found a pink Post-it note, like a crushed butterfly, and picked it up, knowing that it was important. *Calm now, very, very calm, but alert too... he was doing splendidly.*

He put it carefully in his pocket, and hurried home. As he passed the Rose and Crown, he heard his mother's whoop whoop of a laugh, inevitably followed by Tony's dirty snigger. His fingers caressed the Post-it note, curled in his pocket like a fortune cookie. He'd look at it tomorrow, after his training. He'd know what it meant then.

CHAPTER FORTY

The next afternoon, David returned from school, to find the house uncharacteristically cluttered and noisy. Usually, at this time, he had the place to himself, but today someone was fixing the dishwasher, and someone else was fixing the hole in the roof of the summer house that Tony had tried to repair himself, but only managed to make bigger. Tony himself was loafing about the house, trying to make conversation with the dishwasher repairman (embarrassing! With his silly faux accent and his... dramatic... pauses...). This meant that David would have to be very, very careful. His planned activities – music training, organising Precious Memories and making a Future Plan, demanded absolute concentration. Knowing that anyone else was in the house could easily derail the whole thing.

Fortunately, David's room at the top of the house in the attic, looking over the garden, was very quiet. The white walls – he'd insisted on white walls when his mother had decorated the rest of the house in that dreadful terracotta colour – were blank, pictureless. He owned no books, no ornaments. There was no room for sentiment – all his battered toys were in his old bedroom the floor below. The carpet was beige. The bedspread was white and beige, and David washed it himself every week with a special odourless washing powder because strong scents offended him. There was nothing in the place to hint at its occupant. It could easily be a hotel room. Nobody was allowed in. He'd considered soundproofing it, just in case, but thought that might arouse the very suspicion he was trying to avoid. That's why he hadn't put a lock on the door either, though he really wanted to.

'It's like a *tomb* up there,' Tony had told him once.

'I like things to be neat,' David had answered.

'A therapist would have a field day with you, he really would.'

'Don't speak to me like that,' David used his low-threat voice, which he'd perfected through training, though it never seemed to affect Tony, who grinned at him.

'I'm *concerned* that's all. I don't want you to develop abnormally.'

David had said something stupid then – '*You're* the freak!' – but immediately realised that that was exactly what Tony had wanted him to say. He'd goaded him into it so he could bad-mouth him to Mum. And he had, too, because that night she had a Long Talk with him about Being Kind and Accepting Difference and Adult Relationships and… the memory still made him faintly sick. After that, he avoided Tony and Tony, too, backed off somewhat, only allowing himself the odd barb now and again – humming Chic's 'Le Freak, C'est Chic' and smirking.

David's room was his Special Place. Every day he retired to this careful sanctuary and trained his face and body to reflect the same blankness as the walls. Every day he stood before his full-length mirror for exactly forty-five minutes, practising blankness. He'd think terrible thoughts, and examine his face for hints; relive embarrassments and failures, while forcing his shoulders to stay straight, his face neutral, his brow unfurrowed. He was really very good at it. He'd started the training because, a few years ago, he noticed that there was a small but ever widening gulf between what *he* thought the world ought to be like, and what everyone else thought. David's world was uncluttered, quiet, isolated. There was no sex in David's world; no music; no drugs. He had no hobbies. He had no tribe. Lately, he felt that the world of every other sixteen-year-old was a horrible, dark shadow of his own. Their world seemed to be all about friends and music, anger, stupidity and all that boys-will-be-boys stuff that was so tiresome. Alien. The frightening centre of this world, the rotten nucleus, was porn, and David hated that most of all, hated it so much that he'd never let it into his training programme. One, very brief, glance at *Porn Hub* was enough to put him off the whole idea for life.

David knew he was absolutely In The Right, but he also knew that being Right wasn't Normal, and he'd noticed that people cared a lot about what seemed normal; if he didn't master how to pass as normal, his life would be very very difficult. All those childhood trips to the doctor had taught him that. The doctor had said he should see a psychiatrist if this 'anxiety' continued into adolescence, and there was no way David would have let that happen. Psychiatrists were for weaklings and social cripples, and he wasn't like that. He just had... issues with some things, that was all.

For the first few years of his life, he slept below a battery-operated mobile – revolving, twirling circles of red, black and white accompanied by tinny excerpts of Mozart. Later, in conversation with the doctor, his mother seized on this being the cause... *perhaps the music, coupled with those disorienting spirals had created some nightmarish vision in his child's mind?* That would explain the times she found him curled up in the corner of his room, eyes staring, catatonic with fear. The garbled, fearful explanations – just that he had to run from the noise, and run quick; how he'd stiffen in her arms when she sang him a lullaby. He suffered until the age of four, when the mobile was retired, And he was moved into a big-boy bed. He still had nightmares though. And he walked in his sleep, sometimes spent days not speaking to a soul, just lying on his bed, stroking his cat, his face as scrupulously blank as an egg.

Father had spent a lot of time reassuring her.

'He doesn't seem to have any friends,' Mother had said. 'He's so terribly *alone*.'

'He's just his own man,' Father had said, and ten-year-old David, listening behind the door, blushed with pleasure, because Father understood.

'—The school?' Mother was saying. 'Maybe boarding?'

That scared him. Boarding school meant no privacy. It meant noise and enforced sports and choir. To his horror, his father wasn't disagreeing with her. Their conversation petered out into frustratingly opaque phrases – 'Reading the room'. 'EQ'. 'On the spectrum'. Right then and there, David vowed to learn how to behave like everyone else. He had no choice, as they'd send him away otherwise. For the first time in his life, he listened to the way other children spoke to each other, memorised their inflections, their slang, took notes on the clothes they wore, the TV shows they watched, and in the safety of his room, he practised hard until he'd assimilated the act. At secondary school, he noticed that having the right haircut was important, as was how to wear your school tie (Fat Windsor knot, the rest tucked in between shirt buttons). Being bright was OK so long as you weren't too bright, so he was careful to do well, but not too well, in school. Swearing was big. You were expected to swear, at least a bit, and so David learned to drop a few fucks and bastards into his speech, and tried to remember not to hesitate or wince when he did. He rebuffed overtures from obviously Weird Kids, and at the same time kept his distance from the powerful elite, knowing that they, out of everyone, would be best equipped to sniff out his oddity.

The only thing he hadn't mastered by the age of fifteen was music. He could disguise or deny his antipathy towards porn and sports, but music was harder, because music was *everywhere*. Yes, the arrangements of notes were arbitrary, ugly, and prodded him into panic, but he simply couldn't afford to let that happen any more. He was a teenager. Teenagers Like Music.

He started the weaning process via television. Father liked peaceful things like *University Challenge* and *Grand Designs*, and, because these programmes only had short theme tunes, David watched quietly with him, nodding appreciatively at their respective scores, or sharing sparing opinions on the virtues of eco building. It was fine to wince during the music round of *University Challenge*, because it was always opera or something, and nobody liked that.

Gradually, he'd progressed so that now so that he could cope with sudden, unexpected bouts of music from a car radio, or a shop speaker, but he knew he had to do better than that.

A while ago, he'd appropriated the bulky 1980s stereo system from the study and ordered headphones from Amazon, as well as a selection of CDs – compilations, mostly, all of different genres. Beginning with *The Best Classical Album Ever!!!* – a series of relatively soft, short, pieces of classical music, some of which he recognised from adverts, he forced himself to train for forty-five minutes a day, and each day, turned the volume up one notch. He'd managed to get through *The Best Classical Album Ever!!!* in under three weeks, relatively unscathed. *Now That's What I Call Classic Rock!* was trickier. He'd been stuck on the intro to 'Pinball Wizard' all week. Today, he was determined to get all the way through it.

He set the volume at 3, then changed it to 4, and, shuddering, pressed play. Guitars jangled, drums pounded a maddeningly repetitive beat, and he watched himself in the mirror, noting with approval how calm he appeared, even as gorge rose. When the splintering vocals began, rather than turning it off as he always had, he gritted his teeth and turned up the volume to 5, telling himself to *look, keep looking. Stand straight. Smile. Keep your eyes open. Now look around. Bink. Blink. Remember to blink.* He was exhausted by the time the song ended, and covered with sweat, but after he'd stopped crying, after he'd splashed his face and spoken sternly to his reflection, he was ready to start all over again. Then again. Then again.

*

Forty-five minutes later, he allowed himself to stop, and again studied himself in the mirror. Drying sweat on too-tense shoulders. He felt his lungs begin to billow more easily, his fingers stretched. This was good. This was progress. This was all down to Jenny, he knew. The knowledge of her spurred him on...

Now that he had earned his reward, he crossed the room, dragged out 'Precious Memories!' from under his bed, said a little prayer, And clicked open the catch.

David had always been a collector. An archivist really. Two years before, when he was still making the mistake of keeping everything In an unmarked box under his bed he came back from school to see that the cleaner had come into his room and removed it. Nobody understood why he was so upset about what the cleaner insisted was just broken pens and old paper. Later, that night, he'd overheard another one of those anxious conversations between Mother and Fathers, realised how stupid he'd been, and told himself off very sternly. It had been very very stupid to get... upset like that. If he got upset, they'd worry, and if they worried, they might start talking about psychiatrists again, boarding school again. The best way to handle this was to... go full Normal. Be honest. Frank, uncomplicated.

Back in the sitting room, he confronted his worried parents and apologised. The thing was, after watching all of those episodes of *Grand Designs*, he'd found himself fascinated by architecture... it was silly, really, but he'd been making some plans? For the kitchen extension they were always talking about? He wanted to draw up his own plans and show them, and he'd been working really hard to surprise them, but all of his work had been in that box.

'Oh, darling!' Mother cried.

Father huffed with shy pride. 'Do we have a budding town planner in our midst?'

David ducked his head, nodded, smiled. 'But it's silly. I shouldn't have been so angry—'

His mother got up then. 'Not at all. Not at *all*. Now we understand.'

David hesitated, wondered if he could push it just a bit further. 'But secrets are wrong. I've learned my lesson.'

'They're absolutely *not* wrong! Piers? Piers!'

'Absolutely not wrong,' his father said.

David went even further. 'But families shouldn't have secrets.'

'Privacy and secrecy aren't the same thing,' his father said firmly.

David left it at that, but he knew that he'd been lucky. A doctor's letter he'd filched from Jeanine's bag had been in that box (*what was chlamydia anyway?*), as well as two of Tony's cheque books (David didn't know what to do with them, but having them made him feel powerful). If his parents had seen them… He'd have to be a lot more careful in the future, no leaving things out to be discovered. He had to go further than that though: he had to make his parents feel too guilty to even think about snooping again, let alone let a cleaner in his room.

So, over the next few months, if Mum or Father mentioned anything to do with *Grand Designs* or the kitchen, David would smile sadly and back away from the conversation. He wrote some truly atrocious poetry, left it in the sitting room where he was sure his mother would read it. Sometimes he drew – amateurish Skyscrapers or shakily sketched ground plans for eco homes and left them half-finished, half-screwed up, half in the bin. The message was clear, his confidence, badly damaged by that stupid cleaner, and his parents' stupid reaction to his privacy being invaded, had yet to recover.

'He's sensitive.' He overheard Mum telling Tony 'He feels things deeply.'

'Mmmmmph,' said Tony.

'Who knew being a mother would be so hard?'

'*I* did,' Tony replied. 'That's why I've never given birth.'

'Idiot,' Mum said fondly.

'Still, toughening up might be a good idea for him. St Columbus.'

Tony really wanted him out of the house, didn't he? David tiptoed up the stairs and then came back down them noisily. When he opened the door to the sitting room, Tony's annoyance was very gratifying.

'Mum? Oh, hi, Tony. Great-grandad's suitcase? The one with his initials? Would I be able to have it?' David was all diffidence.

'Of course, darling, if I can find it, yes. Why?'

'Oh.' David looked at the floor, then into her eyes with frank emotion. 'Well, you know we're studying World War Two in history?' He saw his mother's expression flicker. She didn't actually know much about what he did in school. She left that to his father. 'Well, I remembered that that was his demob case. I'd like to take it into school to show people…' He watched his mother's face radiate pride, watched Tony squint suspiciously at him. 'If that's OK, I mean?'

Of course it was OK.

A few weeks later, using the same brow crinkle, he cornered his mother when she was alone. *Could he possibly keep the suitcase?* – 'It just feels… right that I should have it. It was so precious to him and' – he played his trump card – 'after losing all my drawings—'

'Darling, we're so sorry about that—'

'Well, I feel ready to start drawing again? And keep them in his case? It feels right to keep precious things in it now. Does that make sense?' David had recently realised that using the phrase 'Does that make sense?' elicited a gentle, sentimental response from women. It was something only a sensitive, serious boy would say.

Later he took the precaution to stencil 'Precious Memories!' on its side, complete with an exclamation point. When he showed it to his mother, she thought it was lovely. After that he really didn't think she or anyone else would rummage through his things – not when he was so sensitive, not when it had taken him this long to get his confidence back. Nevertheless, he always made sure to tape one of Jeanine Finney's long hairs across the clasp whenever he shut it, just in case. That way, if the hair was broken, he'd know it had been opened. Happily, this hadn't yet happened, and David still had all fifteen of Jeanine's hairs in a sealed envelope. He'd stolen her hairbrush from her backpack last year while her back was turned.

Now, with the sweat drying on his shoulders, and the psychic echo of 'Pinball Wizard' in the air, David's shaking fingers took up Jenny's Post-it note. He closed his eyes, cupped his hands around it, felt the adhesive strip, still sticky new, like something just born. He brought it to his face, inhaled. Winter cold, cinders, bike brakes and cigarettes. Then he opened his eyes, unfolded it, sat cross-legged and gazed, listening to its story:

7.55 8.14 8.19 9.10

Times.

Train times? *Where've you been? I've been worried...*

It had to be train times. Trains that ran that regularly always went somewhere major too. She was taking a train to the city.

He closed his eyes again. Heard her voice again.

Mum?

Where've you been?

Mum?

I've been worried.

He heard the laugh of the TV again, smelled the cigarette smoke. In his cupped, shaking palms, the note shivered like a living thing. When he opened his eyes, they were wet.

The Significance of this was almost too much to bear.

He folded the note so as to preserve its careless folds. Then he took a deep breath and upended the contents of 'Precious Memories!' onto the carpet: 'New' items merged with 'Pending' and mixed with 'Always Significant'. Everything had to be assessed and arranged again; Jenny's note had changed everything. The chewed biro he'd taken from the Chinese man's notepad? That had no chance of making it into 'Always Significant' now. The flake of rust from Mr Jackson's car could stay in 'Pending', because he'd collected it the day he'd stabbed Francis, so it had some relevance. The photograph of a laughing woman feeding pigeons in Trafalgar Square he'd found in the graveyard had no place at all. He burned that carefully over a candle and flushed the ashes down the toilet. What to do with this badge that had fallen off Jeanine Finney's bag last summer? Flush that down the loo too. And what about this paper bag of grass cuttings from the graveyard? He'd collected them last August after happening to see Tony and Mother leaving the Rose and Crown together. Tony, slightly gin-coherent, had fallen flat on his wide arse in the narrow doorway, got wedged in. Like Winnie the Pooh stuck in Rabbit's burrow, he'd had to be pulled and pushed, pried loose, and, having absolutely no sense of his own absurdity, he had been furious. The memory of his lank comb-over falling over his furious flushed face, the way that even Mother had to laugh at him, and the limp he affected for the next few days, all added up to one brilliant memory. Was it truly Significant, though? He decided to keep the grass in 'Pending', along with a swatch of red velvet he'd found in the graveyard. For some reason the velvet seemed important.

The compass automatically went into 'Always Significant'. He placed it next to the Post-it note with great reverence.

Later, staring at himself in the mirror, he thought about Jenny, and he waited to get hard, but he didn't, which was a relief. He never ever seemed to get hard, and it used to worry him, but not nowadays, not after the *Porn Hub* experiment. He strongly suspected that all that stuff was overrated.

CHAPTER FORTY-ONE

The next day, Thursday, David took his position behind Jenny's house again. He'd borrowed his father's waxed poacher coat and arranged it around the damp hollow of the rocks for warmth. He even brought a hot drink in a flask and some binoculars that had night vision, but he didn't need to see them to know what was going on: both voices were raised in intensity, but, frustratingly, lower in tone. He decided to risk getting closer, and, once again, hid behind the bins underneath the kitchen window.

'… Do it if you're going to do it! You've been umpteen times, and—'

'We need it! I said I'd get it and I'll *get* it!' Jenny shrieked. With the gruffness gone, her voice rattled with an unpleasant echo of her mother's vibrato. 'He *owes* us—'

The woman said something then, something that David couldn't catch, and then Jenny was out of the door; she was only a few feet away from him, and her breath was raspy, angry. He heard the tired squeak of bike wheels, and cowered further into the shadows.

'Jen!' the mother whined.

Jenny muttered something to herself as she got on her bike.

Her mother shouted from the kitchen. 'Jen!'

'Oh fuck *off*,' Jenny hissed under her breath, and pushed off on her bike.

'Jenny!' The woman came to the door. 'Don't though. Come on, love, just stay here.'

'I'll be back in a few hours.'

'But—'

Jenny sped off then, on her wheezy bicycle.

David hunched in frustration. He couldn't get up and follow her without her mother seeing him looming up from behind the bins, but if he stayed here much longer he'd lose her. The woman stayed in the doorway, smoking, sighing. Eventually she went back inside, and David heard her on the phone.

'Kathleen? She's gone again. Mmmm.' Smoke leaked out of the open window, rested on the heavy air, made his eyes water. 'Ros doesn't still live round there, does she? No? Can anyone keep an eye out for her? She's, yes, she's got it in her head that—' Then the kitchen window shut, and the woman's voice was quashed into a blur.

After a minute, David risked getting up. He dusted off his knees, stretched feeling back into his feet, and, keeping to the shadows, went back to his own bike. If he made good time, there was a chance he could catch up with Jenny. He knew where she was going – the train station – the Post-it note had told him. But after that? He had no idea. But even her poor excuse for a mother thought it was dangerous.

Danger danger danger pulsed through his mind as he skirted the village, heading towards the cycle path that bypassed the centre, ran through the woods, and ran parallel to the main road. Through the gaps in the trees, he could keep an eye on Jenny, racing along the smooth, empty road and, whenever he saw her, his head pounded *Danger.* When he briefly lost her at the roundabout he almost shouted in frustration, then his mind gripped grimly onto determination – *help her help her help her protect her* – and he followed his instincts; he found her again, saw her lock her bike outside the train station, saw her trot through the open barriers, and disappear through the doors of an idling train. With no thought, David followed, dodging into the carriage behind just as the doors began closing with a jolting beep. From the carriage ahead, he could just make out the back of her head, her cascading hair, one jerking, nervous foot in the aisle.

David was used to secrecy, to not being noticed. He watched, he planned, he stayed removed. That's how he liked things. Now, as the train pulled away, he marvelled at his impulsivity… he'd never jumped on a train before. He'd never been out of the village at night before. He had no ticket, and no money to pay for one. If the ticket inspector came along he was screwed… he'd be told off, Jenny would hear it, turn and see him. And even if he got away with it on the journey there was no guarantee that he would on the journey back. He was trapped in this train carriage, speeding towards an environment over which he had even less control. He didn't like the city. He didn't like crowds. He didn't like… too many new things converging all at once, overwhelming him, and suddenly he felt panic; he tasted tears. *I must stay calm and I must stay calm*… but no calm came. He switched mantras: *Man up man up man up*. He'd heard this phrase on one of the soap operas he made himself watch every now and again. Tough-looking balding men with working-class accents told each other to do that all the time in pubs. He shuffled next to the window, hunched into his coat. Someone had scratched 'NO SURRENDER!!' on the toughened glass, and these words hovered over his reflection as he stared at himself. *Man up man up man up*. By the time the train drew into the city station he felt calmer. Older. He hadn't surrendered to panic.

He waited until she'd left before getting up himself, and followed the halo of her hair through the station concourse, out through a side exit, and into the unfamiliar, dark streets. Jenny walked quickly, confidently cutting through alleys and underpasses, and David soon lost his bearings completely, and panic rose again, just a little, but *no, he had to not lose her. Man up!*

But where is she going?

Man up!

And how will I get back? And... No. No. Focus. Breathe. Everything will become clear. Everything was happening for a reason. He just had to remember that: No Surrender... never surrender to fear.

*

She skirted the city centre, walked through a dark, dank covered market and past a derelict pub called Pretty Windows. Then she was walking up a steep hill, past more pubs, mean little off-licences and evil-smelling halal butchers, her pace only slowed when she came to a pub – The Fox. She hovered by the door, looking into the bar, while David edged into the little park opposite, kept to the shadows and watched. Then she broke into a trot, through the park (passing only a few feet away from him) to a small dilapidated terrace crouching behind the mouldering walls of a once-grand church, disappearing into the dark alley running between two of the houses. From behind him, the church clock struck eight.

He sat on a gravestone, closed his eyes, letting the quiet in. *Breathe in and slowly out and wait for a sign.* And there it was, the tiny scratching click of a key. The slight sticking of a door yielding to a shove. She was at the back door of one of the last two houses. He gave her a few minutes to get in, and then moved silently towards the alley and onto the grassy mud, and tucked himself into an alcove by the neighbour's garden wall.

Half an hour later, he heard the door again; he shuffled further into the alcove, and, once again, she passed by, breathtakingly close. She held a carrier bag and was swinging it in tightly controlled little jerks, smiling to herself.

David let a minute go by before following her, and this time he moved more slowly, letting her get more of a head start, because he was sure she was going home now, back to the station and going home. He loitered outside a shop, debating buying a chocolate bar – he could keep the wrapper in 'Precious Memories!' – but then he remembered he had no money, and so he moved on.

At the end of the street, the windows of The Fox shone dimly. As he got closer, David could make out a man, a wiry man in a baseball cap and a polo shirt that clung to a burgeoning belly. He slouched insolently in front of the door, blocking it, clutching a half-empty pint glass in one hand, and a cigarette in the other. To David's eyes, he looked exactly like one of those pugnacious bald men in that soap opera, and he slowed, stopped, because this man was frightening. He didn't know why, but he was. This wasn't a man he wanted to get too close to.

The man let out a sudden bark of laughter. He let his glass drop and shatter on the pavement, and David could see that the man had caught someone, someone passing by, and wasn't letting go.

Jenny.

The fabric of her coat ripped. David winced. The man grabbed her harder, with both hands now, and Jenny, struggling, was pushed up against the wall. The weak streetlight that shone through her hair, making her glow, tinged his face a sickly yellow. Once again, David retreated into a nearby doorway, watched.

'Got there, then?' The man had a smile like a shark. He reached for the carrier bag.

'Nothing.' She tried to move it quickly behind her back, but the man grabbed it with such force that the bag ripped and a photo album flopped out onto the ground along with a money belt designed to clip around the waist. Both grabbed at the money belt at the same time, and Jenny's face was filled with fearful rage, as the man's smile flickered like a faulty light bulb. He won the battle, waved the money belt in her face with one hand, pushed her against the wall with the other.

'Robbing me then?' he said.

'It's ours,' Jenny replied.

'Not this.' He waggled the money belt. 'This isn't, is it?'

'It's—'

He hit her then, one short, sharp punch to the stomach. She doubled over.

'You don't get a fucking thing that wasn't yours to start with, not a fucking thing. Tell Sal that!' he told her.

Jenny, gasping, was trying to straighten up. She stood crookedly, still winded from the blow to her stomach.

'Don't milk it either. Barely touched you,' he told her.

'We want our photos,' she managed.

'Well why didn't you take them when you left?' The man looked at her with amusement. 'If they're so precious, why didn't you take them then?' He glanced down at the album, put one foot on it, and dragged it towards him.

'I *don't* want them.'

He smiled then, almost lovingly. 'Why'd you come back really? Miss me, did you?'

'Fuck off.'

'I think that's what it is. I know you.'

'Fuck *off.*' She tried to hit him, but she was weak, small, afraid. He caught her fist in mid-air, twisted her wrist until she sagged a little against the wall.

'I've not missed you, I'll tell you that. You or her. But if you take any of my stuff again, I might have to pay you a visit…'

'You owe us. It costs money to move,' Jenny managed. 'We need furniture and all that.'

He shrugged. 'Should've thought about that before you left.'

'Marc, come on, please?' she said, and David, hidden, shared her painful shame and winced… begging from this man. Pleading with someone so obviously beneath her. She'd hate herself for this later. 'I'll never come back, just help us out this once—'

His face hardened. 'No.'

Then, with the desperate swiftness of a cornered animal, Jenny lunged for the money belt, grabbed hold of it, tugged. David could see the surprise in the man's face, anger that she was still fighting, and whipped the belt away with one hand, using the other to pin her up against the pub wall by her throat. He stared at her, almost lovingly, and whispered something while he dropped the money belt, stepping on it to keep it safe, and slowly, slowly, put his other hand around her neck. David watched her shadow lengthen against the rough bricks, her toes barely touching the ground, and her eyes large and resigned like a rabbit caught in a snare. When she made a brave attempt to kick him in the balls, the man tightened his grip further until her feet were dangling a clear two inches off the ground, trainers swinging fruitlessly. He brought his face in close enough for a kiss.

Man up man up man up! David's frozen limbs twitched. His brain told him to move, to save her, and he lurched from his doorway. He heard himself shout something, but it wasn't a real word, and he ran into the middle of the road. A car swerved, beeped, stopped only inches away from him. Through the car windows, past the red face of the shouting driver, he could see that the man had released her, letting her drop to the pavement like a doll.

'… off the fucking *road!*' screamed the driver. 'Blind? Off the fucking *road!*'

David got off the road, ran to the shadowy park. Over his coarse gasps he could hear the driver still shouting about him. 'See that? Standing there in the middle of the road', and the car obscured Jenny; he couldn't see what was happening.

Another car, forced to linger behind the first, beeped angrily. Another voice started to shout. By the time both men had stopped shouting, and both cars had moved, Jenny had gone. The man – Marc, that was his name – Marc and Jenny's mother must be Sal – picked up the money belt, pulled up his T-shirt and wrapped it around his hairy mound of belly. His face was grim, angry. He kicked at the photo album, dragged it over the tarmac, over the kerb and into the road, until it's limp pages flopped into the clogged drain. Then the outer door of the pub opened and two drunk women came out, all hilarity and unlit cigarettes, and the man was all smiles. He lit their cigarettes, laughed, stayed on the doorstep flirting with them both. After ten minutes or so, they all went back in the pub, the man with a proprietorial palm on both women's jiggling behinds. The door closed, and the street was once again silent, as if the man had taken all the chaos and noise with him. As if the man was the noise, the chaos.

David remained in this mercifully empty world, shocked, numbed, knowing that this was not True Calm, but Terror Calm. He'd spent his life watching from the sidelines, feeling that, by watching, by learning the rules, he was Mastering The Situation. He didn't have to get involved because he already knew how everything worked. Now, crouching in this cold, miserable park, he understood just how childish he'd been. He had no control over this, no power, no... *guts*. He'd watched Jenny be bullied, attacked, intimidated and he'd done nothing. He could have... run at the man, kicked him... or... hit him with a brick, or... *something*. He could have been a man about it.

He was ashamed of himself.

He made himself get up, cross the road. He picked up as many of the scattered photographs as he could, stuffing them in his pockets. Some had stuck to the mud like dead leaves, some had partially fallen down the drain. The album itself had been squashed flat by traffic, but he picked that up too, hugging it close and heavy in his arms, like an injured pet.

All the way down the hill, through the market, back to the station his mind yammered *manupmanupmanup*.

On the train he brought out the photographs... Jenny as a baby. Jenny in an unfamiliar school uniform – smiling stiffly to hide her crooked eye tooth. Jenny on a swing, a beautiful blur, a younger version of her mother behind, caught off guard, a cigarette close – too close – to the child's face. The mother and another woman – slim, coarse-looking – drinking amber liquid from novelty shot glasses. The man, THAT man, standing before the door of The Fox, smirking at the camera, wearing the same hat. David looked into his eyes, feeling strangely as if the man was staring back, as if they were communicating. He shivered, stuffed the photos back in his pockets.

*

It was late when he got back home, but no one noticed him come in, thankfully. Mother and Tony might still be trying the landlord's patience at the Rose and Crown, and Dad was probably already asleep.

In his room, he lit a candle, put a towel down on the carpet, and arranged the photographs on it. Then he stripped off his clothes and sat naked, cross-legged on the floor, closed his eyes, breathed deeply, listening to their story.

It was the saddest story he'd ever heard.

Then he opened his eyes, looked at the pictures, arranged them into the right order – not chronological order, but the order of their importance. After an hour, the photographs formed a triangle – at the bottom, those muddy pictures of family friends, the thin lady with the coarse face was in most of them. Then Jenny took over – Jenny as a baby, as a toddler, at school, alone on a beach, among a crowd of blurred adults on a bus, sitting on a bar stool.

There was only one picture that didn't fit, and that was the one of The Man. Marc. He didn't want to look at that again, but he had to but he had to.

Evil.

Evil flowed from him.

He placed this photo on a sheet of paper and shifted it away from the others – its own little island of contained contagion.

But still David's naked flesh shivered as the man watched, as the man leered. Those eyes.

David slowly dragged 'Precious Memories!' from under his bed, took out Francis's compass, still marked with blood, picked up the photo, and sat at his desk. The man's evil eyes seemed to mock him, seemed to dare him. But David, relaxed now, had all the power. Slowly, he prodded them out with the tip of the compass, poking them into skull-like cavities that took up a third of his face. Then he outlined them with a gold marker until Marc couldn't see him any more.

He took the remaining photos to the bathroom, dabbed the mud off them as best he could, wrapped them in a towel, and brought them back to his room. They lay next to his bed, like a swaddled baby, close enough to touch, close enough to hear. They'd seep into his dreams, and he'd wake up knowing just what to do.

CHAPTER FORTY-TWO

The next day, at school, David's nerves sang with her proximity. Only three seats away in History. Two in Geography. After the Francis Brennan incident, she'd been put in another Maths group, but he still managed to pass her in the corridor, close enough to see that her hair hadn't been washed, that there were ashy sleepless smudges under her eyes. Her shirt, buttoned up to the top of her neck, was held firmly with her school tie, and David wondered if there were bruises to hide? Perhaps when Marc had pinned her to the wall, he'd injured her? He overheard Jeanine Finney asking if she was OK? 'I hope you don't mind me saying, but you look *awful.*' Jeanine enjoyed telling people prettier than her that they looked awful… Jenny had answered, but he couldn't catch the soft burr of her voice to tell if she was hoarse.

He knew that she walked through the graveyard on the way home from school, so he ran ahead at the end of the school day, and loitered in the church portal, waiting, until he saw her pink coat, a splotch of cheerful colour, coming through the gate. She was walking slowly while rooting through her bag. He closed his eyes, breathed slowly, let his body and thoughts dissolve, and when he opened them again, she was almost in front of him, and he knew what to do.

'Lose something?' He didn't say it loudly, but she jumped back. 'Jesus!'

He supposed he must have given her a shock, coming out of the dark doorway like that. 'Sorry! Didn't mean to scare you. Have you though? Lost something?' And he looked directly at her.

Up close, alone, she almost killed him. Her eyes were a strange tawny colour, only a little darker than her hair and fringed with sooty lashes. That skin, faintly pinkened in the cold. The ruddy full mouth. David, staring, tried not to stare.

'What?' Her voice was husky, slovenly.

'You're,' he pointed at her searching fingers, still in the bag, 'looking for something?'

'Yeah, I left a… book. Somewhere.'

There was a pause. Was she talking about the photo album? Was this her way of telling him she knew he'd followed her that night? *God this was exciting! This was Significant!*

'What book? A library book?' He thought it best to go along with her little game.

'Yeah.' Her fingers stopped fidgeting in the bag. She pulled the strap further up her shoulder and stood straighter. 'Art. Well, not *art*. Photography.'

The photo album! She *was* talking about the photo album! His head felt hot. He closed his eyes and wobbled on his heels.

'Are you feeling OK?' she asked.

'Yes. No, I mean I was out last night and I think I got a bit of a cold, that's all.' He opened his eyes, blinked significantly.

'Yeah, me too,' she answered. And she blinked too. *She blinked too! Did that mean she'd seen him? Did that mean they could drop all this cutesy hinting and talk properly?* He searched her face for clues, saw nothing he could be absolutely sure of, decided to play it safe.

'Can I help you find it? The book, I mean?'

She seemed startled. Then she smiled, relaxed. 'You don't know what it looks like though,' she said.

Man up man up man up. He held out his hands about twelve inches apart. 'It's about this big?' Her face told him nothing. He went on. 'Black? With, like, a gold pattern on it?'

There was a long pause. 'No,' she said.

David could almost feel himself deflating. 'Oh.'

'It was, like, about migration?' She did that upwards inflection at the end of the sentence? Everything was a question? Jeanine did this too. So did David when he wanted to appear normal. Jenny was better than that. David felt the beginning of a headache.

'Migration?'

'Displaced families after war. That sort of thing.'

Now they were back on firm ground! Families moving, war, displacement. He spoke carefully. 'Serious stuff.'

She squinted at him. 'Yeah. Anyway—'

'So, you were out last night, yes?'

She looked him right in the eye and smiled. 'Yep.'

He smiled back. 'Me too. A friend needed help with her history homework.' He beamed inwardly. *God, he was good at this.*

Her posture shifted. She was about to leave. 'OK, well I better—'

A little desperately he pointed at the school insignia on her blazer. *Acta Non Verba* on a shield of gold. 'D'you know what that means?'

'What, this? No.' She smiled at him quizzically. 'What's it mean then?'

'It's Latin. It means "Action not Words".'

She smiled again, and nodded. 'I like that,' she said.

'Me too,' he said.

'OK, then, bye!' She gave him a little wave.

'Bye!' He waved back cheerfully.

It had all gone perfectly.

History. Family. Conflict. It was subtle, but undeniable – she knew he had her pictures and she wanted them back. David wouldn't just give them back though – he'd clean them, arrange them and present them in just the right way, in just the right sort of box.

Back at home he took a desultory look on eBay, but bidding on something unseen felt risky; it might get lost in the post, or Tony might intercept it, open it, say something snarky, and ruin the whole thing. He didn't want to buy some piece of Amazon tat out of desperation either... He wouldn't know if it was the right sort of box until he held it in his hands, but he didn't have time to properly research shops, get to the city, find the perfect thing, bring it home... it would all take too long, and he really wanted to get this done today. He had to. She'd *asked* him to.

A jewellery box would be perfect. Mother had three, but they were all in her room and would surely be missed. Could he *make* one? His memory drifted towards his only attempt at Art – a disastrous papier mâché Christmas decoration in the shape of a snowman that Tony had – accurately – said looked more like a penis... No. He couldn't trust himself to make a box. His mind ran around the house, into the cupboards, the attic, the conservatory, but there was nothing that was *right*. As a last resort, he decided to look in the summer house. Tony probably had a box. He must have a box; he had so much stuff in there, and one little box wouldn't be missed. Even if it was, there was something definitely... *attractive* about the idea of poking about in Tony's things, stealing from him. And so, once Mother and Tony had left for their traditional Friday drinks at the Rose and Crown, David crept into Tony's lair.

The summer house was... frightening. David had never been inside it before, never accepted Tony's slightly ironic invitations to 'have a spot of tea' with him. He knew it was cluttered – but now he could see that it was more than cluttered – it was chaotic, offensively disorganised, and it smelled of old clothes and oil paint, the strong cigarettes he smoked and the stronger incense Tony burned to disguise the stench. It smelled furtive, alien and frightening.

The little kitchen area – a hotplate and a toaster – was greasy and crumb-covered. There were dried smears of jam on the handle of the kettle. Ashtrays abounded, but the floor was still dotted with cigarette butts. David shuddered. Everything teetered on the brink of collapse, like a snapshot of an earthquake in motion, and he wanted to run. He wanted to be sick. *Man up man up man up and THINK though…* This was his quest, and quests were never easy, were they? So, keeping up his mantra, trying to ignore the greasy dirt collecting under his fingernails, he held his nerve, knowing he'd not only find *a* box, he'd find *the* box. He was meant to because it was a Significant thing. He started searching the dimly lit piles of possessions, feeling the panicky anger at the lack of order and logic recede, feeling… adult.

It took an hour, but he did eventually uncover the box, jammed under the chaise longue next to an unopened box of artists pastels and a suspiciously crusty Kleenex. When he prised it out, he recognised it as part of a present Mother had given to Tony the year before – an oblong, black lacquered box, tapering at the base and delicately inlaid with mother-of-pearl and filled with nicotine patches. Tony had laughed, made a show of trying to quit for a while, but was soon back on the fags. The box was damaged now and some of the inlay had fallen out. Opening the lid, David saw that there were cigarette burns inside it; Tony used it as an ashtray. Typical. That was typical, wasn't it? Tony was such a smug little sponger. He took Mother's heartfelt gift and ruined it, just like he deliberately messed up the summer house, the garden (all churned earth and litter), just like he'd ruined their standing in the village – damaged Father's reputation, his self-image. David knew people joked about Tony and Mother, and knowing this made him burn with shame. The only person Tony *hadn't* damaged was David; David was too strong to bend and too clever to break. That's why Tony hated him. It was bound to come to a head one of these days… but David would win then, too, he knew, and Tony would be driven away, banished, like an exorcised ghost. He walked back to the main house, holding the box far away from his body. The hour he'd spent in the summer house made him feel dirty all over, as if Tony's dirt was no ordinary dirt, but a revolting resin that clung and stained. Once inside, he ran, shaking, to the bathroom and scrubbed each fingertip with bleach.

When he felt solid again, he walked slowly to his room to assess the amount of work he'd have to do.

The damage was substantial. The gouges on the top of the box were too deep to polish out and David didn't have any black paint to cover them, so he improvised by making the smaller scratches into flying birds, incorporating what was left of the mother-of-pearl inlay as part of their wings. He turned the largest scratch into an elongated 'J' for Jenny. Carving carefully with the needle of the compass he'd stabbed Francis with; using his special gold marker (the same one he'd circled Marc's eyes with) to carefully fill in the 'J' and the wings, he was pretty proud of himself. Art wasn't his strong suit, perhaps the wings were a little crooked, and the 'J' a little long, but, after all, he wasn't going for realism. No, the more he looked at it, the prouder he felt about the way the birds flanked the 'J' for Jenny, as if guiding her from the black to a new era… *perhaps he should carve a sun in the corner? To make it more obvious?* He closed his eyes and tried to sink into her mind. Discovering the present on the doorstep. The black and the gold – strong colours – respectful colours. He opened his eyes. *No. No sun. A sun would be too overstated. Leave it.*

He lined the inside of the box with the piece of red velvet he'd kept in 'Pending' (*now he knew why he'd kept it!*). He allowed himself to keep two photographs: one of Jenny as a baby, and the other with the now eyeless man in the hat. A third – a woman in brown, out of focus and unidentifiable, he kept aside on grounds of quality. He tied the rest of the photos together with a red ribbon from one of Tinker's old toys, placed them reverently in the box, and sat back, happy, tired, but not finished, because now he had to deliver it, and it had to be handled perfectly.

By the time he'd finished customising the box, it was 10 p.m. He cycled to Jenny's house but, halfway there, it began to rain heavily and, stupidly, he'd left without a waterproof jacket. The rain dripped down his collar, through to his neck, his chest. His jeans clung wetly to his thighs, and his gloveless hands, clenched on the handlebars, ached with cold.

When he arrived, he could see that Jenny was in. Her bike was propped up against the house and draped in bin bags to protect it from the weather. This was perfect. He could put the box on her saddle where only she was bound to find it, and the bin bags would keep it dry...

He circled away, back down the bend of the road, stashed his bike behind some bins, and made his way to her house on foot, being careful to keep to the shadows, and walking on the grass to soften his steps – accidentally stepping into a puddle, soaking both trainers. He took the box from his backpack, kissed it reverently, and placed it, carefully, on the saddle, gazed at it for a moment, and then replaced the covering and backed away. If only there was a way he could be there to see her face when she discovered it! But it couldn't be done without her seeing him. He'd have to settle for coming back early in the morning, hiding at the end of their garden, and hope that he'd be able to catch what she was saying.

*

On the way home, the rain turned to sleet. By the time David was wheeling past the Rose and Crown, he was shaking with cold. Back in the safety of his room his head felt hot and his legs were cramped. *Was he getting ill?* He couldn't *afford* to get ill… He stared at himself in his mirror, telling himself that illness wasn't an option. *Man up.*

He slept badly though, waking, shivering with cold, sweating with heat, and he slept through his alarm, set for 6 a.m., and woke instead at 10, feverish and clammy. *Late, he was late! What if she'd left the house by now?* He pulled on the previous night's damp clothes, put on his trainers, grimacing as his feet sank into the warm, waterlogged sponge. No time for breakfast, no time for anything. He put on his father's tweed jacket, hopped on his bike, and felt the jacket's warmth lie heavy against the fabric of his shirt, itself already damp with sweat. This humid, fetid layer of air enveloped him, heavy as a shroud.

CHAPTER FORTY-THREE

Jenny's mother was standing by the open kitchen window, blowing smoke. 'I don't know what you're so worked up about—'

'Mum, fuck's *sake*! Come on!!' Jenny shouted then. 'How do you think they *got* here?'

There was a silence. 'Well *I* don't know. I don't *know*, but—'

Jenny raised her voice further. 'Oh my GOD! They came from *him*. He brought them here. In a fucking *coffin*! That means he knows where we *live*!'

David, shivering in his little nook at the beginning of the hills, shrank from the swearing, thought *Coffin?*

'We don't *know* they're from him,' the mother answered shortly after a pause.

Jenny, completely visible in the kitchen window, gave an exasperated snort. Angry. She was *angry*? Why? Her mother… her mother must have done something. Invited someone bad over maybe, or… the truth pinched and hurt him; soon he'd have to face it, but he didn't want to. Not yet. No. The mother. Sal? The Bad Man said she was called Sal. She'd said some something to scare Jenny. It was her, it was her—

'Well, who else are they going to be from? Mum? They're pictures of *you* and *me*. Look!' She was brandishing a fistful of photos. 'You and *Kathleen*. You and *me* – Marc was the only person who had them, and now they're here, and how d'you think they got here? Tell me that?'

'Maybe it's a nice thing—' Sal started weakly.

'Oh, for God's sake, Mum, Marc doesn't *do* "nice things"! Why are we here? Why did we come *here*? To get *away* from Marc! It's meant to be a secret where we are, and if he *knows* then we'll have to move again, won't we?'

And David, crouched in his nook, groaned quietly. Seen from this horrible new angle, his noble gesture hadn't been such a good idea after all. Had been probably the worst idea he'd ever had.

'… still could be a nice thing,' Sal was saying.

'It's not nice, it's weird, Mum; it's a *threat* is what it is,' Jenny replied.

'Maybe it's his way of saying sorry?' she replied defiantly. 'Maybe that's what it means?'

'In a *coffin*? Look at it! He's carved fucking crosses on it, and here's a "J". Look at it!'

And David winced and moaned again. His lovingly carved birds looked like crucifixes. His golden 'J' was a threat. *How could he have got this so wrong?* Maybe she hadn't understood what he'd been talking about in the graveyard after all? Maybe – horrible thought, the worst thought – they weren't as attuned as he believed? Maybe—

'We have to call the police. At the refuge they said that if he contacted us we'd have to call the police.' Jenny sounded tired, exasperated.

'No! No, you're not doing that,' the woman sounded more definite than he'd ever heard her before. 'He's on probation, and I won't do that to him, not over something silly like this. He'd lose his job and everything. No, can't do that.'

Jenny let out a little huff of frustration and anger. 'So, what, you want to move again, do you?'

'Well, it's not like we *know* anyone here, is it? Not the friendliest of places.' She was whining, but there was something in her voice that suggested she felt she was on firmer footing. 'I've not met anyone in all the time we've been here, and it gets lonely, I'll tell you.'

'We've only been here a few weeks. And you never leave the house, do you? Why don't you get a job? And I don't *want* to move again! We wouldn't get another house anyway – they only put us on the priority list because of Marc, and if you don't want to call the police on him—'

'I won't,' Sal said firmly and threw her cigarette stub out of the window before shutting it.

David couldn't hear anything now. Hoping that they wouldn't look out of the window and spot him, he moved stealthily down the side of their garden towards the shed that stood adjacent to the back door. He couldn't see them any more, but at least he could hear better. Jenny was saying something about the council.

'… move cause what did they say? We'd be "making ourselves voluntarily homeless".' Her mother must have said something then, because Jenny's voice crackled with anger. '*What* did you say?'

'I *said*,' the woman's voice, though quieter, rang with a kind of rusty authority, '*I'm* the adult here. *I'm* the one in charge, and *I* want to go back home.' She lit another cigarette, pushed open the window again.

'We're not going back home,' Jenny said, her voice wobbling, close to tears. 'That's not happening.'

'All this, just to get your own room,' the woman grumbled. 'Never thought of *me*, leaving my friends and everything. It's all about you, isn't it?'

'He beat the shit out of you, Mum! Did you forget that?' Jenny shouted.

'And none of that happened until you started… acting up. Being cheeky. Accusing him of God knows what—'

'I didn't make anything *up*.' Jenny was beginning to cry harder now. David's heart hurt to hear her. 'You *know* I didn't. You *know* what happened.'

'If he's such a bad lot, why d'you go back there all the time then? If you're scared of him? If he's done these terrible things to you? Why d'you go there all the time?' Sal jeered 'Can't keep away, can you?'

'I went back to get our stuff! The stuff you're always on about – the photographs, all the things you left that you moan about! I'm going back for *you*!'

'Right.' There was a twisted glee in the woman's voice, a 'got you now' smugness. 'You've been back all those times to get "our stuff", but you never *get* any of it, do you?'

'I tried but he caught me!' Jenny was sobbing; her words ran into one another in hitching, tumbling starts. 'He caught me and he hurt me and—'

'He caught you. Right.'

She was all satisfied sarcasm, and David could imagine her pinched profile, her set, mean mouth. Her nasty, cold expression as she watched her weeping daughter with amused detachment. Horrible. The woman was even worse than he'd imagined. And the man – this Marc man – he, too, was not just bad, but vile. Somehow, horribly, David had made a bad situation even worse, had inadvertently reopened wounds that had only just started to heal. He'd brought this evil to Jenny's front door.

The door slammed then, and he could hear Jenny getting on her bike, heard the squeak and sigh of the wheels. Her mother followed, but didn't try to stop her. She lit another cigarette and smoked it on the doorstep muttering to herself. Then she went back inside, and David heard the TV being turned on, the canned laughter from some sitcom. When he got up, his head swam, and he couldn't feel his feet. He muttered to himself: *I'm sick. I'm sick*, but he couldn't be. There was no time to be sick, no time left for anything. He had to reverse this terrible thing he'd caused; he had to right every wrong there was.

David knew where Jenny was likely to be going, but he didn't want to let too much time and distance form between them, and so he ran back home, quickly changed into dry clothes, and emptied his money box: £15. *He might need more.*

The quiet tidiness of the kitchen told him that Mum was still asleep. As usual, she'd left her purse out when she came back from the pub last night. David rarely took money from her purse, and it always made him feel bad when he did, but something told him that today was going to be Significant, and morality had to take a backseat to necessity. He opened his mother's purse: £20 and change. He took the note and left the coins, telling himself that she'd probably think she just spent more than usual at the pub – that was if she noticed at all. And anyway, any money he took from her wouldn't be spent on Tony; that had to be a good thing, right?

Outside, the damp air had turned cold. The mist permeated his clothes and clung to his face, and his limbs felt weakly heavy as he got on his bike and raced towards the station. The dull throb of a stitch spread from his side to his chest, making breathing difficult, and twice he had to stop, gasping, by the side of the road, the traffic pelting past fast, and that rogue thought pushed at him again – *I'm sick, I'm sick* – but it was a weak thought, a thought he couldn't afford to have.

This time he bought a return ticket and, in the train, he worked hard to smooth his mind, calm down. He kept his face carefully blank, and stared out of the window, trying to think of nothing at all, as grey-brown countryside slid past, flat, wormlike. Just ahead were the grimy, unlovely city suburbs; the industrial estates, the empty One Bedroomed Executive Flats built on a promise of prosperity, the lonely billboards: 'Your Ad Here!'

He knew where she would be going. He knew what to do. He knew where he was going. There was no need to worry. He closed his eyes then and let the map of the city spread through his mind; found his path through the city centre, through the crowded market, and past Pretty Windows. Up the hill, past The Fox and straight to the house where Marc lived. By the time the train drew into the station, wheezing like an aged beast, he was so calm that he almost didn't notice how much he was shaking.

Saturday in the city was a new experience for David. The crowds, the noise and the music all threatened his composure. It was dizzying, largely because nothing about it made sense... Some streets were all crowds, while others – seemingly identical to David – were virtually empty. The crowd flowed, eddied, clashed and dawdled; it almost seemed to have a collective mind – a hive mentality that David couldn't tune into, and would never be part of. He was relieved to get away from the centre, relieved to be walking up the hill towards The Fox. Here there were no crowds, and no one on the streets. It was like a plague town.

Once he was at the top of the hill, he took a moment to catch his breath, close his eyes and sink into Jenny's mind. Once he felt connected to her again, he opened his eyes, nodded to himself, and made his way down the alley towards the small overgrown backyard, and crouched behind wheelie bins parked at the edge of the fence. A slat was missing, and through the gap, David could see the garden, the back door, a little of the kitchen window. The vague shapes of two people standing by the sink.

'How'd you get our address?' Jenny said. Her voice was high, strained. She sounded so young.

The Bad Man – Marc – laughed, and sauntered out of the kitchen holding a laundry basket. Slowly, insultingly slowly, he picked up damp underwear, and pegged it fussily on the line.

'How?' Jenny almost shrieked. She was standing on the doorstep now. David could see half of her pale face, saw the tension rippling down her body to one tapping foot.

Marc looked up at the weak sun, and grinned. 'Warming up a bit,' he said. 'How's your neck by the way?'

Jenny took a step forward. 'How'd you *find* us?'

'Want a cup of tea?' Marc asked.

'What? No!'

'Well, I want one.' Marc walked back inside to put the kettle on. David didn't hear anything else until he was stirring his tea, ending with a cheerful little 'tink tink' of the spoon on the cup. Then he wandered back out into the garden, smiling. He clearly wasn't intimidated. 'Spring,' he said.

'I *mean* it! Tell me or I'll get you breached,' Jenny shouted and the air fizzed.

This threat to his probation seemed to rattle him ever so slightly. 'Watch it,' he said.

'Tell me or I'll call them!' Her voice was slightly steadier now. David willed her all his strength, and peered through the gap. She stood straight, brave as a warrior.

'Sorry to disappoint you, love, but I don't *have* your address,' he said, oh so reasonably. 'And I don't *want* your fucking address. Listen, I've got to go to work in a bit, so talk sense if you're going to, or fuck off home, wherever that is.' He put his tea down on the step and resumed putting up the washing.

'The *coffin*?' Jenny managed. 'With the *pictures* in it?'

'I honestly have no fucking clue what you're on about. What pictures?' Marc sounded bored.

'The ones in Mum's photo album! The ones—'

'Oh, that photo album you tried to rob from *my* house? Along with *my* money? Is that what you mean?' His voice had an edge to it now.

'It was *ours*!' Jenny's voice cracked a little. 'Mum wanted the pictures back; they're *ours*!'

'You didn't take it when you moved out, and they're in *my* house, so they're *mine*, aren't they? Not that I care about them, but the money wasn't yours and you tried to take that, didn't you?'

'You owe us—'

'I don't owe you anything. You left and blagged yourself a nice new life. I owe you fuck all. Seriously, get the fuck out. I'm telling you. Try and breach me and I tell them how you robbed me,' he snarled.

'How did you get our *address*!' she shouted.

'I *haven't*,' the man hissed, and moved towards her, not quickly, but it was enough to produce a little yelp of fear. David saw her dart into the kitchen, and come out with one hand holding a paring knife, the blade was about four inches long, and sharp looking.

Marc stared blankly at her, but stopped dead. 'Put that down.'

'Leave us alone!' Jenny shouted at him. 'Don't come round ever *again*!' Her voice cracked. She sounded like a little girl, fiercely frightened, but used to defeat, and David winced at that, and his clasped hands squeezed together, and he tried to send Jenny strength, calm. *You're better than him, you're better than him, please believe you're better than him. You'll beat him, you will.*

When Marc tried to grab her hand, she lunged at him clumsily. The knife sliced into the webbing between his thumb and forefinger, and she let out a little cry and dropped it on the ground. Marc stepped on the blade, and kicked it angrily away towards the garden wall. Then he grabbed her with his good hand and dragged her close, fingers digging cruelly into her wrist.

The pain of this, and the pain of defeat, made her cry, big, angry tears, and this humiliation transferred itself to David, sinking into his mind, his bones. He closed his eyes, shook his head. When he opened them, he saw that the knife had skittered within his reach.

'I'll fucking *kill* you if you come round again! I will!' Jenny sobbed.

'Yeah, right. You and your knife, eh?' Marc's fingers dripped red onto the concrete. The other hand twisted her wrist sideways and up, an unnatural angle. 'Anyone'd think you don't love me any more.' A quick jerk. That's all it would take to break her arm. She made a sudden, brave attempt to wrench herself free, but his grip tightened further. David could see her red hand, the thin, exposed arm with its delicate bones, pulled, pulled further, surely almost about to snap.

'I hate you,' Jenny managed through her tears. 'I *hate* you.'

'You didn't always hate me though, did you?' You used to like a bit of a kiss and a cuddle.' Marc jerked her arm down again now, gave the hand a vicious twist to the side. 'Didn't you?'

'You're hurting me—'

'Want me to kiss it better?' He smiled like a shark, and let go.

'I *hate* you!' she sobbed again, cradling one arm with the other shaking hand.

'If you hate me so much why d'you keep coming round? I could get the wrong idea, couldn't I?' He sounded out of breath now, tired. Drip drip. The blood pattered in coin-sized drops. He lifted his hand, looked at it, grimaced, and then pointed one bloody finger at her. 'Right, I've had enough of this. Don't try to rob off me, or chat any shit. And listen close, cause I won't say it again – I've not been round yours and I don't give a shit where you are, all right? Tell Sal that. And don't even think about breaching me, or you'll be lucky to have an arm left, you get me?' He took one step towards her. 'Get fucked off now, I mean it.'

Jenny, whimpering, backed into the kitchen again. David heard her running to the front door, heard it slam.

Then there was a silence, long, broken only by Marc's heavy breathing. He stooped to the laundry basket, pulled out a tea towel and wrapped it clumsily around the wound on his hand. 'Bitch got me,' he muttered to himself. 'Look at that. Bitch got me.' He wandered around the garden shaking his head, looking like a wounded bear, before drifting back inside. David heard him turn on the tap, running his hand under it, cursing.

David's heart, pumping painfully, seemed to be sending blood solely to his brain, which pulsed, struggled, under the onslaught. It was hard to think clearly. When he looked down, he saw that he was holding the knife in one frozen hand, that it was slick with Marc's blood. He had no memory of picking it up. He hid the knife up his coat sleeve. From the house, he heard the front door slam and, after a few minutes, he tottered cautiously up the alley, down the street, and back towards the little park outside The Fox.

He didn't try to hide. Jenny wasn't here any more; he knew it; he could feel it. He just sat on the bench, staring vacantly ahead, imagining the blood on the blade seeping into the lining of his coat. He sat on the bench for an hour or more. The temperature dropped, the sun began to set. Once or twice he saw Marc through the glass doors of the pub with his red hat on, swinging between the tables collecting empty glasses. One hand was bandaged, and a pink island of blood showed through the white. On cigarette breaks, David heard him tell one person that a jack had slipped when he was working on the car; another that a dog had bitten him. David, frozen, stared at Marc. He stared at everyone. Nobody stared back. Nobody seemed to notice him at all. He was invisible. He'd merged with the air; he was insubstantial as a ghost. He was nothing. He meant nothing. He was absolutely powerless.

If he was nothing, he didn't exist. And if he didn't exist, he was absolutely free. He could do anything. Anything at all, and it wouldn't matter. That was… interesting. A new perspective.

He closed his eyes then, feeling each jagged piece of his soul shuffle, slide, and lock together like a Chinese puzzle box. In his shaken mind, a firm plan rose.

CHAPTER FORTY-FOUR

Marc seemed a little drunk when his shift was over, and unwilling to be alone. He stayed standing and smoking outside the pub door, gesticulating with his bad hand. Someone told him he might need stitches. Marc shook his head, no. Someone had given him some painkillers – 'ones they give to cancer patients' – he couldn't feel fuck all! And he laughed, and so did his friends, and soon they all started walking down the hill to the city centre, to carry on drinking. David followed.

For the next few hours chill turned to cold and the drizzle to a downpour, and David trailed Marc to pub after pub, watching him go in with one group of people, and leaving with others who would, in turn, be replaced with identical hangers-on: drunk, blowsy women, a teenager or two, balding, grim-faced men.

One by one, the hangers-on left, and were not replaced, and by ten o'clock, Marc was alone. He stood on the step of a pub called The Bristolian, wobbling on his heels. He looked old, tired. The stain on his bandage was larger now, more symmetrical, and a brighter red. He stepped into the street, and wandered south, towards the canal. David followed.

The rain had stopped, but the temperature had dropped so that the slicked streets were turning icy. Twice Marc stumbled, slipped. Once he stayed down, breathing hard, laboured as an old horse. And David followed. Marc made it to the water's edge, to a bridge that smelled of piss and damp, the ground scattered with used condoms, like desiccated jellyfish. David, standing on the bank, heard the sound of a zip, a sigh of relief, and the splash of urine against stone; then the click of a lighter and fizz of a cigarette. He heard the traffic. His heart. The soft lap of the water, and his own footsteps on the bank, on the slippery towpath. And he was nothing, and he was free and— *Now. Act. Do.* He stopped about five feet away from the man, saw him turn to face him, and then ran swiftly, smoothly, towards him, the knife outstretched, and jammed it into the soft flesh just below Marc's shoulder. It was easy. It was like he'd imagined it. It was like slicing butter.

'You shouldn't hurt women,' he told him.

Marc jerked backwards.

For a split second, they looked at each other. David smiled at him, and then ran at him with the knife again, getting him this time in the belly, deep; deep enough to feel fresh blood squirming through his knuckles, into his palm; deep enough that it jarred on something solid; stuck into something hard, and his blood-slicked fist struggled to pull it free. Marc made a sound – a kind of animal sound, an angry, lowing noise, loud, but only once, twice and then nothing. He staggered back into the dark, then, back under the bridge like a troll.

Was that it? Had he done it?

David took a step into the darkness. The blood roared in his ears. The puzzle box of his mind clicked and shifted, its smooth surface fracturing along invisible lines; because he hadn't done it. Marc wasn't dead. Marc was on his hands and knees a few feet away, and he was hurt, he was shaken, but he was very much alive.

David watched him clutch at the wall with one bloodied hand, levering himself up; he watched him stand up, and *now, now, and now… What? What now? The man wouldn't die, the man wouldn't die, the man—*

'Saw you today,' Marc gasped. 'Saw you in the park.' He staggered towards David, his filthy, bandaged hand palm up, as if greeting him. 'Saw you. Outside… pubs…'

That triggered the puzzle-box mechanism of David's mind, and everything he'd managed to keep inside – the rage, the fear, the self-hatred – suddenly rushed out, and he was only sixteen! He was only a boy, alone, in a big city where things were loud and frightening and, somehow, he'd stabbed a man and, somehow, the man wasn't dead, and oh God he wished he was at home, in his room, safely organising 'Precious Memories!' Home, where he was safe and things were quiet and—

From far away someone was singing, singing badly. The faulty notes echoed down the towpath and the noise made things even worse... made him panic just that little bit more. He scurried up the bank to the top of the bridge to get away from it.

The singing drunk girl was still far away, but getting closer, and from the top of the bridge, David could hear the sound of Marc's tortured breathing from beneath the bridge and there he was, staggering out from the shadows, wobbling. David, horribly visible just above, still with a knife in one cold, bloody hand, had to think fast. *Man up man up man up.* He kicked at half a loose paving stone, and levered it, creaking, on one toe of his trainer. It was heavy. It was heavy enough. He put the knife in his pocket, picked up the rock using both hands to hold it against the edge of the bridge wall. *Breathe breathe breathe.* The singing seemed far away, but the acoustics were weird here. He had to finish it. He had to do it, now, before the drunk girl got any closer. Marc's red baseball cap bobbed into view. David's body twitched like a dog in a dream. He let the stone drop.

It smashed onto Marc's left shoulder and side of the neck, sending the hat spinning, and he went down on his side like a felled ox, rolling to the water's edge, one hand trailing in the dirty water, one spastic leg scrabbling for traction. The paving stone had cut into his scalp and cheek – a flap of skin hung down jaggedly, a child's quavering 'V', and he lay crumpled on his left side, a few feet away from the bloodstained cap, and his mouth was open as if to shout for help, but only a wheezy, whispery sound escaped him.

David made his way down the bank. He looked curiously into the dying man's eyes. *There must be something there. There must be.*

'… seen you…' Marc managed. His eyes were flat and dull as pennies. 'Seen you before.'

David pushed his body to the edge of the canal with one foot. Half of his body rolled towards the water and dropped in, but his hairy, strong hands clung to the side. Suddenly, one of them grasped David's left trainer with surprising strength, and he felt himself being dragged towards the water by the big man's weight. He kicked at Marc's head wildly, felt the hand tighten spasmodically, and stamped again and again, savagely, until Marc's grip loosened, until his fingers fell away and he sank silently into the dark water.

David picked up the baseball cap. The paving stone had cracked in half with the impact; one half was cleanish and this he placed carefully in the canal. The other half was gore streaked and pieces of it had chipped off into bloody gravel. He scraped up all the pieces and put them inside the hat, along with half of the heavy, blood-covered stone. Then he crouched down, pushed his hands into the freezing water, rubbed them together to get rid of the blood. He didn't have a bag to put everything in, so he just shoved them under his coat and zipped it up. If he hunched, no one would be able to see the bulge.

Then he walked up the bank again, to the bridge, crossed the street, and kept on walking. The singing girl was walking in the same direction. He slowed to let her pass. She was with friends, three young women, blue with cold and loud with booze, on their way to last orders. They didn't look at David. They wouldn't remember he was there. He walked slowly through the city, avoiding the main streets that might have CCTV. He found a carrier bag in the street, transferred the hat, the knife and the rock into it, and headed towards the station.

He caught the last train home, sharing the carriage with a few drunks whose laughter and singing made his head hurt.

When he got home, he stripped off his clothes, and put them in the washing machine on a boiling setting – just in case there were any bloodstains on them. Then he stood under a scalding hot shower, scrubbing at his hands, washing his hair three times.

He hid the bag in the back of his wardrobe. When he got into bed, shivering and burning, he knew was sick.

The next morning, he struggled down to the kitchen, intending to cycle to Jenny's, see if she'd heard the news about Marc, but Mother took one look at him and refused to let him leave the house. He put up a bit of a fight, but he felt weak, too weak to persist, and allowed himself to be led back to his room, allowed Mother to enter, tuck him back into his bed, feel his forehead with one cool hand.

'You're burning up,' she said. 'Did you feel ill yesterday?'

'A bit.'

'Get some rest and we'll see how you are in an hour or so.'

David fell asleep then, a solid, blank gap of consciousness, and came round to the image of a white-faced, concerned Mother holding a cup of water to his lips and begging him to drink something. He felt the water run down his chin and onto his chest, which was sweaty and bare – *why wasn't he wearing a T-shirt? What had happened to his T-shirt?* And Mother was telling him that they had to take it off; he was so hot he'd sweated right through it, and *please, darling, please drink some water, for me? Just try?*

Thoughts and memories of the night before – or was it the night before that? – swirled in his mind like oil on water, and sometimes he thought that maybe he'd fallen in the canal instead of Marc – he was so cold and wet, and *where was his hat? And Tony – what was he doing here? He was NOT ALLOWED in his room! GET OUT OF MY ROOM AND DON'T HURT WOMEN*, and that must have worked, that must have frightened him off, because now they were inside, not by the canal, and Mother was here, not Marc, and Mother held his hot hand in her gentle cool one; she held his hand even though it was dirty – sticky with blood, and he tried to say sorry, sorry, I tried to wash it off, but it must have stained, but she said Shhhh. Calm now, Shush now. She said: 'there's an ambulance coming, darling, don't worry, there's an ambulance coming soon.'

*

At first, they thought he might have meningitis. He retained a dim memory of the needle going into his spine, the strange sensation as the fluid was extracted, the wincing anxiety on Mother's face. The pain in his chest, combined with the fever, eventually led them to diagnose pneumonia, and he was able to leave hospital, weak and woozy, after three days suspended in pharmaceutical calm.

*

'Bed rest, fluids and painkillers for the next two weeks,' Mother said firmly. 'We'll have some Mother and Son time, yes? Movies, and *treats* and—'

The novelty quickly wore off for both of them, though. David didn't like movies, and the fact that his mother didn't know that he didn't like movies irritated him. In turn, the sullen way he suffered through Merchant Ivory classics annoyed her. They played card games which David, humourlessly, won every time, and he wasn't interested in her latest dabblings in watercolour, and didn't want to

join her. Mother and Son time turned out to be a bit of a chore…
but Catherine didn't give up. She was grimly determined to Nurse
Him Back to Health, so he had to Stay Nice and Warm Indoors.

The better he got, the more he resented being watched, fussed
over and assessed. He'd imprisoned himself too – he couldn't even
retreat to his own room because the hat, the knife and that paving
stone were all still there, poisoning the carefully calibrated calm.
All he really wanted to do was sit quietly, alone, or with Tinker,
concentrate on getting strong again so he could see Jenny again
because not seeing her was driving him mad. She must know by
now that Marc was dead, and she must know on some level – on
the indefinable, animal level that connected them – that David
was responsible. But this stupid illness had robbed him of his
reward. It was like reading a book with the last chapter ripped
out. Not that he read fiction, but still. It was infuriating, and his
fury weakened him still more, wore him out. And he had to sit
here and *imagine* the gradual, dawning delight she'd felt when
she realised what he'd done. He had to wait for her gratitude. It
wasn't fair.

And because his anxiously awaited denouement had been so
cruelly postponed, more injustices tormented him. Marc. Marc
wouldn't go away. David would be happily doing nothing, stroking
Tinker, maybe, or squeezing a few spots on his shoulders, and Marc
would swim back, his hands, pale and water-wrinkled, clinging to
the side of the canal, his face, incredulous, smashed, and David
would have to kill him again and again, sometimes three or four
times a day. In daylight, Marc would finally allow himself to slip
into the water, but at night it was a different story. At night, Marc
wouldn't leave him alone, and he *should* leave him alone now. He
had to. He was dead. It was *wrong* to keep hanging around in his
mind like this… it simply wasn't fair. At night, Marc was more
powerful, his shrivelled fingers were stronger, his breath was a rolling

mist of decay, and he dragged David down with him, into the inky freeze, where one day, he knew, he'd stay for ever...

David would wake, shivering and sweating, from these dreams that he knew were not dreams but threats, and he'd reach for the nearest live, warm thing, the thing that wouldn't ask him why he was crying, why he was scared – Tinker. Tinker, with her sleepy eyes, her familiar purr, her warm, responsive body, was the only thing that got David through these nights with Marc.

It couldn't go on like this. He knew what the problem was – the knife, hat and paving slab in his room. They didn't belong here. They shouldn't be here. That was how Marc kept coming back... Marc would bleach out all the colour that Jenny had lent the world.

CHAPTER FORTY-FIVE

It took his mother three weeks of relatively close supervision before she got bored enough to leave David alone. (*She and Tony simply had to go to the quiz night. They'd missed so many. And David was ever so much better now, wasn't he?*) The first thing he did when he had some privacy again was look online for a perfect resting place for Marc's Things. He settled on an old biscuit tin he found on eBay, large, square, with a picture of kittens on the top, one of which looked a lot like Tinker. As soon as he saw it, he knew it was Significant enough to contain Marc.

For the next few days he waited anxiously for the post to arrive; he managed to get it up to his room without anyone seeing it. All in all, he'd done very well. He almost felt like he was back in control… pretty soon he'd be his old self again. He threw the hat, the stone and the knife into the box with no ceremony at all – Marc didn't deserve one – buried the box at the end of the garden, next to the old oak tree, covered the soft earth with leaves, and that night he slept, and he didn't dream.

The Kitten box worked. The next day, the *Post* ran a story about an unidentified body found in the canal. It had become tangled with weeds, and those weeds tangled with a dumped shopping trolley, and it had been in the water too long for a cause of death to be ascertained.

David clipped this article. A week later, once dental records had formally identified the body as Marc's, he also clipped the death notice, and put both in 'Precious Memories!'

For a while, he was safe.

*

Later, both Catherine and Piers looked back on the Tinker episode as pivotal. Before, they'd seen David's secrecy and surliness as being within the bounds of normal adolescent behaviour. But after Tinker, they were forced, painfully, to reassess things, question their parenting, and – most painfully – admit that David was not well.

It had all started with one of Tony's sporadic attempts to earn his keep. He'd decided to 'help out in the garden'. Over a week, he'd begun, and abandoned, digging a vegetable patch, planted rows of daffodils that the frost immediately killed off, and needlessly pollarded two trees. He dragged their sappy branches into a pile, and announced that he was building a bonfire.

Piers looked worriedly at the conifers lining the boundary of the garden. 'Not too close to the end?' and Tony had dragged the branches further in, closer to the rockery that he'd half built a few years before.

But the branches refused to burn. Tony, rapidly losing his good humour, sprayed them with lighter fuel, which worked, but it wasn't the glorious, manly blaze he was after. He added other things – that broken stool in the shed, a few cardboard boxes. The fire rose. The fizz and pop of the branches was loud enough to penetrate David's headphones ('*Now That's What I Call Party Bangers Volume 4!!*') and interrupt his training, and he wandered down to the garden to see what was happening.

'Ah! The Boy David!' Tony shouted. 'Is this a bit too big? Possibly?' He backed away, slightly fearfully from the flames. 'D'you think you could get me the hose?'

And so, David, sighing, had got the hose, and together they drowned the flames before more of the garden was engulfed. A few little patches of flame persisted, and Tony – pointing to his moccasins – didn't want to stamp them, so David did it for him.

Then his boot touched something. Something that both squelched and crunched. He peered, jumped back. Then he began to scream.

There was Tinker's little corpse: one half of her had been reduced to fur, fat and bones all charred and twisted, the other half, her pretty little face, her too-large ears and little pink nose, was untouched. David, still screaming, reached for the unburnt half, picked it up screamed louder when her head and front paws came away from the rest of her, leaving a trail of gory backbone. He turned, still holding her small head like a ghastly trophy, and vomited on Tony's moccasins.

Tony was sincerely sorry! *Awful, awful thing, believe me, I never would have done anything like this on purpose!* He tried to tell David that it would have been quick, and Tinker was old. Old and deaf and probably ready to go. *She probably just fell asleep in one of those old boxes, maybe, and he hadn't seen her, and… David, please, please believe me, I'm so sorry she, she might not even have woken up. It was probably very… peaceful? And please, David? Please? Come into the house. Come into the house and try to calm down. Put her… put her down, now, OK?*

But David didn't put her down, and he didn't calm down either. Tinker's head stayed pinched between his fingers. When his mother tried to remove it, he shrieked and pulled it closer, rubbing blood on his shirt. All three adults crowded round him, trying to help, trying to understand, all confused by the level of his hysteria… they knew he'd liked Tinker, of course, but this much? When he finally quieted, the silence was large and loud. Tony hovered around sporting a nervous, poleaxed smile. Piers busied himself making tea, while Catherine crooned, patted, stroked… they'd give her a decent burial – *even a headstone? I'm sure you can get headstones for pets…*

David stood then, still cradling what remained of Tinker, and told them all, quietly, that he wanted to be alone. He wanted to bury her, privately, by himself, right now.

'It's very dark out there, sweetie,' his mother said doubtfully. 'And very cold. And you're still not one hundred per cent—'

'I want to do it,' David said again, flatly.

'But—'

His father laid a hand on his mother's shoulder. 'Let him do it.' He nodded seriously at David, as if he understood.

Everyone backed away from him then. Father brought him a spade from the garden shed; they all watched respectfully as David, slight, so young looking in the gathering gloom, trudged down to the end of the garden. Soon nobody could make him out, and his mother made to go to him, but his father stopped her.

When he came back into the kitchen, pale, very sad, he said that he wanted to make a cross, and use Tony's soldering iron to burn Tinker's name on it.

'Right-o, of course!' Tony was glad to do something. 'Come with me and I'll show you—'

'No,' David said quietly, firmly. 'I want to do it myself.'

'It's quite a tricky instrument though—'

'How about if I help you?' Piers put in. 'I think I can remember the rudiments? David?'

And so, father and son retired solemnly to the summer house – David standing on the threshold, his back ostentatiously turned to the entrance – and together they burned TINKER on one of the few pieces of wood that had escaped the bonfire. It turned out later to be an unused frame that Tony had been saving for something, and that felt good. It felt good to destroy something of Tony's; it felt good to know that Tony couldn't complain about it either, not after what he'd done.

*

For the next few days David stayed in his room, in a state of blank, crushing sadness. The depression absolutely terrifying. David had never felt depressed before; before Tinker, he'd strongly suspected that depression was just an excuse for layabouts like Tony to do nothing, drink too much and never be held to account for their actions, but now it was happening to him, he had to accept that it was real.

David couldn't move for it, couldn't train, organise 'Precious Memories!', sink into Jenny's mind. He couldn't even leave the house to follow her. He didn't even want to open the windows of his room – the air was fetid, humid in there; it smelled of loss and fear and death. Sometimes, when David woke up, he'd smell the fishy evil of the canal, and he knew that Marc hadn't gone away after all; Marc was still here, and getting stronger all the time, because Tinker wasn't there to ward him off.

The only thing that stirred from his gloomy torpor was extreme irritation and very loud noise, both of which were amply provided by Tony who was entering the annual event he called his Spring Cycle.

Tony's Spring Cycle – 'having a good clean out' – involved great displays of self-conscious endeavour over what could sometimes be weeks. Tony hauled everything out of the summer house and dumped them all over the lawn. Wooden chairs, cigarette-scarred and musty, were piled with papers, with clothes. A guitar was propped up on a djembe drum; a ukulele poked out of a bucket full of cleaning products; why, David didn't know, because Tony couldn't play any instrument, had no musical talent at all. Some of the ugly, muddy daubs he called art were stacked against the door, others lay face up on the grass, staring up into David's room; all those eyes, staring from murky depths, dozens of Marc Doyle's… David stopped opening his curtains and kept his back to the window at all times.

During his Spring Cycle, Tony liked to prop the speakers up at the windows of the summer house and listen to one of his eight records – opera mostly – each scratched and tinny. He even sang along with the godawful noise while he 'pottered'. Tony 'pottering' was horribly compelling and repellent at the same time. The mess of ugly paintings, un-upholstered chairs, and cheap, chintzy fabric in the garden grew ever higher, as Tony wandered around, deciding, loudly, what to keep, what had 'promise', before inevitably cramming it all back into the summer house in even less order than before. On the few occasions even Mother had complained about the mess, Tony had said, 'There's madness in my method', as if it was clever.

Normally, David wasn't around during the entire Spring Cycle. His parents went on holiday together, once a year, religiously, and they always took David too: Greece last year, Egypt the year before – and this meant that David only witnessed the very start and the very end of Tony's yearly foray into decluttering. This year, though, David flatly refused to join them. He didn't want to go anywhere, see anyone, or leave his room. Father didn't think they should leave him, but Mother needed a holiday, and *perhaps it was a good sign? Independence?* Give him his space, he'll come through this… and so they agreed. One week though, not two.

'And call whenever you need to, son?' Father said more than once. 'I'm just at the end of the line, OK?'

When they left, Catherine kissed both David and Tony wetly. 'Behave, you two!'

'Oh, we'll have a grand old time!' Tony told her, and winked at David. 'Won't we, chum?'

Then, when the car disappeared down the drive, Tony went straight to the summer house, and David went straight to his room. And that was the way it was for the next five days. If it had stayed like that, everything would have been fine. But Tony had to push it. It was all Tony's fault – everything that happened later was his fault.

CHAPTER FORTY-SIX

His parents were coming back that evening, but Tony, having promised to complete his Spring Cycle by the time they got back, was only just starting in earnest. He crossed from one pile of crap to another, talking to himself, and David could hear him, even through the closed window, and it made his head hurt. The noise-cancelling headphones didn't help either: while they protected him from some of Tony's noise, they allowed Marc to swim up from the deadened depths of his mind, and David was trapped between Tony's loud chaos and Marc's stealthy silence. Fortunately, David had come up with a plan to defeat them both and protect himself. It was tricky, delicate, and it demanded huge… *what's the word? What's the word? Jesus, it's so loud, so loud? Why so loud, whysoloudwhysoloudwhy—*

For the last hour, Tony had been playing the same aria from *Carmen*, and the scratched record stuck at the same phrase every few minutes. Each time it stuck, it took him at least thirty seconds to notice and pick up the needle, and start it all over again. '*Si tu ne m'aimes pas, je t'aime, Si tu ne m'aimes pas, je t'aime, Si tu ne m'aimes pas, je t'aime…*'

David paced his room like a bear driven mad by captivity.

He couldn't concentrate with that – *screaming* – going on. And he *had* to, it was imperative because, if he didn't, then he couldn't sleep, and if he didn't sleep he'd go mad, and Marc would win and that couldn't happen. Bullies don't prosper. That's the truth; Marc needed to be told—

'STOP IT!' For the first time in a week, David opened his window.

'*Si tu ne m'aimes pas, je t'aime…*'

'TONY! STOP IT!' He couldn't focus.

'*Si tu—*'

He opened the window wider and leaned out. The fresh air made him feel dizzy. 'TONY! TURN IT OFF!'

Tony popped his head out of the summer house and waved. David noted, painfully, that he was wearing a red velvet beret. 'OFF OFF OFF!'

'Back from the land of nod, are we?' Tony shouted over the noise. David pointed furiously at the speakers. Tony nodded. 'Callas!' he called.

'It's SKIPPING!'

'What, can't hear you, let me turn it down – what?'

'Tony, the record's been skipping for ages,' David called, surprised at how calm his voice sounded. 'Can't you get a new needle or something?'

'Has it?' Tony smiled quizzically. 'I didn't notice.'

'You do,' David called. It was more difficult now to keep his voice even. 'You do notice it; you just start it again, every time. You're doing it on purpose.'

'It's a beautiful piece. You're just a philistine!' Tony called cheerfully.

David took a deep breath. 'Tony. I have a headache. I'm still not well. Do you want me to tell Mum that you made me feel worse?'

Tony smirked a little, but said nothing. They stared at each other for a few seconds. Then Tony went back into the summer house, and David returned to his task. The fresh air from the window somehow made the stink in the room worse, he had to breathe through his mouth because of the smell. The wire was sharp against his fingertips; the smell of peroxide made his eyes sting. It had been an... unpleasant task. Unpleasant, but necessary. If he got this right, then Marc's face, with its cheekbone smashed and his eyes – surprised, strangely innocent as he slipped, finally, into the cold water – might leave him alone. No, not might, *would*. Any ghost conjured can be conjured away. You just need the right charm, and he knew that this was the right charm.

After ten minutes of calm, though, the music started again. The same side with the same skip, and *no, don't let it get to you, don't let it – concentrate*! Concentrate! '*Si tu ne m'aimes pas, je t'aime, Si tu ne m'aimes pas, je t'aime*' and for the love of God *turn it down turn it off turn it down turn it off.*

He didn't hear Tony jogging up the stairs and opening his bedroom door.

'You've been shouting? What's happened?'

And David, stunned, looked up at Tony's reddened, droopy face, and he scrambled backwards, his toe catching the bowl of peroxide, tipping it over onto the carpet. Tinker's broken jaw, those carefully prised out, polished teeth, scattered across the carpet. 'You're in my room!' David gasped. 'You can't be in my room!'

But Tony, now pale, stayed. He even tottered in further. 'What's that?' he asked stupidly, pointing at the cat's skull, the partially skinned paws. 'Jesus, David, what've you done?' and David had no answer. His only thought was to somehow get Tony out of the room.

'Get OUT!' he scuttled back on his backside and got up on numb legs. In one hand he held the pliers, and he made an ineffectual launch at Tony with them 'GET OUT OF MY ROOM!'

And Tony did, running back down the stairs, his silly little oriental sandals flapping on each step.

*

When Tinker had died (*when Tony had murdered her*), David had genuinely intended to bury her. He dug the hole and everything, but then she spoke to him – not actually spoke to him, he wasn't crazy – but she… somehow… let him know that even in death she could help. And so he'd filled in the grave, and kept her in his room. When she started to smell, he bought the pliers, peroxide and citric acid online, and read about taxidermy, about witchcraft and lucky charms. He wrapped her in silver foil and put her in a pillowcase when he wasn't working on her, thinking dimly that this would stop the smell from spreading. It wouldn't take long now, anyway. All he had to do was take out her claws, wire everything together to make his gleaming, rattling bracelet – a totem he could secretly wear at night to fend off Marc.

Now David spent long minutes looking for Tinker's teeth in the carpet. In his shaken mind, he thought that if he found them all, and arranged them just as they'd been before, then he could start over. It could still work. Tinker wouldn't let him down, would she?

'Would you darling?' he asked her. 'You're OK, aren't you darling?'

But poor Tinker, stinking and desiccated on the plastic sheeting he'd put down to protect the carpet, was not OK. Poor Tinker. Poor, dead Tinker, who'd wanted to help, who'd given her life to help, had been thwarted once again by Tony.

He picked up each tooth, stuck them in order on a piece of tape, and wrapped them in a piece of foil, placed it in her mouth, and wrapped her half-denuded torso in the pillowcase. Then he said a prayer. He told her how sorry he was, and he began to cry, feeling like a baby, but unable to stop. He cried for a long time, until his despair morphed into anger, which in turn became an implacable, calm rage. *Tony. That fucker Tony. He'd ruined everything, he was doing Marc's bidding for him. The two of them were in it together.*

Perhaps if he buried Tinker now? If she wasn't in the house when Mother and Father came back, David could just say that Tony was lying, couldn't he? This could still be turned around. Also, if he buried her next to the kitten box, she could work her charm still? It was worth trying. So, for the first time since Tinker died, David left the house.

CHAPTER FORTY-SEVEN

David dug beneath the cross, placed her in her grave, then backed away. In the garden, the doors to the summer house were wide open, but Tony wasn't anywhere to be seen. The music was still playing, but quieter. David abandoned the idea of calm. He was tired of being calm. Where had being calm got him? He thrust his hand through the open window and dragged the needle off the record with a nasty ripping sound, pulled the record off the turntable and threw the entire thing across the garden into the bushes. That felt good. He picked up a palette knife from the grass, crossed to the stack of self-portraits on the lawn, and began gouging into one of Tony's eyes, put the knife in and pulled down until the canvas flapped open, just like Marc's skin.

Then he went to the shed for supplies. Lighter fuel, matches, a screwdriver; from the kitchen he could hear Tony on the phone, presumably to Catherine. His voice was urgent, scared. *An emergency, yes, an emergency—*

Scared? You should be. If Tony brought chaos, David could counter with rage. Emergency? *OK. You'll have an emergency. A Grand Old Emergency. That will be my gift to you, Tony. Old chum.*

David walked slowly back to the summer house, taking time to drag the screw driver against another one of Tony's half-finished oils scarring the yellow skin, the foggy pools of eyes. Humming, tuneless as an insect, he sprayed another with lighter fuel and threw a match at it, watching, with great satisfaction, the flames melting his face off. He tried to imagine that the fire was eating through Tony's real face. He sprayed the fuel in joyful zigzags over everything else – Tony's dusty, brittle canvases in the plywood frames, over his cheap, veneered occasional tables, over the piles of receipts, the old newspapers, the records, the radio, everything, and threw a match. Now for the summer house itself; he splashed the doorway, dripped a careful line of fuel in a line back out onto the lawn. Then, taking a deep breath, he struck one match, set alight all the rest of the matches in the box, waited until the box was aflame, and tossed it.

The small flame ran, thin, towards the doorway, caught and rushed inside and soon David heard the *pop pop pop* of Tony's scattered cigarette lighters, exploding like little fireworks inside the summer house, saw the smoke boiling out of the open window. Such an exciting noise! So *thrilling*, so *definite*. He closed his eyes, smiled, and thought to himself, *I should have done this years ago*. The flames rose, thrillingly immense. *I* did this, he thought *I did this. This is what happens when I get pushed too far… This should teach them*. He closed his eyes, grinned. He felt very calm, very powerful. He hadn't felt this good since stabbing Francis Brennan…

But when he opened his eyes, his smile faltered. The fire was… large, getting larger every second. Already it was between him and the house. He could faintly see the outline of his window before the black smoke billowed towards him, smarting his eyes. He heard Tony calling him from behind the wall of flame: 'David! David!' in a panicked bellow, and David felt fear then. All he could see was flame, and all he could smell was black, choking smoke. All he could hear was fire and his own name, and something awful, something shameful – small whimpering animal sounds that he dimly understood were coming from him, which he despised even as they got louder. Smoke had now completely obscured his view of his bedroom window – that neat, empty, fire-less sanctuary that he wished to God he'd never left, and then he tripped over something and landed spreadeagled on the ashy grass, one palm on a melting record, the vinyl burning like napalm. The smoke was thick with all the varnish and dirt burning off the furniture, and David retched and screamed, retched and screamed – screamed in pain and fury because he'd messed this up. He'd made a fool of himself. He'd done it all *wrong*.

Then Tony swam through the smoke. He was shouting and his eyes were red slits. 'David! David, grab my hand! David!'

But David, confused now, stayed still. His instincts told him to hunker down like an animal.

'David!'

And Tony gripped him by the hand and pulled, pulled him with surprising strength along the burning grass to the oak tree. Tony's hair was on fire, and his grip was slippery and burning hot, and David saw, with horror, that Tony's hand was *melting*, and he pulled away then, screaming, and kicked Tony away, back into the flames. He crawled backwards, heard Tony shouting, screaming. 'SHUT UP SHUT UP SHUT UP!' David screamed back, and then something exploded and he lost consciousness.

The fire brigade found him curled up by Tinker's grave, with Tony's sloughed-off palm still in his.

*

He was in the hospital for three days. His burns, aside from the one to his hand, were not serious. However, the fact that he didn't talk or open his eyes, suggested that smoke inhalation had affected him in some way the doctors couldn't be sure of. They had to sedate him to check his airways; he fought them too much when he was conscious.

Eventually he was referred to a psychiatrist, who succeeded in getting him to open his eyes, but couldn't get him to talk in either of their meetings. David did nothing but stare furiously at her.

Shock. *Trauma affects people in different ways... and did he have trouble communicating his feelings usually?*

'He can be withdrawn,' his mother admitted. 'I try to get him out and about – you know, friends, girlfriends and things like that, but he's never been one for... he's more of a loner, I'd say.'

'Is there any chance that he had something to do with the fire?' The psychiatrist's tired eyes rested on hers.

Catherine kept her voice calm. 'It was all just a terrible accident. I'm sure he'll tell you that when he feels better.'

Later, Piers stopped the psychiatrist in the corridor. Suppose, just suppose, the boy didn't recover his speech? Suppose the trauma was such that he might need specialist care? No, no, I understand that the NHS is too stretched... Home care? Well, it's still all a bit of a muddle at home – fire damage and everything... not a quiet environment... And the stress on his mother would be... a more private environment? Where he'd have access to doctors, like yourself, to help him get over this... this *phase*?

And so David was packed off, bandaged and silent, to a private psychiatric hospital.

'It's got lovely grounds,' Catherine told Tony, helping him move what remained of his belongings into David's old room. 'A pool, tennis courts. And he can have individual therapy until he feels more sociable.'

'What shall we do with this?' Tony pointed at 'Precious Memories!' His hand was a patchwork mess of grafted skin, shiny and pink as a pig's.

'I'll put it in the small room, just in the meantime.'

'Burn it, I would,' muttered Tony savagely. He'd lost weight. His Chinese robe drooped on him. Catherine opened her mouth to say something, but nothing came out. Instead she shook her head and moved her son's only personal possession out of the room, where it collected dust under the radiator of the box room for the next few years.

Tony decorated his new room in terracotta stucco. He covered the beige carpet with oriental rugs; one whole wall was dominated by a new sound system, complete with three-foot speakers, and Catherine replaced his melted records with compilation CDs.

CHAPTER FORTY-EIGHT

First it was The Wolsey Clinic. Six months or thereabouts. Then it was Hazlewood Priory. He was there for a long time. Then, after a long gap, it was… what was the last one called? Hillier Private Hospital, that was it, but he wasn't there for long. These places had their own stationery, gyms, a pool, and cable TV in each room. They were more like a hotel than a mental hospital. Mother didn't like him calling them that, but that's what they all were, after all. Once the lights went out, and the whispering started, you couldn't call them anything else.

He went to The Wolsey straight from the burns unit. His left hand, the one they'd had to pick the vinyl out of, was more or less useless, and would be until he had more skin grafts, and the painkillers made him sleep. When he wasn't sleeping, he still tended to keep his eyes closed, and he didn't speak a word. Not for weeks.

He wasn't quite the youngest patient at The Wolsey. There were at least five girls, possibly his age or older, but so shrunken with anorexia they looked like infants. They hung around together and talked about food, huddled over their phones doing image searches of burgers. David thought once or twice that possibly the hospital staff should know about this, and he even thought about telling them himself, but in the end he didn't. It wasn't anyone else's business really. The smiling, complacent staff were big on privacy, and the patients were called guests, and you didn't really have to do anything or see anyone if you didn't want to, and David didn't want to.

He stayed there until Christmas, then he was deemed well enough to go home.

*

When he saw what Tony had done to his old room, he retaliated by setting fire to the Christmas tree, and didn't even try to pretend it was an accident. He made sure that he stood far enough away that the flying, sappy bristles didn't catch him. They caught Father though, and David was sorry for that because he never wanted to hurt his father, and the look on his face, as he batted away the flames that clung to his sweater, haunted David for a long time.

*

He was only at home for a week before his parents decided that he needed to go back to hospital, but not The Wolsey – this time he was sent to Hazlewood, which was a hundred miles away and used to be a monastery or something. Father said that it was the best place for him; he'd get better care… *He wants me as far away as possible*, thought David, with no malice.

*

At Hazlewood he thought about writing to Father – and even began – but the letters didn't make any sense. He was on too much medication and his thoughts weren't ordered enough. He kept the half-finished letters though. He kept everything from this period because it seemed that it might be Significant at some point, but he didn't know how.

He liked Hazlewood more than The Wolsey because there was more of a routine, and his room was white and empty, like his room at home, but smaller. In The Wolsey there'd been pictures on the wall (in non-shatter plastic, fixed to the wall with industrial-strength brackets) and brightly patterned curtains, which he found offensive, but in Hazlewood they got it right. Everything was much more restful, and the people were older too, and less likely to try to talk to you. They had more about them, even though some of them were really very mad indeed. David liked the other patients, enjoyed watching them. He watched one man more than most – a tall, thin dignified character with a twitch in one eye and a crooked mouth that made it seem as if he was winking at you, that you had some humorous secret in common.

The Man with the Twitch stole things, stored things, just like David did. Little things like soap, a phone charger, and three spoons (plastic – not able to be sharpened) a day from the cafeteria, and hid them all under his mattress; David had seen him through a crack in the door. Doors were always open at Hazlewood, and it was remarkable how little people seemed to notice they were being spied on. Every two days, the staff would change everyone's sheets, and everything that The Man with the Twitch had accumulated would be quietly returned to their original owners, the spoons presumably disposed of (I mean, who knew *what* he did with the spoons?) and no one said a word about it, not even The Man with the Twitch, who serenely started all over again, beginning with the three spoons from the cafeteria.

David found this quiet defiance immensely interesting and comforting. He thought of The Man with the Twitch as a walking, winking parable, the moral of which was beautifully simple: abide, never change, anything you lose can always be found again. And therein lay contentment. The Man with the Twitch was very, very contented, David could tell.

The Man with The Twitch, the quiet, karmic silence of the staff, the white, empty room… it all did David the power of good. He understood now that everything had been necessary: being tormented by Marc, by Tony; the fire – *both* fires. He had to be forcibly taken away from that hell and placed in the comfortable limbo of Hazlewood in order to prepare himself for the paradise of his true vocation: Jenny. He had to suffer to be free.

He asked his psychiatrist if he'd be able to have an iPad? Mum wanted to buy him the new one, and, of course, he knew he wasn't well enough to go back to school, but he'd like to keep up with the GCSE syllabus? Keep his hand in? The psychiatrist smiled, and not only allowed him to have an iPad but also allowed him to keep it in his room, and have unmonitored access to it. Private hospitals were great that way. If you had the money, you could do anything.

'Hazlewood works wonders!' Mother told him. 'Dad is so pleased; we're so proud of you!'

As soon as he got the iPad, he found her. It was easy. Facebook. Twitter. Instagram. Jenny had them all. He was both frustrated and gratified by how little of her life she put online though... Jenny wasn't a daily communicant, unlike her friend Freddie who cropped up on her page all the time, a tubby, grinning clown that David disliked on sight.

Freddie Lees-Hill was one of those idiots that posted everything: his address, his phone number, everything. He friended everyone who asked and appeared to have no filter. He posted annoying GIFs of people double-taking in sitcoms, and religiously photographed his meals; he overused punctuation. During the holidays, he was for ever 'drinking anything alcoholic' with Jenny Holloway, which deepened David's dislike into hatred. What was she drinking for? It was illegal to drink until you were eighteen anyway, wasn't it? The law was there for a reason. David would sit, cross-legged in his hospital bed, frowning worriedly at the screen. He stayed away for – what was it now? A year? – and she took up with someone so obviously beneath her. That Freddie was gay didn't make David feel any better... For the first time, David thought that if he'd only managed *not* to set fire to Tony's belongings, and *hadn't* killed the Christmas tree, then that would be him there, 'Enjoying fireworks with bestie Jennifer Holloway', instead of this fat little prick. *It was… wrong. It was just wrong.*

From Hazlewood, David watched Jenny do her A levels (two Bs and a D – *she could have done better. Freddie probably distracted her*), mourned when she accepted a place at a second-string university to study psychology (she was better than Leicester, she was better than psychology, which – and he knew this from experience – was an absolute con), cheered up considerably when she dropped out and moved back home. If she was back in the village, he'd be able to see her there, soon. All he had to do was get out of hospital. But before that, he needed to prepare the ground, and this presented a problem.

If he, as David Crane, sent her a friend request, there was a good chance that she'd turn him down. After all, he didn't know what rumours might have circulated about him in his absence; he didn't know who knew what about the cause of the fires and why he left school before GCSEs. If he asked Mother, she might think he was getting… anxious again, and if she thought that, he might have to stay at Hazlewood longer. But just gleaning bits of information about her from Freddie's page was impossibly frustrating… he had to have some kind of direct contact with her.

And so Ryan Needham arrived on the scene. A tall, rangy basketball player who liked to travel, Ryan was studying at the University of Durham. Good old Ryan.

The best thing about Ryan was that he was almost, very nearly, real. Ryan was indeed a basketball player (he didn't live in Durham but in Idaho). He really had studied anthropology (at a private college in Illinois dedicated to spreading Christian teachings of creationism). But Ryan Needham wasn't, strictly speaking, *called* Ryan Needham. He was Tyler Dodds, a fundamentalist Christian sports enthusiast who, once upon a time, had greatly overshared on Myspace before he abandoned it, leaving his entire life preserved there – like an insect in amber... three years' worth of photographs that David used to create Ryan the Extreme Sports Enthusiast; Ryan the Effortlessly Cool scholar. He grew very attached to Ryan, very proud of his popularity. After giving him fifty or so friends from other fake profiles David created other, real people, wanting to be friends with him too. Most of them pouting girls with heavily filtered profile pictures and obvious self-esteem issues.

David let Ryan accumulate a few hundred friends, real and fake, before targeting a sad, chubby cutter of a girl called Immy – a girl Freddie Lees-Hill knew from university. Immy was pathetically grateful to Ryan for his faintly sleazy comments on her public photos ('Looking hot!!!!!'), and soon (too soon, the girl had no notion of how pitiful she seemed) she was confiding in him... long private messages that David didn't bother reading to the end... 'my parents are divorced/step brother abused me/ boo hoo etc'. Immy made David feel a bit sick, and he grew to loathe her; but she was useful because she could lead him to Freddie.

Finally, after a few months of Immy banging on about her anxiety and calorie counting, David made the decision to have Ryan message Freddie directly.

Bit weird... you don't know me... worried about Immy? Seems depressed... is she OK?

Ryan was nice like that.

And that's how Freddie and Ryan became friends.

They even spoke on the phone – though not often. Ryan was from Brighton, so David would have to practice the accent for a few hours before speaking to Freddie and he always kept the conversation short, and let Freddie do most of the talking. Afterwards, he would feel murderously angry – things were going so slowly, Freddie didn't talk enough about Jenny *and really what was the*

*point what was the point and he really needed to get out of this place
just get out and find her, meet her.* Then he'd make himself think
of The Man with The Twitch, and he'd calm down. Because he
would meet her. He *would* be with her. He just had to be patient,
complete every level, earn his destiny. This was purgatory. He
wouldn't be here for ever.

In the end, Ryan didn't contact Jenny; she messaged *him.* She
was suspicious; she was worried for her friend, and she didn't hold
back – Why didn't he have any pictures of himself as a child? No
one was ever tagged in the photos either, and the library-bound,
scholarly Ryan in updates didn't seem to match the intrepid Ryan
of the pictures. How did he have the time to snowboard in what
looked a lot like Utah? Kayak in a suspiciously sunny lake district?
Run the Berlin marathon? The picture wasn't even of Berlin anyway;
the car number plate was American.

Who are you really? she asked.

And David genuinely had no idea what to say. On the one
hand, he was mortified that his carefully laid plan had already
fallen into tatters; but at the same time strangely proud that she'd
seen through him when no one else had. The more he thought
about it, the more fitting that seemed, because it proved her basic
superiority to others.

She messaged him.

I'm really intrigued, what makes people do things like this?

That sounded hostile. Did that sound hostile? David suffered
through waves of icy panic. He lay on his bed, with his head mashed
into the pillow, going over every mistake he'd made, and every way
he'd underestimated her. When it was time to take his medication,

he pretended to swallow and kept the capsule under his tongue, and spat it out into the toilet, once the nurse left. He had to keep a clear head. He had to think of the best way forward.

She messaged him again.

Freddie really likes you, talks about you all the time. He might even like the Real You if you come clean to him?

Before he knew what he was doing, he'd messaged back.

It's you I'm interested in though not him.

There was a long pause, during which David dug his nails into his wrists, folded over one another in a Möbius strip of anxiety.

Why? She answered eventually.

That simple syllable told him that she hadn't automatically written him off. Wincingly, he relaxed his grip and gently massaged the little half-moon cuts on each wrist.

I didn't want to be weird. I created a fake profile just for fun, but then I saw that this guy was actually your friend, and I wanted to message you.
Yes, but why?

Was she fishing for compliments? David frowned at the screen. Full disclosure? Full disclosure. Well, full-ish.

I went to school with you.
Which school?
He named the one in the village.

You were in my form. We met once in the graveyard. David Crane.
You probably don't remember me.
Oh I do.

She left a five-minute pause, then.

Why not just message me/friend me as you are? Freddie's really
into you. Are you even gay?
No! And I didn't want to lead him on or anything, but now I can't
get out of it, it's all been a mistake I can see that now.

He took a break to hyperventilate, wishing that he hadn't spat out his medication. A few hours of warm, fuzzy catatonia seemed very welcome right about now.

I'm so sorry.
Don't panic. Send me a picture to prove who you are. As for
Freddie, we can work something out to let him down easily. I don't
want him to be hurt either.

She wanted his picture? Why? He had to go outside to take a decent photo, and when he sent it to her she immediately responded with:

Are you in a hospital?

How did she know? He peered at the picture – at the top left you could just see an alarmed door and half of the sign for Cecelia Wing. *Shit, she was sharp…*

I volunteer at a rehabilitation ward.

He replied, all the time thinking *she'll see through this, she'll see through this*:

I had a stroke when I was a child and that's why I volunteer. I had such good care, I'm just giving back really.

He typed, wincing, worrying that he was over-egging things.

God. That sounds harsh.

David passed his iPad from one sweaty hand to the other.

Please don't tell Freddie. I feel really bad about all this. I'm not a bad person, honestly. I'll take the profile down. I'll do it now.
No, don't do that, that would be weird and it'd hurt F more. Just dial it down and don't lead him on any more.
And us?

He asked, abandoning all pride. She replied:

I'm not sure. You'd have to prove that you're sorry and that you're trustworthy.

He replied eagerly:

I can do that!

She left the conversation then without answering. Almost immediately, Ryan received a new Facebook notification:

Freddie Lees-Hill is on Facebook live.

And... there he was, livestreaming himself bellowing: '£2 doubles YES PLEASE!' and, right beside him, there was Jenny, looking straight at the camera, smiling, waving. Freddie dodged out of frame; Jenny blew a kiss at the camera. 'Say hi, Jen! Jen!' Freddie cried, and she did. She waved. 'Hi! Hi!' and David realised that it was the first time he'd heard her voice or seen her move in three years, and the knowledge made him feel faint. He closed his eyes. Tears started. He heard Freddie laughing his hooting laugh. Then the stream stopped, and David was suddenly alone again, in his dim room; She'd actually been with Freddie throughout their whole unmasking-of-Ryan conversation, and hadn't told him anything?

She remembered him from school. That meant that something about David interested her enough to keep her friend in the dark. She'd already thought more of him than she did of Freddie! And how brilliantly she'd handled it! He wouldn't have to be Ryan ever again; he wouldn't have to talk to Freddie ever again. Jenny had achieved, in less than an hour, more than David had in years.

She was even more perfect than he'd imagined.

Over the next year or so they kept in touch. On his birthday, she even sent him a photo of herself, which he immediately wrapped in a clean pillowcase and put under his mattress.

When he left Hazlewood, the first thing he did was get it properly framed, but he didn't put it on the wall of the flat his parents had bought for him. They would notice when they came round – as they did, frequently, not to 'check' just to 'say hello!'– and he wasn't ready to share her with them.

It was only after his father's death had propelled him back into hospital, and after his mother's diagnosis had propelled him out again, that he put it up in his old bedroom, and spent long hours gazing at it, hoping desperately for her, praying that they would meet, properly, soon. That they would be together, for ever, at last.

She wanted that too. Of *course* she did. But, she reminded him that things were complicated, he just had to be patient, that's all. Sometimes he almost fought back. *Why? Why does Freddie take precedence over me? Why can't your mother have people around the house? You can't be that busy – too busy to even meet, when we're only a mile apart?* Then he'd hear the silence on her end of the phone, a frozen, sometimes tearful pause:

'You think I'm… lying?'

'No! No, of course—'

'I don't do that, David. *You're* the one who does that.'

'Not any more – I don't any more.'

'Sometimes I wonder if that's true.' And her voice was so hurt, distant, and sometimes she wouldn't answer calls, pick up messages, and David hated hated hated himself for demanding too much, was joyfully relieved when she forgave him and they started speaking again.

And when she asked for small favours, he was more than happy to oblige her; it was the least he could do. It was only money, after all, and he had lots of money. And as for the last favour he'd done for her, well, it made him feel warm every time he thought of it.

CHAPTER FORTY-NINE

Jenny. The Day After Freddie's Death

'Cheryl, I'm sorry!' Jenny stood quivering in the doorway. 'I didn't know where else to go! '

Cheryl was uncharacteristically flustered. Her hennaed hair showed grey at the roots and her signature silver nail polish was chipped. 'What's happened?' She made Jenny come in, sit down and accept a glass of wine.

Jenny sat tense on the edge of an armchair. 'I can only stay for a minute. I need to get away.'

Cheryl wrinkled her brow. 'Escape is always a short-term answer, what say we—'

'No, Cheryl, please listen.' Jenny hunched forward. 'I'm sorry. I've been lying to you and to Freddie and everyone. It's my fault – everything that's happened is my fault—'

'*What's* happened though? If we talk, maybe we'll discover that it isn't that bad after—'

'Freddie's dead.'

'Oh my god!' Cheryl sagged back against the cushions. 'How?'

Jenny closed her eyes. 'He was attacked, stabbed. I think' – she forced the words out – 'I think David did it.'

Cheryl, rarely silent, was silent as she struggled to comprehend Jenny's words. Her make-up free face was pale and pockmarked as an ancient moon 'Surely – I mean, the police? You have to call the police—'

'I did. I've just come from there.' Jenny took a sip of wine. 'I told them everything. They're going to arrest David, but I don't want to be there when it happens. Freddie – he was always suspicious of David; he never liked him. I thought he was just… jealous. I even told him that. Then Freddie found all these things that David had kept – he'd been spying on me – stalking me for years. Freddie tried to warn me, but I thought that if I just *talked* to David… But David, he went crazy. Violent.' She moved her hair further away from her face, to show her bruises. 'He even *hit* me. Locked me in a room.'

Cheryl's eyes widened. 'Has he hit you before?'

Jenny fingered her cheek, hesitated, nodded. 'A few times. Never before this last week though But, he's ill, Cheryl. I always knew he was… anxious, but I didn't think he was dangerous. I did what everyone does – I forgave him. I thought that I'd provoked it. And he was always so sorry, always so *guilty* that… Stupid… I thought I could help him, but…'

'You're staying here,' Cheryl said stoutly. 'And I'm calling the police. We have to make sure they've got him—'

'No. Listen, I'm not making that mistake again. I've decided to go away somewhere where he can't find me. Just in case he somehow… I mean, he *won't*… but just in case he gets away from the police. He's clever. He doesn't know much about you, where you live, your full name, and I told him we fell out a few weeks ago.'

'Why?' Cheryl was puzzled.

Jenny gestured impatiently. 'He's been acting strangely for a long time. He was very jealous of you. I wanted to protect you, make sure he wouldn't, I don't know, show up at your office and cause a scene. So I lied and told him that he'd been right all along and you were this awful charlatan and I never wanted to see you again.'

Cheryl's expression was an odd mixture of dazed and peevish. 'You haven't said anything about this before.'

'Cheryl, there's so much I haven't told you, OK? I haven't told anyone everything, Freddie knew more than anyone else, and look what happened to him? I can't let anything happen to you too.' She closed her eyes, took a breath. 'I came to give you this.' She handed Cheryl an A4 envelope full of paper. 'I've made a kind of diary, written down some of the things he's been doing. He looks at my computer and my phone, so writing was safer. Some of it might not make a lot of sense, some of it might sound crazy, but it's the truth and I need you to keep it all safe. When I'm sure they've got him, I'll come back, and give it all to the police.' She hesitated. 'And, if anything happens to me, take it to them yourself? OK?' Her phone buzzed then, both women paled; Jenny peered at her phone. 'No, it's OK, it's just the taxi saying they're here.'

'Where are you going?'

Jenny shrugged on her coat. 'I'm not going to tell you, just in case. But I'll call you when I get there, I promise. Be careful!'

'You too!' Cheryl replied weakly. She watched the younger woman hurry out of the door and into the waiting car. Then she bolted the door, poured herself a brandy, and sat down to read Jenny's notes.

CHAPTER FIFTY

Jenny had found the police difficult to read. When she ran through the doors and began panting her story to the man on the desk, she'd seen his expression move from flat boredom, through sudden sharp interest, to something else. Something that might be dark amusement, tinged with disbelief, and she'd said: 'I know it all sounds insane, I *know* that, but please, it's true!' and watched his expression crawl back behind the wall of professional indulgence. She had no idea if he believed her or not. She just had to hope he did.

In the safety of an interview room, she told another officer the whole story. David was violent, obsessive. He'd been stalking her – her friend had the proof, but now her friend was dead. 'I should have come to you then, I know I should, but I thought that if I *talked* to David I could get him to admit things?'

'And you saw these items – the hat, the knife – yourself did you?'

'No,' Jenny admitted. 'Freddie took some photos of them on his phone and showed them to me. They'll still be on his phone? All you have to do is look on his phone and—'

'We haven't recovered Mr Lees-Hill's phone yet.' The officer leaned towards her tiredly. 'So you say you only saw… *photographs* of photographs of you?'

'Yes.'

'Not the original photographs?'

'No, but—'

'And what else? A hat?'

She nodded. 'A red Nike baseball cap. It had bloodstains on it. Marc wore it all the time.'

The officer nodded slowly. 'A lot of red baseball caps around.'

Jenny's face hardened. 'It was his hat. I know it was his hat.'

'How could you tell it was bloodstained from only seeing a photograph? Blood on red—'

Jenny clenched her fists, tried to keep her voice calm. 'You don't believe me.'

The officer smiled patronisingly. 'I'm not saying that, what I *am* saying is that we'd need more to—'

'Look, he's sick. David. He has mental problems; he's been hospitalised.' She let herself cry then, and her eyes wide, pleading, met those of the officer. 'Look at my face! Look at what he did to me!' She watched the policeman's face as he looked at her eye. *Maybe it wasn't bruised enough? She hadn't looked at it since...* 'He has a history of violence, look him up! He's been in psychiatric hospitals! He killed my friend, I know he did! I *know* it was David!' Still that hooded scepticism. Jenny felt tears of rage. One hand clenched the other, hard until her knuckles turned white. 'Look, he's in the hospital with his mother, right now. There's no way he'd leave her there, even to find me. If you go *now*, there's a chance you could get him.'

The officer didn't reply, but looked heavily at her. His expression was smooth, unreadable, and it made her nervous. Eventually, he said that he had to have a word with his colleague, led Jenny back to the reception, and placed her on the hard bench below the noticeboard. He disappeared into the back office behind the reception desk.

She waited for ten long minutes and, from behind the frosted glass, she heard dull mutterings and one sharp laugh. She waited for five more minutes, feeling anger and fear build... were they laughing about *her*? No, they weren't. Of course they weren't. They *were* though… she could feel it. She wasn't believed. She wasn't bruised enough to believe. Her silenced phone buzzed with calls from David. *How long did she have? How long did she have before he found her?* She turned off her phone and went to the toilet, gritted her teeth, and hit herself in the eye a few more times. Then she smoothed her hair, dabbed her eyes, and walked back to the reception area, ripped down a 'Hang Up on Fraudsters!' poster and wrote David's address on the back of it, along with a tearful note:

PLEASE ARREST THIS MAN! HE'S DANGEROUS!

She left it on the reception desk, and walked out of the building, and took a cab to Cheryl's, gave her the notes, then took another cab to the station. She had a long journey ahead of her. It would take two trains and a bus to get where she needed to go.

On the first train, she tried to write. On the second she tried to read, but on the final few miles, shaking on the back seat of the clattering bus, gave herself over to silent thought, as her present looped neatly into the past, pulling her into the heart of Scarborough.

The Windsor Castle was under new ownership, and she doubted if the slightly pitiful hipster couple that ran it now had ever heard of the names Granville, Kathleen or Sal. The shabby fleur-de-lis carpet on the stairs had been taken up; the boards still squeaked. The foyer had been jazzed up with a few forlorn-looking taxidermied animals, mismatched chairs and kitschy mirrors. The hipster decor spread over the whole place, but stopped dead at the boundary of the bar area. Here, it was like stepping back in time. The same creaky stools clustered around the same walnut curve of the bar. Jenny almost expected to see an eight-year-old version of herself, spinning on her stool, kicking the shabby veneer with scuffed shoes, eating crisps, while Sal and Kathleen drank, laughed, sang along to Dusty Springfield on the jukebox, loud enough for Granville to tell them to 'Keep it down – sounds like two cats in a blender!' and both women would stop, mock offended, then carry on, louder than before.

On the cusp of the bar, adult Jenny closed her eyes, smiled, almost hearing the rough affection in Granville's voice, the shy pride. Because they didn't sound like cats in a blender at all – they both had lovely, strong, smoky voices. Beautiful voices.

Jenny hadn't expected to feel... anything really. She'd come up here because it was far away, and she'd checked into The Windsor Castle because it was familiar, that was all. She hadn't expected it to be this affecting. She hadn't... wow. She shook her head in a dazed sort of way. The man behind the bar asked if she was OK.

'Yes. Just... I used to come here when I was little, that's all.'

'Has it changed much?'

'This bit hasn't.'

The barman nodded. 'I think they thought it was cheesy enough in here as it was. They didn't need to do anything to it.' He smiled ironically. 'London. Rob and Jemma? The owners? London.' He nodded again with grim satisfaction. 'Thought they could bring a little bit of Shoreditch to Scarborough.'

'Is it not doing well then?'

The man smiled again. 'Well, put it this way – twelve rooms, twelve vacancies. Eleven now that you're here. What can I get you?'

'Gin and tonic.'

He rolled his eyes. 'We've got this elderflower infused one, and some sloe gin somewhere, and—'

'Have you got any just normal gin? Gordon's or something?' She sat on a bar stool gingerly. 'And not served up in a test tube or something?'

He winked, dug out a bottle of something called Juniper Flavoured Spirit. 'This is the most bog-standard they've got.' He poured it into a normal, un-ironic glass, while the jukebox played the unrepentantly uncool Elton John.

'Hope you don't mind me asking.' He was awkward. She knew what was coming. 'Your eye?'

She touched it with a gentle finger, as if she'd forgotten what it looked like. 'Oh God, is it awful?'

'It's… colourful.'

'Let's just say I… got on the wrong side of someone.' She allowed a brave, sad smile to spread.

The barman shifted uncomfortably. 'None of my business but, boyfriend?'

Jenny nodded, looked down at the bar, let tears thicken her voice. 'I ran away.' Elton John's inane lyrics were the only thing breaking the silence. She could almost feel the barman's discomfort. She waited another minute or so before speaking again. 'Bad man.'

'You've… told the police then?'

She nodded. 'And came straight here.' She took a sip of her gin. 'Sorry. Don't want to make you feel uncomfortable. It's not a very happy topic of conversation, is it?'

'Don't worry about that, love,' the barman said stoutly. 'He sounds like a proper bastard. Sounds like you're well out of it.'

She nodded, smiled gratefully. 'Got to keep yourself safe, haven't you?'

'Yup. Look after number one.'

She finished her drink. 'Listen, just in case someone… calls for me, comes round looking for me, please…?'

'You're safe here, love,' he told her. 'I'll let Rob and Jemma know to look out for someone too, OK?'

She smiled gratefully at him. Her bad eye was almost closed.

CHAPTER FIFTY-ONE

Later, in her densely decorated room, creepily aware that she was the only guest in the whole place, she went over the conversation, and was very grateful it had happened. Maybe it would have been a good idea to mention what happened to Freddie as well though? By way of backup? But it hurt too much to think about Freddie. Freddie couldn't be moved into the 'Practicalities' folder of her brain just now. Maybe tomorrow, but not now. Anyway, it was more normal to tell a little bit of the truth at first, and the rest of it over intervals. People believed you more if you were reserved, especially about violent things… then she did what she'd been avoiding doing all night, and turned on her phone.

No calls.

No messages.

Nothing new from David.

That meant they'd got him. Didn't it? It had to.

Wouldn't the police call you, though? To let you know?

She shook her head at herself. *I don't know. I don't know.* They could be questioning him right now. They wouldn't interrupt it to call her and tell her how they were doing, would they? She told this to herself a few times, hoping it would calm her down. Then she texted Cheryl to let her know she was safe, and after that she had nothing to do except lie on the musty pink eiderdown, tired, a little gin-dizzy, and try to sleep. But sleep wasn't ready to come…

CHAPTER FIFTY-TWO

Jenny. Eight years earlier

Marc and Mum rowed a lot, but it never lasted long. Sal would apologise, Marc would grudgingly accept the apology and then one or both of them would celebrate by buying a bottle of gin that they'd do their best to finish. Jenny had got so used to the pattern now that once she heard the first rumblings of argument, she made plans to be out of the house – preferably all night. Nobody needs to hear their mum having embarrassingly loud make-up sex, after all. This time though, the last time, it didn't follow the same pattern.

Jenny came back from school to find that Sal was hurt. Marc had done more damage than usual. Her face was red and swollen, her left eye pinched shut, and her right eye bloodshot and rheumy. Her arm was sprained too, and three of her fingernails were ripped to the quick. Jenny almost didn't comment on it. Too many times she'd asked what had happened, and Sal's brisk, dismissive replies – 'Oh don't you worry, I gave as good as I got'; 'It looks worse than it is'; 'I just tripped' – were just too dispiriting to take. But today, because it was that much worse, she said something, and Sal didn't offer any depressing explanations. She didn't change the subject when Jenny, hesitatingly, then more forcefully, told her it wasn't right. He couldn't do this. Rather, she nodded, her bruised face averted, a cigarette clutched between two scabbed fingers.

This time, Sal asked Jenny to sleep with her in the big bed.

Jenny waited until she had drifted off, and then tried to secure the house as best she could – double-locking both the doors, and piling up chairs against them; filling the sink with dishes that would fall, crash, wake them if Marc tried getting in through the kitchen window.

At no point did she think of calling the police.

But Marc stayed away all night.

The next morning the house was filled with Marc's sinister absence, and Sal didn't want to be alone, asked Jenny to stay home from school. 'Keep me company, will you? We'll have a nice girly day together, yeah?' Only one half of her face was able to smile, the other side was too tightly swollen. The mismatch was grotesque.

All day they watched TV and ate biscuits, keeping a fearful eye on the door, jumping when the telephone rang.

Later, she asked Jenny to help wash her hair – her arm was too hurt to do it herself. In the bathroom sink, the shampoo lather was filled with loose hair, and spotted with scabs.

Sal, meeting her eyes in the mirror, water running down her neck, tried to smile. She flexed her bruised arm, stroked her black eye. 'I look a state, don't I?' Jenny silently handed her a towel. Sal took it, shook her head, tried to smile. 'Not going to win any beauty competitions any time soon, am I?'

'Mum—'

'Still, if I put some make-up on—'

'Mum—'

'I always feel better once I've got my face on——'

'Mum? Shut up.'

Once again, their eyes, in the spotted mirror, locked. There was a long pause. 'Look, it looks a lot worse than it is, Jen. You know me, I bruise like a peach; you only have to touch me and I... and

it was all my fault anyway. I kept going on and on at him, and…
you know what I'm like. I can be a right nagging bitch—'

'Mum.'

Sal nodded, turned away from the mirror, kept up the chatter. 'I
know it's not right, OK? I know, but it does take two to tango and—'

'Mum. Just shut up now. Shut up, OK?' Jenny, frowning, had
her eyes closed. 'It's got to stop, now. It's getting worse. *He's* getting
worse.' She opened her eyes then, hesitated. 'And it's getting worse
for me too.' She made sure she was looking directly into Sal's face
as she said this. 'Mum? He's—'

'Don't know what you're on about.' Sal's eyes were shiny with
fearful anger.

'He touches me, Mum!' Her voice was loud in the small room.
'He comes in here when I'm having a shower, and he—'

Sal put up one irritated hand. 'Just leave it, will you?'

'He tried to make me touch him too. I've tried to tell you
before, but—'

Up went the hand again, and Jenny watched Sal's injured face
go through a series of painful expressions: shock; horror; pain;
and finally, horribly, jealousy. She looked at her daughter with the
hateful envy of a rival. 'Well, you think a lot of yourself, don't you?'

'What? Mum—'

'Why don't you lock the bloody door, then? If he's… whatever
you say? Eh? Why're you just telling me this now if you're so scared?'
Her voice boiled with fury.

'He broke the lock. The lock doesn't work. Mum, you know
that—'

'And why don't you put a bra on. Tight T-shirt and no bra,
what d'you *expect* to happen? You're just—' But then she stopped,
opened her eyes, looked at Jenny properly, steadily.

Then she took her hand, and silently led her back into the living
room. They sat together on the sofa.

'I'm going to ask you this once,' Sal said eventually. 'Is it true? What you said? Has he been… getting at you?' Jenny nodded. Sal shuddered. A tear leaked out of her one good eye.

'He's been—' Jenny began.

Sal held up one hand. 'I don't want to know. I don't want to hear what he's been doing.' She clenched her jaw painfully, nodded at her knees. 'And, hand on heart, you've not… encouraged him? You're a nice-looking girl, and he's just a big teenager, really, they all are, men, aren't they—?'

'Jesus, Mum!'

Sal closed her eyes, nodded again. 'All right. All right, here's what we'll do. I'll call Kathleen now. We'll go and stay with her.'

'Really?' Jenny was shocked.

Sal nodded. Her face was tired, defeated. 'Go and get my phone, will you? And then get that suitcase out from under the bed.'

'Mum… I-I'm sorry. I mean—'

'Just get me the phone, love, all right? And start packing. He might come back any time.'

'If we called the police they'd come, make sure he didn't stop us—'

'No. The police make everything worse. No. Kathleen'll help. We can do this ourselves. Get as much as you can and pack it up. There's a money belt somewhere; see if you can find that.'

'But later? Should we tell them about, you know, what he's been doing to me?'

Sal turned to her very seriously. 'That's private. All that stuff, that's family stuff.'

'But—'

'Leave it now, Jen, or you can forget about going to Kathleen's, all right? I'm getting you out of here, that's good enough. Anything else that may or may not have happened to you, just try to forget it. OK? What's past is past.' She stood up. 'Chop chop!'

*

An hour later, they crept out of the back door, quiet, so quiet down the alley, Jenny carrying a holdall and pulling a bulky suitcase on wheels that made a noise like pebbles rolling on a tin roof, loud, too loud on the silent street. Sal's injured arm curved protectively around a bin bag containing her hairdryer, make-up and underwear.

When they got to the main street they passed The Fox where Marc was at work. They had no choice.

'Heads down, fast as we can, all right? Right, here we go then.' And Sal scuttled towards the door, the bin bag beginning to slither from her weak grasp. Together they trotted past the door like loaded mules.

'Where're we going after Kathleen's, Mum?'

'We'll sort something; I'll sort something.' She gasped. 'Just keep moving— shit!' The bin bag slipped, mascara rolled into the gutter and eyeshadow shattered. Sal cried out, knelt painfully down to pick it all up.

'Mum, just leave it!' Jenny hissed. 'Come on, just leave it!'

'I'm not leaving it!' Sal said. 'It's new!' And she walked a few paces back towards the pub, following the silvery trail of eyeshadow.

'Mum!'

Then, with horrible suddenness, Marc was there. A big man, just running to fat around the middle, but still agile, still dangerously strong. Jenny instinctively dodged into a doorway, but Sal froze. Mark pulled her up by one elbow. Jenny watched the resolve start to leak out of her mother, like stale air from an old balloon.

'What's this then?' he asked calmly. 'Where d'you think you're off to then?'

Sal began to babble. The laundrette. The new one? The one on Ladysmith by the pool hall? There's an opening-week offer. Half-price service wash after five. Thought I'd take the sheets.

Marc smiled faintly, plunged his hand into the bin bag, and pulled out a bra.

'See?' Sal said. 'I told you, it's just… clothes,' He reached in again, brought out a mascara wand, held it up questioningly.

'How'd that get in there?' Sal managed.

Marc dropped it, stepped on it lazily, cracked it like a bug. Then he took the bag out of Sal's shaking arms and dumped everything out onto the pavement… toothbrushes, a hairdryer, tampons, more underwear with its popped and worn elastic. Finally, her phone dropped with a clunk. He stepped on it, all the while smiling gently.

She began to cry.

Marc smiled even more gently, took her bad arm, twisted it. Sal was whimpering now, promising to go home, saying it had all been a mistake and please let go of my arm you're going to break it, no you are, you're going to break it, don't break it.

A bus trundled past, a whole top deck of pale moon faces gazed at the man pulling the crying woman by her injured arm, with no curiosity, no surprise. The few people on the street said and did nothing; at best they lingered at a distance, concern on their faces, as if, somehow, concern was action enough. Others just kept their heads down and walked. One man even loitered behind Marc, trying to pass him, before crossing the road and going on his way.

None of this meant anything to anybody.

She'd fallen now. He pulled her up. There was dirty water on her knees where she'd been kneeling on the pavement, and she was chattering again, and Jenny hated the chatter more than anything, because Marc liked that. He liked it when you panicked and begged; she knew that first-hand. He was breathing hard. He always breathed heavily when he was excited, when he was about to win. She knew that too. His left arm, wrapped around Sal, looked loving and intimate, but he dug the dirty nails of his right hand into the soft meat of her upper arm; her bruised face creased in fresh pain as he talked to her, softly, reasonably; it was time to go home. Stop making a fool of yourself now, and it was this – Sal's inevitable, depressing submission, head bowed like an ox before the axe – that filled Jenny with a rage she'd never felt before. They were going to go back. They were going to go back home, back to the unlocked bathroom door, and the hand in her knickers. Back to the screaming and the tears, but it would be worse now because this time they'd actively rebelled – Marc would make them pay for that. Marc would make them pay, and Sal would make her pay double. The jealous hatred Jenny had seen in her face – as if they were love rivals – told her that.

No.

No.

Jenny let the rage flood into her, let it intoxicate her, and it was a glorious feeling. And she ran at Marc hard as she could, pushing the suitcase in front of her like a battering ram. It slammed into his shins, making him stumble into the road and slip on some rotting leaves in the gutter. Jenny came forward then, watching him struggle on his back like an upturned insect, trying and failing to pull his shirt over his paunch. His hat, that stupid fucking hat he wore to hide his bald spot, had fallen off, and he was groping for that too. Behind her, she could hear Sal whimpering about her make-up.

Look at them both, scrabbling about in the dirt like apes.

They were cunts. Both of them. Scum. And they weren't going to drag her down with them any more.

Jenny kicked kicked kicked Marc in the head, on the shoulders, missing most of the time, but not stopping until she saw blood. She was shouting, screaming things she didn't even hear or understand, and then Sal was clawing at her, telling her to *stop, stop it or you'll kill him, stop it!*

And now there were other people, pulling her off him, dragging her backwards. A group of men ran to help him, carried him out of

the road, *you all right mate? You all right mate?* And it almost made
her laugh. Where were they when he was hurting Sal? Where'd
they been then?

That was the turning point. That was when whatever had been
left of Child Jenny died. From then on, though she tried to hide it,
she hated Sal. Hated her weakness, hated how she'd hidden behind
Jenny's skirts, asking for protection one minute, and abandoning
her to abuse the next. From then on, too, she hated Men in general,
because they were all hypocritical bastards who clubbed together,
protected each other, would happily stand by watching a woman
get beaten on the street, and only step in when the tide turned and
the man was getting the worst of it.

Jenny grabbed the suitcase from the gutter. One of the men
tending to Marc half turned. 'Stop! Stop her!'

And Jenny and Sal ran, rain in their faces, every step a victory.

Jenny wished she'd found the money belt though… He owed
them.

CHAPTER FIFTY-THREE

Kathleen let them stay the night at hers.

'But tomorrow you'll have to go. He's a clever bastard is Marc; he'll find you, and he's from bad stock. Remember I went out with his cousin, and he ended up in Rampton? No offence, love, but I don't need a visit from another Doyle.'

It was Kathleen that called the helpline, got them their place at the refuge. It was Kathleen who helped them move into their gloomy room at the back, and strutted around like a little general. 'It's big, isn't it?' She looked at the cornicing. 'Needs a bit of a dust around the corners.' She looked critically at Sal. 'You look done in. Have a rest. Have a lie down. Me and Jen'll have a cup of tea together. There's a place up on the hill that looked like it did a nice breakfast. Jen, get your coat, it's spitting out there. Chop chop.'

*

Outside, Kathleen spent a few seconds studying the building. 'You'd never know, would you? What it is?'

'Well, nobody's meant to know what it is. Safety,' Jenny answered.

Kathleen pointed at the security camera poised above the doorway. 'That gives it away though, doesn't it?' She sighed, and moved briskly on. Jenny had to trot after her.

*

Kathleen was one of those women who liked to tell people that they 'don't mince words' and 'tell it like it is'. She expected children to get over themselves and understand the world around them with clear, hard eyes. She treated them like miniature adults; that was probably why her own daughters were so intimidating. As soon as they sat down, she got straight to the point.

'Right. I need you to look after your mum. She's been through a lot,' Kathleen said seriously. 'She's been through too much. It does things to you. But you, you can take it; you're like me – you're tough, that's why I'm telling you this.'

'No, I'm not,' Jenny muttered.

'Oh, you *are* though, like it or not. And, you've got to get her to stop drinking so much.' Kathleen sat back. 'No drinking, no calling him, none of that. You've got to keep an eye on her. And don't look at me all gormless. You've got to step up.'

Jenny looked at the tabletop, clenched her jaw. 'I can't,' she managed, and her voice was slightly more forceful.

Kathleen's eyes widened in exaggerated surprise. 'What d'you mean, "can't"? 'Course you can. You're very capable. You're like me. Now, what'll you have? Bacon sarnie?'

'I mean I shouldn't *have* to look after her,' Jenny said. 'It should be the other way around. She should be looking after me.'

Kathleen scowled at her. 'Now you're just feeling sorry for yourself. She has looked after you! Look, you've always had a roof over your head, a meal on the table. Plenty of kids don't have that, you know,' Kathleen said sharply. 'She gave up a lot to have you. Think on that. She didn't have to have you at all.' She paused significantly.

'So I have to be grateful she didn't abort me, is that what you mean?' Jenny's voice was raised.

'Shhh!' Kathleen flapped her hand, looked around anxiously. 'Keep it down. And no, that's not what I meant. I mean that you and Sal, well, you're a unit. A woman has a baby, and that's... that's a special bond. Nothing comes between you.'

'Marc did.'

Kathleen's face creased with irritation. 'Yes, but not any more. Now it's just you and her, isn't it? She did the right thing *eventually* and she's going to need you. You're her darling.' She smiled, held out a hand, patted Jenny's cold fist. 'Yeah?'

'Let me tell you something.' Jenny tried to keep her face still, tried to keep the raging emotions from showing, knowing that, if she cried, Kathleen would dismiss her as a baby and stop listening. 'Marc. He didn't just hurt her. He hurt me too. He did things to me. I told Mum, but' – she looked up – 'she didn't *believe me*; she said I was jealous of her, trying to split them up. She said I'd let it happen. She was jealous.' Tears started then; she couldn't help it. 'So, you know, I'm really *not* her darling, Kathleen.'

Kathleen's face stiffened. Her mouth opened, then closed. She made a show of getting out her cigarettes.

Jenny raised her voice just a little. 'She's never looked after me, and now you're asking me to carry on looking after her, even though—'

Kathleen closed her eyes and made an irritated gesture with her unlit cigarette. 'Why're you telling me this now?'

'I'm saying it because ... I need to.' Jenny's voice broke. She dug her nails into her palms, hoping that the pain would distract her from more tears. 'I can't feel safe. I can't relax because, deep down, I still don't think she believes me, and I think she'll go back. She loves him more than she loves me. And I-I *hate* her for that, Kathleen. I'm sorry, but I do.'

Tap tap tap went Kathleen's cigarette. Jenny heard the click of her lighter, the approaching footsteps of the waitress, 'You can't smoke in here,' and Kathleen's righteous indignation: 'Oh for God's sake, one ciggy? And I'm right by the door!' and she knew that

Kathleen had deliberately lit up just so she'd have to step outside for a few minutes to buy herself some time, some kind of wiggle room, a way to think how to refute Jenny and back up Sal. Of course. Sal was the priority – always helped, coddled. And Jenny? Well she was just a supporting player who should be grateful for being given any role at all.

It wasn't fair.

When was it ever fair?

Jenny felt the two sides of her nature meet and clash. One half – the bruised, guilty half – adored strong, cynical Kathleen and treasured her spare, infrequent compliments: that she was a good girl, she was tough, she could cope with everything thrown at her. The other half – unwillingly precocious and bitter – bristled with contempt at Kathleen's failure to believe her, protect her, take her side.

All this was depressingly familiar.

Then, suddenly, watching Kathleen greedily sucking down the smoke, her profile all vexed angles, raw bones, a new Jenny stirred, and this Jenny had had enough. This Jenny promised herself, with dispassionate clarity, that *none of this will ever happen to me again.*

Fuck Sal.

And fuck Kathleen too.

They're never going to do the right thing. They don't care about you, so you better start caring about yourself. You better do whatever you've got to do to make sure you're safe, that no one can harm you, ever ever ever.

You're the priority.

You're the only one that matters.

You're cleverer than all of them. I bet you can make them do anything.

This new Jenny watched Kathleen come back, sit down again, stiff with tension. The tension indicated that she'd wrong-footed

Kathleen, unsettled her. New Jenny turned this over in her mind, savouring it. She stayed silent, waiting for Kathleen to speak.

'OK. What did he do? Marc? No, wait.' She held up one hand. 'No. Second thoughts I don't want to know.'

'I'll tell you though.'

'*No.*' Kathleen looked her hard in the eyes. 'I don't want to hear it. There's no point. It's over now, isn't it? Whatever it was that happened to you, you survived it and it's all finished with.'

Despite herself, pain welled. Old Jenny's eyes widened, tears shone, nearly spilled before New Jenny stepped in, squashed it all down. She looked at Kathleen, silently. *Fuck you Kathleen. Fuck you.*

'Yes, I survived it,' she said after a while.

Kathleen smiled. ''Course you did. You're tough as old boots. Like me.'

Jenny smiled back. *Fuck you Kathleen.* 'I'm glad I'm like you, Auntie Kathleen.'

Touched, Kathleen smiled again, softer. She took her hand. 'I'll tell you this: if you let her go back, it'll all start again.' She gently rapped their joined hands on the table for emphasis, and sat back, looking expectantly at Jenny.

'We won't go back.'

'Damn right you won't. You'll leave, go to another town, get another school, all that. If you don't, then you'll end up back there with him.' Kathleen sighed. 'I love your mother dearly, but she's a stupid mare when it comes to men. She doesn't have the sense she was born with. But you, you've got sense. You can sort it all out – you're very capable.' She paused, looked up expectantly, but New Jenny didn't feel like giving her what she wanted right then. Instead, New Jenny let the silence lengthen, and watched as Kathleen become more and more uncomfortable. She thought she could buy her off with compliments like 'You've got sense'. Stupid. Stupid patronising—

'Jen? I said you're very capable.' It was interesting, New Jenny thought, how Kathleen really couldn't cope with silence. *Let's see how she copes with non sequiturs, shall we?*

'My dad. What was he like?' she asked suddenly. 'Didn't you go out with him, too?'

Kathleen looked rattled, confused. 'What? Your dad? He was nice looking. Nice-looking man. Nice skin – his mum was from Dominica, I think? Anyway. Nice skin. Daft though. Why?'

'But what was he *like*?'

Kathleen stared at her. 'I just told you!' she said.

'I mean, as a person, what was he like?'

Kathleen rolled her eyes. 'Oh for Christ's sake, Jen. *I* don't know. Nice enough. Daft though. Liked football—'

'Where is he now, then?'

'Oh God knows? *God* knows. Soon as you came along he went. That's what happens, isn't it? Or sometimes they *don't* leave and, believe me, that's worse.'

'I was just thinking how funny life is, though; I mean, it could've been you that had a baby with him, and not Mum. I could have been *your* daughter, and not hers.' Jenny smiled vaguely. 'I always thought you were a good mum.' She watched Kathleen's reaction, noted the confused irritation driven out by flattered gratitude, thought she might as well push it a bit further. 'It sounds awful, but, you know, when I was little? I sometimes wished you were my mum.'

'Oh Jen! Come here!' Kathleen reached over for a brief, awkward hug. Her clothes smelled of cigarettes. Her breath smelled of pennies. 'Listen, my love. You're just as much a daughter to me as Maraid and Ros. OK?'

Who would have thought it? Kathleen – the dyed-in-the-wool cynic, this abrupt, unsentimental force of nature – rolled over if you stroked her ego the right way. 'Tell me what to do, Auntie Kathleen? Please?'

Kathleen sat back, wiped her eyes. 'Right. This is what I've always told my girls, so pay attention: women have to stick together. We're all born strong, but life kicks it out of most of us, and the ones who are strongest have to help the weaker ones. Like carrying a toddler when they're tired.' She shook her head bleakly. 'It shouldn't be that way, but it is. Sal's like a baby, and it's your job to carry her. It's not fair, but fair's got nothing to do with it. She's your mum, and that's what you do.' Kathleen sighed again. 'Men are always going to take advantage of people like your mum. They always have and they always will. But not you. It won't happen to you.'

'Why not?'

'Because I'm going to tell you now how to avoid it.' Kathleen smiled craftily. 'When it comes to men, they'll always take advantage. It's their nature, so you've got to do it to them before they do it to you. Take them for everything they've got – in a nice way, you know, and, if you can't do that, then get the hell out of it. This Marc thing – whatever it was that happened – it taught you a valuable lesson.' She crinkled her eyes in a conspiratorial way. 'Don't fall for the talk, the presents, none of it. *Take* them, say thanks, but don't ever think you owe a man anything, and if they hurt you, hurt them back, worse. Do whatever you have to do. Does that make sense?'

It did make sense. It made a lot of sense. Jenny took her hand then, felt her hot, dry fingers. She said: 'I love you, Auntie Kathleen.' And, right then, she meant it.

Outside, Kathleen buttoned up Jenny's jacket for her, and back at the refuge she hugged her again – two hugs in fifteen years and both in one day.

'You're a good girl, Jen,' Kathleen managed, dabbed her eyes, stepped back. 'Now, remember what I've said, all right? You've got to do it to them before they do it to you. All right. Call me whenever you want, OK? Promise?'

Sal wasn't in the room when she got back. The bedclothes had been shoved aside and the pillow was cool.

'Mum?'

A horrible certainty was edging into her mind.

Sal was standing with her back to the street, in a lone phone box just behind the refuge. She must have picked it because it was so secluded. That was the thing about Sal – she was cunning in that way. She even had Kathleen fooled on that one. Jenny crept up behind her, closer, closer until she heard Sal's breathy telephone voice on their old answer machine: 'And if you will leave your number, I will be sure to get back to you as soon as possible.' Sal took a breath, about to speak. She was already crying.

Jenny grabbed the hand holding the receiver and smashed it against the toughened glass. Then, breathing heavily, grabbing Sal's injured arm, she dragged her out into the cold still air and all the way back to the refuge. Sal cradled her arm, whimpered: 'You're hurting my bad arm, grabbing me like that', but that only made Jenny dig her fingers in more, pull her along quicker. When they got back to the refuge, she marched her up the stairs to their room, propelled her towards the bed, all without saying a word.

Sal curled up and kept on crying. It was almost like she was enjoying herself, savouring it, cuddling and cooing to herself on the bed like a big baby, while Jenny, silent, watched, and as minutes ticked, she found herself understanding Marc, thinking, maybe, just maybe, it wasn't all his fault... Sal loved being the victim, the child, just as much as Marc loved being the bully, the Man. The more pathetic she got, the more contempt he had, and the more contempt he had, the happier she was. He hit her because she deserved it. Because she asked for it. She fucking loved it. That was what kept them together, and that's what would make her go back, again and again, unless Jenny stopped it. But pleading wouldn't work. Speaking sense wouldn't work. There was only one thing that Sal understood.

And so Jenny watched her mother's genuine tears stop and the fake ones begin. She watched her rock herself like a baby on the rumpled sheets, muttering to herself that she was so lonely and so sad and only wanted her stuff back and just thinking about you and how'd we end up here and why do bad things happen to good people and…

Jenny crossed to the bed, knelt at her feet. Sal looked up, hopefully, pathetically, through damp eyelashes. 'You don't know what it is to be lonely, Jen. You don't know—'

'Fucking shut up,' Jenny told her quietly.

'Don't say that.' Sal's eyes widened. 'Don't talk to me like that—'

'Here's what's happening. We're moving away. You'll never see him again. If you behave well, I'll get your stuff back, but you're never seeing him again, all right?'

'But—'

'No,' Jenny said. 'Listen to me now. I've had it. I don't care how you feel. I don't care any more. I'm doing this for me, and you're not going to fuck it up.'

Sal's mouth pursed. She looked like an angry baby. 'Selfish—'

Slowly, almost dreamily, Jenny pulled one arm back. Sal watched her fist warily. 'What're you—'

Then Jenny slammed her fist into Sal's quavering chin, paused, then did it again. Paused, then did it again, and again, until her bunched knuckles hurt, and her arm felt weak. Sal fell back, crying now with real pain.

*

Jenny walked slowly down the stairs into the kitchen to get some water. One of the residents, a woman called Karen, with rivulets of scar tissue running down her face where an ex had thrown boiling fat on her, stood by the window sipping tea.

'You all right, darling?'

'Yeah. Yeah, well, Mum's got a migraine. Stress. She's really depressed.'

Karen's ridged scars contracted, rippled. 'Oh, poor love. I've got some painkillers – you want some?'

'Oh, really, you can spare them?'

'Oh, I've got loads. Take 'em like Smarties.' She laughed a little sadly. 'They're strong though – dihydrocodeine? She won't do much but sleep if she's not used to them.'

'I want her to sleep, to tell the truth. She needs it.'

'Oh, bless you.' Karen's ravaged face was gentle. 'She's lucky to have you, she really is. Come with me.' She led Jenny to her room, dark and humid. Pictures of her children – all of whom were now fostered – had been tacked up on the wall above the bed in the shape of a heart. Beneath them, in careful, tumbling letters, she'd written 'My Angels' in lipstick. She gave Jenny the pills, almost a full packet. 'You only get one Mum, don't you? Got to look after her.'

Jenny nodded. 'I know. She's my best friend.'

Back upstairs, Sal had stopped crying, and was sitting on the bed, watching the door expectantly. She had a bloodied tissue in one hand.

'I'm sorry, Jen.' Her speech was slurred with blood – two teeth had loosened and she'd bitten her tongue.

'Don't make me do that again.'

Sal shook her head, grave as a child.

'Because I will. You know I will now, don't you?'

'Yesh.'

'Say you understand then.'

'Yesh. Yesh I unnerstand.' A thin trickle of blood ran down her chin.

Jenny shook out two pills. 'Take these.'

'Whudardey?'

'Painkillers.'

Sal took them, and obediently lay down. There was a look of dazed gratitude in her eyes. It was the same expression seen on the faces of released hostages, facing the cameras after years in captivity.

CHAPTER FIFTY-FOUR

Sal stayed supine. She signed where she had to sign, called who she had to call, and did it all under Jenny's supervision. Only once did she speak up – *leave the city? All her friends?* But Jenny silenced her with a look. One of Kathleen's admirers, a jolly man called John, drove them up to their new house in his car. Their belongings barely filled the boot. Kathleen kept up a brisk and cheerful commentary as the fag ends of the city slid past the windows in muddy daubs. It was lovely where they were going. *You've been there, John? Haven't you?*

'Oh yes. Lovely. It's like something out of Miss Marple up there. Very picture-squeue,'

'"Picture-squeue". You're funny, John,' Kathleen said perfunctorily.

Jenny smiled, nudged Sal, who smiled too.

Those first few weeks were rocky, but Sal seemed to have learned her lesson. It helped that Marc died so soon after they moved. She lost all interest in going back to the city. She lost interest in everything, while Jenny thrived. She was a clever girl, pretty, popular enough. When she got a place at university, Sal told her she was proud, and Kathleen sent her a novelty mug from Tenerife – where she'd moved a few years before – with 'Don't Mess with this Tough Bitch!' on it. The design melted off in the dishwasher within a week.

Things fell apart at university, though. Living in Halls of Residence mirrored and magnified her sense of difference. The other students drifting together in little eddies and tides of privilege made her... angry. They were more rooted than she could ever be; they had a kind of animal sense of security that Jenny thought she'd managed to achieve by moving to the village, and now understood that she'd never had at all. Maybe it would have been easier if she was with Freddie, but he was in London having a great time at his own university. When they spoke, she tried to sound cheerful, but afterwards she always cried.

She was out of her depth here. Not such a Tough Bitch after all.

She only lasted two terms. One afternoon, in a tutorial on the developmental effects of neglect, she felt something inside her switch, as if her response system had short-circuited. She stared around the table and nothing made sense – the earnest, pale children in the room seemed alien; the words were only words; the whole exercise was witless. When she tried to speak to the tutor afterwards, she couldn't make him understand why she was so upset, and she could see that her emotions frightened him, which made her hate him.

She came back home at Christmas to find that, in the few months she'd been away, Sal had changed, and for the better She looked years younger, had lost a stone, and hadn't had a drink in weeks. Jenny found this more unsettling than welcome. It meant that *she* was the only broken person in the house. She retreated to her little pink bedroom that felt like a used womb.

And weeks became months until Sal asked her to leave. *She wasn't going back, was she? Face it. Why not sign up with temping agencies? You can't stay here on no money, you know. Why d'you want to stay here anyway?*

So, Jenny, in a fit of masochism, moved to the city – the same city she'd left when she was fifteen and had never been back to since. Too many bad memories. Strangely though, once she was there, she liked it. She never came across old faces; she never went to their old area. The centre had been gentrified enough to (almost) make it seem like a different city to the one she'd lived in and left.

The menial jobs she took were strangely soothing. Simple, transactional work, with no grey areas and no reason to think. Jobs where she was obviously the cleverest, the quickest. It did wonders for her self-esteem. This strange hibernation lasted for two years, until Freddie finished university, came back, and took it on himself to drag her out of her burrow. It was good to have him back, even though he tended to bully her into self-improvement. She was so bright! *For God's sake, don't sell yourself short! Therapy? Why not? Jesus Jen, you can't go on like this!*

And so she'd let herself be talked into seeing Cheryl, and the thread of her life untangled, smoothed and strengthened. Over the months that followed, Cheryl made her understand that what had happened at university was in many ways an inevitability. It all came down to her childhood – the chaos of living with Marc, the pain of being a parent to a parent, the crushing pressure Kathleen had brought to bear at that pivotal point of assumed escape – look after Sal, carry her, That Is Your Role. How on earth could she come into her own with Sal always waiting in the wings, ready and willing to ruin Jenny's successful Second Act?

Each week, Cheryl picked up Sal, turned her over like some dead crab on the beach, stinking of rot, and she and Jenny would let rip… *A terrible mother. A selfish mother. A damaging person; toxic.* And so what if she'd stopped drinking? So what if she was fine now, had a job, was independent? Why did she wait until Jenny left home to turn into a functioning adult? Jenny had every right to take her desires as reality, just so long as she truly believed in the reality of her desires.

Jenny revelled in this power that was both intoxicatingly novel and strangely familiar. Later, she realised that she'd had the same fleeting feeling once before, when her fist had connected with Sal's jaw all those years ago.

Then, something happened that changed her life for ever.

Ryan Needham.

There was something weird about that guy. She didn't trust that guy. He was too perfect. Freddie was just too nice to see it, but Ryan was playing him. Manipulating him. After a particularly invigorating session with Cheryl, on a whim, Jenny messaged Ryan – if he was even called Ryan – and, feeling like she was in an episode of *Catfish*, told him she knew he was a fake. And it felt good. It felt really good to… win. To call a man out on manipulation, watch him squirm, watch him try and fail to defend himself…. he'd only done it to get close to her, and he was so sorry… it was pathetic. For the next few minutes she was content to watch him tie himself in knots over Messenger. Oh, they went to school together did they? Like she gave a shit. He was sorry, was he, and he didn't mean to hurt anyone? Well, he might not have meant to, but he had – leading someone on like that for months on end. Jesus. Then she asked for a photo. If he was fool enough to send her one then he really was as stupid as he seemed.

When he *did* send her a photo, she laughed aloud again. Now she had a face to go with the name, she recognised him straightaway. David Crane: that creepy boy who'd dropped out of school. Who, she faintly remembered now, had stopped her in the graveyard once and made awkward conversation about World War Two. He'd got better-looking in the last few years, but still. He was back in the village, looking after his mum. That rang a bell – that big house. The cleaning company Sal worked for, they cleaned it. Mrs Hurst had told her… Rich. They were the richest people in the village.

This put a new complexion on things.

And so she kept the conversation to herself. She made 'Ryan' disappear from Freddie's life, nursed Freddie through his (*frankly, over-the-top*) grief, while keeping in touch with David. After all, it wasn't often that a rich, easily controlled man came along. He cried out to be cultivated. Kathleen would have been proud.

Over the next year, David, smitten puppyish, could always be relied on to help with her rent, and her bills. He was undemanding too. He rarely questioned her explanations for not meeting face-to-face and, on the few occasions that he pushed back a bit, all she had to do was withdraw, not answer a few texts, and he'd quickly back down and apologise.

She was very careful to keep all four of her cheerleaders apart from each other: Andreena was acquainted with Freddie, but not with Cheryl, and knew nothing about David. Cheryl knew about Freddie's existence, but they never met, and Jenny made sure David's surname was never mentioned in their sessions. Freddie knew of Cheryl, but not David; David already knew about Freddie and Andreena and knew that she saw a therapist, but he didn't know her name – at least not until Freddie let it slip at that disastrous dinner party. Keeping the three main struts of her support network in this atomised state appealed to her for the simple reason that, if they didn't meet they couldn't become friends, opening up the potential for one or all of them to shift their focus from where it should be: on her.

CHAPTER FIFTY-FIVE

It was the blog audience that really completed everything. Jenny was special, she was brave. She was extraordinary. David said the same in his infatuated emails and rare phone calls, as did Freddie in their heart-to-heart chats, and Cheryl in their counselling sessions. Andreena prayed for her, and all that was great, but all that was behind closed doors. When Sal got sick, and Jenny moved back to look after her, *You Can't Go Home Again* assumed a new importance. Her readers said the same things her friends did, with a crucial difference – they said it in public.

They lapped up her posts about the stresses and strains of caring for an invalid. *While training to be a counsellor too? How did she do it?* At every stage, they were there to tell her how brave, honest and inspirational she was. They competed with each other to give her the most compliments, they vied for her attention, shoring up her carefully crafted image of gutsy sweetness. The appreciation was so strong, the approbation so addictive, that soon, very soon, *You Can't Go Home Again* became her main outlet, her greatest delight.

But, as always, fate intervened, complicated things. And the complication had a face, a voice and a name: Sal.

It wasn't *all* lies, Jenny sometimes reasoned to herself. After all, Sal *had* suffered a stroke, but it was very minor. After a few weeks she was mobile again and her speech was just fine. She could eat solid food. She needed no help getting in and out of the shower. In fact, Sal became so inconveniently *not ill*, that Jenny was running out of excuses to stay with her. And she *had* to stay. If she left, Freddie, Cheryl, Andreena and David would know she'd left, and if they knew, then she wouldn't be able to carry on with the blog – the best bit of her blog – the 'caring for a sick mother' bit that got her all the sympathy, and if she wasn't Saintly Blogger 'Jay', then who was she? Just another, ordinary twenty-something part-time student, juggling jobs? How could she go back to that?

The stronger Sal got, the more irritable and vicious Jenny felt towards her. And the nastier Jenny was, the more Sal, after years of relative sobriety, relied on alcohol to cope with the discomfort of living with her daughter. And she began having accidents – genuine, drunken accidents – slips in the bathroom, a tumble down the stairs, a sprained wrist, a bruised hip, which Jenny, on her blog and to her friends, packaged as stroke-affiliated injuries. Some of the accidents weren't accidents though. Sometimes Sal would... act up. Push back, and Jenny would be forced to restrain her a bit. Nobody came to the house; Jenny made sure everyone knew that Sal was too frail for visitors, and nobody had any reason to question Jenny's version of things. On the rare occasions she allowed Sal out of the house, they were always together – Jenny gripping Sal's arm firmly, telling her, loudly and often, that she was doing very well, but she was still sick so-we-should-go-home-now. Back at home, Jenny hid the keys, disconnected the phone, and kept Sal weary with sleeping pills, but that couldn't go on for ever. She knew that, even as she willed it to.

In phone calls with Freddie, sessions with Cheryl, at lunch with Andreena, she allowed herself to be comforted, mothered. It was just so good to *talk*. It felt so wrong to be moaning like this when Mum was so sick. She didn't know how they put up with her!

'Oh darling, don't be silly. Can I help? Maybe I can look after her at the weekends? Give you a break?' Freddie would say.

'No, she'd be too embarrassed. She needs help on the commode and... she couldn't do that with you. She doesn't even want to see anyone. Thanks though,' Jenny told him, blinking back tears of gratitude.

'You're like a daughter to me,' Andreena would tell her.

'I'm blessed,' Jenny would answer.

'You have the power,' Cheryl intoned. 'Remember that, to access your strength centres, you have to believe. You can get through this! You are a Strong, Beautiful Soul.'

'Do you think so, am I really? *Really?*'

'The strongest soul I know!'

And David? David was simple. She barely had to lie to David at all. He was only concerned with Jenny; her friends and family held no interest for him. On the rare occasions he asked after Sal, she downplayed The Stroke and highlighted The Drinking Problem, sensing that, as a carer himself, he might be able to see through some of her tales. The quiet but palpable antipathy she detected in his voice was particularly gratifying because, well, in a very real sense, she was almost telling him the truth. Almost. And it was such a relief, almost telling someone the truth.

No. David was very straightforward. She'd broken him in like a horse. He'd believe anything she told him. He'd do anything for her; he told her that. He'd said that many times.

On the night the snow fell, she gave him the opportunity to prove it.

CHAPTER FIFTY-SIX

Jenny. The Night the Snow Fell

The slate grey day was heavy with snow, and Sal had been drinking steadily from midday; little sips during the *Judge Judy* marathon; sloppier swallows by *Diagnosis Murder*; and, by four, she was hungry. *What happened to that bacon in the fridge?*

'You must have had it already,' Jenny told her.

'No. And that crusty bread, that's gone too.'

'There's some soup left – have some of that.'

'Soup's not enough. I was looking forward to that bacon. Can you go to Tesco?'

Jenny looked irritably out of the window. 'It's snowing.'

'I just really fancy some bacon,' Sal said plaintively. 'And we need more milk too. It's not that bad – it's more sleet than snow. Go on, Jen, be a love.'

Looking back, Jenny saw that that phrase 'be a love' was suspiciously affectionate. Sal was trying to appear oh-so-guileless, oh-so-sweet. At the time though, she didn't notice. She was just irritated at being interrupted. She was working on a blog post. The theme was family dynamics, and making sure that the sick relative still felt valued and in control, despite being forced into an infantile state by their illness. Jenny had been…

experimenting with blended foods – butternut squash and apple
are Mum's favourite, and we have a laugh about the role reversal.
I just finished scraping the mush off her face,

She wrote:

and she started to laugh, and then I did too. That's the thing, she's still my mum, with her sense of absurdity and humour. She's still here, thank god, and we're closer than we've ever been.

She stopped typing, read the last few lines and smiled. It was a lovely, gentle smile.

'Jen! What about this bacon then?'

Jenny's gentle smile hardened into a grimace. She closed her eyes in weary irritation. 'I'm not going out now. Not in this. Have some soup!'

Sal wavered towards the door. 'All right then, I'll go. I'm not scared of a bit of snow.'

'What? No, you can't go!' Jenny stared at her non-disabled mother, imagining her trotting about Tesco on her very not-disabled legs.

'Where's my coat?' Sal made a show of opening the cupboard. 'Where's my heavy coat…'

'All right, all right, I'll go.' Jenny stood up, shoved Sal aside and got out her own coat. 'But if I freeze to death out there, it's on you. Bacon. That's it, right?'

'Bread too. And butter, and milk, and—'

'I'm not getting loads of things,' Jenny told her.

'But we might be snowed in,' Sal whined. 'Get some frozen stuff, at least.'

'Jesus,' Jenny muttered.

'Why're you in such a bad mood?' Sal asked.

'I'm not. I just don't want to go out in the snow,' Jenny said evenly. 'I'm busy. College work.'

'Well, shouldn't you go to college some time? You have to go every now and again, don't you?'

'It's not that kind of college.'

'I hear you on that computer all the time,' Sal said.

'Bacon, bread, milk… anything else?' When Sal shook her head, all docility, Jenny left the house, and hunched into the driving snow, leaving the closed laptop on the kitchen table. *Stupid. Stupid thing to do.*

The house was quiet when she came back. The TV was off, and Sal, a fresh gin in a smeary glass by her elbow, was sitting in the dim kitchen, her pale face illuminated by the computer screen.

Jenny froze in the doorway, then slapped on the light. 'What're you doing?' Sal didn't answer. 'What're you *doing*?' Jenny screeched, and lunged towards her, tugging at the laptop. 'That's my private college work—'

Sal held on hard. '"Adult nappies",' she read. Her voice a cracked falsetto. '"This has been one of the hardest things for Mum to deal with, and, frankly, for me too".'

'Mum, that – it's— it's just a story – it's a creative writing thing, for— for college—'

'"But it's something you have to do, isn't it? My mum is my best friend after all".' Sal went on in that sing-song way.

Jenny moved forward again. 'Give it here.'

Again, Sal jerked back.

'Oh, and look here, you've got a message – a comment: '"You're so brave, not only to care so brilliantly for your mum, but also to write about it with such compassion",' Sal read.

'Give it *here*,' Jenny grabbed Sal's arm, but again, with surprising strength, she resisted, and backed away towards the stairs, holding the laptop in front of her.

'"… feeding Mum like a baby… Helping her out of the bath… closer than we've ever been–".'

Jenny ran at her then, grabbed at the laptop, and this time Sal let it go. Her wondering expression was tinged with disgust. 'College work. You must think I'm daft.'

'It's… it's creative writing,' Jenny managed.

'It's creative something,' Sal said. 'How long have you been doing this? Making out I'm sick? And why? Why?'

'You are sick,' Jenny muttered. The computer pinged. Another comment. StaceyC told her that she was amazing.

Sal moved back to the table, picked up her glass with one shaking hand.

Ping.

Take care of yourself Jay!
Ping.
Such respect for you lady.

It took a herculean effort for Jenny to shut the laptop and put it on the work surface behind her. Without it she felt… defenceless. Almost scared. Sal wasn't looking at her. Everything was quiet, still.

'I bought you bacon,' Jenny said eventually. 'And I got some of that ham you like too. And eggs and… and… burgers. You were right, it's good to have some frozen things in. We've got beans, haven't we? And—'

'How long have you been telling people I'm a fucking vegetable?' Sal's voice shook with quiet anger.

'I *haven't* been saying that,' Jenny was indignant. 'It's about being a carer and—'

Sal snorted. 'You? Caring? That's funny.'

'I came back to care for you—'

'I never wanted you to come back though, did I?' She stared at Jenny. 'I told you *then* I didn't need you to move back. I was

fine on my own; I was *better* on my own. But you came anyway…
why? So you could make out you were this great carer? Jesus, Jen.'
She shook her head, and took another drink. 'That's sick, that is.
Is that why you don't let me out? You don't want people to see that
I'm all right? Is that why no one comes round?'

Jenny thought quickly. 'You're sicker than you think you are,' she
said. 'They told me at the hospital. They said that you'd probably
think you were fine, but that really you weren't – you *thinking* you
were better was actually part of the illness.'

Sal shook her head. 'And that's the best you can do, is it?'

'I came back to look after you! Not many people would've done
that, not for a mother like you!' Jenny heard her own voice, ringing
with falsehood, and suddenly she saw just how much trouble she
was in, looking at Sal, so still, so disgusted, so capable of blowing
this thing wide open. 'And anyway, I didn't use any real names,'
she said then. 'It's all anonymised.'

'And that's meant to make me feel better, is it?'

'Well—'

'And what about other people – your friend Freddie, does he
think I'm ill? And Mrs Hurst – did she really let me go, or did you
tell her I was too sick to work?'

'Too sick to work…' Jenny muttered. Shame bloomed red across
her cheekbones. She closed her eyes to keep in the tears. She heard
the splash of gin, the crack of ice, and when she opened her eyes,
Sal was smiling. A strange smile. Sinister.

'You've not changed much, have you?' Sal said.

'What d'you mean?' Jenny asked guardedly.

'I mean you were always one for making things up. You always
were a good little actress. People always believed you. *I* believed
you.' The smile twisted. She took a long drink. 'All that shit with
Marc—'

'Mum, don't do this.'

Sal shook her head. 'Had us all going about that, didn't you? Even told Kathleen, didn't you?' Long gulp. Quick refill. 'Made me move, lose everything. All so you could get your own room.'

Jenny closed her eyes. 'It wasn't about getting my own room. That's not what it was about.'

Sal nodded. 'All because of jealousy too. You wanted Marc and you couldn't have him, so you split us up, got us here, and you got your own room, and me all to yourself. That's what it was. And now your dream has come true, hasn't it?' She made a wide gesture. Gin slopped in a small arc.

'It's never been my dream to live with you, Mum, believe me,' Jenny said scornfully.

'But, I thought we were "closer than we've ever been"?'

'How much have you had to drink anyway?'

Sal took a sloppy drink. 'Thing is, you never told me *exactly* what it was Marc'd done, did you? Just hinted. Hedged around it.' Sal smiled nastily. 'You've always been clever like that.'

'I didn't make anything up,' Jenny said quietly. The tears had gone but inside her shifted the old, cold panic. She thought of Cheryl: *Strength Centre – go to your Strength Centre*. 'You want to know what he did? He put his fingers up me.' The kitchen throbbed with silence. Sal kept steady, sceptical eyes on her. 'He did that twice.'

'And that's it? Fingers?' Sal said flatly.

'It hurt. He wanted to hurt me. He was a… bad man, Mum. He was really bad and he was getting worse and—'

'And again, why didn't you tell me at the time if it hurt so much?' Sal asked nastily.

'He-he told me not to. I didn't want to make you sad.' She heard her voice, heard the thin pathetic pleading of a child in it, hated herself for it, hated her for hearing it.

'Make your mind up,' Sal sneered.

'It's true. And it might not seem like a lot, like abuse to you, but—'

'Well now he's dead, so he can't defend himself, can he?' Sal said. 'Lucky, that.'

Jenny stiffened. 'It's the truth.'

'Yeah. Like your "creative writing" is the truth. I'm at death's door, and you're Mother Teresa, that sort of truth. Jesus.' Sal shook her head. 'I always knew there was something wrong with you.' She stared at Jenny. Her face cold. 'You wouldn't know the truth if it killed you.' She got up from her chair. The unforgiving strip light showed the grey twinkling at her roots and cast skull-like shadows from her brows.

'Where're you going?' Jenny whispered.

'Out.'

'It's snowing. Mum, don't be—'

'You're going to let me alone!' Sal shouted. It was as if all the drinks in her system had formed a sudden hive of fury. 'I've had enough of you… *keeping* me here. Shut away. You can fuck off!' She turned messily, and tried to put on the nearest coat, Jenny's, but put her arm through the wrong hole, cursed, turned it round, and did the same thing.

'Sit down, you're hammered,' Jen said.

'I'm not sitting down. I'm going out. I'm going to the pub. Without my *walker* or *wheelchair*, or whatever the fuck else you've been telling people I need. Where's my shoes? What've you done with my shoes?' She wandered towards the cupboard, located her own coat, wrapped her chiffon scarf with the roses on it around her neck, and then stumbled against the bannister on the way up the stairs, hit her head on the wall, bloodying her nose. 'Shit!'

'Mum.' Sighing, Jenny got up, went to her. 'Just sit down will you?'

'No!' Sal threw out one stiff arm. It knocked Jenny off balance, and her head hit the wall, in turn knocked the framed photo into splinters. 'Look what you did there! Where're my shoes?'

'Mum, no, just sit down—'

'Bugger it, I'll just keep my slippers on,' Sal muttered to herself, and lurched towards the back door, pulling the coat around her shoulders like a shawl. Then she plunged into the cascade of whirling snow, colliding briefly with the recycling box, swearing at it, and carrying on.

Jenny's mind ran at full pelt. If she ran after Sal now, Mrs Mondesir might see them, Sal would talk, and everything would be over. On the other hand, if she allowed Sal to get to the pub, people would see that she wasn't ill – pissed, but not ill. Freddie would find out through local gossip, and he'd be so disappointed. He'd never forgive her. Andreena wouldn't want to be her second mum any more. And what about Kathleen? Jenny didn't see much of her nowadays, but still, she needed to know that Kathleen approved of her, was proud of her. Cheryl? Christ… Cheryl could get her thrown off the course for this. Bye bye career and hello to a long life of temping. She'd lose her blog audience: that precious support network of all those people who loved her, admired her… Jenny opened her computer and scrolled: fifteen new comments.

When things get too much for me, I re-read Jay's latest piece and it always, without fail, gives me courage. She has the kind of honesty that I can only dream about…'
'Please make sure you look after yourself, Jay.'
'You're such a diamond! Never stop shining!

She turned the computer off. One tear plopped onto the keyboard, then another. God she'd miss these people. She'd miss this so much. The only person who wouldn't turn on her was David. The only person she'd be left with was David. And he was very helpful with money; he was devoted to her but, she had to admit it… David was *weird*. He had been weird in school. You don't forget someone like him in a hurry; he stabbed a kid with a compass, for God's sake! And then there were the fires, all the rumours that went round about that. No. Hitching her wagon to David's star would be… a last resort. David was someone you needed in your corner, but not the only one on your team. A little bit of David went a long, long way.

The harsh light of the kitchen shone on the dirty linoleum, the smeared glasses, the cheap bottle of gin, and she hated this place. She hated Sal. All those years ago, Jenny – a child – had stepped up, saved them both, got them here, given them a whole new life. And now, all these years later, Sal still didn't appreciate it. Not only did she not appreciate it, she brought up the Marc thing again, calling her a *liar*. Even now, when the bastard was long dead, she didn't dare go against him. What sort of a mother didn't believe her own child? Called her own child a liar? What kind of a mother…

She went to the loo, stared at herself in the mirror until the welcome tears of self-pity started. Then she noticed the beginning of a bruise coming out on her chin from where Sal had flailed at her, and that intensified the tears. She looked just as bedraggled and put upon as she felt. *Poor Jenny, all alone. Drunk Sal, bad Sal. Shittest Mum Ever.*

Pull yourself together, Jen. Come on now, if you leave now you'll be able to catch her. Even if she's already in the pub, she's drunk enough that she won't be making sense. Whatever she might have said, no one would believe her. After all, you're the one with the bruised face, and she's the town drunk. There's still time. You can still stop this, just… just find her, muzzle her. That's all. That's not too hard, is it, now – what? *What was that?* A noise from the garden… A fox, or a dog or something? But not quite that… and there it was again. A pained sound.

She stood on the toilet, opened the frosted window and peered out into the snow; she heard that same wail again in the hills, and something reddish flapped – The snow was coming down so fast it was hard to make out what it was.

'*Jen?*'

How'd she end up there?

Thank *Christ* she's there though, and not the pub… Lucky. Lucky.

With renewed energy, Jenny ran back downstairs, shoved on some shoes and opened the back door, stiff against the snow, ran out into the garden, through the gap in the fence, and into the whirling monochrome of the hills.

'Mum?' She said it softly. 'Mum? You there?' Just a little louder, and she heard in response a faint cry that she moved towards slowly, being careful not to trip. The rocks here were sharp, and if she fell she might not get up again.

'Mum?'

'Jen!' The cry came again, weaker, quieter, even though Sal was closer now. 'Jen! I'm here. Come… come and help me. Hurt my leg…'

Jenny stayed where she was. 'What's happened?' she asked.

'I fell down. My ankle. Hurt my leg. Jen, come and help me up!'

'Why're you out here? I thought you were going to the pub?' Jen asked, almost conversationally. 'You'll miss last orders if you're not careful.'

'Don't take the piss. I got… confused… the snow turned me round. Jenny, give me a hand, please? Jen!'

And Jenny looked up into the sky at the falling snow. It felt like she was racing through space, shooting past stars. It felt like she was the only person alive.

'Jenny! Love, please!'

An image came into her mind – a long plank over a cliff, Jenny astride it on safe ground and Sal perched over the ravine, teetering. 'You said some bad things about me,' Jenny said after a pause. 'Say sorry.'

'You what?' Sal's pain-filled voice was filled with wonder. 'What? I'm hurt, I can't feel my leg now – come and help me!'

'The stuff about Marc – you know it's true. You always knew. Admit it and I'll help you up.'

'Sssorry! Sorry! Jen I—'

'Tell me you always knew.'

'I didn't though, Jen, love, just get me up, will you?'

'Admit that you always knew.'

In the dark, she could hear Sal trying to get up herself – that creak of pressure on fresh snow. Jen heard dragging steps, and a muffled fall, a little yell of pain, and a sob.

'Jen! Where are you?'

'You can't tell anyone that you're well either. The blog. You can't talk about that to anyone, OK?'

'There's something wrong with you!' Sal managed. It sounded like she was trying to heave herself up again. 'There is. You're not right!' Jenny sighed, took a few steps back. 'No! Jen, listen. I didn't mean anything, love, I didn't. I won't tell anyone either. You're right, and I'm wrong, and… just, please, help me up, OK?'

Jen left a pause. She could hear Sal's exhausted gasps. Fear and pain mixed with gin. She sounded tired. She sounded too tired to shout any more. 'I'll have to go back for a torch,' she said.

'What? What you need a torch for? Just, help, will you?'

'I'll be a minute. Don't go anywhere.'

'Ha bloody ha,' Sal muttered.

When she was halfway back to the house, Sal called once, just one cry, weak and kittenish. Jen waited for another few minutes, body tensed in the cold, waiting for a scream, but didn't hear another sound. Then she walked back to the house as quickly as she dared. It was freezing out there, her feet were numb, even through leather boots… Sal in her thin coat and slippers would probably have frostbite by now. When she got back into the garden she noticed that her boot prints were already obscured by snow.

In the bright kitchen, she sat.

Time ticked…

CHAPTER FIFTY-SEVEN

Jenny. The Windsor Castle, Scarborough

Waking up in The Windsor Castle, Jenny didn't at first realise where she was. Then everything came swimming back to her, and her heart began to pound painfully. She reached for her phone. Nothing. No calls. No texts.

What could this mean? If it meant anything, could it be good? After a few minutes of panic, she forced herself into the shower, then forced herself out into the drizzling cold of the morning to the one and only cafe already open on the seafront. It was called Kirsty's Baps, and Jenny thought instantly of Freddie, how funny he'd find that, and he'd laugh his honking laugh, pause, take a photo and put it on Twitter. But thinking about Freddie was simply too painful at the moment. *Don't do that. Work your way up to that.*

The cafe had one other customer: a malodorous man in a trench coat. His hands, palsied, shook, and his tea dripped onto the Formica tabletop. When the waitress – one of those creamy-skinned adolescents with starfish mascara and a faintly insolent smile – drifted over, Jenny ordered tea and toast and changed seat so she could look out of the window at the sea over the railing, merging sinuously with the grey horizon. She'd never been here in winter before. Summers. Summers with Mum – the first week of August staying at The Windsor Castle, bacon sandwiches in the morning in the quiet dining room. Lights out at ten and the creaky floorboards and the sound of the waves.

God she was tired. So tired. Even though she'd slept she hadn't rested, and everything she thought was fixed… wasn't. *If David had been arrested, surely she'd know by now? If he hadn't been arrested, why hadn't he called her?* She'd come to Scarborough to escape for a day or two, but now it felt more like she was imprisoned here, in a foggy vacuum, cut off from the world, powerless. God, what a mess. More than a mess. There wasn't a word for what this was.

If only she'd handled things better, been more careful around David, never introduced him to Freddie, or maybe introduced him earlier? All those times she resisted meeting up with David by using Freddie as an excuse… 'Freddie's a bit jealous.' 'Freddie's a bit sensitive.' 'Sorry, I'm out with Freddie… yes, I promise you'll meet each other. When the time's right. He's so protective of me…' All because of her long-cherished strategy of keeping friends separate, having her cake and eating it. Then she messed it all up by clumsily unveiling David at the funeral as The Stranger Who Gave Me an Alibi, and she hadn't properly prepared the ground either. *Of course* Freddie would ask about David's past, about school, *of course* he'd think it was strange they'd never met before….. She'd tried- clumsily- to get them off the topic of school by talking about the cat limping, but that hadn't worked. For god's sake, why hadn't she been more careful? Coached David a bit more? Prepared him? *Here's what we say when he asks about school… here's what we say when he asks about That Night…* If she'd only bothered to do that, David wouldn't have opened with that stupid hole-in-the-heart-doing-GCSE's-and-A-Levels-at-Hazlewood story. Freddie wouldn't have even *heard* the name Hazlewood, and he wouldn't have had any suspicions to go on, and none of this would've happened. *Stupid.* Even then, though, it might still have worked if she'd just done everything more gradually, casually… after-work drinks with Freddie, *David, want to come along?* Fred, the Alibi Man just texted me – Rose and Crown? If she'd just done that…

Then Freddie wanted to arrange the dinner party, and it was such a big deal, and David was nervous, and when David got nervous he could be… odd. Even though they'd had many conversations about it, he was strange about psychiatry in front of Freddie… he hinted about that picture of her… made a fuss about childhood photos, had basically been a poster child for Asperger's. The whole evening was a slow-motion car wreck, and she could tell, from the tone of Freddie's *text*, that David had freaked him out on the drive home too. It all mushroomed from there.

If it wasn't for that night, Freddie wouldn't have started digging around and David wouldn't have gone nuts about him digging around. If only she'd handled it better from the start, Freddie might not have noticed how strange David was on the night she'd deliberately double booked them- he might have overlooked the suits, the shoes, the hairdresser… he might have thought it was cute rather than controlling… Then none of this would have happened, Freddie would still be alive and… There. That did it. She let herself sob. Freddie was dead. The shock had worn off, leaving brutal grief and now her voice would be the right kind of broken when she made the call to Graham and Ruth.

She'd tell them as much about David as they needed to know.

They'd tell her that David had been arrested.

They'd sob together. And then she could go back home. Grieve with them. *She didn't have anyone else now, did she?*

She headed to the beach, to make the call as privately as possible. Someone answered almost immediately, but it was an unfamiliar voice and her tears turned traitor and dried in her throat.

'Can I help you?'

'Who's this?' Jenny managed.

'Jane Westergaard. I'm a friend of the family,'

Jane. She was a barrister. Jenny had met her once or twice. A tall, tweedy lesbian with no discernible sense of humour. She had a way of resting her grey, pebbly eyes on someone, and gradually widening them, until her face assumed an expression of baffled intrigue. She was Freddie's godmother. *Well, not any more.*

'My name's Jenny? Freddie's friend Jenny? Can I speak to Graham or Ruth?'

'It's not a good time,' Jane told her drily.

'I just wanted to call… to see how they both were; I know what's happened,' Jenny said lamely.

'They're not doing well, obviously,' Jane told her. A pause gathered. The cold wind carried the senseless yapping of a dog – and the equally senseless bellowing of its owner. 'Where are you?' Jane asked.

'I'm… I had to get away. Look, maybe you can help me. My boyfriend—'

'David?'

Jenny stopped. 'How d'you know David?'

'He's just left the house.'

Jenny stopped still then. Her body flushed with, sudden, scalding heat. 'What was he doing there?'

She heard a squeak – the sound of wicker under Jane's weight – she must be sitting on the log box in the kitchen. 'He came to see Ruth and Graham. Pay his respects.' There was blithe condemnation in her voice.

'Look, Jane? There's something about David. Perhaps you're the right person to talk to about this, I don't know. David is—,' Jane's voice was muffled. She was answering someone. There was a rustle and Graham was on the line.

'Jenny? Where are you?'

'Look, I need to tell you something about David—'

'Come home.' Graham sounded heartbroken. 'David's worried sick. We all are—'

'What d'you mean? Graham—'

'He told us that you ran away from him at the hospital; he told us about the problems you've been having.'

'What?'

'It's to be expected, what with your mother dying, and now… with Freddie.' He stopped then, but his breath still whispered like a much older man.

'What's he been saying about me?'

'That you struggle with stress. That you can become a little detached from reality. Look, Jenny, I really can't—' Graham's voice fractured.

'He killed Freddie!' Jenny shouted. 'I know he did! I even went to the police—'

'Yes, we know you did, David told us.' Graham's voice hardened just a little. 'And you ran away from there too.' He sighed. 'Jenny, come back. You're not well. At least call David, plea—'

She hung up then.

David was worried sick. Kind, dependable David. Doggedly loyal David who still loved her despite her mental problems. He was good. He must have sailed through the police interview, if it even got that far. Now he would be trying to find her. And he was very good at finding her – he'd done it many times, after all.

CHAPTER FIFTY-EIGHT

David. The Night the Snow Fell

It was David's private sorrow that fate had forced him, again and again, into deceit. He comforted himself with the thought that his lies had all been to one end: to keep Jenny happy and safe. All these small Wrongs forming one large Right.

She'd come back to the village months ago, and yet they still hadn't met face-to-face. The problem was that Freddie was going through a 'hard time' – bad break up – and she didn't want anyone to see them together, tell Freddie. It was a bit silly, but Freddie really needed her at the minute, and he could be a bit possessive... she needed just a little more time... get him over his break-up first and then, gradually, introduce him to the idea that she had a boyfriend. David could understand that, couldn't he? And David, floating in a sudden bubble of joy (she said he was her boyfriend! She *said* it!) told her that, yes, of course he could understand that. And it wouldn't be for long, anyway, would it?

'Only a few more weeks,' Jenny said. That's what she always said. It was beginning to seem like it was never going to happen... 'I so nearly did it today! I was about to say how I ran into you in the village, but then he started getting all upset about his ex, and I just couldn't do it.' There was a sad smile in her voice. 'Don't hate me! You hate me, don't you?'

'Of course I don't hate you,' David answered. 'I-I *love* you.'

'You're so sweet to wait like this!'

But, after a while, the situation began to torment him. After all, he lived a mere mile away from the love of his life but he couldn't see her! Sal was sick. Sal was drunk. No, you can't come round and see me, David, she's... it's awful. Tomorrow? But it was never tomorrow either. Sal was sick, or Freddie was needy, or the house was a state, and she was *so sorry*. He was so patient. *Please don't hate me!*

It was driving him mad. It was too much. So he made a decision – if he couldn't meet her, then at least he could see her. Just for an hour or two, while Mother slept.

It was strangely exciting, how familiar it was – just like the old days with the same old hiding places – behind the bins at her kitchen window, and at the dip at the end of her garden by the hills, prepared as always with night-vision goggles, a thermal coat, gloves, even a pad to kneel on. Sometimes he filmed her silhouette, recorded her voice. This time it was safe because she was safe, and there was no haring off to the city, no Marc to deal with.

The night the snow fell was the fourth time he'd watched. He almost didn't go, but something told him he must. Something told him that this was a Significant Night, and so he kissed Catherine's sleeping cheek, and made his way through the village, happy, happy, and the snow made everything beautiful, so beautiful, disguising the dirt. On the way the present and past collided in his mind, briefly merged, then pulled apart. The same image, the same memory. It happened again and again. He was sixteen and a recent growth spurt had pulled his school blazer tight across his shoulders, tighter still as he spied the pink paper, crushed like a butterfly in the middle of the street, and reached to pluck it up. Then, for a fraction of a second, he hovered between the decades, neither boy nor man, and then sank back into adult David, who only had to wait a little while, just a while longer, to go public as A Real Boyfriend. And again and again, and then there he was, teen and adult, crouched by the bins and the same incessant TV chatter, the same cigarette smoke drifting out of the open window, the same raised voices from the kitchen saying the same words: '… just to get your own room…'

He heard it all. He watched Sal barrelling out of the door, stumbling, weaving with drunk defiance towards the hills. He followed, of course he followed. He found the chiffon scarf, bloodstained and already half frozen, pointing like an arrow to the slumped form of Sal; he knew why he was there, and what he had to do. Time looped, merged. Everything was as it should be.

And when, days later, Jenny called him to tell him that the police had been asking questions… she had no alibi, but she hadn't done anything – *'course she hadn't done anything…*

'It's just… it's so horrible, David,' she had whispered. 'Mum dying and the thought that anyone thinks I did anything… if you could just… say you saw me that night? Tell the police that?

Of course he could say that. It was true after all.

CHAPTER FIFTY-NINE

Jenny. The Windsor Castle, Scarborough

An hour after speaking to Graham on the phone, Jenny was standing at the desk of The Windsor Castle, trying to settle her bill. Rob, the wispy hipster owner, frowned and prodded at his iPhone. 'Can't get it to connect.' His smile was whimsical, maddening.

'I have to leave, now,' Jenny told him, not for the first time. Her small bag leaned against her leg. 'I have to. Look, can you just… I don't know, email me the bill? I'll pay it, I promise.'

But the hipster looked at her with rehearsed weary cynicism. 'Where would I be if I let all my guests check out without paying?' he said.

'God, I don't know. The owner of a completely empty hotel? Oh, wait…'

The hipster clenched his jaw, nodded at the bar with professional impatience – another rehearsed-looking gesture. 'Craig will give you a complimentary latte if you take a seat in the snug.'

'You don't understand. I. Have. To. Leave. I've got to! Just – look, come with me to a cashpoint? Yeah? Just please.'

'You can have a complimentary bagel also.' He smiled like he'd used some magic words. 'Locally milled organic spelt.'

Half an hour later, Jenny was on her third complimentary latte, poking holes in one hard-as-concrete organic bagel, and trying to jump-start her tired brain into thinking like David's. She'd never had trouble with that before, but now he had slipped out of her control, gone rogue. God what a stupid phrase, though. There was nothing roguish about David; in his own way he was the most conventional man alive. He wanted his poor urchin girl to turn into a princess; he believed in the Happily Ever After. Crucially, he believed in *her*. He believed that she was brave, and strong, and true, and this is what she'd been trading on all this time. They hadn't even had sex, for God's sake. Girls in David-Land didn't have sex until they were safely married, and this suited Jenny because she'd privately decided that there was no way she'd let that happen. David might be handsome, rich and in good shape, but he made her skin crawl. Her plan was always to leave him eventually. Perhaps she'd been silly to move in with him when he asked, but it had seemed like a good idea at the time... it was a way to keep him happy and it meant that she wouldn't have to worry about rent, do any more stupid temping jobs and carry on wearing shit, cheap clothes. Her mistake had been that she got used to it, got too comfortable. It was the same trap she'd fallen into when she moved back in with Sal – convenience and comfort had superseded plain good sense. She'd stayed, even when she knew he was losing it, even when Freddie had started finding things out about David, things, like the psychiatric hospitals, that even she didn't know about.

But even *then* she'd been stupid enough to think she could still control things – control David by doing what she always did – withdrawing love, frightening him into obedience. 'I'll handle David,' she'd told Freddie just two days ago; she'd sailed off to do just that. So sure of herself, arriving at the station, pulling out all the stops... a sad disappointed smile that she let wither on her face, no eye contact, monosyllabic replies, until by the time they were back at the house, David was frantic, stammering: *what had he done?*

She thought she had him then. 'I don't know. What *have* you done?'

He swallowed hard. 'You were out all night, I was worried.' He looked at her, pleading. Jenny, her mouth a line, stared at her knees. 'Where were you?'

'Freddie's,' she admitted finally. She looked up at him then, saw how guilty he looked, decided to go for broke. 'You really fucked up, David.'

He winced. 'Don't swear.'

'So Ryan's back, is he?'

'Freddie started that – he messaged… he wanted to get some dirt on me. He was trying to split us up, Jenny – and anyway, I used an encryption thing for Ryan and it's all erased now.' David was babbling.

'It's not "all erased" though,' Jenny said sharply. 'Freddie had plane times. Why did you keep the plane times? Why? Do you want to… hurt me?' She said it softly, but kept her eyes hard on his sweating profile.

'I'd never do that,' he replied huskily.

'Because between Ryan and the plane times, Freddie's started to ask about… that night. The night my mum died.' She let a few tears into her voice. 'David, you said you'd help me, and how is this helping me? I asked you to do one, simple thing, and just tell the police you saw me. That's all I asked.'

'I'm sorry,' David mumbled. 'I shouldn't have kept those things. I-I have trouble throwing things away… I—'

'He's got more than the plane times and the Ryan stuff.' She kept her face averted. 'He found some things in your garden too.'

David slowed and swerved. 'What things?' He pulled over into a lay-by. 'What kind of things?'

Jenny frowned, wondering how far she could afford to take this. *Pretty far*, she thought. David was scared, grovelling, anxious to make things right. Her instinct was to dump everything on him, make him feel as guilty and responsible as possible. Confuse him.

Make him the bad guy, the killer, the stalker, the one who causes problems. The more confused David got, the less dangerous he was. And so she took a gamble.

'A hat, and a knife. He took photos of them too.' She turned in her seat and stared at him. 'And a newspaper clipping. Do I have to go on?'

'I can explain all that. I wanted to tell you earlier—' David sounded eager.

'No!' she shouted. 'I don't want to know. It's just *another* thing I'll have to worry about, and you've given me enough worry.' She left a long silence. 'I don't know what to do, David, I really don't.' She shook her head. 'That's why I went to Freddie's, to try to sort out your mess. I've been up *all night* trying to convince him not to call the police about the things he's found. I've been up all night defending you, David. Because I love you.' She stopped. He sounded like he was crying. Good. 'And I did that *even though* you've put me in danger.'

He looked up, voice choked with sobs. 'How? I would never do that? How?'

'You *know* how. If he shows the pictures to the police, they'll talk to you, and they'll dig around the plane times; they'll find out about Ryan, and your alibi won't stand up any more.' Her voice rose. 'I asked you to tell them you saw me, not to keep a fucking paper trail about it!'

'Don't swear.'

'Well I'm pissed off though, David? You said you'd look after me, but you haven't. You've made things worse!' She looked with satisfaction at the way his face creased with tears, and pressed her advantage. 'David, because of you they might arrest me. You're my alibi, but if they don't trust you, they'll come after me again. Think about that. They might take me away from you. And it'll all be your fault.' Dispassionately, she watched David cry. After a minute she told him to pull himself together, and get them home.

She'd told him off in the same way you would a dog, to get him back on his best behaviour. Then all she had to do was find Sal's scarf, the plane times, and destroy them along with the photos on Freddie's phone, and everything would be all right.

And so she told him off, she made him feel stupid and ashamed, and then she blithely went for a nap thinking that now he'd been taught his lesson, things would go smoothly. She never expected David to kill Freddie.

CHAPTER SIXTY

David. Under the Bridge

David felt so grateful to Jenny. Yes, she was angry, yes she was upset, but she had every right to be. Instead of leaving him, she'd given him another chance. But his brain was fogged and slow, and there were too many tendrils to clutch. He didn't want to get rid of everything; the idea filled him with painful panic. Everything he'd collected, preserved and revered reminded him of how much he'd achieved: Marc vanquished; Sal disposed of; Jenny saved. They formed the stage of his life's purpose; he needed them.

In the attic room he collected the phone he'd used when he was being Ryan, and put it in his pocket. Then he went to see Mother. She was awake, and it was one of her good days. She held his hand as he knelt by her, patted it and smiled.

'You're tired,' she said.

'Yes.'

Pat pat. 'All tired out.'

'Yes,' David said. Then: 'Jenny's upset with me.'

Pat pat. 'And why's that?'

'I made a mistake. I made a stupid mistake.'

'Well, I'm sure you can sort it out,' his mother twinkled at him. 'You've always been a very resourceful boy.'

David swallowed hard and looked at the carpet. He didn't want Mother to see him cry. 'What should I do?' he muttered.

In his back pocket, Ryan's phone beeped with Freddie. Catherine winced and closed her eyes. 'Such an annoying thing. Such a horrible, horrible thing.'

'Yes, he is,' David told her, and silenced the phone.

'You must do as you think best,' Catherine told him with great solemnity. 'You always know what to do. You always do the right thing.'

And David nodded. He felt his mind calm.

They made plans to watch *University Challenge* that night, at eight. He brought her some soup, and watched her eat it, and then gave her a Nytol, telling her it was a vitamin pill. When Catherine began to get sleepy, he helped her into bed, and kissed her forehead.

He then crushed up four risperidone and added them to a special smoothie – carrot, lime and kale – Jenny's favourite. Upstairs, Jenny was wrapped in a bathrobe, rubbing at her damp hair.

'I made you your special juice,' David said humbly, put it beside her bed. 'I am sorry.'

She sighed. 'I know you are. I just wish you'd think about things before you do them.' She looked at him in the mirror. She took a sip.

'Is it nice?'

She took another sip. 'Mmmmm. It's all right.'

'I am sorry. I am you know.'

She frowned at him. 'I'm going to have a rest and then head back to Freddie's.'

'OK,' he said humbly, and left the room.

Half an hour later she was lying like a carved angel on her bed, half under and half on top of the duvet. He tucked her in, gave her a kiss. When he backed out of the room again he turned the key in the lock.

The pills would hopefully keep both Jenny and Mother asleep until he came back. Back in Catherine's room, he gently placed his noise-cancelling headphones over her ears; if by any chance

Jenny woke and started to shout, Mother wouldn't hear and get upset. He felt awful about tricking Jenny this way, but he knew that she'd be so relieved that he'd sorted everything out, that she'd forgive him. Once again he was pleasantly surprised at just how well he coped during a crisis.

He took out Ryan's phone. It was a message from Freddie:

I can meet anytime. Tonight?

David replied:

OK the Narrowboat at 8? There are things about David that I think you should know. I've told Jenny too.

Freddie asked Ryan:

How do you know Jenny?
Will explain tonight. I want to help. Please don't talk to anyone/ tell anyone about this.

David pressed send.

Then he took a spade and trowel from the shed and began to dig up the Kitten Box.

Driving through the less salubrious area of the city, David stopped at a poky little place called Da Fone Shop. There he bought an unlocked phone and a sim card with cash. Back in the car, he texted Freddie.

> *It's Jen, I'm using this phone. DON'T call the other one! Will explain later. Have you heard from Ryan?*

Freddie replied immediately.

Yes, where are you? Is everything OK?

I'm with him now. Lot's happened but need to tell you face-to-face… don't worry though we're both safe

Freddie would bite at that.

Meet now then? Come here?

We're driving. Narrowboat nearer and your place might not be safe. Will explain I promise XOXO

What's happening????

David smiled and turned off the phone.

*

It was eight o'clock, and David's legs were cramping from slouching in his car for the last few hours. He hadn't wanted to get out and walk about the city in case he got picked up on CCTV. He'd parked in a street that backed onto the canal. There were no houses close by, no cameras, but even so he'd taken the precaution of taping cardboard over the license plates.

He closed his eyes, breathed deeply. Opened them.

Now.

Ryan messaged Freddie:

Is Jenny with you?
No! She was with you, wasn't she? What's happened?
We got separated she said she was coming to see you, look around for her.

David was sweating suddenly.

She's not here I would've seen her What's happened?
Find her!
What's happening?

David could practically hear his squeal. Then the text to 'Jenny's' phone came through

CALL ME!

And the first act had concluded; it was time for Jenny to take the stage.

Come and get me something bad's happened I'm under the canal bridge behind the pub please come now!

He wasn't sweating any longer. A strange calm descended. He opened the car door and stepped out into the cold air, towards the canal, and the bridge – the same bridge under which Marc had died. He carried the same knife too. There was a beautiful symmetry to that.

'Jen?' Freddie shouted.
He was near.
David swapped phones

QUIET! Ryan messaged.
I've found her Please hurry!
Then: *I can see you, stay there.*

Freddie's figure loomed through the mist. He stopped a few metres away with his back to David, and David closed his eyes.

The smell of piss under the bridge. The lap of the water. The faint music… it was just as it had been all those years ago with Marc. And then he ran smoothly at Freddie, knocked the phone out of his hand, and thrust the knife just below his shoulder blade. Freddie spun round, and David had time to register the recognition on his face, had time to smile at him. When Freddie slid into the water, he hardly made a noise, surprising for such a fat man.

David found Freddie's phone and turned it off. Back in the car, he removed the sim card, and put it in a plastic bag along with Ryan's phone and the unlocked mobile he'd just bought. Then he removed the cardboard from the license plates, slowly drove out of the road, and headed towards the motorway. It was a roundabout way to get home, but he couldn't risk being seen driving in a crowded area.

Halfway home he pulled into a farm track, tied up the bag and smashed the phones with a hammer so no pieces of them could be found in his car. Every few miles he delved into the bag, took a pinch of the debris and threw it out of the window. Ryan, Freddie and 'Jenny' were soon scattered across fifteen miles of muddy country. He'd burn the sim cards later.

He arrived back at home just after ten, washed the knife carefully, scrubbing the serrations with a Brillo pad, put it in a clean plastic bag and hid it under the sink. He should get rid of it, he knew, but… *tomorrow. Do it tomorrow. And the hat too.*

Both Jenny and Catherine were asleep. He walked around the house putting all the clocks back two and a half hours, put Catch-up TV on ready to go, and then gently shook Catherine awake.

'How long have I been asleep?'

'Quite a long time,' he told her. 'It's nearly eight.' She blinked slowly. 'Do you still want to watch *University Challenge*?' She was tired. He levered her out of the bed, put her slippers on her unresisting feet. 'Come on, let's go to the sitting room.'

'It feels later. It feels like it's the middle of the night,' she said, shuffling beside him. The grandfather clock in the hall struck eight, just as they sat down.

Jenny woke to find David lying beside her.

'What time is it?' She sat up. 'How long have I been asleep?'

'For the past twelve hours,' David told her.

She put the light on. Her face was flushed, her hair tangled. 'Shit, I was meant to call Freddie.'

'It's too late now,' he told her.

'What d'you mean? "Too late"?' she said sharply.

'I mean it's midnight,' he said.

'I'll text him then, where's my phone?'

'I looked in the car, but I didn't find it. It'll turn up,' he said and smiled reassuringly.

She looked hard at him. The light from the bedside lamp shone through her hair, creating a nimbus of light, dazzling. 'I've got a headache,' she said. 'And I'm hungry.'

He scurried off to make her some toast and brought it up on a tray, along with some paracetamol and fresh orange juice.

Her expression softened. 'You are good to me,' she said.

'I try,' he muttered. 'And when I don't succeed, I try to put it right; you know that, don't you?'

She looked at him keenly and gave one sharp nod. 'I do.'

CHAPTER SIXTY-ONE

Jenny. The Day after Freddie's Death

When Jenny got the call from Graham, her shock and grief were absolutely genuine. It had never occurred to her that David would do something as insane as kill Freddie.

She had to think quickly, lay the ground. Escape.

After coming back from seeing Freddie's body, she made her notes about the hospital visit, wrote about her fear that David had drugged her and killed Freddie. She'd give them to Cheryl once she managed to get away. Hopefully this, coupled with knowledge of David's stints in the psychiatric wards, the pictures on Freddie's phone (if the phone was found), as well as the stuff David still probably had buried in the garden, would help catch him and keep him caught. Hopefully all this would outweigh the one thing David had that might reflect badly on her: the chiffon scarf. She hadn't been able to find it. God knows where he'd hidden it.

The fact that David had the scarf meant that he'd been there the night Sal died. If he was close enough to find the scarf, he was close enough to have overheard Jenny's promise to come back, and close enough to see that she didn't. That meant David knew that she'd left Sal in the snow to die. And he hadn't said a word.

CHAPTER SIXTY-TWO

Catherine was having one of her bad days. Jenny sat with her, listening to her mutterings, trying to work out what she knew, what David might have told her. They stayed in the room together all day, until Catherine began to feel frightened. She didn't like Jenny. She didn't like her didn't like her didn't like her. *Get out of my house!*

'Keep your voice down,' Jenny told her.

'Piers!'

'Piers died,' Jenny told her flatly. 'And so did Tony.' She was sick of this woman. They were sick of each other.

'I know you,' Catherine told her. She narrowed her eyes, sat up straight in her chair. 'You're fired.'

'Believe me, at this stage of the game, if I could leave, I would,' Jenny told her.

Catherine paused. Wilted. 'Need the loo,' she whispered.

'You need the loo or you've already pissed yourself?'

'You're fired.'

'OK. I'm fired. Let's get you to the loo…'

But once outside the room, Catherine tried to run. With a hoarse cry she dashed blindly towards the darkened hall. Jenny ran after her, caught her by the nightgown, but the woman slapped at her arm.

'I don't *like* you I don't *like* you!' And ran to the bathroom.

Jenny followed her. Rage, tired rage, made her grab Catherine by the hair. She kicked the door shut behind her.

'Piers!' cried Catherine, and Jenny slammed her head onto the side of the sink.

Catherine fell like a dead thing. She looked like a dead thing. *Shit. Shit!* Jenny put an ear to her chest – *was that a heartbeat? Yes? Was it?*

'Catherine? Catherine? Answer me!' One eye half flickered open. 'Catherine, listen to me. You fell. You tripped and you fell, OK. I'm helping you. I've been helping you.'

'...tripped...'

'That's right. You tripped. That's right. David! David!'

'David, listen, calm down, listen. David, she needs to get to casualty. David, call an ambulance! I'll stay with her, I'll stay...'

*

By the time the ambulance came, David was completely hysterical, while Jenny, though shaken, was the epitome of calm. She explained what had happened, stayed with Catherine long enough to make sure she said the same thing, and, as they strapped her to a stretcher, and levered her out of the house, Jenny ran upstairs, shoved some underwear, her wallet and phone into a bag. She dug out the notes for Cheryl that she'd hidden around the bedroom and shoved them into an envelope Finally, she approached the mirror, took a deep breath, and hit herself sharply on the left cheek, opened her eyes, closed them, and hit herself again in the eye until it watered in pain.

'Jenny!' David's panicked call sounded from downstairs.

She shook her hair down from her ponytail, letting it cloud and partially obscure her face, and in the back of the ambulance kept her head down and held David's hand. She whispered to him that everything was going to be OK. She promised him that things would work out. To Catherine she said: 'It was just a fall, just a fall.'

Half an hour later she was running towards the police station, her hair back in its ponytail, the bruise just coming out around her eye.

CHAPTER SIXTY-THREE

David. The Day after Freddie's Death

The police did speak to David, but only because he called them. His girlfriend had gone missing that afternoon and her phone was turned off. This was really unlike her. Yes, of course he'd come in. *Was she OK? Was she there?*

In the station he was able to tell them that Jenny had… problems. She'd always been an anxious, imaginative person – sensitive and dreamy. Her mother had recently died, her best friend had just been killed, and seeing Catherine injured and in the hospital, well, it might have been too much for her.

'It'd be too much for *anyone*,' he said seriously. 'I shouldn't have let her come to the hospital with me, too many associations. God.' He shook his head. 'I completely respect her privacy, but did she tell you where she was going? She's… she's not well.'

But the police didn't know. They suggested he contact family members. *Good idea, yes. He'd do that, thanks.*

'Can we ask you where you were two nights ago?'

'Yes, of course. I was at home. Jenny took a long nap, and I watched *University Challenge* with my mother.' He smiled. 'She has dementia, but she still got a higher score than me. Why?'

'Routine enquiries. Anyone close to Mr Lees-Hill is being asked the same thing.'

David nodded. 'I understand. I didn't know him very well but what a horrible thing. You know he was gay? Could it be a hate crime?'

'We're looking at everything.'

David nodded again. 'Jenny was obsessed with the attack. Last night she had terrible dreams about it. She seemed to think they were real…' He shook his head. 'Please, if she gets in touch with you, *please* tell her to come home. I don't know if she told you but we're actually engaged.' His smile faltered. His sad, sad eyes misted. 'I always thought that if she had a real family – a family of her own – it would help her get over all the horrible experiences she's had. Please, tell her I love her? Just in case she calls.'

He told Ruth and Graham the same thing when he went round to offer his sincere condolences. They weren't to be upset if she called, and he was… florid. Losing Freddie had tipped Jenny over the edge. He'd just been talking to the police about her. She'd gone missing. 'But I don't want you to worry. She'll come home. But if she calls you and tells you where she is, please let me know?'

He thought he'd handled this very well. Very well indeed. He didn't blame Jenny for leaving – well, he *did*, but he could understand it. She was distraught, overtired, she needed a break. When people were… in a state of shock, they sometimes acted out of character. Now that everyone knew how fragile she was, they'd be more gentle with her when she got back, more forgiving.

She hadn't been herself for a few days – she'd spoken so sharply to him when he'd picked her up from the station – almost as if she hated him. She'd been under so much stress lately, and a whole night with that emotional leech Freddie had exhausted her. David should have been more understanding… All those years living with vampires like Sal and Freddie had made it hard for her to accept the love and respect that she deserved. Now that he'd freed her of them both, her gratitude was being poisoned by fear: fear that she didn't deserve him, fear that she'd become a burden to him.

It made total sense in a tragic sort of way.

Fortunately, he had a perfect plan to not only get her back, but make her understand how much he loved her, how safe she'd be from now on.

Half an hour later, he was driving quickly northwards, brain humming, nerves quiveringly awake. The kitten tin with the hat and the knife in it sat next to 'Precious Memories!' on the back seat. In his pocket was Sal's scarf. Together they'd burn it all, and start afresh. Scarborough. There she was, pinned on a map. Lucky he'd put that tracking software on her phone… No, not lucky, he shouldn't put himself down like that. It was planning, foresight. He was a Good Boyfriend who'd always had her safety at heart. Always. Each minute brought him closer to Jen's pulsing dot, and the closer he got, the calmer he felt.

CHAPTER SIXTY-FOUR

Endgame

They sat in the car, 'Precious Memories!' between them.

'We can do this later?' David said anxiously. 'We could go to a hotel, and you could have a rest?'

She smiled gently 'No. You've come all this way. Let's do it now. I think it's the right time.'

So he showed it all to her, explained it all to her – the train tickets, the photographs. God, it was so good to be honest, come clean, even show off a little.

'Really? You didn't know I followed you? Really? I followed you all the way to your house.'

'I didn't see you,' Jenny said after a pause. 'You're... very good at following people.'

'Thanks! And I saw you pass that pub. What was it called?'

'The Fox,' Jenny said softly.

'The Fox, yes. I saw him hurt you. I...' He shook his head. 'I'm still ashamed of myself. I didn't help you. I should've helped you.'

'That's all right,' Jenny managed. 'You don't need to... feel guilty.'

'Really? Honestly? I've felt bad about that for *years*. Anyway, I collected as many of your photos as I could. They were all over the road, and... I got as many as I could. And I gave them back, d'you remember?'

'In the coffin? The box like a coffin?' Her voice was still soft.

He groaned humorously, nodded. 'God. Sorry about that. It was only once you'd got it that I realised it looked a bit coffin-like.'

'You saw me get the box too?'

'Mmm. Well, not *right* when you got it because I overslept, but yeah.' His smile faded. 'I didn't mean to scare you. It was meant to be a nice thing, but you thought it was from Marc, that he was threatening you, that he'd found you, and, well, I had to make it all right again.' He took her hand carefully. 'I had to. You went off to see him and I had to make sure you were safe, so I followed you again. You're sure you want to hear all this?'

She nodded then, and smiled. A sweet smile, if a little tired. 'It feels… great to finally understand everything. But, I've got a bit of a headache. I need a Coke and some paracetamol maybe. There's a shop around the corner, I'll just nip out,' she said.

'I'll come too.'

They walked to the corner shop. While David chatted happily, Jenny made sure to look straight at the security cameras. All four of them.

Back in the car he anxiously watched her take the pills. 'How long have you had a headache?'

'Oh, it's not bad, let's carry on talking.'

'Have you eaten?' he asked. 'You need to eat.'

'I will. I promise. Can we drive somewhere else now though? Somewhere quiet, near the sea, and you can tell me everything?' She smiled. 'It's time I knew everything, don't you think?'

And so they drove to a miserable scrap of land on the edge of a caravan park. The windows fogged and the air grew humid, but Jenny didn't take her coat off – he hoped she hadn't caught a chill?

'No, no,' she reassured him. 'I'm fine, I promise. Tell me about this. Is it…?'

'Yes. Marc Doyle's hat.' David looked at it, his expression a queasy mix of pride and hatred. 'After I sent the pictures back? In the box? I followed you to his house, and I saw him hurt you again. It made me so… mad. And you were being so brave, and there was I, cowering behind a wall, doing *nothing*… so I stayed. After you left, I stayed, and I followed him too.' He smiled fondly at the memory.

'Where did you follow him to?' Jenny asked softly.

'To the canal,' David answered her dreamily. 'It was raining. Remember the rain that night? I was soaked through by the time I got to the canal. I caught a rotten cold, not a cold, worse. I even ended up in hospital, it was pneumonia, d'you remember I was off school—'

'Tell me about the canal'

'Oh, yes. So I already had the knife; I picked it up in his garden,' he told her. 'And the knife bit went OK, but he didn't fall down. And so I had to think quickly. You know what I did?' He smiled gleefully in recollection.

'No. What?'

'I ran up to the top of the bridge and I threw a rock at him! A big one.' David pulled it out of the kitten box. 'Look, here it is.'

'And that's how he died?' Jenny asked softly.

'Sort of. He was like Rasputin though!' David laughed, shook his head. 'I mean the knife hurt him but didn't, you know, put him down; the slab put him down, but even then I still had to push him in the water, and he didn't sink for ages, and—' He stopped, his smile faded. 'I'm not going on and on, am I? Talking too much?' he asked anxiously.

'No. No, carry on. I've… always wanted to know what happened.'

'Don't want to bore you.'

'You're not.' She coughed, paused. 'What about Freddie?'

David's face darkened. 'I'm sorry about that.'

'Are you?'

'I shouldn't have let it get that far. I should've told him to back off and leave you alone. He was bad for you. He fed off you.' David's voice rose. 'And he stole from me, spied on me. And he frightened Mother.' David shook his head.

'Tell me, David. How did you get him there?'

'*I* didn't. Ryan did. You know this though—'

'Yes, but it was all so… stressful. I might have missed some things. Can you tell me again? If you don't mind, I mean? If I hear the whole story in one lump, it might make me… understand a bit better.'

David nodded soberly. 'OK. So Freddie texted me – sorry, he texted Ryan.' He smirked. 'And he said all these awful things about me. He'd found things. You *know*. And I didn't want him to,' David screwed up his eyes and mouth, searching for the right phrase, 'make things more difficult. He'd done that enough. He was going to carry on doing it, too.' Then he paused. The smirk almost faded, disappeared. 'I know this might still be… difficult to hear. But he'd seen the scarf. Your mum's scarf? I couldn't let him tell anyone about that. Obviously.'

Jenny stiffened, coughed, took a sip of Coke. 'What scarf was that?' she asked carefully.

'The scarf she had when she died. The one with the roses.'

'And how did you get hold of that?' *Careful, very careful.* She put one cold hand in her pocket.

'Because I was there,' David told her. 'I was there, when, you know…'

'When she died?'

'Yes.'

Jenny left a long pause. 'Have you told anyone about that?' she asked.

He shook his head. 'No. Nobody.'

'How long… how long did it take?' Jen's voice was shaky.

David placed a hot hand on her knee. 'Not long. Once I got her up, it was easy to push her down. And it was quick. I mean, I don't think she suffered.'

'*You* did it? But—' she stopped then. 'Tell me what happened with Mum.'

'I don't really want to talk about this.' David was solicitous. 'It's too painful for you, and you're tired and—'

'I'd like to know.' There was force in her voice.

David, hesitated, capitulated. He told her how he had listened to Sal crying, a weak, pitiful sound, an annoying sound, and then something told him to get up, get up and approach her. When he saw the scarf, he almost didn't bother with it, but then something told him that it was Significant, so he stooped, picked it up, wound it around one hand. Then he advanced towards the sniffs and moans and found her, half frozen, her nose clotted with slushy blood, one leg caught on something buried in the snow…

He had stopped a few feet away and lowered into a squat.

She'd fixed him with one exhausted eye. 'Hurt my leg.'

David had tilted his head, smiled.

'Help me up?' Sal had gasped. One hand made a feeble attempt to push herself up. David did nothing. She raised her voice. 'Help me up! Please!'

He had tilted his head again. 'Oh, d'you need help?' He extended one hand. She grabbed it with surprising strength. Her other hand made clawing movements in the snow. One woeful eye winced. 'Nearly there,' he'd told her.

'My foot's caught!' she gasped again. 'Can't feel it.'

David had stayed silent while fate flooded in. He closed his eyes. Opened them.

'You should've been a better mother.'

Sal had stared at him. 'What?'

'What?'

'Whadyousay?' Sal was exhausted now. The cold had crept to the centre of her, shutting pieces of her down, one by one. 'Whuyousay?'

'I didn't say anything.' He smiled back. 'Lean on me.' He helped her up. It had been like picking up a sack of manure. Sal had been weak, wobbled and dragged one mangled foot behind her. She'd smelled of gin and indifferently brushed teeth. David turned her away from the house, further into the hills, but she'd been too cold and drunk to notice. She *had* noticed one thing though…

'Zatmyscarf?'

'Yes.' David had looked down at his still wrapped hand. 'D'you want it back?'

'What? Yes, I want it back.'

David had smiled broadly. 'Well, you're not getting it back.'

Sal sagged, stopped, looked at him, then looked around. 'What? We're not… we're not … right direction, where're… we going?'

'Let's walk. Nearly there,' David had said cheerfully, holding her arm firmly, painfully, but not hard enough to leave a bruise. 'What?' Sal asked fearfully. Her eyes held an expression that he'd only ever seen before in dying animals: a dulled, wary acceptance. 'Why? Where we going?'

'Don't worry' David had said. 'You're with me now.' And he had given her a hard shove down into one of the deepest hollows, a place he knew was treacherous with boulders, and watched as Sal slid messily down, clutching uselessly at the snow. He heard the sound of her head hitting the rock. He saw the movements her legs made – those strange, scurrying motions one sees on the gallows. He had wondered if she'd bleed, and if so, whether he'd be able to see it from there.

'I waited for an hour and she didn't move.' David reached for Jenny's hand. 'And I knew then that she was—'

'Dead,' Jenny whispered.

'Yes. Then, I went to find you, but you'd already gone to Freddie's house, and then, of course—'

She removed her hand from his and shrank back against the car door.

'You see? I *told* you. It's too much information for you, *you're sick, and, you're tired*, and—' He ducked his head, trying to look into her eyes. 'Did I do the wrong thing? Jenny?' She was shivering in her coat, shaking. She gave a low moan, shrunk into a crouch. His chest constricted with alarm – *what was wrong, what was wrong? Jenny? Je—*

And then her boot smashed into his nose.

'Jenny? Wha—?'

Her heel slammed into his temple, then his throat, and she was screaming, shouting. 'You killed my mum!' And she kicked, and kicked and kicked until his head fell against the steering wheel, and the sound of him trying to breathe through his broken nose filled the car. She paused then. Closed her eyes, concentrated, opened them and shouted: 'Don't! David!' The shout became a scream, a different type of scream – a fearful scream. 'No!' as she grasped the knife that had killed both Marc and Freddie, and thrust it into David's throat, ground it in using all her strength, and then wrenching it back out, turning away from the splash of his boiling blood, letting her screams merge into whimpering, weeping.

After a minute, she put her hand in her pocket, brought out her phone and tapped to stop record.

Then she stopped crying, shook herself, took off her coat.

David, a mass of meat on the steering wheel, stared at her with fading eyes as she gritted her teeth and turned the knife on herself, scoring defensive slashes on her forearms. The blood gurgled from David's neck, and his eyes grew dimmer dimmer dimmer, watching her check her face in the mirror, watching her tear some hair loose from her ponytail, punching herself in the face, wincing, then again. He was still alive when she got out of the car, as she walked across the isolated car park, while she jogged and then ran towards the lights of the pub she'd noticed on the other side of the caravan park.

He died just as she fell through the door, gore-streaked and screaming for help.

CHAPTER SIXTY-FIVE

Between the phone recording, the blood-soaked contents of 'Precious Memories!', Jenny's statement, and the diary notes she'd given to Cheryl, the police drew the obvious – the only – conclusion about David: his long-standing obsession with Jenny was psychotic and murderous. He had a history of mental illness and violence – he'd stabbed a boy in school, set at least two fires in the family home, and had been under private psychiatric care for years. Not only had he killed Marc Doyle, he'd killed Sal so he could get closer to Jenny, and when Freddie voiced his suspicions, he had killed him too.

It was a terrible story. It was an irresistible story. It had everything – obsession; abuse; murder; arson; insanity; and more murder. It had stalking and police negligence – It had Beauty and the Beast (David was conspicuously good-looking, but that didn't figure in the headlines much).

Jenny was a heroine, a gutsy virago who had done the police's job for them – putting herself in danger by drawing a confession out of the bad guy, recording it, and when he turned on her too, fighting back and winning. She was remarkable! She was so, so brave! And, later, she comported herself with such dignity at Freddie's funeral, sitting in the front pew, between Ruth and Graham, her bandaged arms around their shoulders, her bruised face eloquent, heroic.

After the funeral, she stayed in the village, in the same house where she had lived with David. When Catherine was released from hospital, she went to collect her. She wanted to look after her. David had given her power of attorney, and now, *who else was there? Catherine couldn't be put in a home! Why should a sick old lady have to suffer for her son's crimes?*

Jenny gave a few interviews but never in the house. Catherine knew nothing about what had happened, and even though she was less and less compos mentis these days, any chance mention of David might still distress her. Catherine was a victim, just as Jenny was a victim, and she needed all the love and help she could give her. None of this was her fault. It was nobody's fault.

In a TV interview she was asked: 'But surely it is someone's fault? David Crane committed these crimes, it's his fault, surely?'

Jenny's forehead puckered. She looked just to the left of the camera, her eyes misty. 'All I can say is that David... he was very ill. He was very ill, and because of this illness, he did some terrible things. It's the illness that needs to be taken seriously. We can't run away from this any more. And she showed both scarred forearms to the camera, gave a sad smile. 'Look what happens when we try?'

ONE YEAR LATER

CHAPTER SIXTY-SIX

Mrs Mondesir waited anxiously at the vet's. Huck had been limping – *and not because he's overweight, like the vet said. Well, it wasn't just that anyway.* A thorn stuck behind one paw pad had got infected, and they'd kept him in overnight, and God knows how much that was going to cost, but you don't have a choice do you? Dogs. They're like your children.

She had one eye on the frosted glass of the examining room, and the other on a day-old copy of the *Daily Mail*. She'd seen it before. Everyone in the village had, but she picked it up again, it passed the time waiting for the vet. Lovely photograph of Jenny Holloway –really, she looked beautiful, but then newspapers employ special hair and make-up people don't they?

> An exclusive interview plus extract from *You Are My Everything: One Woman's Journey* by Jenny Holloway and Cheryl Hasani, Page 6.

Mrs Mondesir rustled the pages eagerly, and there was Jenny, gazing at a photograph of herself as a child.

> Jenny Holloway strokes the crumpled photograph.
>
> *Her eyes fill with tears, and they do throughout our interview, but she always presses on. 'It's hard. I still have nightmares, but I truly believe that truth is the best medicine.' She looks out from under her long eyelashes. 'Mum always said that if you tell the truth then nothing can hurt you.'*

Using diaries, notes, letters and excerpts from her award-winning blog *You Can't Go Home Again*, Ms Holloway tells her remarkable and harrowing story – abused and neglected in childhood, and later stalked and threatened by the love of her life – yet she refuses to succumb to bitterness and hate, rather, she wants to educate.

'I wrote the book to raise awareness. As a survivor of abuse, I was looking for someone to love me. When I met David, I thought he was my saviour. I think a lot of women think that, don't they?' she says softly. 'I didn't ask the questions I should have. I didn't stand up for myself. I wanted the fairy tale.' She smiles sadly. 'But—

'We have Huck, here?'

Mrs Mondesir stood. The paper dropped beside her. 'Is he all right?'

'Well we cleaned the wound. He'll be a bit grumpy for a few days. There's a week's worth of antibiotics and some painkillers you can give him with food.'

Huck let out a bark.

'He heard you say "food". Didn't you, eh?' She chucked him under the chin.

'And diet-wise—' the vet began.

'It's all lean chicken I give him,' Mrs Mondesir interrupted. 'He eats better than me.'

The vet put up her hands in mock surrender. 'Any more trouble, give us a call.'

'Oh, I shall. I shall, won't I, Huck?' She tucked him under her arm.

The paper slipped from the bench to the floor.

After a while the receptionist picked it up and used it to line one of the litter trays.

A LETTER FROM FRANCES

Hi!

I hope you enjoyed *Liars*. I had a good time writing it!

If you did enjoy it, and want to keep up to date with all my latest releases, just sign up at the following link. Your email address will never be shared and you can unsubscribe at any time.

www.bookouture.com/frances-vick/

The idea of *Liars* came to me after I had a conversation with an interesting but… difficult… acquaintance. I called her out on a few lies she'd told me and others, lies that, though they seemed meaningless to her, had nevertheless caused quite a lot of problems… Anyway, after a few minutes of counter accusations, bluster and rage, she stopped, thought, and said a very curious thing: 'I don't lie. I tell what ought to be the truth. There's a difference.'

And I thought… Wow.

People who trade in manipulation and deceit cause and prolong so much anger, so much fevered anxiety. I wonder, do they do it because they just like causing trouble? Maybe they don't attach too much importance to their actions? Or is it because – like my acquaintance – they believe they're making necessary improvements – their 'Truth' trumps a more boring/painful reality?

That got me thinking: Are you entitled to make your own truth? If so, what has to be sacrificed to make that happen?

Everyone in *Liars* tries hard to improve on their truths – from Tony believing that he'll get back on his feet one day, to Sal believing the best of Marc. Jenny and David take it further: they are snared by their separate and mutual contrivances, and it's the accumulation of lies that is so toxic. They won't give up on their fantasies, even to the point of murder.

Some quick questions: How much – if any – sympathy do you have for David? Was Freddie a good friend, or a meddler? What future do you see for Jenny? Did your opinion on the characters change throughout the book? I'd be interested to hear what you think.

Once again, thanks for reading. Feel free to get in touch with me on Facebook, Twitter or via my website www.francesvick.com.

A new book will be out soon – well, as soon as I get these people out of my system!

Cheers!
Frances.

ACKNOWLEDGEMENTS

HUGE thanks to the team at Bookouture – particularly my editor Kathryn Taussig, Noelle Holten and Kim 'Publicity Dynamo' Nash, as well as all the other Bookouture authors who have been so supportive (and funny as hell). Thanks also to Kate Barker who has been very generous with her expertise and advice, and all the while politely putting up with my apparent inability to be anywhere on time.

Finally, to my husband, and my kids, Ralph and Sandy – I love you! Thanks for everything.